Summer in
Napa

Also in Marina Adair's St. Helena Vineyard Series

Kissing Under the Mistletoe

Summer in Napa

MARINA ADAIR

Published by Montlake Romance
PO Box 400818
Las Vegas, NV 89140

ISBN-13: 9781611099737
ISBN-10: 1611099730

For my grandmother,
who taught me that fluffy
biscuits and a flaky crust
are the true ingredients to
happily ever after.

CHAPTER 1

If there was one thing Alexis Moreau knew, it was how to make an entrance. Timing, posture, and that enchanting smile that had been passed down from Moreau mother to Moreau daughter for over five generations were key to a lasting—and impeccable—first impression.

Which was why, after driving three and a half days across the country, Lexi planned a middle-of-the-night arrival and snuck into the vacant apartment above her grandmother's bakery. She needed a good cry, a hot shower, one of Pricilla's famous éclairs, and at least ten hours of solid sleep before she could face the residents of St. Helena.

Unfortunately, she found a bottle of her grandmother's Angelica stashed behind a rack of day-old pastries in the bakery kitchen, which was the only way to explain how she woke up on the bathroom floor, eyes swollen shut, wearing yesterday's clothes and half of an éclair.

She stumbled into the bedroom to grab her things and shower, then remembered that her dress—the outrageously expensive sundress from Neiman Marcus that she'd charged on Jeffery's account, the same one she intended to wear when she walked out onto Main Street to announce that Alexis Moreau, former prom queen and current five-star chef, was back—was sitting in the trunk of her car.

Maybe they would be so dazzled by her Moreau smile and culinary prowess that they wouldn't notice her bare ring finger?

Yeah, right. They would take one look at her custard-stained sweats and realize that Lexi had gone from overachieving to barely surviving. And for a girl who, until recently, had received a gold star in the game of life, that didn't sit well with her current, and rapidly depleting, average.

Lexi looked down at herself, picked a curl of chocolate from her cleavage, and groaned. "Crap."

Her return home, much like the past six months, was turning out far differently than she'd envisioned.

Most people only got one shot at their dream. Lexi was about to get her second chance at running an acclaimed eatery, and she wasn't going to blow it. Making the right impression felt like the first step toward her new life.

She looked at the dozen or so boxes piled in the corner of her childhood room and forced herself to breathe. The last thing she wanted to do right then was unpack what was left of her marriage to find an outfit that didn't have melted ganache on the rear.

So, tossing her pants in the hamper and her custard-smeared tank top in the trash, she riffled through her grandmother's closet, coming up with a handful of old concert T-shirts, an aqua pantsuit in size twenty, Lexi's favorite pair of cutoffs from senior year, and her prom dress.

She grabbed the shorts and her grandmother's shirt, which said *Hoff This* under a smiling David Hasselhoff giving the finger, and tugged them on. The shirt came down to her thighs and her shorts came up to her butt, the last in a long list of things she wished she could reverse.

Lexi looked at the clock and her heart went heavy, because erasing the past ten years wasn't going to happen. Neither was ignoring the fact that her grandmother was expecting her in less than an hour, or that she would have to face her family and friends eventually. But when she did, it was going be on her terms. And in that damn sundress. Which meant she needed to get to her car.

Lexi grabbed her car keys and headed down the rear stairs. Cracking the door open, she glanced around, her shoulders relaxing slightly when she saw that the alley next to the bakery and the back parking lot where she'd parked her car was reassuringly empty.

She had snuck in and out of this apartment so many times as a teenager there was no reason that her heart should be pounding out of her chest right now. It was like riding a bike, right? The only difference was that back in high school, she had snuck around so that no one would know she was having sex with Jeffery, and now she was going stealth because she didn't want people to know that Jeffery had stopped having sex with her a long time ago.

"A quick grab and dash. That's all."

Coast clear, Lexi took a single step toward her car, then stiffened at the sound of feet pounding the pavement, followed by the instant clang of jangling metal. Both sounds were wild and hurried. And both sounds were moving.

Toward her.

"Shit!" Lexi reached back for the doorknob, twisted—nothing.

Shit. Shit. Shit!

It was locked. In her grandmother's mission to protect Lexi's teenage virtue, Pricilla had installed safety measures: a doorknob that was extremely loud to open, with a lock that was always engaged.

Lexi patted down the sides of her shorts, as though expecting to find magical pockets containing a set of apartment keys. Sadly, she found neither.

"Come here, boy," a distinctly male, and distinctly familiar, voice called out. Followed by a playful bark that sounded much closer.

Lexi froze, and last night's pastry dinner declared war on her stomach.

"That's it, come on. Good boy." Claws clicked excitedly on the pavement. A dog tore around the corner. He was some kind of mastiff-Thoroughbred mix with paws the size of a polar bear's and covered head to tail in mud. And he was headed directly toward her. "Damn it, Wingman, I said come!"

This could not be happening.

Fear had her feet moving—and fast. Lexi would rather explain to her grandmother that she had snuck into the apartment than face *him.* She shot around the corner of the building and, deciding that running didn't make her a coward, made a beeline down the alley next to the bakery, hoping to slip in the delivery door without being noticed.

She got to the corner of Main Street and stopped, her stomach plummeting to her toes.

The one-lane road was backed up with a line of cars that went past the Paws and Claws Day Spa, made its way beyond Bottles and Bottles—the local pharmacy *and* wine retailer—and continued toward the highway and the bright-green sign that read:

WELCOME TO ST. HELENA, CALIFORNIA
POPULATION 5,814
BLENDING POETRY IN A BOTTLE SINCE 1858

The sidewalks were even worse. The brick-and-awning storefronts and lamp-lined streets were filled with tourists, tourists, and more tourists, who were admiring the rows of old wine barrels filled with seasonal flowers and taking in the large banner advertising the St. Helena Summer Wine Showdown. Wine-tasting season was in full swing, and people were out in masses, which meant that Pricilla's Patisserie would be overflowing with locals, weekend warriors, and Sunday shoppers.

The second she walked into the bakery, she would run into a dozen people she knew, all with a dozen inappropriate questions that would lead to a dozen or more rumors about how Lexi had come crawling home—a divorced failure.

A gentle breeze blew past her, carrying with it the smell of freshly baked choux pastry. Lexi followed the scent and found that both of the windows her grandmother used to ventilate the rear kitchen were opened a crack.

She pried the first window open, her body turning on adolescent autopilot as she hoisted herself through. She got that same old high school thrill until she realized she didn't have the same old high school hips and found herself ass up, wedged between the window casing.

"Oh God, no." Lexi rocked, trying to gain enough momentum to tumble to the other side of the windowsill. "Please, no."

Seconds ticked by, and sweat beaded on her forehead. She clawed at the sill and kicked at the planter box she stood on, mentally willing her hips back to prom night—but she didn't move, or lose, an inch. No matter how hard she tried, she just couldn't squeeze herself through the window.

Refusing to give up, she looked around the kitchen, hoping to find something, anything that might help. But nothing useful was in reach—except for a fresh tray of éclairs, which sat just to her right.

Her body sank, dangling like raw dough over the windowsill. It was no use. She was stuck. Trying to move forward while dodging your past was clearly impossible. So she did what any reasonable woman would do under the circumstances: she reached across the table, plucked a petit-éclair from the tray, and shoved the entire thing in her mouth, making sure to lick her fingers clean in the process.

She was reaching for her second pastry when something cold and wet poked her in the butt. She yelped. There was a bark, a sniff, and the wet again.

"Shoo," Lexi hissed, waving her free hand even though the dog couldn't see. "Go away."

"He was just saying good morning."

Lexi froze, considering her options. When she realized she had none, she snapped, "Well, you should teach him some manners."

"Says the woman mooning half of St. Helena," the silky smooth and way-too-amused voice behind her said, as though she wasn't aware that her fanny was flapping in the wind.

"Plus, as far as Wingman is concerned, you were offering him up a doggie high five."

Closing her eyes, Lexi composed herself and went for enchanting—something she'd once excelled in. Hell, she'd been cheer captain *and* valedictorian.

But that was all before. Before the end of her marriage. Before she lost her restaurant. Before she found her husband trussed up like a Thanksgiving turkey in nothing but her award-winning *noix de coco brûlée* and a hard-on, while her sous chef Sara used a basting brush and caramelizing torch in ways that were illegal in thirty-seven of the fifty states.

And before she turned her head, looked up through the window, and found herself staring at the one person in town who had never found Alexis Moreau enchanting. In fact, Marco DeLuca, entitled playboy and total meathead, had gone out of his way over the years to let her know just how annoying he'd believed her to be.

Ignoring Marc's smart-ass grin and Wingman's breath on her thighs, Lexi realized that with her new diet of cynicism and foolishness, enchanting was no longer her. So she did the next best thing. She grabbed another éclair and—

"No, he doesn't do well with—"

—chucked it out the window. Barking and jumping ensued, accompanied by a lot of scrambling, mainly on Marc's part.

"No, boy. Drop it. That's right, custard's—"

Wingman went wild at the word, barking and panting with excitement. Lexi knew how the dog felt; she felt a bond forming between her and the canine.

"Get the custard," Lexi cooed.

"Don't say that word."

"What, *custard?*" Claws tapped the concrete as though Wingman was jumping up and down.

"Stop it," Marc directed at her, and then, "No, very bad. Let go, it gives you...Aw, Wingman!"

The window next to her squeaked open. By the time she turned her head, Marc was leaning in, his forearms leisurely resting on the windowsill, earbuds dangling around his neck, and his alpha-male swagger stinking up the kitchen.

"Heard you were coming home."

The way he said it, with an added little wink for extra sting, made her wonder just what else he had heard. Damn it. This was supposed to be a covert homecoming.

She grabbed the last éclair off the table and took a bite.

"I hope you brought enough to share with the class."

She could have told him that there was another tray on the far wall, but Marc had been a permanent pain in her butt ever since she moved to St. Helena with her mom freshman year. He'd either teased her mercilessly or ignored her completely, a hard accomplishment, since Marc loved everything with boobs.

She looked down at her breasts and paused. They weren't huge, but even in her grandmother's baggy T-shirt, they filled out the top nicely. Jeffery had never complained.

Then again, he had also left her for a loafer-wearing vegan who—although she had a bizarre food fetish—looked more like a librarian than the "other woman."

She took another bite and pondered. Whatever she and Marc used to have, confusing as it was, was just that—history. After she'd filed for a divorce, Lexi had gone from "pest-like friend" to "easily forgotten" in Marc's eyes. And it had hurt.

Even worse—for Lexi—Marc was not only loved by women, respected by men, adored by the elderly, a real hometown freaking hero, but he was also her ex-husband's best friend. Had been since preschool.

With a shrug she shoved almost the entire éclair in her mouth. Mumbling around the bits of flaky pastry and heavenly filling, she said, "Sorry, last one."

Marc reached through the window, snatched the remaining bite—the last and *best* bite.

"Give it back." Lexi's arms shot out to stop him. Only Marc was faster, and meaner. Palming her head with his free hand, he held her down while he savored the last piece.

Lexi swatted him away. "Does everyone get such a warm welcome?"

Reaching through the opened window, he wiped a glob of filling off the side of her mouth. Licking it clean, he smiled. "Only the ones who wear their breakfast, cream puff."

"I'll be sure to pack a napkin next time. And it's an éclair."

When Marc's hand made its way back toward her lips, she quickly wiped her mouth on her right shoulder. The white cotton came away with custard and chocolate smears.

"As great as it is to see you again, I'm kind of busy."

All traces of humor faded, and his eyes went soft. "I can see that. Need some help?"

Yes, she was about to beg. The offer seemed genuine enough, the last seventy-two hours had left her on the brink of tears, and for some bizarre reason Lexi wanted to give in to Marc's charm and gallantry.

Then Marc came up behind her and, pressing his body against hers, leaned over and reached around her to scrape some leftover filling off the tray. Never one to disappoint, he stepped back and ran a cream-coated finger down the back of her thigh before whistling, "Come here, boy."

Not caring if she kicked Marc, Lexi started pumping her limbs like a teeter-totter. She might not be the most athletic girl on the planet, but she could still inflict some damage.

"Hold up, you're going to hurt yourself." Warm, strong, and incredibly unsettling hands rested on her upper thigh, stopping her movements and sending her heart into overdrive. Not to mention making everything below her belly button tingle.

Oh, so not good. Over the years she'd seen many a girl rendered downright stupid by just a single flick of his panty-melting smile. Lexi was not, and never would be, one of *those* girls.

His hands drifted higher so that his fingertips brushed the bottom edge of her shorts. "Now push back against me, and I will slide you out of there."

"Nope. I've got it."

"You sure, cream puff?"

Oh yeah. The last thing she needed was his help.

Marc pressed forward, close enough that she could smell his soap. "It'll only take a minute. Then we never have to talk about it again."

"I'll manage."

"Yeah, while I'd love to sit back and watch you try, it's nearly ten, which means the Wine Train is about to disembark and its passengers will soon make their way down this alley, and your grandmother's expecting you any minute. So stop swinging those legs at me, and I'll help your stubborn ass out."

When she didn't budge, except to swing harder while aiming lower for more satisfying results, he said, "Or I can just shove you through to the other side. Either way, cream puff, I'm getting you out."

Running into Marc with her hair in a messy knot, last night's makeup on her face, and the unsettling feeling that he knew the truth behind her recent divorce was bad enough. Having him rescue her so he could call Jeffery later to laugh about her humiliating homecoming made her want to throw up.

But just like she'd known six months ago that she couldn't hold together her marriage, Lexi now knew Marc was right. She couldn't get out of the window by herself, and the Wine Train whistle was sounding closer by the minute, so she lowered her legs and reached back for his hands.

Alexis Moreau was a never-ending pain in Marc's ass—always had been. She was smart, stubborn, and sexy as hell, exactly how Marc liked 'em. She was also his best friend's girl, or ex-girl, which in man speak translated into hands off, something his brain had always known, but his dick had a hard time accepting.

If she hadn't seemed close to tears a moment ago—or seemed as though she would rather ram him in the nuts than accept his help—he would have kept walking. And that was exactly what he was going to do, right after he got her out of the window, made sure she wasn't hurt, and found the spare key to Pricilla's apartment, which he was certain was hidden under the garden gnome.

That was his plan, anyway, until he placed his hands on her waist, gently slid her from the window, and registered what she was wearing. The usually coiffed and primped prom queen was in a pair of butt-hugging cutoffs—which he assumed at one time had been jeans—a thin white shirt, and not much else. She was a big, rumpled, blonde mess, and by the hollowness he heard in her mumbled "thanks" when he set her on her feet, he'd bet it wasn't just a physical thing. Odd, since she'd been the one to walk away from her marriage and Pairing, the upscale New York restaurant that she and Jeff had opened a few years back.

Then Lexi bent over and reached sideways through the window to grab an éclair off another table inside, angling her body just right so that he got a near-perfect view of *her* pairing, pink bra and all, and her failed marriage was the last thing on his mind.

He stood back and smiled, not even bothering to pretend he wasn't staring when she twisted farther to reach the treat, the movement tugging her shirt up and her shorts down low enough to prove she liked her lace matching. God, she was killing him.

"I'm guessing you're okay then?"

"What?" She turned her head to look at him, those big green eyes wide in question. He merely dropped his gaze to her ass sticking up out of the window. "Oh, um, I'm fine. Just hungry." She extracted herself from the window, sans the éclair, and straightened, pulling her too-long tee down.

Sad to lose his view but desperate to get out of such close proximity, Marc told her about the key under the gnome and turned. He was about to leave when her hands settled on his arm and—goddamned son of a bitch—her touch sent a hot sexual zing shooting through his entire body.

Marc liked women. All kinds of women. He liked the way they smelled, the way they felt, the way they sounded calling out his name. He especially liked the last part.

He just couldn't like *this* woman, not in *that* way. Not in any way other than as a friend.

Ever.

Yeah, good luck with that, he told himself, remembering how he'd said those same exact words on graduation night, when he'd found her crying under the bleachers because Jeff, wanting to start college a free agent with open possibilities, had broken up with her. A week and some lame advice later, Lexi had left, following Jeff to New York with hopes of saving their relationship.

Lexi must have felt something too, because she jerked her hand back and eyed him cautiously. "You promised me earlier that we'd never talk about this again. Did you mean to anyone?"

Marc looked down the alley at Mrs. Lambert of Grapevine Prune and Clip and her partner in crime, Mrs. Kincaid—who, from the looks on their faces, had been watching the entire event unfold—and wondered how Lexi intended to keep her window fiasco a secret. St. Helena was a small town located in the heart of the Napa Valley, with two blocks of downtown, two gas stations, and only two commodities: wine and gossip. Now that two pairs of the loosest lips in the county were firsthand witnesses, those who hadn't been there were bound to get a stellar reenactment by lunch.

Lexi ignored the women and stared up at him, pleading—and with one look at the anxious way she worried her lower lip, he understood. She wasn't talking about the town; she was afraid this would get back to Jeff. Which made no sense at all.

Last he'd heard Lexi hadn't given a rat's ass about Jeff's opinion, which was one of the reasons their restaurant had been foundering in the year or so leading up to the divorce. But if she wanted her morning kept a secret, who was he to ruin her day?

"Deal."

"Thanks," Lexi whispered.

Marc's phone chirped. He didn't move to answer it.

"I'll let you get that and"—she paused and offered up a pathetic smile—"thanks."

Marc should have taken the opportunity to get the hell out of there. Instead, he found himself sending the call to voice mail without even looking at the screen. "Look, when the rest of your stuff gets here, let me know and I can help you unload."

He should be putting space between them, not offering to get all hot and sweaty in her room. Even if it was just from moving her boxes.

"Except for my dress, I already unloaded everything." Marc looked at her gnat-sized car and frowned. As if reading his mind, she continued, "I got a really fair offer for the house as is, with the furniture, which worked for me. I bought everything to fit that house, and it meant less for me to move."

"You sold your place in New York?" That surprised him. Every time he went back east to visit, Lexi was remodeling or decorating or refinishing some part of that house. It was a cozy little brownstone with a tiny backyard in one of the more family-centric boroughs. And Lexi had loved it. Jeff, on the other hand, had been pulling for a plush loft uptown near their restaurant.

"Hard to start over when you're dragging the past with you. Plus—"

Marc's phone rang. Again.

"You should probably get that," she said, already backing away.

Marc looked down at the screen and groaned. Wingman growled. It read "Natasha Duval." It also said that he'd missed three calls from the very same.

Shit.

He'd been playing phone tag with Natasha all week. Okay, maybe he was avoiding her calls. He hadn't spoken to her since, well, the week before Valentine's Day, when they'd run into each other at a party she was catering. Natasha had been wearing a tight red dress held together by a single scrap of ribbon that she made clear she wanted him to untie, so he brought her back to his suite at the hotel and diligently unwrapped her. At the time it had seemed like the perfect arrangement.

She wasn't looking for serious, a good thing, since he didn't do serious. Ever. He'd made that clear.

Apparently not clear enough, because the phone rang again and Wingman instinctively curled up on Marc's feet and whimpered. Another reason to send her to voice mail: Natasha didn't do dogs.

"When are you going to learn?" Lexi lectured from beside him. "You can't just keep ignoring women and hope they'll go away."

"You know what? You're absolutely right." He handed her the phone. "Here."

She shook her head while backing away. "What are we, in high school? No way. I stopped being your winggirl when Bethany Jones called me crying about how you were her soul mate and I had to tell her that you were gay."

"I still can't believe you said that." Or that Bethany had bought it. Marc rested his palm on the brick wall, sending a flirty wink at a brunette wearing a push-up bra who passed by the alley. Push-up flushed and looked away.

Gay, my ass.

"Come on. One last call," Marc heard himself beg. "Then we'll be even."

"Even? You said we wouldn't ever talk about this." She gestured vaguely to the window.

The phone rang, louder and more obnoxious than the last time. Marc felt his left eye twitch.

"Doesn't mean that we both won't know you still owe me one." Marc hated pulling that. He had no intention of holding Lexi's inability to climb through a window over her head. But he also had no intention of dealing with Natasha right now.

Not before his morning coffee and chocolate croissant. Not when Marc was trying to prove to himself—and his brothers—that bowing out of the family wine business and dumping every cent he had into renovating an old hotel, which was becoming a serious money pit, was a smart move. And not when the most prestigious blind wine tasting in the country, the St. Helena Summer Wine Showdown, was just six weeks away and being held in his hotel. He couldn't afford any distractions.

He couldn't afford to fuck this up.

The phone gave one final ring and went silent. Marc exhaled and, after making sure the phone hadn't somehow connected, sagged against the brick wall, relieved.

It immediately rang again.

Marc rolled his head so he was looking at Lexi, making sure to turn on the charm. "Come on, cream puff."

"Don't aim that at me." She pointed to his face. "I'm immune." Didn't he know it. The one woman who couldn't be charmed was the only one who mattered.

Forcing an unaffected smile, one that he'd mastered after fifteen years of watching Lexi and Jeff together, he played his winning card. It was a crappy card to play, but suddenly this wasn't about avoiding Natasha as much as it was about getting back to where he and Lexi used to be.

"You don't have thirty seconds to help an old friend out?"

Something painful flickered in Lexi's expression. Marc didn't know why he suddenly felt like shit, but his gut got that squirrelly feeling he hated. The one that came when he knew he'd screwed up. Before he could figure out what he'd done, Lexi held out her hand.

"Fine. I'll do it. But then we're even. Agreed?"

"Agreed."

He handed her the phone. She didn't take it. "But I'm not pretending to be your spiritual life coach."

"All right."

"Or your nonna, sister, stalker, or any other woman who has possession issues." Marc nodded. "You have fifteen seconds to explain the logistics of this latest conquest. Go."

"Fine. We spent a few nights together. She wanted more. I said no, too busy focusing on my hotel and the Summer Wine Showdown. We parted friends. Now she's calling again."

"That's all of the story."

"Yup."

She reached over and, instead of taking the phone like he'd expected, hit speakerphone. "Marco DeLuca's office, how may I help you?"

The phone remained silent.

"Hello?" Lexi prompted.

"Um…yes." Natasha's voice sounded through the phone. It was pinched and pissed and, unless Marc was mistaken, jealous. It also was nasal and annoying, something he'd never noticed before today. "I'm calling for Marco."

Lexi gave Marc a where-do-you-find-these-women roll of the eyes. "Unfortunately, he's in a meeting right now. Can I take a message?"

"A meeting?" Natasha's tone all but said *liar, liar.* "Well, when he's done with his *meeting*, make sure he closes the window. I would hate for someone to sneak into the bakery and steal your secret recipes."

The phone went silent.

Lexi blinked at the phone and then him. "Why do I get the feeling that there is so much more to the story than you are letting on?"

"When have I ever lied to you?" *Well, besides the time you asked me if following Jeff to New York was a good idea and I said yes.*

"Never." She frowned. "But I still don't believe that this woman spent just a few nights with you and now she's all stalker."

"Believe it." Marc smiled. "I'm that good."

"She's watching you. She threatened to steal my grand-mother's recipes! What kind of women are you dating?"

She stopped, raising a hand. "You know what, never mind. I don't care. I am so over men and their choices in women."

Someone cleared her throat—loudly. Lexi jumped at the sound and let out a yelp when she turned and saw Natasha smiling at her from the end of the alley.

Lexi slowly turned back to face him, her mouth gaping open, her eyes forming two pissed-off slits. "You. Slept. With. Natasha. Duval?"

Marc shrugged, feeling way more anxious that he was letting on. "I was clear with her, nothing serious."

"She's been trying to corner you into *serious* since sophomore year." Oh yeah, he'd forgotten that. "When you made me break up with her for you. Twice." Lexi looked down the alley and gave a little wiggle of her fingers and shouted, "Hey, Natasha. Long time no see."

Natasha gave an eat-shit smile in return. No wave.

Lexi turned back to Marc. "Make that three times. And she's still here. Like that freaky cat off *Pet Sematary*."

"I can hear you," Natasha said, pointing to her wireless earpiece with her long red nails. They looked like claws. Sharp, red claws made for sinking into a man and never letting go. Marc shivered.

Natasha pocketed her phone and swished her way toward them, her hips working double time, then plastered herself to Marc in a hug when she got close enough.

"Hey, Marc," she said too sweetly, finally pulling back from the hug.

"Hey, Natasha," he began, stepping away from her. To avoid saying something stupid, like agreeing to another date, he focused on her eyes and away from her cleavage. She subtly shifted, crossing her arms and smashing her breasts together, and "Sorry about not getting back to you" came sputtering out of his mouth.

"That's okay, I get it. The Showdown is next month, and I know you've been swamped with trying to get your celebrity judge and a new caterer"—her eyes flickered to Lexi, and Marc felt his heart literally slam into his chest—"which is why I was trying to set up a time to chat. There's a guy I cater for sometimes, anyway he's an editor at *Martha Stewart Living*. I told him he should do a spread on your hotel for their summer-getaway issue."

Natasha was positioning herself and trying to use their history and her connections to lock down the Showdown catering gig, which pissed him off even further, but he was willing to agree to anything if it meant getting rid of her before she said something that would make Lexi's homecoming even worse.

"That's great. How about dinner?"

"Really?" Natasha sounded way too happy for a no-strings former fuck buddy. "I can't wait. Plus, I want to hear all about your trip to *New York*." She emphasized the last words with a pointed glare. At Lexi. Whose lower lip trembled. *Ah, shit!* "That is, if you're done with your *meeting*."

"Oh, we're done," Lexi said.

CHAPTER 2

*D**one* was such an understatement, Lexi thought as she took off down the alley toward Main Street.

"Screw the dress." And screw her homecoming.

Lexis tugged her T-shirt farther down her thighs, turned right on Main Street, and stormed toward her grandmother's shop. It was the one place in her world where Lexi had always felt safe. And all she wanted to do was crawl into her *grand-mère*'s arms and settle in for a good cry—and maybe some homemade fudge.

"Hold up, will ya?" Marc yelled after her.

Lexi kept right on going, even though Marc had no trouble keeping up. With his long legs, she had to take two steps for his every one to ensure she made it inside before he got to her.

"I see you still walk fast when you're mad."

"I'm not mad," she said truthfully.

She was livid, and she didn't understand why. Lexi knew why Marc had gone to New York recently, and apparently so did Natasha. It wasn't as though she'd expected Marc *not* to go to Jeffery and Sara's wedding. Since Marc was Jeffery's oldest friend, she assumed he'd be the best man—just like he had been for *their* wedding.

The problem was that the divorce had only been finalized Friday, the same day as Jeff's rehearsal dinner. The rat bastard couldn't even wait a day to move on with his life, to erase almost fifteen years of memories from his mind. And the knowing glance Natasha shot her meant everybody in town already knew. It also meant that, although Jeffery had promised no one back home knew about the affair, there was the distinct possibility that he'd lied.

Big shocker there.

Lexi reached for the door handle and heard the familiar jingle of the bells on the other side, welcoming her home, when Marc's hand covered hers. "Really? Then why do you look like you want to hit me?"

It wasn't his hold that had her halting in her tracks, or even his smart mouth, it was the softness in his voice and the way his thumb traced gently over her bare finger.

"Look, Jeff called and asked me to be in the wedding. He's been my best friend since preschool." The word *friend* made her heart ache. At one time she'd considered Marc her friend, even through all of the teasing and pranks—but friends didn't just disappear. "I couldn't say no."

"I never expected you to." But she had expected him to check in on her, even if it was just a phone call to make sure she was okay—which she hadn't been. She had been scared and hurt and heartbroken. And since all of her friends in New York were somehow connected to the restaurant—and Jeffery—she had also been completely alone.

To an extent, she understood. Divorces were messy, awkward for everyone involved. But Lexi hadn't been the one to cheat, and yet she had lost everything. Looking back on the past six months, she realized that Marc's silence had hurt the worst. "Thanks for the help, but I can take it from here."

"Look, it's obvious you had a rough night."

Lexi looked down at her clothes. Did she really look that bad? Marc's grimace said she did.

"How about you come back to the hotel with me—" Before she could even roll her eyes at his cheesy line, he put his hands up in a show of innocence. "Just for a nap and to get something other than chocolate and sugar in your system."

Lexi looked down Main toward the Napa Grand and couldn't help but smile. The once-dilapidated hotel stood elegant and proud. The windows, no longer boarded over, were framed with beautifully handcrafted edging, and ornate marble casings hugged the corners of the building. Even the original stained-glass panes over the circular entry had been painstakingly recreated. It was incredible.

The first time she'd gone inside the hotel, Marc had convinced her that it was haunted. They had snuck in the through the broken window in the back by the loading dock. Even at fourteen, Lexi had been pretty certain that he just wanted to charm his way into her panties, but confident that her panties weren't easily charmed, she'd agreed. To her surprise, instead of making his move, Marc had taken her by the hand and led her around the place, explaining the history of the hotel and how it had, at one time, been an important asset to the Napa Valley. Then, after swearing her to secrecy, he'd explained how one day he was going to buy the building and restore it to its original state.

In a rare show of uncertainty, he had gone on to explain that it was a dumb idea, since DeLucas made wine, not hotels. Too late, Lexi had been captivated by his vision; where his family saw cobwebs and rotted boards, Lexi saw what Marc did: something magical, tying this generation to a time that was simpler, full of elegance and class.

She looked at the intricate glass dome over what she remembered to be the ballroom and smiled. He'd accomplished that—and more.

Suddenly everything seemed so overwhelming. She really wanted a nap. A stealthy lowering of the head and quick whiff confirmed that she was in desperate need of a shower. More than anything, she needed to pull it together so she could be on her best game if she expected to face her grandma and not crumble.

"I'm really sorry," Marc whispered, his fingers threading with hers in a sign of support. Was he sorry for not calling? Or because Jeffery had left her for a bowl of chicken noodle soup? That's what Sara was—comfortable, nurturing, and homey—with a dash of kink.

Whatever the reason, the small offer brought tears to her tired eyes. Yeah, regrouping before the onslaught of questions sounded nice. Until she realized that Marc was staring down at her with a big dose of pity. Just like Jeffery had when he'd told her he didn't even want to try to make it work, that he was already in love with Sara.

"I'm fine, actually," she said, pulling her hand away. Because she was not some woman who crumbled every time a man broke her heart. She was not her mother.

Lexi ignored Marc's raised brow, and the fact that she was standing on Main Street in her grandmother's shirt and people were starting to recognize her and wave. "Thanks for the offer, but I'm good."

"Lexi, wait." Marc's hand shot out, grabbing her elbow. "I can't let you go in there."

That was all she wanted right now. To hug her grandma, make her way upstairs to her room, and get away from the probing eyes. She wanted to be alone. With an éclair.

"I wasn't aware that you were my newly appointed social advisor. See ya later, Marc."

She opened the pastry-shop door and took in a deep, calming breath. Cinnamon, vanilla, and the smell of home only made holding back tears all the more difficult. Especially when she took one step inside, looked past the life-sized cardboard cutout of *Baywatch*-era David Hasselhoff in red trunks, chest hair, and a plastic lei, past the glass display case filled with petits fours and truffles, past her utter humiliation to lock eyes with Pricilla, who, dressed in a grass skirt and crocheted coconuts, looked as startled to see Lexi as Lexi was when a good portion of the town leaped out from behind the counter and yelled, "Surprise!"

Everyone froze with smiles in place. Arms out wide.

A party popper exploded.

Her grandmother shifted on her orthopedics.

And without a word, Lexi took one step back, then another, turning on her third step to run—straight into a solid mass of warm, manly muscles.

"Easy there." Marc's arms came around her to help steady her, she was sure. It actually threw her off more than the surprise party. Or the fact that the portion of the town that was here was the male half. "You run now and everyone will talk."

"But I'm a mess," she whispered into his chest. "And why are there so many men here?"

"Our grandmothers have been conspiring again," he whispered back, and she could hear the smile in his voice.

Pricilla and ChiChi Ryo had been trying to marry off their grandkids for years. All in the name of procreation. And now that ChiChi had her a new granddaughter, with another one on the way, Pricilla desperately wanted someone to dote on. Lexi had thought her grandma would give her at least a few months to ease into being back home and single. Apparently not.

"You could have at least warned me." He thankfully didn't mention that he had, in his high-handed way, tried to warn her.

"And miss all the fun?"

"Yeah." She looked down at the disaster she had become. "Fun."

Then Marc did the most un-Marc-like thing ever. Instead of telling her how stubborn she was or pointing out the fact that she matched the *Baywatch* decor, he tucked a finger under her chin, lifted her gaze to his, and said softly enough that only she could hear, "You are Alexis Moreau. Student-body president, prom queen, valedictorian, and the most distinguished pastry chef that St. Helena High's culinary-immersion program ever graduated."

She didn't know about the last part; her grandmother pretty much took that title. But the conviction behind his words, his belief in her, almost made it feel real. Back straight, chest high, sending crumbs scattering to the ground, she fluffed her mop of hair and, ignoring Marc as he swiped a glob of éclair filling off her top, cocked her head slightly to the side—and went for enchanting.

"Now, turn around," he whispered, taking her by the shoulders and spinning her to face the awaiting guests. "Flash that sexy girl-next-door smile."

He thought her smile was sexy?

"And show them that you are here to kick ass and take names." Then, with a resounding smack on the rump, he said, really loudly, "Bring on the bachelors."

Two hours, eleven minutes, and three éclairs later, Lexi lay on her grandmother's floral couch, a plastic lei pressing into her cheek as she smothered her face with the throw pillows. She had a headache, a stomachache, and a date lined up for every night of the following three weeks, five for this coming weekend. It wasn't enough that Jeff was enjoying *their* time-share in the Keys with his new wife, or that when they came home Sara would be cooking in Lexi's kitchen, serving *her* customers *her* special menu. Now Lexi was back in St. Helena, a divorcée with a grandmother who thought she was too pathetic to get her own dates.

"I don't think chocolate's going to fix this one," Pricilla said, sounding bewildered by her own statement.

Lexi pulled the pillow off her face and glanced up to see her grandmother in the doorway, all soft curves and frosted tips. Wearing a concert tee and a black pleather skort, she looked more like a geriatric roadie than one of the most distinguished pâtissiers in the country.

She came bustling over, two teacups dangling from one hand and a bottle of Angelica in the other. It was barely past the lunch hour, too early to start drinking. Especially since Pricilla put her own Parisian twist on her Angelica, meaning she fortified it with cognac so it was strong enough to cure copper pots.

"I was hoping that the party would have lasted a little longer," she said, setting the teacups next to a plate of miniquiches on the coffee table. She filled each cup to the rim before swatting Lexi's legs off the couch and taking up residence in the now-vacant spot. "You shooed everyone away before Chad Stevens showed up."

"Chad Stevens?" The guy who used to sit across from her in homeroom? He was popular, good looking, played football, and smelled like Ovaltine. He also had boundary issues, meaning he took issue when other people expressed that they had boundaries.

"He's been asking about your arrival for weeks. Did I mention that he works at Stevens, Stevens, and Stevens?"

"He's a lawyer?" The idea that a guy like Chad, even though he came from a family of suits, was a legitimate part of the judicial process made her pick up her cup by the dainty handle and chug.

If it was afternoon in St. Helena, it was happy hour in New York.

"And quite the looker, if you ask me. Tall, dark, wears custom suits. I always liked a man who took the time to have his clothes tailored. Your grandpa, God rest his soul, always wore his clothes pressed and tailored."

"I thought Grandpa owned a tire shop."

"Didn't mean that he lacked the respect to dress like a gentleman," Pricilla chided.

"Grandma, it's sweet that you went to all the trouble to throw me a party and"—she choked on the next words—"*arranged* for me to meet some nice men, but—"

Pricilla grabbed a quiche and, before Lexi could seal her lips closed, shoved it in, silencing any further disagreement. "There's more on that Match site. After ChiChi and Lucinda helped me post your profile, we had nearly a hundred winks—and all local."

Oh God, there were more men? She needed another refill. And a quiche.

"You don't even own a computer."

"I do now. Gabe's new wife, Regan, has us ladies all teched up and web savvy. I even have a smartphone for when I'm out and want to use the Twitter. My handle is HotBuns, one word with the circled little *a* before it, if you want to follow me. I'm up to seven thousand followers."

"Grandma, I'm just not ready to jump back into dating yet," Lexi said, and lame excuse or not, it was true.

After Lexi interrupted the great basting debacle of her marriage, her confidence took a serious hit. Up until that moment, she'd assumed Jeffery's lack of interest in sex was due to the long hours he was working, not that *her* sex appeal lacked interest.

She used to consider herself a romantic. Not anymore. She'd been there, done that, already returned the T-shirt.

"And going out with a bunch of guys that my *grandma* set me up with will make me look even more pathetic," she added.

"Oh, honey. I didn't place that ad because I didn't think you could find your own gentleman friend. I did it because I knew you would bury yourself in work and spend every night alone in this apartment wondering what went wrong in New York." Pricilla set her cup down and wrapped a meaty arm around Lexi's shoulders, tugging her close. "But I'd like to hear why *you* think you're pathetic."

Lexi wrapped her arms around Pricilla's waist and snuggled in deeper. She smelled like flour and alcohol and home. One sniff and Lexi felt the tears threaten. "I thought we had a good relationship, me and Jeffery, but he never even told me that he was interested in culinary foreplay."

"Of course not, dear," Pricilla cooed, smoothing a hand down Lexi's hair. "You are a good Catholic girl, and he respected you too much for that."

"We haven't gone to church since I was seven." Lexi sniffed. "Plus, Jeffery respected Sara enough to *marry* her."

"In a hotel. With her best friend as acting as officiant. She's probably a Protestant."

"She's going to run *my* kitchen."

"Which means that you got to come home and finally help me turn Pricilla's Patisserie into what we always dreamed it could be."

Lexi had fallen in love with food at a young age, the tastes, textures, and different combinations fascinating her. By the time she was in middle school, she knew a career in the culinary arts was her future. And opening the Sweet and Savory Bistro, with her grandmother, had always been at the center of that dream.

"You and I both know that this town needs a place where locals can share a meal without all the fuss and fanfare of the Napa Valley. Simple food for simple people," Pricilla went on.

It was also a simple solution to Lexi's financial problems. She owed her grandmother a great deal of money, and this was the perfect way to pay her back—for everything Pricilla had done for her over the years.

"I know, and I'm excited that we finally get to do this."

Jeffery had promised that after college they would move back to St. Helena, but then he found the perfect vacancy in Manhattan for their dream restaurant and put in an offer without consulting her. Wanting to make her marriage work, she had believed him when he promised they would only need three years to get Pairing up and running and then they could open their West Coast location and move home.

Then again, he'd also promised to honor and to cherish.

Three years had turned into six, and Jeffery showed no interest in moving home. He also showed no interest in her opinions on how the restaurant should be run, how going organic and local would help boost sales, or how not making time for *them* could ruin their marriage. The only thing he had listened to her on was their unique menu and the unexpected pairings of flavors, something the restaurant had become famous for and something that Lexi was extremely proud of. And that menu was the only good thing she had salvaged from their marriage.

"But parading around with a different guy every night isn't my style. Plus, what kind of man agrees to go out with someone's granddaughter?"

"I met your grandfather that way," Pricilla scoffed.

"You met Grandpa at the track. Betting on a race."

"Yes, well, my grandfather taught me how to place bets. I was very good. And Perkins"—Lexi felt Pricilla sigh—"he was so handsome. Walked right up into the stands between races and asked me if he could have the privilege of escorting me to dinner after the last race. We stayed up until nearly midnight talking and holding hands and sharing dreams about the future. We married three weeks later."

The dreamy look that her grandmother got whenever she talked about Perkins made Lexi's heart ache. What would it be like to have a love affair like that? Sure, Lexi had loved Jeffery, but never with the fierceness that her grandmother displayed.

"I didn't know Grandpa raced?"

"Oh, he didn't race. He was in charge of the tires. But after we married he opened up the tire shop, and two years later he'd made enough money to build me the patisserie. When your mother came along, he added this apartment so I could keep early baker's hours and still be with the family. We never liked to be apart for long."

Lexi hadn't been able to get Jeffery to agree to be in the same room with her for more than an hour unless it was at the restaurant. "I just need time, Grandma. I haven't even been divorced a week. The last thing I want to do is end up like Mom."

Lexi's parents had divorced when she was seven. Since then Evelyn Moreau had been in love a total of fifteen times, engaged eleven, married to six different men, and lived through seven divorces. Husband number three was stupid enough to also be divorcé number six. And last Valentine's Day, Evelyn Moreau had been stupid enough to say yes to her twelfth proposal and follow a retired podiatrist to Palm Beach.

"If I hadn't spent thirty-nine hours in labor with her, and if her daddy hadn't died when she was just a child, I would have shot her by now." Pricilla sighed. "Honey, you could never be like your mother even if you tried. You're hard-working and driven and just about the sweetest, most loyal person I know. Which is why you would never ask me to go back to those nice young men and cancel their dates. They are looking forward to seeing you, and it would be rude."

Grandma was right; Lexi was never rude. She prided herself on that…although when it came to Marc, she couldn't seem to remember her manners.

"Fine, I will go on the dates"—she held up a hand as Pricilla practically quivered with delight—"but *only* the ones that I have already agreed to, no more. And no more Match.com, got it?"

"You always were stubborn." Pricilla leaned over and kissed Lexi on the forehead. "Think of it as preparation for Mr. Right."

"Mr. Right?" Lexi's stomach suddenly hollowed out. The twinkle in her grandmother's eyes only made it worse.

"How are you supposed to know what you *are* looking for if you've only ever really dated one man?" Pricilla stood and gathered the dishes. "Your mother's problem was she would never go out with a Mr. Wrong, so everyone became Mr. Right. If you date a bunch of different men with no pressure about the future, you won't mistake a Wrong for a Right ever again. That way you'll know a Right when you meet him."

Lexi ducked into Picker's Produce, Meats, and More, grabbed a bar of specialty chocolate, and managed to sneak past the owner, Mrs. Craver, who was arguing with Mr. Craver—her estranged husband, who also happened to be the butcher.

Normally Lexi would say hello and politely inquire as to how things were in the grocers' business, but today she was in a rush. She needed some kind of citrus for her citrus-infused chocolate sauce and a few minutes to pull herself together before she went back to the bakery, where three very opinionated grannies were setting the table for lunch.

Lexi had wanted to thank Pricilla for letting her stay in the apartment, and ChiChi for giving her grandmother a place to live until Lexi found her own pad. What she hadn't wanted was to endure an hour-long interrogation about yesterday's date with Mr. Monday Night, especially since Mr. Monday Night had turned out to be every bit a Monday: jarring, exhausting, and a calamity of errors. He was cute in that finance-guy kind of way and late in that my-meeting-ran-over-and-it-will-never-happen-again kind of way. The only thing he did get right was the never-going-to-happen-again portion of the evening.

When she'd decided to move back to St. Helena and Pricilla had insisted on Lexi taking over the apartment completely, she had believed her grandmother's intentions to be pure: A quiet place for Lexi to grieve and reassess. Now, after seeing her list of bachelors, the only thing Lexi had reassessed was Pricilla's motive—she didn't want her granddaughter to have to fiddle with a sock on the doorknob.

Well, Grandmère, *you moved out in vain*, Lexi thought. She was done with knobs, fiddling or otherwise.

Her heels clicked on the barn-style wood floors, stopping right before she reached the white painted line that separated Mr. Craver's part of the store—the butcher's shop—from Mrs. Craver's part—everything else. The specialty grocer had been around since 1894 and the Cravers for about as long. Marilee asked for a divorce about a year after they were married, and Biff denied her request on the grounds that the divorce would make his wife happy. Livid, Marilee painted a white line down the middle of the store and told her husband that if he ever crossed the line she'd claim crime of passion. And the fighting had been going on ever since.

Lexi dropped two Valencia oranges into her basket and then paused, looking at the sour oranges two barrels over. She picked one up and smelled it, the bitter scent tickling the tip of her nose. The blood orange might be too sweet, but was the sour one too acidic?

She didn't know. And that made her nervous. Today's lunch was special because it was the first time she would be cooking for her grandmother since Jeffery left her for chicken noodle soup. Too bad that it was not the first time since discovering the affair that Lexi had been unsure of what ingredients would work best. Not a good sign for her future as a Michelin-starred chef hopeful.

"Bought some of those last week. Biggest mistake of my life."

Lexi turned and found Nora Kincaid, current treasurer of the Daughters of the Prohibition and a big enough busybody to give ChiChi a run for her money, hunched over her shopping cart, her teeth bared in what appeared to be a smile.

"Why's that?" Lexi asked, even though she knew better. But she was having a crisis of the culinary kind and needed help.

"Bitter, I tell you. Made me salivate until my Harvey though I'd gone rabid." Nora grabbed the orange and set it back in the barrel with a disgusted tut, and Lexi wasn't so sure it was the salivation that had led Harvey to that conclusion. "If you ask me, things here have been going downhill ever since Marilee started selling produce from Chile."

Nora shot a glance at Marilee, who was standing behind the cash register, and dropped her voice. "I hear it's because Biff told her that real Americans didn't sell foreign wares and he would have nothing to do with it. She told him that real men don't need so many little blue pills to make it happen down there and then started importing things from all over."

Nora leaned in closer. "My Harvey never needed any of those blue pills. His plumbing works just fine, and I do my job as a wife."

"Um, congratulations," Lexi said, looking around, not sure what she was supposed to say.

"Oh my. This is awkward, isn't it? I didn't mean to imply—" Nora glanced down at Lexi's bare ring finger, and before Lexi could defend herself against the nonimplication, Nora changed the subject. "Nonetheless, I'm glad I ran into you."

Lexi wasn't sure she could return the sentiment.

"Your grandmother signed on to provide all the pastries for the Book Walk this Saturday."

"I saw it on her calendar." The Book Walk was run by the Community Action Committee and helped the library raise funds for new books. Pricilla had been the food vendor of choice ever since Lexi could remember.

"Last month we advertised her being there, and she only showed up with enough pastries to feed a handful of people," Nora sniffed. "So unless you can promise me provisions for half the town, I'm going to have to give her contract to someone else."

"What?" Lexi stammered. "No, my grandma loves that event." She had no idea what the real story was, but if Pricilla was shorting her customers, then it wasn't good. "There'll be more than enough for everyone. I promise."

"Good, because my grandson Grayson is taking you to BoVine Thursday night, and he doesn't like flaky women." The woman gave Lexi a slow and thorough once-over. The wag of her head told Lexi she'd come up short. "He's also never needed a blue pill. But just to be safe, try dressing to inspire, dear."

Lexi looked down at her dress. It was fun, cute, and showed just enough cleavage to be flirty. She set her basket down and tugged at the neckline of her dress. Still not satisfied, she gave another tug.

"Any lower and Mr. Craver might just fall over the counter."

She looked up. Nora was gone and—

Great.

Marc leaned against the display housing cucumbers and zucchini. Dressed in a pair of cargo shorts, a gray shirt that hugged his muscular chest, and a navy baseball cap, he held a bag of beef jerky, a power drink, and enough raw testosterone to make what should have been vineyard casual look ruggedly sexy—and extremely inspiring.

"It's the hair," he said, and she agreed. He had really great hair. Even though it was only peeking out the back of the cap, she knew it was dark and thick, and she understood why women would want to run their fingers through it—other women, that is, not her.

She'd given in to lust with Jeffery, and look where that had gotten her. Nope, not a cycle she was interested in repeating anytime soon.

"I meant *your* hair," he said, reaching up and taking out the elastic band she was wearing. Her hair came loose and tumbled down her back.

When he ran his fingers through it a few times and then pulled it forward over her shoulder, his hand grazing her bare skin, her body started to tingle. And when he murmured, "Hair like yours should never be pulled back," that annoying tingle became a full-blown hum.

No way in hell, she thought, taking a step back. *Not him.*

She didn't have the time for men right now. And she didn't have the experience *with* men to tangle with a guy like Marco DeLuca—ever.

Her first thought was to grab her oranges and run. Then she remembered that Marc loved food almost as much as she did. That she still hadn't figured out what was wrong with her sauce. And that she was tired of running from men.

Sexy hum or not.

She grabbed a dark-chocolate bar from her basket and broke off a square. "Open up." He did, and she shoved it in his mouth. "Now smell this." She placed the Valencia orange to his nose.

"It smells really"—he cracked a smile—"orangey."

"Orangey? That all you've got?"

"Fruity?" He shrugged matter-of-factly, but his eyes were twinkling with humor.

"Never mind, smell this." She grabbed the sour orange and put it to his nose.

His nostrils flared, and he scrunched up his face. *Dang it.* Why was this so hard? She was picking out an acid for her sauce, for God's sake. It was Cooking 101.

"What were you hoping for?"

"Well, not fruity or *orangey*, and definitely not—" She mimicked his disgusted expression, and he laughed. "I was hoping for more tart, I guess. It's for a sauce to go over a pepper-crusted lamb chop."

He turned the bill of his cap backward and surveyed the choices. Lexi was too busy trying not to survey him to notice how many varieties of oranges the store offered.

"How about this?" He broke off a chunk of chocolate and held it to her mouth. When she didn't open, he teased it across the seam of her lips until she parted them on a gasp. He slid the chocolate in and she nearly moaned, because of the chocolate or the fluttering going on in her girly region, she didn't know.

Marc reached behind him, and when he turned back around, he stared down at her with those intense brown eyes and cocked a brow. She figured *what the hell* and opened.

"Oh my God," she moaned, savoring the bitter and tart and dissecting each individual taste. "Is that a kumquat? I never would have thought to add that. It's incredible."

"Yes, you would have. You made me a chocolate cake with these things on the top for my eighteenth birthday."

She had. How had she forgotten that? And why had he remembered?

"How many do you need?" he asked, smiling smugly.

"About twenty, I guess. They're so small."

Marc bagged her citrus and dropped it in her basket. Bending over, he grabbed the handles and strode off—with her groceries.

"What are you doing?" She followed behind him.

"What else do you need?" He didn't slow down.

"What I *need* is to carry my own basket to the counter and pay so I can get home."

"Great, checkout it is." He never broke his stride and wouldn't give up the basket.

"Fine," she conceded, looking at his groceries, "but I need a few things first."

CHAPTER 3

Marc smiled as she led him around the store, those heels of hers slapping the ground and a delicate, feminine scent lingering behind her. "A few things" didn't even begin to describe what she was buying. She loaded up the basket with a loaf of herbed focaccia bread, a block of wasabi gouda, adding an apple and some kind of bone that Biff wrapped specially for her. He had no idea what she was going to use it for, a broth maybe, but the way she carried it instead of dropping it in the basket told him that it was important.

Then she added in a jar of fig preserves, and Marc wondered what he was doing. He had run into the store to grab a quick lunch, which he'd done. And now he was good to go.

Hell, he needed to go. Needed to get out of this store. Away from Lexi before he did something that he wouldn't be proud of—like break man law and kiss his best friend's ex-wife.

Plus, instead of playing "carry the hot girl's books to class" he should be in the truck, halfway out of town already.

He'd promised a buddy in Sonoma that he'd drive over the hill and pick up ten cases of wine slated for the Showdown wine tasting.

He'd been looking forward to getting out of town since last week. No office meant no e-mail, no phone calls, no BS. Just him, his dog, and a winding country road.

Then he saw Lexi in that sundress and those shoes, looking frazzled and adorably irritated, and his plans changed because she appeared as though she needed the time away as much as he did.

Maybe more.

He'd overheard Nora giving her a hard time. Saw the look on Lexi's face when she was trying to figure out what was wrong with her dress. And wanted to tell her she was perfect, that nothing was wrong. Hell, Lexi could be inspiring in a freaking potato sack. Then he'd touched her hair and, Christ, all he could think about was touching her more.

"That all?" Marilee asked, snapping Marc out of his daze.

Mrs. Craver was glaring at Lexi, who was too busy repacking what the bag boy had already packed up to answer. She carefully separated everything in two bags, so intent on her project she didn't realize they were holding up the line.

"I think so," Marc said, taking out his card and adding his items to the total.

He signed the receipt and grabbed the bags when Lexi looked up. "I have to pay."

"Already did, cream puff." And with a "good day" to Marilee, he ushered her out the door.

They were halfway to his truck, Lexi digging through her wallet and following him blindly, when Wingman spotted them.

"Wingman, stay," he commanded, and like any good dog, Wingman leaped out the window with a bark and ran—right up to Lexi.

Squatting down, she hugged the lucky mutt and didn't even complain when he licked her face.

"You shouldn't run around like that. You could get hit," she cooed, and Wingman, being a male confronted with a soft, curvy female, dropped to his stomach and rolled over, letting her give him a nice belly rub.

When the dog was all but moaning, with his eyes rolled back into his head, Lexi stood and extended her arms. For a split second Marc though she was offering him a belly rub.

"My bag. I've got to get going."

Bag. Right. "I've got it."

"Yes, well, you're going there"—she looked pointedly at his truck and then to the bakery across the street—"and I'm going there."

"Great. Then it shouldn't take too long. Let's go." After locking Wingman back in the cab of the truck, he walked across the parking lot, biting back a smile when she came clacking up behind him.

"I can carry my own stuff."

"Never said you couldn't."

"Fine," she huffed. "At least tell me how much I owe you."

Marc reached the curb and stopped. "I have a better idea." It was a stupid idea. One of the worst ideas he'd ever had. "My buddy's wife just went into labor, and I said I would pick up his wines for the Showdown. Buy me a tank of gas, come with Wingman and me for a ride, and we'll call it even."

She didn't ask where he was going or when he'd be back, just stared at the bakery, which housed three silvered grannies staring back, and said, "Okay."

"Really?" And just like that he went to half-mast. The image of her riding next to him on his truck bench, straddling the gearshift—

Ah man, he was toast. That mountain would force him to change gears at least twenty times each way. Which meant he'd be brushing up against her thigh at least twenty times each way. And man law or not—that was way too tempting.

Before he could rescind his invitation, she nodded and looked up at him with those big, mossy eyes and he was lost.

What the hell had just happened?

He was supposed to offer, and she was supposed to refuse. It was how they worked. How they had always worked.

"I mean, if you can wait," she began. "I'm making lunch for our grandmas and Lucinda as a thank-you for, well, everything. And they're waiting on me."

So that's what they had told her.

"It will be about an hour. Is that okay?" she asked, resting a hand on his arm.

"I can wait." Hell, if she kept touching him like that, he'd wait all afternoon. Not that he'd be waiting that long. He'd give her two minutes tops, and then they'd be on the road.

They crossed Main Street, and when they reached the other side, she took the smaller bag from him. "This is for you. It's healthier than the beef jerky. Plus, the fig jam on that gouda is incredible. Oh, and—" She dug through the bag, coming up with the bone. She unwrapped it. "This is for Wingman."

"Marc?" A sugary voice came down the street and right into the moment.

He watched as his newish assistant, who was stacked, blonde, and looked like she was more adept at navigating a pole than a spreadsheet, made her way past the hotel and toward them. Even though she was dressed in the standard Napa Grand uniform of a black skirt and fitted blazer, in the sunlight, seeing her through Lexi's eyes, suddenly there was nothing standard about the way it fit.

"Hey, Chrissi," Marc said. "Have you met Pricilla's granddaughter? Lexi, this is Chrissi."

"Ohmigod," Chrissi squealed. "I love her chocolate croissants. The ones with the tiny pieces of sea salt sprinkled on the top. Yummy."

"It's nice to meet you, Christie," Lexi said.

"Chrissi, with an *i*," she corrected, and Marc felt his left eyelid twitch.

"My apologies," Lexi said, sliding him an amused glance.

Chrissi blinked up at Marc with her big eyes, and her even bigger breasts strained against her blazer. "I've been trying to find you. Gabe called, something about a missing case of wine. And I ordered lunch. Your favorite. It's getting cold."

"Well, then, I won't keep you," Lexi said, giving his arm a little pat. "It was nice to meet you, Chrissi."

Marc watched her walk off, knowing what she was thinking, knowing that she was wrong, and hating that he cared.

Thanking Chrissi for lunch and apologizing that he would be out of the office the rest of the day, he took off after Lexi.

"I still have your kumquats," he shouted.

Lexi stopped under the red-and-white-striped awning of the patisserie. When he caught up, he said, "And you stole my lunch."

"Actually, I *left* so that you could *get* to your lunch."

Marc looked up at the sky and counted to ten, letting her words settle. Surprised by how much they rubbed him the wrong way, he actually had to go up to fifteen. "It's not what you think."

"I didn't say anything."

"You didn't have to." Marc kicked at the ground, irritated that he was irritated.

"I get it, remember?" she said softly. "I'm the one who breaks up with girls for you. As long as she's a consenting adult, you don't have to explain yourself to me."

Exactly. So why did he want to so badly?

"For the record, Chrissi is my assistant. She holds a double degree in marketing and hospitality management. And although she's a little flighty and way too perky—"

He stopped when Lexi snorted at his word choice.

"Sorry, go on." She placed a hand over her mouth, but he could still see her eyes glistening with humor.

"She's bilingual, great with customers, and was hired by my sister-in-law."

With that, Marc spun on his heel, took two steps, and stopped. Yeah, it looked bad; he got it. And it sucked. So he stalked back. "And I don't sleep with my staff. Ever."

And he stormed off for the second time. Only this time he didn't make it more than a step when he felt her hand on his arm—again. And this time he couldn't ignore that some serious sparks of lust shot straight down to his groin at the simple contact. "I never thought you would."

Then why did he feel like he was lacking?

He released a breath and faced her. "People change, Lexi."

"Okay," she said, her expression soft and genuine, which pissed him off even more.

Because it wasn't okay. Nothing was okay. He'd never felt the need to give an explanation before. Not even to his brothers. So why was he chasing her through town to give one? Now that Lexi was back in St. Helena, something had changed, and he wasn't sure how he felt about it. Hell, he wasn't sure how he felt about anything.

With a soft smile, she held out her hand. "You still have my kumquats."

He handed them over. "You're not going to come with me, are you?"

"I promised the grannies. And even though it would be fun to ride around like old times, the longer I avoid..." She stared at him a moment. A long moment, before finally shaking her head. "Maybe another time."

"What if I told you that there is no lunch with the grannies? That this is a setup for your Mr. Tuesday Lunch?"

"What?" Lexi made her way to the window and cautiously peeked in. He knew what she would see. Jay Sanders, a decent-enough-looking middle-school history teacher. He would be nice and charming and laugh at her jokes. He'd stick to bland crap like kids and travel and his favorite movies. And he'd be a safe bet.

"There was no Mr. Tuesday Lunch. How did you know?"

Marc came up beside her. "Pricilla runs a blog with everyone's days on it. Bios. Everything but their criminal records." From inside, Jay waved and so did Pricilla. "Go for a ride with me, Lexi."

Lexi gave Mr. Safe a hesitant wave back, and Marc had his answer.

He shouldn't have felt disappointed. But he did. "I guess I was wrong about people changing. Have fun on your date, cream puff."

"What can I get you? The regular?" the bartender asked.

Every Thursday night for the past eight years, ever since the youngest DeLuca brother, Trey, became of legal age to partake in public, Marc and his brothers had met at the locals-only bar, the Spigot. After a couple rounds of pool and a couple more rounds of beer, they would come up with a couple really satisfying ideas on how to catch and castrate their sister Abby's SOB of a husband.

Six years ago Richard, who suffered from wandering-dick-and-sticky-fingers syndrome, got caught having an affair. Shortly after, he disappeared—taking with him twelve million dollars and their sister's heart. The four brothers had sworn to get both back.

Tonight was a Wednesday, though, and Marc hadn't come to shoot a game, the shit, or otherwise. He'd come to unwind—alone. He'd managed to avoid a meeting with his brothers, claiming that the first shipment of wine for the Showdown was expected to arrive, which it had. It had also taken three extra guys and an afternoon of paperwork to get the cases settled properly in the wine cellar.

Okay, so maybe the paperwork took a little longer because he still couldn't get his mind off what Lexi had said yesterday. More specifically, what Lexi hadn't said. She'd stood there silent while he justified how he'd chosen to live the past ten years—to her!

The more he thought about it, the more irritated he got.

So he'd grabbed his keys, locked up the office, and found himself standing at her back door, ready to explain just how much he'd changed. And apologize for his parting remark.

Then he realized that he didn't do explanations—or apologies. They were too close to the truth, which made things too serious—another thing he didn't do. He also reminded himself that this was Lexi, the woman who'd been married to his best friend. The same best friend who had not only helped Marc get through the single most painful experience of his life, but had stood by his side as Marc spun himself out of control. Jeff had never judged Marc for his reckless behavior after his parents' deaths, like his brothers had. Never told him to grow the fuck up and get serious about his future. No, Jeff had understood that Marc needed to lose control before he could find it again, needed to deal with the pain of losing his parents in his own way.

So instead of knocking he kept walking, straight through town, straight through the bar, and straight through his second drink.

He'd barely started on his third when two familiar and, by the looks of them, pissed-off Italians flanked him on either side. Not bothering to hide all their big-brother bullshit, Gabriel and Nathaniel, the oldest of the DeLuca boys, elbowed and pressed in on him as they took their seats at the bar.

"You want to tell me what the hell you were thinking?" Gabe said in greeting.

Since Marc wasn't sure exactly what he was being accused of, though he was pretty sure he was guilty on several counts, he remained silent. When he picked up his beer, purposefully tuning out his brothers and tuning in to the ball game playing on the plasma screen behind the bar, Nate slid the day's issue of the *St. Helena Sentinel* in front of him.

Marc looked down at the headline advertising the St. Helena Summer Wine Showdown and felt himself relax. They weren't here about Lexi or Natasha or the fact that two contenders had almost pulled out of the Showdown because his "qualified" assistant had forgotten to send them the proper paperwork.

"You'd better start explaining, and fast, since I'm about two seconds from kicking your ass, stealing your beer, and moving the Showdown to the family winery."

"I heard that the second trimester's rough," Marc said, biting back a grin and sliding his beer toward his oldest brother. "I didn't know all the nagging and hormonal crap was contagious, though."

Gabe shot him a look that was intended to intimidate him into compliance, but all it accomplished was making Marc laugh. Even after their parents died and Gabe stepped up to run the family winery and raise his younger siblings, he'd always managed to keep his easygoing attitude—that was, until his new wife announced that they were expecting. Regan, outside of a few bizarre cravings, had had an easy pregnancy so far. Gabe, on the other hand, was a complete mess.

"Regan's not nagging," Gabe defended.

"Says the man who has a flat of Rocky Road ice cream stashed in his truck," Nate said, waving the bartender over.

"Which is melting." Gabe looked down longingly at the beer before slowly sliding it back toward Marc with a mumbled curse.

Marc took one look at the constipated expression on Gabe's face, noticed the three gray hairs that had sprouted overnight, and slid the beer back. "You go ahead. You need it more than I do."

Gabe held out a weary hand, waving off the beer. "Can't" was all he said.

"Since Regan was totally alone through her first pregnancy with Holly, Gabe said he wanted to be a part of every step of this one." Nate managed to hide his smirk but not the tone in his voice that said *dumb-ass*. "If Regan is awake, so is Gabe. If she wants ice cream, it's what's for dinner."

"If she can't drink alcohol, neither can he?" Marc added, seeing where this was going. *Dumb-ass* didn't even begin to describe what Gabe was if he willingly agreed to that setup.

Gabe rested his elbows on the table and dropped his face into his hands. "I haven't slept in three weeks, my pants are tight, and I swear, if I have to eat one more pickled-beet salad, I think I'm going to puke."

But he'd man up and do it. Gabe had already proven that he would do anything if it meant making Regan happy.

"So can you explain to me what kind of idiot agreed to this so I can go home, snuggle with my wife, and eat a bowl of Rocky Road while watching another Nicholas Sparks movie?"

"There he goes, being all hormonal," Marc joked.

"You think he's bad, wait until Frankie gets a hold of this. She's going to castrate you. Slowly," Nate said.

Marc picked up the paper and studied it, at a total loss for why his two brothers were looking at him like he was in deep shit. Sure, he'd approved the article, even had Regan look it over to make sure it would pop. Nothing.

Gabe opened the paper and once again rested his head in his hands. "Fourth column, down at the bottom. Third name under the Tasting Tribunal."

Marc scanned the article, found the list of judges for the blind wine tasting, and drew a blank. "Simon Baudouin, so what?"

"So what?" Gabe snapped, looking up and pinning Marc with a glare. "You want to tell me how the hell *that* happened?"

Marc couldn't understand what had his brothers so pissed. A hundred years ago the DeLuca and Baudouin families held the first annual St. Helena Summer Wine Showdown in the dining room of the Napa Grand as a way to settle a friendly dispute over whose wine was superior. Over the years the tasting grew to include the entire valley, and it eventually became a platform for winemakers and enthusiasts from around the globe to compete and show off their new wines. It was also where his grandparents met and fell in love, and even where his parents had their wedding.

And had the Napa Grand not closed its doors twenty years ago, this year would have marked the hotel's centennial year of hosting the event as well as his parents' fortieth wedding anniversary. Which was why Marc had agreed that, even though his hotel wasn't quite ready for an event of this caliber, the Showdown needed to be brought home—back to the Napa Grand. It had long outgrown the opera house two towns over in old town Napa, where it had been held the past twenty years.

"There's always been one DeLuca and one Baudouin on the tribunal," Marc defended. "It's written in the bylaws.

So if Frankie's bitching because they only get one spot, tell her to suck it up."

"Frankie doesn't bitch." An extremely loud and extremely ticked-off voice echoed throughout the bar. "Frankie delivers a donkey kick to the nuts."

All three brothers turned toward the entrance, took one look, and instinctively dropped their hands to cover their goods because there—dressed in a shirt that read *Bite Me*, shredded jeans, and a pair of steel-toed boots—stood Francesca Baudouin.

"Ah shit," Nate whispered.

Frankie was tall, curvy, supposedly tattooed, and hot in that I-can-maim-you-with-my-bare-hands kind of way. She was also considered one of the most promising up-and-coming vintners in the valley, which ticked Nate to high hell—and she was the granddaughter of Charles Baudouin, placing her on the wrong side of the sixty-year-old Baudouin-DeLuca feud.

"Is this another one of your stupid jokes, Nathaniel?" Frankie demanded when she'd made her way across the bar and right into Nate's face.

No one knew what Nate had done to get on Frankie's shit list, but whatever it was had landed him permanently at the top. Not a good list to be on, since Frankie was a master grudge holder—and dartboard champion.

"Why are you looking at me? I make wine. He's the one planning the Showdown," Nate said, pointing to Marc and selling him out. So much for brotherly support.

"Yeah, well, if your goal was to humiliate me, the DeLucas get a gold star." She held up a copy of the newspaper as proof. "Do you know how hard I've worked to be taken seriously in this industry?" That she'd had to work twice as hard to gain any respect from her family went unsaid.

"No one's questioning your qualifications, Francesca." Nate's expression was soft, but his body was ready to respond should Frankie start donkey kicking. "We were as shocked as you were when we saw the article."

"How can you be shocked? You were the ones who ran the list, which pretty much says that a dog is more qualified to represent my family than I am."

"A dog?" Marc gasped.

"Simon is old man Charles's bulldog," Gabe supplied, picking up Marc's beer. The foam hadn't even touched his lips when he stopped and with a mumbled curse slammed the glass back down.

"This is going to make the Summer Wine Showdown look like some kind of redneck moonshine crawl."

"You really didn't know?" Frankie asked, her eyes narrowed in disbelief.

Marc put his hands up in surrender. "I followed the bylaws to the letter. Five people sit on the Tasting Tribunal: the mayor, the wine commissioner, a celebrity judge, and one member from each founding family. We chose Nate. Your grandfather chose Simon."

Which made no sense at all. Sure, a lifetime ago Charles Baudouin and Geno DeLuca had been the best of friends; they had also fallen in love with the same woman. And Charles had chosen Geno's wedding day to publicly express his undying love for Marc's grandmother, ChiChi. The ceremony continued, a lifelong friendship ended, and the feud between the DeLucas and the Baudouins began.

Although the dog would complicate things for Marc and his family, it would also hurt the town's reputation. And Charles Baudouin might despise the DeLucas, but he loved St. Helena.

"My grandpa did this?" Frankie held the paper limp in her hand, and had she been any other woman, Marc would have sworn she was about to cry.

"Looks like it." Marc shoved back in his chair. "I worked my ass off to get the town behind hosting this event at my hotel. Not to mention I have so much money tied up in this thing if it goes under, I go with it."

"Christ, Marc, you said you had this under control," Gabe said, going all brother-knows-best.

"It is under control," Marc defended.

"You have a fucking dog for a judge."

"I'll check the bylaws tonight. See if there is a clause that states the representative has to be human."

"You should have done that *before* you announced to everyone that you were going to host the Showdown." Gabe shook his head. "This is why I told you to wait a few years, to make sure your foundation was laid so you could handle it."

"The town council approached me about hosting the event, remember? And *this*," Marc said, pointing to the headline announcing the Showdown, "will shave five years off my ten-year plan. I knew the short timeline was going to be a challenge, but I would have been an idiot to turn them down. They wanted it brought back to the Napa Grand for the centennial, and it's a chance to really show what the hotel can do."

"You're willing to bet everything you've built because you want to challenge yourself? And you choose the most high-profile event you can find to do it?" Gabe shook his head.

"A lot of people are counting on this fund-raiser," Nate said in his most inoffensive tone, which Marc took immediate offense to. The only thing missing in this touching moment of brotherly bonding was the youngest DeLuca. Thankfully for Marc, Trey was in Madrid, selling a hotel chain on DeLuca Wines as their house specialty of choice.

"We are talking hundreds of thousands of dollars that this town needs," Gabe said, as though Marc didn't already know. The Summer Wine Showdown was elaborate, exclusive, and at a thousand dollars a plate, the dinner and wine tasting raised close to a million dollars every year for the local hospital and schools. Which made it a high-visibility event, and if it went bad, it would go bad under the watchful eyes of every media outlet in the food, wine, and travel industries.

"Did you even think about how this will affect the family if it goes south? Ryo Wines is one of the main sponsors, and the last thing Abby needs right now is her company connected to another disaster."

Marc wanted to laugh at his brother's family-first speech. Hell, just last Christmas Gabe had given the family an ultimatum: either welcome Regan and her daughter, Holly, into the family or he'd walk. A hard thing to ask since Abby's husband, Richard, who had been carrying on an affair with Regan for over a year, was Holly's biological father. Regan hadn't known that Richard was married, but the affair had shattered Abby's world regardless. Now that Regan was officially a sister-in-law and expecting the first DeLuca great-grandbaby, Marc was surprised that Abby hadn't relocated to one of their Santa Barbara properties.

Not wanting to argue in front of half the town, especially on a topic as delicate as Regan and Abby, Marc picked up his beer and took a drawn-out pull, making sure that Gabe saw every last drop disappear. Then he licked his lips and considered ordering another one just to mess with his brother.

"I want to see this work," Gabe finally said. "For everybody."

"I can do this." Marc had to do this. It was the only way to prove to his family, and himself, that walking away from his role in DeLuca Wines was a smart move. That he wasn't that same impulsive screwup he'd been after his parents died. That he'd grown into the kind of man his father would have been proud of.

"I don't doubt that you will. I'm just afraid that one day you're going to play it too fast and too risky and end up blowing something important." Gabe shook his head, then changed his tone—trying for light. "At least tell me you found a caterer."

"Handled," Marc lied.

Gabe took one last look at Marc's beer. "Hopefully better than you handled announcing a dog as a fucking judge."

CHAPTER 4

Saturday morning, with her eyes barely open, two trays full of pastries in her hands, and a light dusting of flour in nearly every crevice, Lexi pushed through the back door of the bakery. She made her way to her car and managed to locate her keys and pop the trunk, only to realize that there was no way all of the pastries were going to fit.

The grannies were already at the Book Walk. Her best friend, Abby, wasn't answering her phone. And Lexi still had two dozen trays left in the kitchen.

She checked her watch and wondered what the time limit was before Nora Kincaid, who had been adamant about timeliness, was justified to act on her promise to publicly pop Lexi's cream puffs. Not long, she imagined, since the event started in ten minutes.

Maybe if she dropped the backseat down she could make it in two trips.

Lexi set the trays on the roof and crawled into the car. Unlatching the seat locks, she pulled. And pulled. With a frown, and a whole lot of stomping, she went around to the trunk, leaned in, and started pushing.

"Well, look who it is, Wingman. Our friendly neighborhood backside."

Lexi looked over her shoulder, surprised to see Marc, his brown eyes twinkling with amusement as he leaned out the widow of his pickup and watched her struggle. She was less surprised, however, at the annoying fluttering that started low in her belly just because she looked at him. Irritated, but not surprised. The man was sexy as sin, and he knew it.

He wore his dimpled grin and enough stubble to show that he hadn't bothered to shave that morning. Which shouldn't have bothered Lexi. But it did. And that made her nervous.

"Go away," she mumbled, focusing on the back seats again. Because divorcées who couldn't make it work with the sure thing had no business getting bothered by the hometown playboy.

"Heard you might need a hand," he said. "Actually, heard you might need a truck to lug all of the pastries."

"You heard?" She didn't turn around.

"Yup, ChiChi called an hour ago saying you'd need a ride. Pricilla about ten minutes after that."

Which meant their grandmas were trying to set her up on yet another date she hadn't agreed to. With Marc.

"I've got it handled," she lied. "You can go."

"Nah, we'll wait. It's not every day that a guy gets a morning flash of red lace before he's even had his coffee. Huh, Wingman?"

Wingman panted loudly from the passenger seat.

With a squeak Lexi jerked up, smacking her head on the top of the trunk, her hands smoothing down the back of her dress. She reached the hem and stopped, pinning him with a glare. "I'm not wearing red today."

"No?" He rested his forearm on the windowsill and shrugged matter-of-factly. "Well, a man can dream."

"Does this whole 'let me guess the color of your panties and then you'll be charmed into taking a ride with me' shtick really work?"

He paused for a second, as though surprised that it hadn't. Then the dimples were back. "I can see you're still a crabby morning person, which is why I brought coffee." He held up two cups, and she nearly drooled at the scents of hazelnut and vanilla wafting out of his car window. She'd already had a cup, when she'd first gotten up and started baking. That had been five hours ago.

She walked over, snatched a coffee, and took a sip, her eyes closing at the heavenly flavor. "Thank you."

"You're welcome." Opening the door, Marc stepped out of the cab, went around to the passenger side, and opened the door for her. "Hop in and I'll load up. It'll only take a minute. Then we can be on our way and I won't even make you admit that I saved the day."

He took her elbow to help her in, and wouldn't you know it, little sparks of attraction shot straight down to her toes. "I'm not getting in your truck."

"You can get used to the idea on the way to the high school."

When she didn't budge, except to take another sip of coffee, he slammed the door and leaned in, close enough that she could smell his soap mingling with the scent of frustrated man. She liked him frustrated; it left no room for the smooth-talking stud boy.

"Christ, woman, you are the most stubborn person I have ever met. I know that you've got more trays in that kitchen than you've got space in your trunk. And while I'd love to sit back and watch you and your *white* silk with little pink dots on them try to make it work"—he gazed down at her, satisfaction lighting his eyes when she gasped—"you're already late, and I promised my nonna I'd see that you and your incredible cream puffs made it to the high school safely. So for both of our sakes—" He ran a hand down his face as the muscles in his neck tensed and coiled.

When he spoke again, he wasn't charming; he seemed desperate. "Please, Lexi, scoot your stubborn ass inside or I'll be forced to put it there, and it might just end up on my lap."

Lexi swallowed. Who knew a frustrated man could be such a turn-on.

"Might want to scoot over." Marc patted the bench seat next to him.

"Not going to happen." She stared out the front windshield, arms crossed, lips pursed.

God, she was prickly. And hardheaded. And knowing that the only thing she had on under all that attitude was a scrap of white silk and a soft heart was a total turn-on. Which was why, after he'd gotten halfway to his buddy's house the other day and realized that Lexi had been smart to turn him down, he'd ordered himself to stay away.

Although she took risks in the kitchen, in her personal life Lexi played thing safe, and there was nothing safe about their history or the sparks flying between them. And unless someone was looking to get hurt, they had no business spending time together, so last night he'd decided to back off.

Then morning came and ChiChi called, explaining how Lexi needed his help—and here he was driving her to the high school in his pickup.

"All right, suit yourself." Marc put the truck in drive.

He had no sooner pulled out onto Main Street when Wingman leaped over the backseat of his extended cab and onto Lexi's lap.

"Wingman!" She put her hands in front of her face, shielding it against the thrashing tail.

"He's used to riding shotgun. So unless you want wind-blown hair and drool on your shoulder, you might want to reconsider."

He patted again.

Three tail smacks to the forehead later, Lexi slid on over, her legs daintily straddling the gearshift. They came to a red light, and Marc downshifted. Without thinking, he relaxed his arm and his thumb accidentally grazed her bare knee. He heard her breathing catch.

Neither said a word the rest of the drive, but the tension in the cab increased with every shift of the gears until Marc thought about pulling over and letting her take his damn truck. He didn't do the good guy act very often because, well, he pretty much sucked at it.

But Lexi deserved a good guy right now. And he wanted to be that guy for her. Which meant that this thing between them could never happen. What she needed was a straight-up friend—and not one with benefits.

With a resigned sigh, Marc pulled into the parking lot and drove around the back of the school. Truck in park, he turned to face her at the precise moment she turned to face him. Her lips parted on a gasp, he went rock hard, and it took a moment to register that they were close enough to kiss—and she wasn't slapping him.

She didn't speak and neither did he, as he remembered just how cozy the cab of his truck could be.

"This can't happen," she whispered, looking up at him, and *holy fuck*.

"Then stop looking at me like you want to crawl in the back of the truck and get comfortable."

She blinked, her eyes zeroing in on his lips. "Pretend that I don't. That's what I do."

"I've spent my life pretending with you. It's getting harder," he whispered and noticed she'd moved closer. So he did too. And the second her eyes fluttered shut and her lips parted for his, he dipped his head and—

"Shit," he mumbled, leaning back in his seat and running his hand down his face.

"What?" She blinked up at him, all fuzzy and confused. "Why did you stop?"

Because I never should have started. Because you were my best friend's girl. Because karma hates me.

"Because we are about to be joined by our grandmothers."

"Oh." She looked at the back window, and her eyes went round. Wedged in between him and Wingman, her only shot at escape was through his door, so she started shoving at his chest. "Oh my God! Will you move already! If they catch us like—" She gestured wildly back and forth between them as though he wasn't aware that he was sitting there with the windows fogged and a fucking hard-on.

He reached for the door handle when she added, almost horrified, "What if they add you to my list of bachelors? It wouldn't just be a one-time thing. They would get their hopes up."

And he froze. Hand still on the door, he pinned her with a look. She had a problem with *him* being on that stupid list. After all the boneheads and stuffy suits, she had a problem with *him*?

"How about this, cream puff." He reached his free arm across the back of the bench seat and smiled. "You agree to one dinner with me and I'll move."

"What? Why?" Her eyes narrowed on his hand, which had slid down to cup her shoulder. "That is a terrible idea and you know it."

It was a terrible idea, on so many levels, which was why he persisted. "One date. To clear the air." He'd show her what a real date with a real man was like. And there wouldn't be any favorite-color-and-number talk.

When it looked like she was going to take her chances with the grannies, she added, "Just as friends. So, none of this—" She picked up his hand by the finger, unwrapped it, and tossed it off her shoulder. But her nonchalant attitude didn't fool him. He could see her eyes frantically darting to the rearview mirror as the threat of orthopedic shoes crept closer.

His hand, now free, found its way to her thigh, where he gave a gentle squeeze. "Only if you beg."

She looked over her shoulder and blindly batted his hand. "Fine. Lunch. Tomorrow." She swore, and it was adorable. "I can't tomorrow. I have lunch with Mr. Second Sunday."

"Monday then?"

"Can't," she grimaced. "Drinks at the Martini House followed by dessert. There'd better be chocolate. I've got a movie date on Tuesday. How about Wednesday? Wait, anytime but morning."

Marc took a calming breath. He wasn't used to being wedged between other men. "Great. Wednesday night it is. Your place. I'll bring the wine." He opened the door and stepped out, reaching back to assist her.

She didn't take his hand. "Wait. You're asking *me* out and you expect *me* to cook?"

"Would you rather I take you to some froufrou restaurant so you can complain about how you would have done things differently?"

She opened her mouth and then closed it.

"Face it, you're a food snob. Plus, you always have more fun when you cook the meal."

She frowned, and he silently smiled. He'd nailed it, and she knew it, and that made her nervous. Hell, it made him nervous. "How do you know that?"

"Cream puff." He stepped into her, making her knees part a little in the process. "There isn't much about you that I don't know."

Lexi pulled her car into Stan's Soup and Service Station. She needed gas, a glass of wine, and a bowl of Stan's soup du jour—unless it was chicken noodle. Her day had started off with a coffee date. Mr. Wednesday Morning was a nice enough cork-machine operator from Yountville who loved cooking and foreign films and knew his way around an engine—a bonus since Lexi's car had picked up a strange pinging sound in Chicago that had turned into a high-pitched squeal by Salt Lake City. Unfortunately, Mr. Wednesday Morning also had a thing for Velcro sneakers and still lived with his parents, which should have made it easy to decline when he invited her to his mom's Tupperware party. But saying no would have been rude, especially since he'd had his mom on speakerphone when the invite was issued.

Lexi hopped out of the car and had just started the gas pump when her phone rang.

"Hello?"

"Morning, Lexi. It's me."

She waited for the gut-wrenching pain to hit, but when all she felt was growing irritation, she thunked her head against the side of car. Five times. Once for every time "me" had called since she'd left New York nearly three weeks ago. "Jeffery, why are you calling?"

There was an amused pause where she could almost hear his head wagging from side to side, and she just knew he wore that silly-Lexi playacting smile. "You promised you'd call when you got settled."

"No, you *told* me to call. I reminded you that we are no longer married and accountable to each other."

"That hurts, Lexi. We may not still be married, but we'll always be friends. And friends look out for each other. I just wanted to see if you were all right, how the patisserie is doing, and if you needed anything."

What she needed was for him to stop calling. Maybe it was immature, but being friends with the man who'd traded her in for an eco-friendly model wasn't something she was interested in. She understood that many people managed to keep a relationship with their exes, but Lexi just couldn't stomach the thought. She finally had the chance to follow her dream, and she'd be damned if she was going to run her plans, or life, past anyone this time.

"You're on your honeymoon. Shouldn't you be"—she couldn't say it—"with Sara?"

"She's right here." *Of course she is.* Sara not only stole Lexi's husband, her kitchen, *and* her life—she was apparently the bigger person. "She agrees with me. Maintaining a healthy relationship is important for everyone involved."

Instead of explaining in great detail exactly where he could stick his healthy relationship or warning that the only thing he should worry about maintaining was the three thousand miles between them, she explained the facts, hoping they would sink in. "Listen carefully, Jeffery. We are no longer involved. We are divorced—from each other—no kids, no ties, nothing in common."

"That's hurtful, Lexi. We have a past, fifteen wonderful years, and the restaurant."

"You have the restaurant, and I—" Lexi paused. A glimpse of a tailored suit with a briefcase caught her eye from across the street. *Crap!* "I have to go."

She ended the call, dropped to all fours, and held her breath, stuffing her phone in her back pocket when it rang again. Jeffery hadn't been the only annoying caller this week. Chad Stevens had called her cell, the apartment, even the bakery asking for her. She'd hidden behind a crate of watermelons at Picker's Produce, Meats, and More when she saw him walking from aisle to aisle, as though hunting her down. She'd also ended her second Monday-night date early, right in the middle of chocolate-hazelnut fondue, when she spotted Chad, in the parking lot, writing down her license plate number. When Chad had turned toward the entry, looking like he was ready to walk in and find her, Lexi ran out the back, claiming a headache and cursing Chad Stevens. Not that she could envision herself long term with the date in question, a man who headed up the local LARP coalition, but there had been chocolate.

Telling Chad to go away should have been easy. But Lexi had promised Pricilla that she would honor her date with Chad—*only* if he personally told her the official meeting time. Which meant he had to track her down. And Lexi figured that if she could avoid him long enough, he'd give up. Find some other divorcée to stalk.

After a long moment, she chanced a peek through the window, only to find Chad staring back, studying her car. "Get a clue," she muttered.

"You could always write him a note." She could tell from the golden-boy tone and the way her stomach did stupid little flips that Marc was directly behind her. "I think I have some binder paper in my backpack. The wide-ruled kind. Oh, wait, I left it in the car. Want me to grab it?"

Wingman barked his approval.

"I think I can manage without, thanks," Lexi said, turning back around and resuming her seat on the hot asphalt. Wingman's whole body shook excitedly as he loped over. He nosed at the ground and around her legs, and when he couldn't get to her rear end he settled on a big, doggie face lick.

"Wingman, come. Sorry about that, he's all muddy from the trail."

Wingman rolled into her and plopped down—right on her feet. Mud dripped off and speckled her jeans.

"He's not that bad."

"Really?" Marc looked across the street and frowned. "He's a total tool."

"I was talking about the dog."

"Good, because you can do better than Chad. In fact, I've got a friend. Nice guy. Single, loves to travel, owns a hotel, handsome as hell. In fact, I think you already have a date with him tonight. He wanted me to ask what you were planning on wearing, and suggest something with no straps, bra optional."

"Really?"

He shrugged.

"It's not a date. And I'm not listening to you right now," Lexi said, also *not* noticing how his running shorts hung low on his waist and highlighted his impressive thighs. Or how his shirt, a little damp from the heat of the morning, clung to his broad chest as it would to someone who'd been pounding the pavement, which she'd guessed he'd been doing before he decided to poke his unwanted nose in her business.

"Stevens, huh? Never figured him for your type." Even with his mirrored sunglasses on, Lexi could feel Marc staring straight at her, pinning her with a gaze that made sitting still impossible. "A little too handsy for the prom queen, if you ask me."

"Maybe I like handsy." Wingman pressed farther into her legs, letting out a protective growl and sending a big glob of mud splatting to the ground. "Plus, Chad and I were friends back in school." Okay, that was a lie, but there was no way he would remember that she hated Chad.

Marc pocketed the sunglasses, his whiskey-brown eyes flickering with amusement and—crap! He remembered. "You kneed the poor bastard sophomore year when he tried to get up close and personal with your pom-poms."

It had been junior year, when she and Jeffery had broken up for three days because she had tried out for the cheer team and it conflicted with her ability to support him from the stands on game night.

"He helped me put up my posters for class president, senior year." Another time that she and Jeffery had taken a break.

"He liked to look up your cheerleading skirt. But hey, who am I to stop true love?" Marc looked over the top of the car and waved. "Hey, Chad. How's it going? Are you looking—"

Lexi grabbed Marc's hand and yanked him to the ground. "Can you not? I have enough people trying to run my love life."

"So you admit that there is a love life." When she didn't answer, except to drop her head to her knees with a frustrated grunt, Marc leaned against the car next to her, close enough so that their thighs brushed. Wingman rested his snout on Marc's running shoe. "Ah, too much of a love life."

"My marriage officially ended two weeks ago. I have a bakery that needs to become a bistro, and my grandma has set me up with at least two first dates a day. Although they are nice enough guys, I don't have the time, or interest, to date right now. My apartment is overflowing with flowers, and the idea of another cup of get-to-know-each-other coffee makes me want to cry."

"Easy solution. Call your bachelors and tell them no."

Lexi had never been good at saying no. Her whole life she'd worked hard at making people happy. A lifetime of revolving parents could do that to a girl. "I can't."

She paused, waiting for Marc to laugh at her, disagree with her. For him to say that it was as easy as looking them in the eye and saying, "N. O." To point out that people did it every day and, in fact, it was something she should have mastered by high school.

But he didn't do any of those things. He didn't do anything at all except lean his head against her side door and patiently stroke Wingman. In silence.

Also not good with silence, Lexi felt compelled to add, "I promised my grandma I would fulfill all of the scheduled dates that she had agreed to. It would be rude to cancel on them now."

"My thoughts exactly," Natasha said, her heels slapping the concrete as she approached. When she was certain that the towering effect was in place, Natasha stopped, her hands on her hips.

Today she was dressed in cream-colored pants, with matching pumps and a summer jacket, an ice-blue silk shell, and enough sparkly accessories and bad attitude to make Lexi squint.

Natasha turned her eyes on Marc. "I thought we were meeting for lunch at eleven thirty?"

"We are," he confirmed innocently.

"Really?" Lexi whispered.

Marc ran a hand over his face and sighed. He avoided Natasha's gaze, instead fiddling with the cuff of his shorts. Marco DeLuca, total ladies' man, was squirming, and not in a good way. In fact, he looked slightly harassed, and Lexi suddenly wondered if he was hiding from his love life as much as she was.

"Oh, because it's eleven fifteen and you're dressed for the gym. BoVine has a strict dress policy," Natasha said, then turned to Lexi. "By the way, I forgot to tell you the other day how sorry I was to hear about you and Jeffery."

"Thanks, but I'm doing well," Lexi lied. Natasha was only sorry that she hadn't yet had the chance to rub it in, and by the sparkle in her eye she was getting ready to do exactly that. Especially since Lexi had witnessed yet another rebuff from the great playboy himself.

"I mean, divorced and thirty. Sounds rough. They write articles about people like you."

"Twenty-nine. Remember I was a year *behind* you. And Jeffery and I parted amicably. Actually, we're still close," Lexi shot back. "Oh, and I love those pants. Are they cream? No, too yellow. What color are they? It's hard to tell with the sun in my eyes."

"These, well, they are more of a custardy color—"

Wingman's ears perked up, his tail started beating the concrete, and he let go a single bark.

Natasha took a step back, obviously startled.

"Lexi," Marc warned.

"I'm sorry, I didn't hear. What color did you say it was?"

Eyes firmly on the dog, Natasha took another step back and said, "Custard—"

The words had barely left her lips and Wingman was up. He charged Natasha, his tail flicking mud in every direction as his big dirty paws landed right in the center of Natasha's ice-blue heart.

"Oh. My. God," she shrieked as she backed into the gas pump. "Get him off!"

"Down, Wingman," Marc said, but Lexi noticed that he took his time getting to the dog to haul him off a very angry Natasha. "Down."

By the time Marc got Wingman settled, Natasha was sporting two enormous doggie prints on her silk and two pissed-off slits for eyes. And they were zeroed in on Lexi. "You did that on purpose!"

"I guess you'd better go get cleaned up. I hear that BoVine is uptight about who they let in."

"Lexi? That is you!" Chad said from behind them, sidling up to the group and giving her a big hug, his hands sliding a little far south for Lexi's liking. "It's so great to see you. I was waiting for you to come out of the station, and I had almost given up." He looked at his watch. "I have to be in court in an hour. I'm just so glad that I finally ran into you."

He hugged her again, his hands slipping—again.

A low, threatening growl sounded, and Chad slowly backed away.

"Good boy," Marc whispered and gave Wingman a ruffle behind the ears.

"It's good to see you too, Chad," Lexi said, patting her thighs in a silent call for Wingman, who dutifully walked over to sit on her feet and lean into her legs. Chad would have to get past her keeper if he wanted to cop a feel.

"At first I thought you were avoiding me, running out of the supermarket, not returning my calls, but then I told myself that you were probably busy getting settled. How is the bistro coming along?"

"You know about the bistro?" Not that she had kept it a secret, but she hadn't advertised it either. She had finalized the blueprints and design with her designer last week, perfected her summer menu, and met with the contractor—twice. Until they broke ground on the remodel, and she knew what her grand-opening date would be, she was keeping a low profile.

"Well, yeah." He reached inside his jacket and fished around in the pocket. He pulled an envelope out, shoved it in her face, and smiled. "For you."

Wingman barked in warning, but Lexi took the offered envelope. It was official looking, with the Stevens, Stevens, and Stevens corporate seal on the upper left corner. And it was heavy—way too heavy to be an invitation to the yearly office party. "What is this?"

"Alexis Moreau," Chad began, "I hate to be the one to inform you, especially since I am planning on picking you up a week from Saturday for a picnic and maybe a little dip in the lake, but you've been served."

After Lexi swallowed back the bile that rose at the image of the kind of dip he had in mind, she asked, "Served? I don't understand." Her divorce was final. The assets divided. What the hell was going on?

"Jeffery has gained a court-ordered cease and desist that prohibits any use of recipes served in his restaurant Pairing."

"Those recipes are mine." They were *all* hers. And they were all that she had. "I created them." She had breathed life into them, and they into her.

Experimenting in the kitchen had been the only time she felt truly happy in New York. She couldn't keep her husband satisfied, couldn't be a mother, couldn't recognize who looked back at her in the mirror most days. But she could cook.

"Actually, the recipes are assets of the corporation that now owns the restaurant."

"What corporation? Pairing is a family-run business."

Ignoring her last comment, Chad looked at his watch, stepped forward as though to kiss her good-bye, and wisely settled on an awkward shoulder pat when Wingman bared his teeth. "Gotta run, Lexi. Pick you up at nine." And he was gone.

Natasha straightened her top and smiled. "I better get going since lunch is in a few minutes. Great to see you, Lexi. And I am so happy to hear what an amicable divorce you and Jeffery had. It warms my heart. Really."

CHAPTER 5

It was official. Marc was a stalker.

It had started out innocently enough, a quick glance out his office window at the precise moment that a light flickered on across the alley. He'd never noticed before that his office window, situated on the northwest corner of the hotel, afforded him a perfect view of Pricilla's apartment, and if he angled his chair just so, he could see directly into her kitchen. If he stood he was able to steal peeks through the breakfast nook area and get a great view of Pricilla's dining table. And if he stood up and pressed his face to the window, he could see all the way through to the family room and partway down the hall toward the bedroom, which was currently housing a tight little ass that he had the pleasure of watching swish its way around the house.

That night, he should have packed up his things and gone upstairs to his suite. Instead he'd watched her move through the kitchen, her bare feet and legs dancing around the room to Louis Prima as she took out nearly every pan and utensil in the house and spent hours cooking enough food for a large dinner party, only to take a single bite, dump it in the trash can out back, and start over.

That had been six days ago, after she'd been served, after she'd posted a note on her door canceling their dinner, and after she'd refused to return his calls.

That look on her face when she'd been handed those papers still got to Marc. She'd been shocked, then confused, then hurt, which made Marc equal parts confused and pissed—at himself for not making sure Jeff had handled his shit. Marc assumed that Jeff had made it clear to all involved that after the divorce the menu would remain an asset of Pairing. He'd also assumed that when he finally saw Lexi again, the sexual pull between them would be gone.

He'd been wrong on all accounts.

Marc paused for a moment, just watching her. Elbows-deep in a saucepan, she whisked for a good three minutes, her forehead scrunching when she took a little taste with a spoon. Quickly she opened the cabinet to her left, reaching up on her tippy toes and tugging this morning's ensemble of choice, a dark-blue tank top and striped cotton boxers, high enough up her body to expose a tiny strip of torso and a whole lot of leg.

Nope. The pull was still there, and he was still watching.

Marc swore and angled his chair so that he would be forced to stare at his computer, as though she wasn't right behind the window, whisking her flambé or whatever, with her breasts gently swaying because she'd decided to roll out of bed this morning and forgo a bra—again.

The movement startled Wingman, who was sleeping under Marc's desk and awoke with a grunt. He grunted again before rolling over to offer up his belly for a rub.

Marc gave it a valiant effort, staring at an e-mail from Natasha outlining exactly why she would be a brilliant pick to cater the Summer Wine Showdown. He'd put off his reply, hoping to find a solution that didn't involve a clingy woman—a clingy woman he'd slept with.

He'd called every chef he knew and a few dozen he didn't. Either they were booked or too damn expensive. His own chef, who was pissed that Marc still hadn't hired him a sous chef, refused to do the event, claiming it wasn't in his contract.

The easy solution would be to call Jeff, ask him to recommend someone local. More than a thousand spectators, members of the media, and celebrities were due to start arriving in just under a month, but no food had been ordered, and he didn't have enough staff to handle the event—and he still hadn't been able to call.

At first he told himself that it was because he didn't want to interrupt Jeff's honeymoon; his friend deserved a little alone time with his new bride after a hellish year. Then Marc watched, day after day, as Lexi struggled to find peace in the one place she used to thrive, and his reason for not calling was out of sheer preservation—of his and Jeff's friendship.

Every time she stood and stared blankly at her ingredients, every time she sat at the table alone, only to leave her meal untouched and turn in early because he could tell she didn't know what else to do, he formed another question for Jeff. Questions that, Marc knew, had answers he'd hate.

His only option was to hire Natasha. The more he thought about it, the more logical it seemed. She was talented in the kitchen, and although a little experimental for his taste—culinarily speaking—she was a simple solution to his professional problem.

Marc had wasted the past week staring out the window, accomplishing jack shit, and he knew that the town council and his brothers were going to be all over him if he didn't nail down the food. And soon. All he needed was for Gabe to find out he'd turned down a reputable caterer because he hadn't been able to keep his dick in his pants.

With a heavy sigh, Marc made his decision. Natasha wasn't the perfect fit, but she was the best option he had. He'd opened her most recent e-mail and had read through most of it when a door slammed closed and echoed through the alley.

Wingman buried his snout under his front paws and whined.

"I know, buddy," Marc said, ruffling him behind the ears and going to the window.

He and Wingman both watched as Lexi slowly made her way down the alley, feet bare, garbage bag in hand, and shoulders slumped in defeat. She opened the lid to the trash can and ceremoniously dumped the bag, most likely containing the entirety of what she'd been cooking up for the past two hours, inside. She was about to replace the lid when her back went rigid. She stopped, slowly turned her head, and—looked right at him.

"Shit."

Marc jerked to his right, plastering his back against the wall. The sudden movement and elevated energy sent Wingman into a barking fit.

"Shh," he hissed, sounding panicked, and not wanting to draw any more attention to his window. "Sit."

Wingman obeyed and sat at his feet, waiting, with big doggie eyes, for his reward. Marc reached in his pocket, and Wingman inhaled the bribe without even chewing.

She'd seen him. He'd been spying on her like some kind of pervy teen, and she'd caught him. This was worse than the summer when he was supposed to build Mr. Weinstein a new shed and instead had spent most of his time watching his new trophy wife do her morning laps—naked. He'd been fifteen. Mrs. Weinstein had known he was there. And it had been thrilling.

This felt like an invasion of privacy, though. Which was why, instead of pretending it was a coincidence and waving like a normal neighbor would do, he slunk into the shadows. Now, on top of everything else, he was going to have to come up with an excuse, one that wouldn't get him arrested, to explain away his behavior.

"Last boy I caught doing that found himself one peanut short," Grandma said. Not his grandma, but Lexi's.

Marc thunked his head against the wall because Pricilla wasn't smiling and she wasn't alone. No, all three grannies stood inside his office door, each silver coif shaking, while they tutted simultaneously, their expressions ranging from amusement to threatening eternal damnation. But all of them seemed to imply the same thing: Marco DeLuca had been caught checking out the neighbor's wears, and he was in trouble.

"I didn't hear you come in," Marc said, casually walking around his desk to hug ChiChi and company, but going the long way so he didn't have to pass in front of the window.

"Of course not, dear," ChiChi said, giving him a peck on the cheek and taking her seat. "You were too busy peeping on the new neighbor."

"I was not peep—" was all he got out before Pricilla pulled a piece of fudge out of that crocheted bag of hers and shoved it into Marc's mouth.

"I don't take well to lying either," Pricilla said, penciled eyebrows arched so high they all but disappeared into her hairline.

Marc couldn't respond. One, he didn't want to lie, and two, the fudge was incredible. He wondered if this was one of Pricilla's originals or if it was a Lexi creation. A smoky hint of bacon teased his tongue while a bite of cayenne warmed the back of his throat. Marc smiled—savory. Definitely Lexi's, then.

"What can I do for you ladies?" Marc mumbled around the melting chocolate even though he knew he'd regret the question.

These grannies were professional busybodies with only two things on their corporate agenda: their grandkids' business and the business of getting some great-grandbabies. Most of the time one goal overlapped the next, and when that happened everyone in town was bound to suffer. So if they were here before the lunching hour, something was up. And it wouldn't bode well for Marc and his siblings.

"We hear you've gotten yourself into a fix," Lucinda Baudouin said, taking a seat and opening her enormous bag. She pulled out a fluffy white cat wearing a sailor suit, complete with hat, neckerchief, and irritated growl, and set him in her lap.

Wingman jumped to attention, his ear going up and his eyes going wide. He lowered his body to the floor with his tail standing straight up, and then he went completely still.

Mr. Puffins's tail, on the other hand, puffed out like a porcupine's, ready for battle. Wingman barked once. The cat's eyes narrowed on a low growl. Wingman ran behind Marc's desk and hid.

"Harrumph," Lucinda tutted, handing Marc a printed-out copy of an e-mail.

He took one look at the e-mail and almost asked Wingman to move over. The e-mail was one that he'd drafted and sent to the dean of the Napa Valley Culinary Academy, asking for a temporary chef for the Showdown. An e-mail that was supposed to remain confidential.

"How did you get this?"

All three women straightened with pride, but it was Lucinda who spoke. "Broke into Janice's work computer. Regan helped us." Two more things that Gabe never needed to hear about.

"What were you thinking, sending *this*," ChiChi chided, grabbing the e-mail and waving it in his face, her head shaking in disappointment, "to that woman? You want the whole town knowing that you don't have a chef for the Showdown?"

"I sent it to the dean. How was I supposed to know a Baudouin would get her hands on it?"

"Janice has been working there for over twenty years," Lucinda said, as though Marc should be up on every damn Baudouin in the valley.

Marc ran his fingers through his hair. He should be. Just like he should have known this would happen.

Although Lucinda was a Baudouin and ChiChi had married a DeLuca, neither was willing to throw away a lifelong friendship over a silly feud. That didn't mean Lucinda was above using her family ties to the academy's associate dean to gain information, especially if ChiChi asked.

"Does anyone else know?" *Please say no.* The last thing he needed was Gabe up in his business, going all big brother for the next few weeks. Or worse, old man Charles finding out and, like ChiChi said, somehow using it against Marc with the town council.

"Not even Janice," Lucinda clarified, straightening Mr. Puffins's neckerchief with a tug.

Marc raised an unconvinced brow.

All three ladies exchanged panicked looks. Pricilla pulled out a truffle and handed it to ChiChi, who took a nervous nibble before giving a defeated nod.

Lucinda patted ChiChi's knee, much the same way as she did her cat, and said, "Janice has been having online relations with a man."

"A man who had, up until last month, been having relations with me," ChiChi snapped, lips pursed into a tight line.

"Sweet Jesus," Marc murmured, wanting to cover his ears. He looked at his sweet nonna with her white hair, designer churchwear, and little round reading glasses hanging from a diamond-encrusted chain and grimaced. Then he turned to the window, judged its size, height, and drop to the ground, and quickly determined that a broken leg would be far less painful than finishing this conversation.

"Marco DeLuca," ChiChi scolded, making the sign of the cross. "I raised you on a vineyard, not a farm."

"Sorry, Nonna. I just...Can we not—"

Pricilla pulled out another square of fudge, eyes narrowed in warning.

"Put it away, Pricilla. We didn't come here to talk about whoopee. We came here because we have a proposition," ChiChi said with an innocent smile that had Marc looking at the window all over again. The only thing stopping him was the thought that Lexi might still be in the alley.

The last time ChiChi and her friends had a proposal that involved his hotel, it had ended with a drunken bachelorette party, a small bedroom fire, and a confused group of firemen who'd come for a convention on fire safety and left with wadded-up bills in their jeans.

"The Daughters of the Prohibition is about to be hijacked," ChiChi said. "Isabel Stark and that woman you've been keeping company with have been asked to head up the junior league. They think that just because Natasha's good at lighting your fire that you'll hire her to heat up your kitchen too."

"For the Showdown," Pricilla added.

"I'm not sure who I am hiring." Marc snapped his laptop, and the e-mail to Natasha, shut. "And just because Natasha and I are friends—"

Mr. Puffins let loose a low and gravelly growl that vibrated his hat.

And Pricilla waved the fudge in his face.

Right, lying.

ChiChi released a breath, her shoulders sagging just a bit, and for the first time Marc saw just how old his nonna had become. She looked small and fragile and so unlike the bold force that had molded his life.

"It is important to this town that this year's Showdown remains true to the founding fathers' ideas. That we abide by the traditions that were set before us. A lot of people's dreams have come true at this event."

"A hundred years of dreams that those ladies are willing to overlook to make room for newer, shinier things," Pricilla added, her hand clutching her chest.

"The Summer Wine Showdown was always about family and friends and community," Lucinda said. "We understand that you need a little flash to get the celebrities and media. That they bring in more money for the hospital and school. But some things, the ones that seem silly to your generation, matter because they are the heart of the event."

"And you think if they have a say in the catering that it will change the event?" Marc asked, because he heard what the grannies were saying, but he didn't understand how something as simple as a caterer would affect the bigger picture.

"This town is a family, Marco." ChiChi leaned across the desk to take Marc's hand. "Family is about sharing wine, breaking bread, remembering the past. Your grandfather and I met at the Showdown. Your parents, God rest their souls"—and there she went with the sign of the cross again—"had their wedding there. Along with a few dozen other people over the years, who are all looking forward to reliving those moments, remembering those who have passed."

ChiChi broke off with a sad shake of the head.

"If the junior league gets their way," Pricilla stepped in when it appeared that ChiChi couldn't finish, "there will be deconstructed this and imported that. The Showdown will turn into one of those celebrity events you see on TV. It won't be about the people of this town and celebrating their appreciation for food and wine and agriculture; it will be about how far up the exclusive places to live list we can move."

"Are you asking me not to hire Natasha?"

"No, we are asking you to let us pick. Let the Daughters of the Prohibition hold a tasting where we invite local culinary artists to showcase their appreciation of local cuisine and culture. You get to focus on the rest of the event, and we can make sure that the people of this town are represented in the food chosen."

Meaning his brothers couldn't blame him for thinking with the wrong head, no matter who got chosen. It also meant one in a long list of problems disappeared. Normally he wouldn't even consider entertaining any brainchild of the granny brigade, especially if it meant bringing them into the middle of something that could potentially sink his entire career, but he was rapidly running out of solutions.

"Deal," Marc said, wondering if he'd just made a huge mistake. He figured that everyone had to have at least one brilliant idea in their lifetime, right? Maybe this was theirs.

Lexi stared up at Jeffery with his bedroom eyes, easygoing smile, and adorable dimple marking his right cheek, and then she sucked in a deep breath and blew. A wad of tissue paper splatted with force across his left nostril, particles breaking off and speckling his upper lip.

Lexi smiled, tore off another piece of tissue, and rolled it around in her mouth, letting it soak up the spit.

"You shouldn't have chosen a head shot. Then you can't do this," said Abigail DeLuca, resident spit-wad champion and fellow woman scorned, putting the straw to her lips and aligning it with lethal accuracy before hitting her estranged husband, Richard, in the goodie bag.

Abby, with her olive skin, big brown eyes, and perfect white teeth, was a miniature version of her brother—only with a bunch of curves and a cute, pert nose. Although compact, she had the body of Ginger, the face of Mary Ann, and, when riled, the same capacity for total destruction as Scarface. She was also Lexi's oldest and dearest friend.

Abby tucked a stray auburn curl behind her ear and smiled. Picking up another perfectly rounded ball of tissue from her arsenal, she dropped it in her mouth for a second before aiming and—

"Nailed him! God, that feels good." She pointed her chin toward the two blown-up pictures of their cheating spouses, each hanging from the bakery rack like shooting targets. "If you want I can print off another picture for you. Full body."

"Nah." Maybe it was the fact that for the past few years she and Jeffery hadn't been on the same page, sexually speaking, but nothing about Jeffery's full body screamed feel-good to her.

"I talked to Tanner yesterday."

"Hard-Hammer Tanner," as he had been aptly named, was successful and sexy and very single, which made his company the number-one choice for the women of wine country when it came to additions and remodels. Something Lexi had discovered *after* Pricilla hired him. When he'd walked in, all muscles and impressive tool belt, Lexi hadn't known if he was a stripper or the real deal.

"I called him to see if he got the new blueprints. I had them sent over a week ago and never heard back."

After winning an award for designing Ryo Wines, a boutique winery that Abby and her grandmother had opened last year, Abby started talking about branching out, working on other kinds of projects. When she heard Lexi was moving home, she offered to design Lexi her dream eatery—and Lexi jumped at the chance.

Abby was also a classically trained pianist and one of the most sought-out piano teachers in the town. Okay, in a town this small, she was the only piano teacher. So when she began angrily tapping out "Flight of the Bumblebee" on the bakery table, Lexi knew her friend was mad.

"Imagine my surprise"—taptaptaptaptap, taptaptaptap—"when he told me he'd been fired."

Lexi's heart did some tapping of its own. "I didn't *fire* him. I merely changed the timeline." *To sometime in the unforeseeable future.*

"Yeah, well, you should have told me! I'm not only the designer, Lex, I'm your friend. We used to share everything."

Talk about laying on the guilt, Lexi thought. She and Abby had met the first day of freshman year when Abby stuck a wad of grape gum in her hair because Lance Burton had offered to walk Lexi to second period. Lexi cut out the gum, stuck it to Abby's chair and consequently the butt of her designer skirt, exposing a side of the DeLuca Darling that wasn't so darling or demure and landing them both in the principal's office. Two weeks of detention later, they were as close as sisters—and they sometimes still fought like ones.

"As for Hard-Hammer Tanner, I think he was afraid you fired him because he was a man," Abby added.

"A man?"

"As in single, potential date material. Or in your case, potential blind date, fixed up by grandmother, unwanted-bachelor material."

"Oh God," Lexi groaned, sticking her finger into a fruit tart and licking off the filling. She was so pathetic that she couldn't even fire a man without people thinking it was about dating.

"So, you want to explain how you went from kicking Jeffery's ass to putting the bistro on hold?"

Lexi shook her head.

"God, he can't even get his cake to rise. There's no way he can claim those recipes are his," Abby fumed.

"Jeffery never claimed that he *created* anything. He argued that a menu is a crucial asset to any restaurant. And since the restaurant was only ever in his name and I never executed an agreement stating exactly what I was bringing into the business and therefore could take with me when I left, the judge agreed."

"Bullshit! Contract or not, you were the reason that restaurant was a success."

"No, my menu was the reason it was a success." It was the main reason she had decided to not fight him for the recipes.

The past few months had been filled with several difficult realizations. For one, Lexi was embarrassed at just how trusting and stupid she'd been in assuming that "to honor and cherish" extended to all aspects of her and Jeffery's marriage. When they'd opened Pairing, he'd only put his and his mother's names on the papers, claiming that it was his mother's equity that afforded them to open the doors, and promising that when they could stand on their own he'd replace his mother's name with Lexi's. God, if that hadn't been a sign to run, she didn't know what was.

Time and again he'd discounted the amount of sweat equity Lexi had put into making their restaurant a success—or that *she* was supposed to be the Mrs. Balldinger in his life. Yes, his last name should have been another red flag. Instead of pressing the issue for her name to be added to a silly piece of paper, she'd naively assumed the marriage certificate was enough, and, not wanting to risk a confrontation in an already stressful time, she had nodded politely, thrown herself into creating the best menu on the West Side, and sat back while Jeffery made one bad decision after another. The worst being a year ago, when the restaurant began to struggle and she'd agreed to borrow a significant amount of money from Pricilla.

When she lost the restaurant, it was as though she had lost a part of herself, the part that made her fearless in the kitchen. That she couldn't pay Pricilla back only made the situation worse.

"So you aren't going to fight him?"

"And risk Pairing going under? No way. I mean, I lost the menu and it sucks, but if Jeffery lost the restaurant he would default on the loan and Grandma would lose everything."

"I thought you paid off the loan."

"The equity from the house wasn't enough because Jeffery insisted on going with the bigger meat supplier and nearly sank us."

"Imagine that," Abby said, rolling her eyes. "Jeff suffering from meat envy."

Yet another ongoing problem for her ex. But this time his need to measure up nearly put Pairing out of business. Insisting that to become a five-star eatery they had to act like a five-star eatery, Jeffery ignored that the fake-it-till-you-make-it theory had never really gone well for them and dumped their local meat supplier to go with a larger, more prestigious one.

Bo Brock's meat man, to be exact.

In theory it had been a smart move, but since Jeffery was, well Jeffery—and not superstar chef Bo Brock, with his thirteen Michelin stars, cable network, and Emmy-winning primetime show—the supplier required a six-month advance purchase. What Jeffery didn't know was that Brock was boycotting the supplier because they were under investigation for maintaining unsanitary and inhumane conditions of their stock.

When the story broke, Lexi was stuck with more than a hundred and fifty thousand dollars' worth of grade-A meat, and a grade-A ass of a spouse who didn't understand why serving factory flesh in a city where PETA reigned supreme was a bad business decision.

"It gets worse." Lexi took a breath. "When Pricilla offered her help, I only agreed because I thought she was just going to cosign a loan for us. Turns out the bank just approved us for a partial."

"Shut up!" Abby jerked to the end of her seat. "That rat bastard son of a bitch borrowed the rest from Pricilla?"

"Out of her retirement account." Even saying it made Lexi's stomach churn. "We managed to pay off a huge chunk of it when I sold the house, but we still owe Pricilla around twenty-five thousand dollars, and the bank at least sixty."

"Oh, Lex," Abby said, patting her hand.

"Yeah, so now you see that I just need to come up with a new menu. A better one," she said, as though it was that easy. It had taken her years to compile enough five-star recipes for Pairing, and although she knew it was possible to do it again, she didn't know if she had the fight left in her.

She'd attempted to alter them, put a different spin on her favorites, but nothing had tasted right. It didn't matter how hard she tried, superior ingredients would go into her kitchen and chain-style entrées would come out. It had been that way since the separation. Jeffery hadn't just stolen her menu; he'd turned her palate bitter.

"So, what's your backup plan?"

"You don't want to know," Lexi said, dropping her head to the table with a grimace.

"Oh, I'm sure I already do. It probably includes you"— Abby jabbed a pointy finger into Lexi's forehead—"slaving away in that kitchen and baking macaroons for the rest of your life."

"Just until I get Pricilla paid back and Jeffery pays off the loan, which he assures me will happen over the next twenty-four months. I figure it's smarter to take the cash I set aside for the bistro and put it toward what I still owe Pricilla, then start saving again once the bakery is turning out a higher profit."

"I have a better plan. One that isn't dumber than you marrying him in the first place."

Abby had never liked Jeffery. In fact, she had declared war on him in the fourth grade when he used her Barbie collection to stage a lifelike reenactment of Hiroshima—Barbie being on the losing end of a blowtorch. But when Lexi fell in love with the rat, Abby set aside her severe dislike and tried to make nice for her friend's sake.

"Want to hear it?"

"No." Lexi realized that her friend had been building toward this moment the entire evening. She'd come here with an agenda in mind and, if history served, Lexi was about to get pressured into doing something she'd regret, that would land her in jail, or that would leave her with Q-tip–length hair and orange skin. Or quite possibly all of the above.

"The Daughters of the Prohibition are in charge of the food for the Summer Wine Showdown's wine-tasting event, and I may have told them that I have a friend who is an excellent cater—"

Lexi crammed an entire petit four in her friend's mouth, silencing her. "Don't say the *C* word. You know it gives me gas."

Catering was something Lexi had promised herself she'd never do again. She had done it early on in her career to help pay the bills while Jeffery was still in grad school.

"Cater—" Abby slapped her hands over her lips, blocking Lexi from shoving another minicake in her already full mouth. "It would generate income, *and* you would have an audience to try out your new ideas on."

It would also be a huge step in the wrong direction. Call it pride or ego, but going from having her own kitchen and staff and creating one-of-a-kind plates for customers back to carting around chafing dishes and serving poached salmon on a bed of asparagus was not going to happen.

"Think about it, the Daughters of the Prohibition, Garden Club, PTA—they are all the same women, and they dictate the social scene of St. Helena. If one hires you, they'll all hire you, claiming that they single-handedly discovered your talent. Not to mention all of the press that comes with the Showdown. It's a win-win, Lex, and you know it." Abby clapped her hands as though the conversation was over.

"Let's say, just for a second, that I am actually considering it...which I'm not...but let's say, baking food in Costco-sized quantities for mass consumption was something I was interested in pursuing. I don't have a kitchen big enough to handle it."

"Prepare to be dazzled." Abby shoved the plates aside and rolled out a set of blueprints, almost identical to the one on Lexi's computer except this set was color coded and labeled. "We alter the redesign, building it in stages as money comes in. See right here." She pointed to a green section labeled "Stage 1." "We would build out the back storage space here and add the secondary kitchen like we had originally planned. It would give plenty of room to cook and prep, and you could be up and running in two weeks, tops."

"That fast?" Lexi asked, surprised; the original timeline was six weeks. She looked at the blueprints, and her heart pinched. God, she wanted to see this come to life. She wanted to cook with her grandmother in this kitchen. More importantly, catering would buy her the ability to pay Pricilla and the bank back, even if Jeffery flaked.

But there was still one big problem. "I don't have the time to oversee the remodel and come up with a menu for the Showdown."

"I do."

"What? No." Lexi shook her head. "You are so busy with Ryo Wines."

"ChiChi has it handled. Plus, I don't want to run a winery. I'm a designer, and I want to design—your bistro. And I'm not letting you just give up!"

"I'm not giving up, Abs." She wasn't. In fact, she had already created a new schedule that placed her in the bakery kitchen to increase production and had reached out to a few farmers' markets to boost sales.

"You are so. I can see it in your face," Abby accused through bits of cake and fondant. "You're going to let that rat bastard son of a bitch win. You're going to let him steal your dream of opening the bistro just like you let him do after high school."

"I repeat, am not. And *did* not." Lexi snatched her straw and started rolling spit wads. "I went to culinary school after high school, just like I said I was going to."

"Yeah, but you went to school in *New York* even though there is an internationally recognized one right here in St. Helena. Which offered you a full scholarship, by the way."

"New York is the mecca for culinary arts."

"You didn't care about that school. From the day I met you, all you ever talked about was opening a bistro with Pricilla, what it would look like, what you would serve. Then Jeffery got into *his* dream school in New York and you were about to start your dream career here. A few well-placed comments about how long-distance relationships don't last, a calculated breakup after graduation, and you started packing."

Lexi opened her mouth to argue and immediately shut it. Was that true? Was that how it had looked to everyone else?

"God, Lex, you were so determined *not* to be your mom and have an entire fleet of exes that you clung to the first guy who showed interest and gave up everything you wanted to keep him."

Lexi wanted to scream that Abby was wrong, that she had left St. Helena behind and married Jeffery because they were soul mates and that's what people in love do for each other. But soul mates didn't divorce. And Jeffery had never once considered staying in the Bay Area for school. In fact, every move or decision in their relationship had been the one that had most benefited Jeffery.

Tears burned at her throat. She'd had so many people float in and out of her life as a child that she'd thought there was something wrong with her. That she was missing whatever it was that other little girls, whose mommies and daddies never left, had that made them lovable. Even as an adult, she'd tried to convince herself she wasn't lacking some kind of crucial trait, and that she was enough. So she'd dedicated herself to Jeffery. Then he left.

Lexi covered her face with her hands. "Oh God, you're right," she sniffled through her fingers. "I'm a total pushover. Just like my mom. A man shows the slightest bit of interest and I drop everything to please him—even my family. What kind of person does that?"

"A person who doesn't want to give up on someone because she knows what it feels like to be walked away from," Abby said, licking the top off one of Pricilla's passion-fruit-and-pineapple petits fours. "Don't give up, Lex. Don't let him win."

Abby leaned in and dropped her voice. "Do you remember that time we went skinny-dipping?"

Lexi did remember. It had been a few months after Abby's parents died. "Jeffery was so mad when he found out. He never believed me when I told him that I didn't really want to do it."

"I knew you didn't. You're way too uptight for that." Abby ignored Lexi's protest and continued, "But I did. And you knew it. You also knew that the only way I would ever get in a car again after the accident was if it meant doing something wild and irresponsible. So you stole your grandmother's car, picked me up, and we went skinny-dipping in the lake."

Lexi gave a chuckle. "I kept my underwear on, and we broke into Mr. Patterson's pool because you couldn't wait to get to the lake. Thank God he didn't report us."

"He lived on *Lake* Drive, and if you hadn't been laughing so hard he would have never caught us." Abby went serious. "The point is, we did it together. I got over my fear of cars, and you did something crazy, like grand larceny and showing some skin in public, a totally unvaledictorian thing to do."

Lexi shifted in her seat, mushed a piece of icing with her fingertip, and waited for Abby to go on.

Abby sat back, arms folded, a cocky smile curving at her lips.

"Wait?" Lexi said, wiping at her tears. "*That's* your big plan: go skinny-dipping?"

Abby nodded. "Our plan is to go big. Together. We go forward with the new kitchen. And by *we*, I mean that I will handle most of the remodel while you cater your way to a full grand opening. By next year you'll have a bistro, a new menu, customers, and Jeffery doesn't win."

Abby looked at her expectantly. What she'd outlined was not only plausible, it was brilliant.

"Think about it, Lex. You get the chance to reinvent yourself. Your life, your cooking, your career, everything would get a clean slate. You can be Alexis Moreau instead of Lexi Balldinger."

Lexi had been Mrs. Balldinger for so long, she was afraid that Alexis Moreau no longer existed. Or worse, what if she didn't recognize her? But the idea of rediscovering that girl who loved to laugh and cook and had dreams, big dreams, was less terrifying than living the rest of her life as a failed Balldinger.

"All right, I'm in. I'll *go big*"—Lexi threw air quotes around the last two words—"if you agree to file for divorce."

"What?"

"If I have to spend the next six months alternating between dating and cater—" She shivered, unable to finish the sentence. "If I have to *win*, so do you, and that means flipping Richard the finger and taking your life back."

Her friend's face went completely white.

She placed a comforting hand on Abby's shoulder. "I'm sorry that the bank account in the Caymans turned out to be a dead end. I know how badly you needed this to be over so you could move on. And I get it, divorce by publication would mean that you would have to put an ad in the local paper stating what a bastard he is and that he walked out, but at least you could finally start over. Maybe even go out on a date."

"A date?" Abby snorted. "He'd better not scare easily."

A big part of the reason Abby had fallen for Richard was that he was the first guy her brothers didn't threaten, maim, or scare away.

"Fine." She flapped her hand nonchalantly. "You find me a man who can handle the DeLuca four, and I'll go on that date."

It was a lie, and they both knew it. Abby wasn't only a Roman Catholic, she was also a DeLuca, which meant that she, just like her brothers, took their vows seriously. Oh, the DeLuca men didn't live like monks in any sense of the word, but the moment they found *the one*, it would be forever. Of that, Lexi was certain. Just like she was certain that until the divorce was official, Abby would conduct herself like a married woman.

"I'm serious, Abs. We both go big, and we both win our lives back. Together."

Abby shrugged noncommittally.

Lexi picked up two chocolate éclairs, one for each of them. "Swear on the éclair."

"What are we, in middle school?"

Lexi, eyes never leaving her friend's, kissed both éclairs before offering them up.

"Fine." Abby finally leaned in, kissing both pastries before grabbing one and cramming the entire thing in her mouth. "I'll call Hard-Hammer Tanner tomorrow." She forced the words through a half cup of cream filling and chocolate glaze. Lexi froze, éclair halfway in her mouth. "To set a new start date for Monday. Jeez, just because I'll soon be divorced doesn't mean I'm going to start dating. And if I did, it would not be with a guy like him."

Lexi was too busy licking her fingers to point out that every time her friend mentioned Hard-Hammer Tanner she got agitated—and really pissed.

CHAPTER 6

Marc was in his office, staring out the window and wondering how he'd managed to get himself in the middle of this fucked-up situation. His celebrity judge, Bo Brock, wasn't returning his calls, Natasha was still trying to nail him down—catering job or otherwise—and Abby was finally divorcing the jerkwad. A great step for his sister but terrible timing for him, since her full-page "Have You Seen This Dick?" announcement, complete with a picture of Richard, ran concurrently with his Summer Wine Showdown ad.

Now he had to deal with the fact that his best friend was suing his sexy new neighbor because Jeff had made promises he shouldn't have. And if Jeff didn't deliver on those promises, Marc's brothers were going to rip him a new one, because it would cost everyone involved a ton of cash.

"Do you really need *her* recipes?" Marc asked, angling his chair so that he would be forced to stare at his computer rather than watching the window, hoping to see a construction crew hard at work, or catch a glimpse of Lexi in her apartment cooking in something other than pj's, anything to reassure him that she was okay.

"Christ, Marc, how many times do I have to explain this?" Jeff's voice came through the speaker on the phone. "They aren't her recipes. They belong to the restaurant, always have, and I own the restaurant. She got the house. I got the restaurant."

They'd been arguing about this on and off for days. Ever since Marc had gotten up the balls to call his friend.

"Yeah, well, *this* is a small town, and people here don't give a rat's ass what some New York judge said or about a house she no longer lives in."

There was a tense pause. Marc closed his eyes and leaned back in the chair. He hated fighting with—well, anyone. It was easier to just stay detached.

"How is she doing?" Jeff asked, and for the first time in an hour his old friend was on the phone. Jeff wasn't a bad guy; he was just always so focused on newer and shinier things that he had a hard time noticing other people's shoes, let alone walking in them. "I've tried calling her, checking in, but she doesn't seem receptive to me right now."

Marc knew the feeling. And telling Jeff about how devastated Lexi had been felt like a betrayal, but he had to tell his friend something to make him see what this was doing to her. "She's stopped construction."

Jeff was quiet for a long moment. When he finally spoke, his voice was low, confused. "I don't understand. That's all she ever talked about. Hell, there were a couple times over the past few years she threatened to bail on the marriage so she could move home and open that bistro." The admission surprised Marc. Jeff had alluded to Lexi being unhappy in the marriage, but he'd never been so blunt about it before. "When she decided to sell the house, I didn't even ask for any of the proceeds because I knew she'd need the money for renovations."

"According to Abby"—who had threatened to fly to New York and kill Jeffery, very slowly, with a pizza slicer—"Lexi doesn't want to sink all of her money into a bistro when she doesn't have a winning menu."

Wingman's ears perked up at the sound of Lexi's name. So did Marc's pulse.

"So, I ask again, is there any way you can do this without her recipes?"

"I wish, man. But the deal depends on *that* menu." Which was what Marc had feared. "When I first met with Montgomery Distributions, I was still clinging to the hope that Lexi and I could make it work, especially if we landed the deal. Monte had a few other restaurants he was talking to, and it was Lexi's food that raised Pairing to the top of his list. We weren't the biggest or most financially set of the competition, but we had the best food. To change the game now...there's no way."

Last spring, Monte, founder and CEO of Montgomery Distributions, had been in town to meet the youngest DeLuca, Trey, whose tendency toward wanderlust had him out of the country more than in. It also had him at a wine sellers' convention in Prague—when he should have had his ass in St. Helena—negotiating a deal with Monte that would take DeLuca Wines from specialty shops to supermarkets around the globe. Marc, already feeling guilty for skirting his responsibilities in the family business to get his hotel stable, had agreed to cover for Trey and entertain the man.

Over a friendly glass of DeLuca zin, Marc learned that Monte not only specialized in wine distribution but that he was also looking to expand into the specialty-food sector, to bring five-star, fine-dining cuisine to freezer sections everywhere and pair it with the perfect wine. Monte had the contacts and the interest; all he needed was a restaurant and winery to partner with. And Jeff needed the kind of money that a deal like this could bring. It seemed the perfect fit.

Gabe had disagreed, adamant about not mixing friends and the family business. But Jeff had always talked about expanding Pairing, taking it to a national scale; he just lacked the backing and support to get there alone. Marc knew what that felt like. In fact, Jeff was the only one who had wholeheartedly supported Marc's decision to buy the Napa Grand, which was why Marc had wanted to see this partnership work. So at the risk of pissing off his brothers, he'd made the introduction. Only now he wasn't so sure that he'd made the right decision.

"Does she know about Monte? About my family's role in the deal?" At this point, Marc wasn't sure he even wanted to know.

There was a long pause, as though Jeff was weighing his answer.

"No."

Marc felt his body relax a little.

"I didn't think it mattered," Jeff said. "She had already checked out on the marriage and the restaurant. I knew she'd move home, and I didn't want to drag you into the middle of everything."

Funny, because the middle was exactly where Jeff had stuck him the minute he asked Lexi out sophomore year—even though he knew Marc had a thing for her. And the middle was starting to piss him off. Sure, Marc had had a weakness for just about anything with pom-poms—still did—but Lexi's pom-poms were different. They always would be.

"I know this is a lot to ask," Jeff went on. "But you guys used to be friends, and this deal needs to close. Until that happens, I need you to keep an eye on Lexi, make sure she doesn't sink this just because she's pissed at me."

"So you want her to be pissed at me? Because the second she finds out we even *talked* about her—"

"She's going to be pissed either way, Marc. That's just Lexi." Not the Lexi that Marc knew. Then again, he had never been married to her.

Marc closed his eyes and leaned back in his chair. So much for not wanting to stick him in the middle. But Jeff was right: this deal couldn't fall apart. Not now. Not after Marc had defended his decision to bring Jeff in on the deal to his brothers. But the thought of Lexi's dreams shattering didn't sit right either.

It's just a cookbook, Lexi. Get a grip.

But she couldn't. Just like she couldn't believe that after almost twenty-four hours of culinary bliss, *this* was happening.

Last night, after covering her ex in a mosaic of spit wads and promising Abby she wouldn't give up, Lexi had called her *grandmère* and agreed to cater for the Daughters of the Prohibition.

Yes, she hated catering. But she loved her grandmother. And with Pricilla being the only real family Lexi had, her grandmother's dream of a bistro trumped everything, so she got her butt in gear, threw on an old CD mix she'd found from high school, and stayed up all night cooking, experimenting, and for the first time in months finding a sense of peace.

In fact, the more creative she got with the traditional Summer Showdown menu, the more her creative block seemed to crumble. Which was why, when she looked up from her Pacific sea bass sashimi with papaya and avocado mousse to find three innocent, smiling grannies, a cat trying to pass for a sunflower, and a worn leather book that predated even Pricilla, Lexi got a bad feeling in her gut.

Forcing an innocuous smile, Lexi threw a towel over the dish and said, "What are you guys doing here?"

They didn't answer.

Lexi watched the inquisitive eyes studying her hidden appetizers, the cat sniffing wildly, and she stepped forward, placing her body between the welcoming committee and the entry to the kitchen.

"What's that?" Pricilla asked, smoothing down her halo of gray after ducking under Lexi's outstretched arms, which were now braced on either side of the kitchen counter, to pull off the towel.

"Oh, that? Nothing. Just dinner." Lexi dropped her arms when ChiChi and Lucinda, who was carrying Mr. Puffins, skirted around the other side of the counter. All three grannies and the cat huddled around and stared suspiciously down at the dish, as if they were expecting it to walk off the plate.

Mr. Puffins looked hopeful.

Pricilla, proud.

The other two—completely at a loss.

"I think it's fish," ChiChi said to the others as though Lexi wasn't standing two feet away.

Lucinda, needing a closer look, set Mr. Puffins on the counter. She extended one bony finger—everything about the woman was sharp edged—and poked the fish, frowning when it jiggled. "How long did you cook it?"

"It's, um, sashimi." When all three ladies pursed their lips in confusion, Lexi added, "Raw fish."

The grannies shared a silent look of concern while the cat gingerly sniffed the air, his eyelids going heavy and his whiskers working overtime. At least someone appreciated good fish.

"It isn't perfected yet. I'm still tinkering with the balance of the papaya—"

"We have reservations," Lucinda pronounced, grabbing Mr. Puffins before he could take his first lick of the mousse.

"But you haven't even tried it!" Lexi said, feeling her entire body deflate.

"At Stan's," ChiChi cut in, smacking Lucinda on the hip with the back of her hand. "For dinner. We have reservations at Stan's for dinner."

"I didn't know Stan took reservations." Nor did she know why she was calling them on the lie. Two minutes ago she would have given her left ovary to get them, and that recipe book, out of her kitchen. But it hurt that they were dismissing her plate on design alone. "Isn't it more of a serve-yourself kind of place?"

ChiChi draped a regal hand down her form to highlight her cream pantsuit as though her St. John ensemble was solid proof that they had reservations for a bowl of soup at the service station.

"I'd ask you to join us, dear," Pricilla said, gently rubbing Lexi's shoulder. It was a sign that she knew Lexi was upset. "But you have your date with Vince."

Lexi looked down at her striped pajama bottoms, at the well-used kitchen, at the fresh ingredients still waiting to be transformed, and groaned. She had totally forgotten about her dinner plans with Mr. Friday Night Lights, who was old enough to have played in the actual football game that inspired the book.

"I got so busy cooking I lost track of time. I'll just call him and reschedule." She pulled out her phone, hoping the ladies would take the hint and give her privacy—or better yet, leave. And take with them the traditional Showdown recipe book, which had been created by Lucinda's and ChiChi's mothers and had served as the culinary bible for every Showdown since.

"Nonsense, child, we're just dropping by. Wanted to bring you this." ChiChi opened the book to the first page and slid it closer to Lexi.

Lexi studied it for a long moment, not touching it. One look at the diagram of how to poach cod in milk was enough to cause her head to pound. It started as a slight pulsing behind her right eye, but by the time she got to the instructions for roasted squash and fig mash, a sharp pain crept down to the base of her skull.

"The tasting is set for Wednesday at seven at the Back Barrel," Pricilla said, clapping her hands. "Bring one appetizer and one entrée with a side dish."

"Of course, for the Showdown you'll need to make each of the different courses for guests to choose from, including the traditional fish, pork, and beef entrees," Lucinda added.

"Traditional. Of course." Lexi reached out, intending to pick up the menu, which ChiChi seemed so insistent that she hold, but only managed to trace a shaky finger across its bottom edge, fearful that if she actually grasped the book it would go off like a live grenade, demolishing all creativity and culinary ability in a seven-mile radius—and all of the progress she'd made last night.

She looked at her beautiful dish, with its bright-orange drizzles and brilliant-green mousse, and straightened her shoulders. Abby was right. It was her life. Her cooking. Her clean slate.

"I was actually going to play with the menu a little. Update it. Take the traditional and make it retro."

"Retro?" ChiChi said, her face going white.

"Yes, a remodeled menu for a remodeled venue." *And a remodeled me.*

"Remodel this—"

"Why, Lexi—" her grandmother intercepted Lucinda, who was moving toward Lexi at an alarming pace. "A little updating would be nice." Pricilla shot a reprimanding glance at her two cohorts before giving Lexi a placating smile. It was the same smile Lexi had received when she was nine and told Pricilla she wanted to add mango to her summer tarts. "What a great idea. Perhaps salmon instead of the cod."

Lucinda nodded.

ChiChi forced out, "Salmon sounds lovely."

Lexi snorted. It did not sound lovely. It sounded safe, boring, the kind of thing one would expect at a catered event. And salmon was even worse than cod for a large group. It was a fish that needed to be cooked to order, freshly prepared and immediately served. Not poached in mass quantity only to sit in a lukewarm bath of milk sauce.

"But I wouldn't go too far," Lucinda warned. "The other girls received their menus last week. And I know that they are thrilled by the opportunity to pay tribute to the history behind these dishes."

"Other girls?" Lexi gasped. "Abby made it sound like the job was mine if I wanted it."

"She is just confident in your ability. We all are," ChiChi soothed, patting her hand. But the gesture wasn't soothing. Nor was the presence of all three grannies smiling serenely at her over oval-rimmed glasses.

Lexi knew that getting the Daughters of the Prohibition to agree on a different menu, one that used the traditional ingredients with a fresh spin, would be a challenge. But she had no idea that she'd have to audition for the job against other caterers who were content to ruin a delicate fish by boiling it in milk.

"Don't worry," Pricilla said. "None of these girls have your training or palate. The tasting is merely a formality."

"Formality my butt," Lexi mumbled after the grannies left. Who needed training or a palate when the recipe was so explicitly detailed, complete with a diagram showing how the fish should be placed atop a bed of five balanced asparagus spears and at a forty-five-degree angle to the half cup of whipped mash?

Bo Brock's hotel reservation had been canceled. Marc hoped to hell it was some kind of glitch and not his celebrity judge pulling out. But the fact that he wasn't returning any of Marc's calls felt like a rock in his gut.

Marc pulled up a fresh e-mail and began typing, outlining the exact terms of their agreed-upon contract, when a light flicked on across the alley. He turned in his chair just as a figure walked across the room toward the stove, drawing him in. A figure with really great boobs, wavy blonde hair, and an ass that had kept him awake all week.

Gone were the pajama bottoms and stained tank from earlier. In their place she wore a slinky red top that dipped way down in the front, and he wasn't sure if she was wearing slacks or jeans, didn't care. They looked damn sexy on her. They also covered her bare feet, which she was currently slipping into a pair of red strappy heels, helpfully bending over to give him a great view of her lacy bra that made looking away damn difficult.

She fastened the shoes around her slim ankles and picked up a bottle of—well, shit, that girl had guts—Pricilla's homebrew. She hopped up on the counter, then poured a cup, a full cup, and went to take a sip, then stopped. She glanced out the window and, before he could turn back to his computer, looked right at him. Then she did the damndest thing—she lifted her glass in salute, offered up a sad smile, and drained the entire thing before refilling it.

Wingman whined.

Marc leaned down and patted his head. "I know, boy. I want to go over there too. But keeping an eye on her and keeping my distance are two separate things."

Both were equally stupid.

"How about a man night? You and me and a couple bloody steaks. I'll even let you have some of my beer."

Wingman didn't answer, just stared across the alley.

Finishing her second drink, Lexi slid off the counter, set the cup in the sink, and wiped her hands across her mouth. Then she smiled over at Marc and gave him a little wave. He waved back. And his smile came out stupid and big.

"Too bad man night excludes the girl next door," Marc mumbled, right as his phone rang. He looked at the screen, saw Trey's number, and hung up.

He didn't have time to listen to his kid brother lay into him over something he had or hadn't done. He was too busy trying to figure out where Lexi, who had grabbed a small handbag off the table and sashayed her ass out of sight, had disappeared to. And why she wasn't returning his calls.

Marc walked to the corner of his office and peered out into the parking lot at the back of the bakery. He didn't see Lexi, but he did see a tool in slacks and a polo strangling a bouquet of roses on her back stoop.

"Dumb-ass," Marc muttered. Lexi hated roses. Thought they were cliché.

His phone chimed that he had a voice mail. He dialed and listened.

"Answer your phone, will you? I need to get a hold of your buddy." Marc could tell by the way Trey said *your buddy* that what little love there had been between the two was long gone. Not good. "I know he's away on his honeymoon, but he still owes me some financials. Monte is on my case about it. So if you hear from him, tell me what he says."

The message ended. Marc hung up. He could tell Trey exactly what his *buddy* had said.

I know this is a lot to ask, but you guys used to be friends.

Marc and Lexi had never stopped being friends. In fact, Marc, abiding by man law, had vowed to keep his distance from her, and over the years he'd done his sex proud. But when Lexi stepped out on her porch, too-big grin in place, tottered a bit on those heels, and then stumbled right into Mr. Friday Night's arms, *friend* was the last person Marc was capable of being. Especially when Dumb-Ass pulled her closer, resting his hand pretty damn low for a first date, and tugged her toward his shiny sports car.

Wingman growled, baring his teeth and his obvious dislike for Lexi's date.

"Me too," Marc said.

The silver-streaked hair, corporate-branded shirt, and overcompensation with a spoiler told Marc that this was Vince Jones, a local dot-comer who specialized in social media and younger women. He was twenty years too old and Lexi was already three shots too far gone for this to be a good idea.

Wingman jumped at the window, barking up a storm and practically foaming at the mouth to rip the guy apart.

"Give me the first shot at him." Marc grabbed Wingman's leash and was already reaching for his keys when he added, "If he's too stupid to listen, I'll give you ten minutes in a dark room with the guy."

Which was how Wingman ended up eating kibble for dinner and Marc found himself at the Spigot, wedged between an irrigation specialist and an investment banker, nursing a warm beer and watching Lexi wobble around on those ridiculous heels while Vince supplied her with enough tequila to get an entire crew of vineyard workers hammered.

Lexi licked the tip of a dart, took aim, and leaned over a bar stool for balance, causing the denim to stretch even more tightly across her incredible backside. Marc zeroed in and choked on his beer when she threw the dart and gave an excited little wiggle. He couldn't see what she was aiming at, but it must have been a bull's-eye because she started bouncing up and down on her toes—and then all thinking became impossible.

God, the woman had an incredible body.

A low, appreciative whistle sounded from his right, and Marc realized that the irrigation specialist—and half the freaking bar—was just as interested in the sight of Lexi jumping up and down while holding a weapon. But when Dumb-Ass leaned in, getting all up behind her to help line up her next throw, it took everything Marc had not to do some lining up of his own.

"I'm her Friday after next," the investment banker bragged, swirling his glass of cabernet. "Got tickets to see *Phantom of the Opera* in the city. Also booked a room at the Fairmont. Just in case it gets late."

"I hope they're refundable," Marc muttered, dropping a ten on the table for his drink and a text to ChiChi about inviting Pricilla and her granddaughter to their family dinner that Friday.

Lexi, out of darts, said something to her date and then disappeared down the hall in the direction of the ladies' room. Vince flagged down the waitress to place another order, his grin a little too confident for Marc's liking.

Marc made his way through the bar, saying "hey" more times than he wished since everyone knew everyone here, and glanced out the window. He took one look at Vince's car and smiled. Not only did it serve as a public service announcement to women everywhere that the man needed help in the form of a little blue pill, it also sagged drastically to the right.

"Hey, Vince, hate to interrupt," Marc lied, taking him by the shoulder and pointing toward the front window. "But I think some idiots were out there messing with your car."

Actually, it was only one idiot. And he was digging himself in deeper when it came to Lexi, because no matter how many times Marc told himself to keep a safe distance, there he was, repeating history and inserting himself between Lexi and another man. Only this time he wasn't sure that he would be satisfied staying stuck in the friendly middle.

"What the—" Vince didn't even wait for Lexi to return before going off to check on his car. He exited the bar, letting loose a whole lot of questionable language when he saw exactly how flat his right-side tires were. Even flatter than Marc had intended.

Marc followed him outside. "You got a jack?" He knew damn well that a Mercedes SLR wasn't the kind of car you just up and change the tire for. Not to mention Vince wasn't the kind of guy to even know where the jack was, should he have one. "Otherwise it might start to bend the rims."

"Shit." Vince was on it, frantically reaching for his phone while trying to use the weight of his body to push against the car and lift it a little—his drunk and sexy date no longer even registering on his list of things to think about.

Marc crossed his arms and leaned back against the right side of the car next to Vince, going for casual and pretending to do his part to help. The Benz groaned under the pressure. So did Vince when the shop said it would take fifteen minutes to get there.

"How about you stay here and wait for the guy while I go fetch your date for you?" When Vince looked up confused, Marc jutted his chin toward the window. Inside, Lexi had returned. So had the waitress. Lexi tossed her blonde curls over her shoulder and the shot of tequila down her throat.

"She must be a handful. I've never seen her drink like this." Marc patted Vince on the back before heading toward the door. He reached for the handle and paused. "You know, if you want, I can take her home. It'd be no problem to drop her off on my way to the hotel."

Vince hesitated, watching Lexi bend over and line up her next shot. Her silky number rode up her back, and the dart flew right past the board, taking out a beer mug on a nearby table.

"You know what, never mind. I wouldn't want to ruin your fun. So I'll go keep her company while you wait for your guy. I'll even make sure the bartender gives her a plastic bag—just in case."

Marc stepped inside, smiling when Vince called after him, "No. You're right. She's having fun, and I have to get this taken care of." He nodded to his car. "Tell her I'm sorry and I'll make it up to her."

"You got it," Marc said over his shoulder, and then lower, "and good luck with that."

The guy was a bigger dumb-ass that Marc originally thought if he assumed he'd get a second chance like the one he'd just blown. No, Lexi wasn't one to get drunk—often— and Vince wouldn't get another date with her. Marc would make sure of that.

Determined to keep it light and easy, Marc made his way across the bar, slid onto the stool next to Lexi's empty glass, and watched patiently as, dart after dart, she carefully aimed, drew back, threw—and hit the wall, a chair, the floor. By the time she had cleaned out her ammo, she'd also cleaned out the entire section of customers.

She slowly backed away from the dartboard, stopping abruptly when she turned and found Marc waiting for her, glass of water in hand. She still held a single dart, which she pointed in his direction.

"You." It came out part greeting, part accusation, and completely slurred.

"Me." He flashed his best bad-boy grin. The one that showed all his teeth and made his normally hidden dimple stand out. The same one he'd learned early on that no woman could resist.

"God, it's like I stepped in a big hunk of...of you and everywhere I go it stinks up the room."

No woman except Lexi.

"And that"—she motioned to his face with the dart and continued—"is insulting. I'm not one of your women, so the charming little smile and flash of dimple won't make me forget that you're trying to screw with me."

Marc didn't know what had happened to make that sweet Lexi from three hours ago, who had waved and smiled to him through the window, vanish completely. In her place was a woman with a dart aimed to lodge in some poor guy's jugular.

"And you chased my date away!"

"I did." No point in lying. Sure, she was mad, but not about Vince's departure. Just in case, Marc covered his neck when he said, "Cream puff, if I'm screwing, there won't be any trying about it. And trust me, you won't forget."

She rolled her eyes. "You're in my seat."

"So I am."

"Move."

"As you wish." He scooted back—an inch—braced his feet on either side of the stool, and patted the now vacant part of the seat. "We can share."

To his surprise she didn't toss the dart to maim, nor did she shove him off the chair. Instead she walked forward, wobbling a little, to right between his legs, nudging them farther apart with her hips and stepping so close he could smell her perfume. It was light and floral and it took everything he had not to lean in for a better whiff. He worked hard to ignore just how far the vee of her top dipped into her glorious cleavage.

But when she looked up at him, her eyes full of hurt, all he could feel was the way his chest clenched up on him and his heart kicked into a painful overtime.

"So what? So you can *share* with Jeffery exactly where I am and how he can serve me?" Her eyes never left Marc's as she drew her hand back and, steady and sure, chucked the dart. Marc leaped off the bar stool, narrowly dodging the pointy tip, which wasn't aimed at his jugular but at somewhere much more tender. "Or wait, he already did that. Maybe this time you just want to laugh with him about how easy it was to chase off my date so I'd sit here looking like a fool in front of everyone, waiting for him to come back."

And with that she stormed out of the bar, leaving Marc checking for puncture wounds. His goods were still intact, but he wasn't so sure about the rest of him.

Dropping enough money on the bar to cover her drinks, he followed her out the door—because when it came to this woman that's what he did: followed and watched. He'd spent the past fifteen years watching her from a distance without getting caught, and he was tired of it. She was upset and probably embarrassed about being stood up, but he'd be damned if he would let her walk out of there thinking he'd set out to purposefully hurt her.

It didn't take him long to catch up; her legs were short, the drinks were straight up, and those heels were slowing her down. She was just rounding the corner of the bar when Marc reached her.

"Look, I might act like an ass sometimes." He took her hand to slow her down.

"Sometimes?" She tried to break free, but he held firm, trapping her hand against his chest and bringing their bodies flush.

One hell of a zing shot through him, and he had a hard time remembering how to breathe. When he saw Lexi's chest doing a dance of its own, he knew this crazy attraction had sucked her in too. And that scared the crap out of him, because whatever had passed between them in the cab of his truck felt like high-school hormones compared to the insane heat arching between them now.

"I will admit that, although a rarity, it does happen more than frequently around you." He relaxed his grip and cleared his throat. "But I would never, never laugh about anything that makes you sad. Understand?"

At his words, her hand flattened against his chest. He didn't let go, and she didn't move except to sag closer into him. "Then why are you here?"

Because even though I can't have you, I can't stay away.

"Because I wanted to make sure you were all right." His eyes ran over her top, which showed more skin that it covered.

Even drunk she still managed to look sassy and sexy and hot as hell. But sexy as she was, this wasn't the Lexi he knew. "And you should be thanking me. I chased off a guy who was willing to front the bill to get in your very drunk pants."

"I'm not drunk." She plucked at her top and took an unsteady step backward, whether to gain distance or because she was swaying on her feet, Marc didn't know. Either way, she was about to tumble right out of those strappy heels and onto her sexy ass. "Fine. Maybe I'm a little tipsy."

"A little?" He mimicked her tone as he dropped his free hand to her hip, pulling her closer and holding steady a good portion of her weight. "Cream puff, I haven't seen you mainline tequila since prom, and that didn't turn out so well for me or the interior of my car." That got a little smile out of her.

"What's going on, Lexi?"

"You knew he was going to sue me, and you didn't say anything. I didn't have time to prepare." She shrugged, her smile now small and sad. "I get that you're his best friend, but I thought we were friends too."

Were friends, as in past tense. Not what he wanted to hear.

"I had no idea he was going to sue you. I assumed that all the assets had been taken care of in the divorce," he said. "And Lexi, we *are* friends."

"Friends call, Marc. They check in on each other. Especially when somebody's world falls apart."

"I didn't know what to say."

Somehow, "I'm sorry that your marriage is over, but even though I never stopped wanting you I still can't ever have you" hadn't seemed like a good opening. So he'd put off calling her after she left Jeff, telling himself to give her a few days to recover from the blow. But then days became weeks and then months, and finally when the silence had become a knot in his gut, he'd heard from Abby that Lexi was moving home.

"I'm sorry I didn't call, and I'm sorry that Jeff is such an idiot that he can't see what he's doing to you. But your world can only fall apart if you let it." He pressed a finger to her puckered lips.

"Now before you go and say something to challenge my masculinity, all I am saying is that the Lexi I know would get pissed that her plan, for which I am sure you had every last detail figured out, has just been shot to hell, and find another way. Not use it as an excuse to give up."

"God, what is it with you DeLucas? I'm not giving up," she argued, but he didn't hear any fight in her voice. "Tanner starts on the remodel Monday, and Abby is determined that we will open. Eventually."

"That makes me happy." Not the part about Tanner walking around her shop lifting heavy things and carrying a hammer, but that she was going forward with the bistro. "The question is, does it make you happy?"

She shook her head. "I have to cook salmon," she said, and to his horror she started crying. Not over Jeff, not over her bistro, but over salmon.

Normally he didn't mind when women cried. He knew just how to hold them, kiss away their tears, and then eventually distract them with mind-blowing sex. But Lexi was different. This whole fucked-up situation was different. And for the first time since, well, since graduation night, when the same woman had cried in his arms, he had no idea what to do.

He remembered how crushed Abby had been after Richard left. She had cried all the time, and the only thing that helped was chocolate ice cream and his nonna's hugs. He didn't have any chocolate ice cream, and ChiChi was playing poker with her friends. So he opened his arms and pulled Lexi close, wrapping one hand around her lower back and gently patting between her shoulders.

Then he said, "Salmon isn't so bad."

"It is when it's poached and served on a bed of blanched asparagus," she sniffled and, to his surprise, wrapped her arms around his waist, pressing her soft cleavage into his chest and burying her face in the curve of his neck. Not sure what to do next, he went quiet, knowing that the women in his life lived to fill gaps of silence.

Sure enough, after what felt like fifteen minutes, Lexi finally spoke. "Our grandmas invited me do a tasting with a few other caterers at the next Daughters of the Prohibition meeting."

She sniffled.

He gave another comforting pat on her head.

They both stood in silence. For a long-ass time, because of course Lexi couldn't be like other women and spill her secrets. That would be too easy.

"That's great," he finally said, hating himself for giving in. Men liked quiet. Welcomed it, even. But with her, he had no idea what he liked anymore. All he knew was that if she was catering that event, she wouldn't hide in her apartment all day, wouldn't have time to date a bunch of tools, and he wouldn't have to deal with Natasha.

"No, not great. They invited the celebrity judge for the Showdown to join them." Sniffle. "Probably because Bo Brock is so hot."

Lexi thought Bo Brock was hot? Marc was suddenly hoping that the guy was reconsidering. Hell, he might just tell Brock he'd found another judge.

"Abby and I figured that if I catered the event it would be a great way to test my new recipes while building a name for the bistro."

"Then why the tears?" Marc asked, running his fingers up the back of her neck and easing out some of the tension. He must have hit a sensitive spot, because she gave a little moan and snuggled closer and Marc gave up.

No matter how many times he patted her back or tried to picture Abby in his arms instead of Lexi, he couldn't come up with a single brotherly emotion. The only thing that was coming up for him was a big problem in his pants, and if Lexi swayed any closer she was bound to notice. And wouldn't that just make everything a hell of a lot more complicated.

So when she added, "They're deciding who gets to cater the Showdown, and if they like my food it will be me," Marc took her by the shoulders and nudged her back a little so that they were no longer touching.

"That's incredible. Do you realize how much press you could get out of that?"

"That's what Abby said." Her lower lip quivered. "But they want me to serve salmon," she cried. "On a bed of asparagus! How can I make the most boring dish ever and impress them? I mean—"

She froze, her big green eyes large and wet. "Oh God." She doubled over and covered her face with her hands as though embarrassed for him to see her break down. Her back shook with emotion, and she was making these little mewling sounds that damn near broke his heart.

Marc squatted in front of her, tucking her hair behind her shoulder, and whispered, "Aw, honey, don't cry anymore, you're killing me. We'll figure this out. You and me. I promise. Hey," he coaxed when she just kept convulsing. He pulled his shirt out and offered it up. "Give a good blow, wipe your tears, and then I'll take you home. We can talk about this in the morning. Okay?"

Lexi lifted her head slightly, looked up at him with those incredible eyes, and then, for the first time since she'd been served, she reminded him of the girl he knew and loved. She moved her hands and threw up all over his shirt.

CHAPTER 7

A clicking sounded in the distance. It echoed through her head, pounding over and over. Lexi groaned, and even that hurt.

Pulling the covers tighter to her, she squeezed her eyes, trying to convince her brain to reattach to her skull. The clicking stopped, and she felt a hand slide into her hair, then rub tiny, moan-worthy circles at the base of her skull. Snuggling in deeper, she melted around the warm body she was holding and felt herself lulled back toward sleepiness. She also felt something wet on her pillow.

Lexi froze. The heavenly fingers stopped and then disappeared. The clicking started up again, and every detail from last night came rushing back in HD. Unfortunately, she'd not only lost her dinner all over Marc's shirt, she'd also lost signal somewhere around the time Marc slung her over his shoulder and carried her up the stairs to her apartment.

Desperate not to wake up her bedmate, Lexi gently slid her left hand—the other was stuck beneath his body—under the covers and did a quick walk-of-shame pat-down. She'd never done the walk of shame, hard to do when you'd only ever been with one man, but secretly she'd fantasized about it once or twice.

Yup, completely naked except for a bra.

Abby would be so proud…until she heard that the shame in question was her brother.

Eyes closed, she took stock. She was practically naked, her arm asleep and trapped between the mattress and her ex's best bro, and the room spun so fast she was pretty sure she was still drunk.

Had she really slept with Marc DeLuca? And if so, why couldn't she have been sober enough to remember the experience? For the first time in her life she had done something wild and irresponsible, and she hadn't even been present for the main event. Worse still, she was trapped and would have to face him not knowing if she was even any good.

She was such a failure.

Slowly she tried to slide her arm out. When he didn't budge except to grunt and roll closer, she threw the covers over her head and decided to feign sleep until he got bored and left.

"Unless you're willing to chew through your arm, I'm pretty sure he'll outwait you."

Lexi pulled back the covers and immediately threw them over her head again. Her eyes were dry and irritated, and she didn't know what made her feel worse, the sun piercing her brain through her retinas or the sight of big brown eyes staring back at her.

"Rise and shine, cream puff." Marc ripped the sheets back, and Lexi gasped.

She was lying in a puddle of drool, next to a man who was very much dressed in shorts and a tee and sitting on top of the covers, while she was spooning his dog for all she was worth. She grabbed the sheets back from Marc and covered herself.

Wait! He was in different clothes. Maybe they did...

"Why are you dressed in"—sheets to chin, she eyed his new clothes—"*those?*"

Marc looked up from his laptop, and the clicking stopped. "I could take them off, but I think Wingman might get a little jealous. He's not really into sharing. We're working on that though, huh, boy?"

Boy barked, his tail thumping the mattress.

"No, I mean, where are your shirt and pants?"

"In the dryer. They got a little dirty last night, so I went to my place and grabbed a few things after you passed out."

She groaned, remembering just how his pants got *dirty*. Turning her head back to look at Wingman, who was panting happily in her face, she asked Marc, "What are you even doing here?"

"Holding your hair while you went to church for most of the night. Listening to you snore for the rest of it. I brought you some coffee. It's on the nightstand."

"I don't snore. And"—she sniffed hazelnut and vanilla— "thank you."

"Then there was the moment when you decided your jeans were too tight. That was a highlight. Almost as good as when the shirt went flying. But my favorite part"—Marc set his laptop aside and leaned in close, his lips grazing her ear when he whispered—"was when you shimmied out of that red thong."

"I did not!"

"Really?" He held up his hand. A pair of red-lace panties dangled from his finger.

"Give those back!" She grabbed the panties and, shoving them under the sheet, slid them on. He might not be able to see under there, but she wasn't taking any chances. "Now go away."

A knock sounded at the front door.

Lexi shot up, taking the blankets with her and sending Wingman flying off the edge of the bed. He landed in a tangled heap of paws and tail and looked around, his big doggie eyes wary and confused.

"Expecting company?" Marc asked with an amused smile.

"No, and why are you smiling like that? What if it's our grandmas? They come over sometimes on Saturday for breakfast. One look at us and—"

There was another knock.

Lexi scurried to grab her robe and put it on, checking the time on her cell before shoving it into the terry-cloth pocket. Marc, on the other hand, stretched and leisurely got out of bed. They reached the door at the same time, Wingman barking excitedly at their feet.

She shoved Marc back. "Are you crazy? One look at you and the whole 'We are good, God-fearing people' speech will begin. By afternoon ChiChi will be at the chapel picking dates and Pricilla will be baking our wedding cake. So stay here. And no matter who is at the door, *don't* come out. Understand?"

Marc just nodded, awfully calm for someone who was usually paralyzed by the threat of forced commitment. Which was good for Lexi, because although she doubted it was the grannies on her doorstep—they would have just let themselves in through the bakery's stairs—she didn't want her bachelors getting the wrong idea about sleeping arrangements. And if Marc was seen leaving her place in the morning, rumors would fly—guaranteed.

"Coming," she yelled, rushing down the steps as she tightened the belt of her robe and answered the door. And froze. Because there, on her porch stoop with a single red rose and a lecherous smile, stood St. Helena High's reigning panty peeper. "Chad?"

Chad swooped in for a kiss. He went for the lips, but she managed to deflect him to the cheek.

"Morning, beautiful." His smile faded a little when he took in her attire. He shot a glance at his watch. "Am I early?"

"Early?"

"For our date."

Had he seriously thought that she would go on a picnic with the man who served her? She took in the red-and-white-checkered picnic basket and convertible running idle and realized he had.

"I called you last night to confirm. I left a message. We have a busy day planned. You and me, a little driving, wine tasting on the way to the lake. I even have reservations at that new Italian place in the hills. How fast can you get ready?"

"I am so sorry that—" She paused. Because she realized that was a lie. She wasn't sorry. Although he didn't seem so creepy right now, bouncing on his toes and holding the flower and acting all excited about their date, he had *served* her. He had helped Jeffery screw her out of her recipes and then acted like he'd done nothing wrong. She hated people like Chad—almost as much as she hated roses. "This date isn't going to happen. Ever. I should have called to cancel, but it slipped my mind."

"Why?" One word, but there was one heck of an accusation behind it.

"Um, why can't I go out with you? Or why did it slip my mind?"

Chad just raised an angry brow.

"Do I really need to explain? You represented my ex-husband in a claim that cost me my recipes."

"But it's Saturday," he said, petulantly. She was surprised he didn't stomp his foot.

He took a step inside the door. Lexi tried to hold her ground, but it happened so fast. One minute he was on her stoop and the next he was in her apartment.

"And your stupid client nearly cost me my bistro."

"Nearly? You're still opening the café?" He was back to smiling again. "Good. Jeff will be happy. He wants you to open it. So do I. See, it all worked out."

"Bistro. And wait!" She must have misunderstood him. "You talked to Jeffery? About me?"

"Of course, you were the defendant in our case." This was getting way too weird. "I also told him we had a date."

"And he encouraged this?"

"Yeah." Chad looked suddenly lost. "He said it was good for you to get out. Told me to bring you this." He stuck the rose out. "For you."

Lexi stared at the rose. She didn't know what hurt more, Jeffery trying to set her up with another man or that after fifteen years he still didn't know she hated roses. The one thing she was sure about was that if Jeffery was messing with her life, it was for his benefit only. "Look, thanks for the gesture, but—"

She broke off. Oh God, she was going to cry. Her head felt like it was about to explode, her ex-husband was playing matchmaker, and after she'd given all of her adult life to a man, he still didn't know something as simple as what kind of flower she liked.

"Morning, sugar." A strong hand slid around her waist, bypassing the lip of the robe and sliding home to caress her bare belly. Marc pulled her back against him, pressing his nose into her neck and delivering a wet kiss that had her thighs quaking.

Snappy retort ready, Lexi turned her head and looked up at Marc, who was looking back at her with an expression that was so innately male, her mouth went too dry to speak. His cocky posture, the possessive way he draped his arm around her—Marc was all but pissing on her apartment to show Chad exactly where the line was.

"Hey, Chad." Marc extended his free hand. Chad reciprocated, and Marc used the solid hand-to-hand contact to shake Chad right back out on the porch stoop. "Oh man, I am so sorry. We forgot to call you. Didn't we?" He looked at Lexi, who shot him a hard glare back.

She didn't need a man setting her up, didn't need a man guilting her into a date, and she most certainly did not need a man lying for her. In fact, she didn't need a man, period.

Lexi opened her mouth to tell them exactly that when Marc's fingers slid higher, right to the sensitive skin underneath her breast, tickled and then pinched. Lexi gasped and twisted, bringing her hand up to grab his, and her butt flush with his groin. To Chad, it would have looked like he was copping a feel, but she knew there would be a small bruise come tomorrow. The big jerk.

"Sorry, buddy, but Lexi and I are busy today. We have to cancel."

"We?" Chad took in the possessive way Marc was holding her and how she wasn't resisting him—yet. He looked as confused as Wingman had when he'd been tossed out of Lexi's warm bed onto the cold floor. "But it's Saturday. I'm Mr. Saturday."

"Yeah," Marc said, and Lexi could feel his chest puff up and smell the testosterone seeping into the air. "Well, I'm her every day."

"Her what?"

"My what?" Lexi snapped, turning to face him, and every argument she had stuck in her throat.

Marc wasn't just standing behind her. He was practically naked. Gone were the shirt and shorts from earlier, and in their place were black boxer-briefs, a bad case of bed head, and a whole lot of naked skin and impressive muscles. One muscle was particularly impressive, but she didn't know if he was revved up by *her* or by the battle-of-bigger-dick syndrome. Either way, she found it hard not to lick her lips.

"Her Mr. Every Day." He spoke as though Lexi wasn't standing right there. "Meaning if it ends in fucking *day*, it's mine, buddy." And with that Marc slammed the door.

"What was that all about?" she snapped, shoving Marc, who moved a whole half inch. Sure, Chad was a jerk, but she had been handling it.

Marc didn't answer. He just stood there in his underwear, looking slightly shocked and a whole lot baffled by his own behavior.

Afraid she'd be too tempted to stare at his nakedness, Lexi squinted through the peephole and watched as Chad stormed across the parking lot to his car. He made a big deal of chucking the rose—and kicking it—before getting in and screeching away.

Chad was livid. It kind of made her smile to see him pout and stomp his foot, but Lexi kept her face stern when, hands on hips in her best intimidating pose, she asked, "What was the point of that?"

Laid-back Marc had returned and was scrolling through his phone, not even sparing her a glance. "That you didn't want to go out with him, that if you did he would spend the day trying to cop a feel, and I don't share well with others. Especially not my girlfriends."

"You don't do girlfriends."

"I know. Which is why I think this possessive streak of mine is throwing us both a little. That's okay, we'll get past this." He looked up from the phone, an irritating grin on his face.

"Hey, give it back," Lexi said, realizing that it was her phone he was messing with. She grabbed for it, but he held it high over his head, out of her reach, still clicking away with that stupid grin on his lips. The one that used to drive her insane—still did, but in a totally different way now.

"I'm being serious, Marc." When he went back to pushing buttons, she faked as though she was giving up, walking away, then spun and jumped for it. Even though she was taller than average, her five eight was useless when paired against his six three. He was also a whole lot faster than she, and snaked his free arm around her neck to hold her down. She folded at the waist, the pressure bending her until her shoulder was pinned to his hip. All he needed to do was add a noogie and it would be just like old times.

With a frustrated grunt, she stopped struggling, gave a firm elbow up to the ribs, and he released her. She stepped back.

"Fine. Play your stupid games, but realize that in about two hours everyone in town is going to hear that you were at my house this morning wearing last night's stubble"—which he wore incredibly well—"and think that we are really a thing."

"Cream puff, we are a thing, and I give it ten minutes, since your Facebook status says you're in a relationship." Marc handed her the phone, and she looked at the screen. Sure enough, he had updated her status on Facebook. He had also posted a comment from his account to her wall reading: "Lexi, make me the happiest man in the valley and allow me to be your Mr. Every Day."

There were already seven comments: five urging her to say yes, one from her grandmother reminding her that handwritten cards to her remaining bachelors would be correct etiquette, and a nasty one from Natasha citing how hacking into another person's account and posting on their behalf was illegal.

Thirty seconds and people were already talking.

Her stomach fell to her toes, making her hangover that much worse. How could he do this? Everyone in town would soon figure out that it was a stupid prank, and she would look even more pathetic than the girl whose dates were grandma-approved.

"Is this some kind of sick joke?"

"No joke, Lexi. And before you type in no and break my heart in front of the world, just think about—"

He stopped talking, and she wondered if he was actually giving her time to think about it, which wasn't a good idea, because all she could think about was finding her straw and some toilet paper.

Then she realized that his lack of verbs and articles was due to a severe lack of terry cloth on her end. His eyes were glued to the front of her robe, which had come open during their tussle and was showing off quite a lot of skin and red lace. And the way he was looking at her, as though he found her sexy and beautiful, made her stomach do a silly flip. Just a little one.

Lexi had forgotten how good it felt to have a man look at her like she was a desirable woman, like all she had to do was nod her head and he would take her against the wall, hangover and all. Lord knew Jeffery hadn't looked at her as more than a roommate and head chef in years. She took her time adjusting her robe and tightening the belt.

Even after it was securely closed, Marc took a while to look up. And when he did, instead of the same stupid line or that little wink she'd seen him give hundreds of girls, he cleared his throat, and if Lexi wasn't mistaken, his ears were tinted slightly pinker than normal.

"Think about it, Lexi," he said, sounding so unaffected it made her wonder if she had, in her need to feel special and beautiful, imagined the entire moment. "It's a great setup. You pretend I'm your boyfriend, and you don't have to go on any more dates. No more dates means you get to focus completely on the bistro and creating a menu."

"I don't need a *pretend* boyfriend," she said. Now those silly little flutters from a moment ago left her feeling just silly. And defensive. Why did everyone assume she needed help in the man department? "If I wanted one, I could get him on my own. And as for my dates, I have everything under control."

As though on cue, her phone rang. She looked at the screen and groaned. It was Mr. Wednesday Morning, probably calling about his mom's Tupperware party. She'd meant to call him, explain about the Daughters of the Prohibition tasting and hope he'd understand. No way could she come up with a unique way to serve salmon on asparagus if her last night to experiment was spent burping lids and touring his Velcro collection.

Before she could answer, Marc had her phone. "Hello?"

Lexi frowned.

Marc winked.

"Oh, Corbin. Yeah, it's Marco." A long silence. "Yeah, Mr. Every Day. I'm still waiting. You know women, they like the chase." After Marc uh-huhed and yupped the call to death, he said, "You got it. Yeah, you too."

He hung up. "That was Corbin. His mom invited the minister's wife to her Tupperware party, and she was concerned that Corbin was bringing a taken woman."

"Will you stop meddling?" She grabbed her phone back. "I have this handled."

"Really? Because you're so worried about being rude that Corbin would have been down on one knee before he realized you were just being polite."

She looked at the screen, which was conveniently open to her Facebook wall, showing nine more comments, including one from the minister's wife and three of her bachelors asking if they were still on next week. "And if I type yes, then what?"

"Corbin finds a new date, and you have tomorrow night free to cook us salmon eleven different ways. Plus, he kind of has a thing for the cute new pharmacist over at Bottles and Bottles, who his mom also invited."

God, it would be so easy. Three little letters sent into cyberspace would release her from any more get-to-know-you coffees and want-to-invite-me-in wines. She'd already had to answer so many questions about why she got divorced, if she was over Jeffery, was she ready to find love again, or, the worst, was she looking for a little rebound action. It was a simple solution and oh so tempting. It was also scary to think of placing her trust in another man...a man whose smile alone had the ability to melt the panties off women everywhere.

Marc loved women and sex—simultaneously and in excess. Lexi didn't multitask all that well, and she wasn't all that sure that she was even any good at sex. Not that it was on the table. Plus, having your husband cheat on you was bad enough. Having the town know that your fake boyfriend spent his nights with other women would be humiliating. Not that they would know he was fake, but if she couldn't even keep a family guy like Jeffery satisfied, there was no way people would believe she could catch and hold the St. Helena Stud.

No, Lexi had learned the hard way what could happen if you didn't clarify the other person's expectations in an arrangement. She wouldn't make that mistake again.

"Okay, hypothetically, I say yes. How would this even work?"

He looked surprised that she was even considering this. "You say yes, we see each other in public a few times, and the town thinks we're dating. Your grandma and the bachelors lay off, and you get to focus on work."

"Dating defeats the purpose. I need time to cook."

"After a few public lunches and taking Wingman to the park—" A bark of agreement erupted, and Lexi patted the dog's head. "People will get the point. Then when you disappear for days on end in your apartment to cook, I'll be working on the Summer Wine Showdown. Everyone will just assume we are in the honeymoon phase and can't keep our hands off each other."

"They'll think we are sleeping together," Lexi said, her voice going a little shrill.

"Sleeping will be the last thing they'll think we are doing," he said in a low, seductive voice that sent chills all over her body. She didn't like that her heart kicked in at the idea. Or that her panties might have gone a little wet.

"I want to be able to cook and experiment"—she held up a silencing hand—"*man free*. Not have everyone think that I'm another one of your many women. I mean, what happens when you get caught with Cindy or Mandy?" *Or Cindy* and *Mandy.* "Would I have to break up with myself for you?"

"First off," he said, taking a step forward and looking really pissed and a bit hurt, "when I am in a relationship, I don't cheat. Period."

Marc took another step closer. Lexi took one backward.

"How would you know? You've never been in a relationship."

"I just know." Marc was so close that she took a final step back. As her heels rammed into the bottom stair, she tipped backward and should have landed with a boom. But when she opened her eyes she found herself upright, pressed between the entry wall and one surly Italian.

"Um, okay." She swallowed, trying to casually lean back against the wall and failing dismally.

"After the bistro is open and the Showdown is over, we'll go our own ways, just tell people it was an amicable parting," he clarified.

"That didn't work so well for me before."

"Okay, you do the breaking up, then. Just don't make me look like a total ass." His hands went to her waist, and he splayed his fingers low over her hipbones. "I blew it, okay. When Jeff told me he'd moved out, I didn't know what to do, how to help you, so I did nothing. And I hate that. You're my friend, separate of Jeff. I can help this time if you'll just let me, Alexis."

He'd never called her by her full name before, so she'd never known how incredibly hypnotic it would sound falling from his lips. Nor did she anticipate the quiet pride she felt at his reminder of who she was…who she wanted to become again. Which was why she forced herself to ask, "So is this like a pity relationship?"

"No pity, Lexi."

"And what about Jeffery? What will we tell him?"

"Let me handle Jeff. And this isn't about him or your grandma or the bachelors. This is about you and your business, and dating me gives you a polite way out, lets you focus." He cupped her cheek, running the pad on his thumb across her cheekbone. "You were my wingman for years. Let me be yours. Then we'll be even, I promise."

When he put it like that, so simple and honest, it was impossible to resist. She found herself not *wanting* to resist, so she snuggled a little closer. "What do you get out of this? I mean, besides making it even?"

He sighed, bringing her into a full embrace to rest his cheek on top of her head. "Is this just between us?"

She did some sighing of her own, melting into his warm, naked chest. He smelled like sexy morning man and felt even better. Unable to stop herself, she wrapped her arms around his middle and whispered, "If this is going to work, everything has to stay between us."

He was silent for a moment. They both knew that her words were part statement and part question. Trust was a two-way thing, and she was giving him hers and asking for his in return.

After a moment, his hand swept up her back to tangle in her hair. "My brothers were right." She knew how hard that must have been for him to admit. He hated being wrong, especially if that meant his brothers were right. "I'm in over my head. The Showdown is a mess. I have a dog as a wine expert, might be short one celebrity taster, and if Abby doesn't stop running those 'dick' ads, people will start asking for refunds and we won't even get any attendees."

"You'll figure it out," she said, placing a hand on his forearm. "It's what you do."

He laughed. "I have no idea what the hell I am doing or how the hell I can fix this. This event means a lot to St. Helena and to my family. I need to focus."

She'd meant what she'd said; he would pull it off, of that she had no doubt. He was born for this job. But what she couldn't grasp was how their fake relationship would benefit him.

She tilted her head back and stared up into those dark mahogany eyes. She must have looked as confused as she felt, because he flashed her a badass smile and added, "You're not the only one with admirers who are distracting, cream puff." Oh, right, Natasha. And probably countless others who were sex-on-a-stick with enormous boobs. How could she forget? "I need time to work this out and a date for all the events that don't require work."

His words hit home—hard and painful. He wanted someone who wasn't a distraction as a front while he saved the Showdown and a date that he didn't have to worry about mixed feelings with while mingling at the events. In a way she was using him too, so it shouldn't have hurt that he would have to fake the romance in their fauxmance, but it did. Because she wouldn't have to pretend. What woman would? Marc was sexy and smart and funny and so far out of her league. He always had been, and this was a clear reminder.

Ohmigod! She froze, her hands started sweating, and her face burned red. She would be his beard—and he wasn't even gay. Alexis Moreau had gone from prom queen to divorcée to a straight man's beard. How pathetic was that?

She detangled herself from his warmth and stepped around him. Plastering a fake smile on her face, she typed "YES" to their fake relationship.

"Good girl. Now come here and give your boyfriend a kiss."

"Fake boyfriend," she corrected.

He tapped his cheek with a single finger. "Make it official."

She rolled her eyes and pressed a chaste kiss to his cheek. "Thank you."

Before she could move out of arm's reach, he grabbed her face and planted a big smacker on her lips. "You're welcome."

"Congratulations, you've got yourself a girlfriend. Now just don't go getting all clingy on me."

She meant it as a joke, but when he answered, "I'll try," as though it wouldn't take much effort on his part to stay detached, she forgot to laugh. She did let out a yelp, though, when he dropped his hand and gave her a swift smack on the ass, saying, "Now go on up and make your man a nice big breakfast."

"I'm going back to bed," she said, walking up the stairs to her apartment, swaying her hips a little more than usual and making the hem of her robe swish higher up her thighs. Since Marc was below her on the stairs, she was sure he was getting a pretty good view. Sex wasn't going to happen between them, but she'd be damned if her fake boyfriend didn't think she was distraction worthy.

Marc groaned. "Even better idea. Let's go, boy." He whistled for Wingman, who loped up the stairs and down the hall behind them.

"Alone," she clarified when she got to the bedroom door. She took one look at Marc, who wasn't smiling anymore. The man was all but pouting. Even Wingman let out a little whimper when she slammed the door.

"Come on, boy," she heard him say through the door. "Day one and we're already couching it."

Great. Now she felt terrible.

"You know what?" She opened the door, and both boys whipped around to face her. "Maybe some company wouldn't be so bad."

She let out a quick whistle, and Wingman barreled toward her and into the bedroom.

"Traitor!" Marc grumbled. Lexi stifled a smile and shut the door.

CHAPTER 8

Marc had a smoking-hot girlfriend. Well, a smoking-hot pretend girlfriend. Problem was, he didn't know what to do with her.

Women he knew: knew how to charm them, undress them, make them moan with pleasure, and, most importantly, how to get them out of his house before the sun came up. Girlfriends, on the other hand, were a foreign species to him. Lexi had been right, he'd never really committed to any one woman. In fact, it was something he'd successfully avoided for most of his adult life.

Until now, anyway.

He knew what he *wanted* to do with her, but that violated man law. Needing to get out, take in a view that didn't include what was across the alley, he grabbed his cleats and gave Gabe a quick call to see if he needed to pick anything up on the way.

In the DeLuca family, every Sunday between September and February was dedicated to family, beer, BBQ, and football.

All the other months they swapped out watching football for playing football. It had been that way since they were kids and, thankfully, this week was no different. Marc could really use some brotherly bonding time, especially the part when he got to beat the crap out of Gabe on the field. The thought made him smile.

So when Gabe told him that Sunday football was canceled because Regan wasn't feeling well, Marc assumed the worst.

"Is she okay?" Because it would have to be pretty bad to cancel a tradition that had been going on since Trey turned three.

"Yeah, she's just feeling a little cooped up and frustrated. I've been so busy trying to get Ryo Wines on track and make sure the deal with Monte goes smoothly that Regan needs some adult time, and Holly is desperate for family time."

Right, the daily reminder that Gabe had a family outside of his brothers and Abby. Marc should have been pissed, like he usually was. But instead he found himself feeling jealous.

"So what are you guys going to do?" Marc asked, wondering how he had gone from avoiding entanglements with women who called too soon after sex to asking how his brother made his wife feel better. God, he was becoming one of *those* guys.

Gabe was the last person he wanted to engage in a conversation about women, since it would most likely lead to a lecture on when he was going to grow the hell up. After their dad died, Gabe became more like a father than a brother, and Marc went off the deep end for a few years, partying too hard and taking nothing too seriously.

Problem was, Gabe still viewed Marc as that screwup with the attention span of a gnat, and Marc was sick of Gabe shoving all his big-brother crap in his face. But big-brother complex or not, Gabe was the only DeLuca who had managed to maintain a healthy relationship with someone of the opposite sex. The guy had not only convinced a woman who despised him to walk down the aisle, he'd also gotten Regan pregnant, proof that they still had sex *after* the I dos.

As Marc figured it, his brother must be doing something right, since he was pretty sure, pregnant wife and all, Gabe was still getting laid on a regular basis. Because the guy smiled—all the freaking time. Whereas Marc had been couched in the first ten minutes of boyfriend bliss and spent his Sunday morning half hard and wholly frustrated.

"I was thinking a walk in the park. Maybe a picnic. Holly could play in the sand, and the walk would do Regan good. Her back has started hurting her."

"That's it?" It seemed way too easy. "Just a walk?"

"Yeah, playboy, just a walk," Gabe laughed. "Regan isn't one of your women who wants a five-star meal and bragging rights to the St. Helena Stud."

"Christ, Gabe, I wasn't judging you." Although Gabe apparently wasn't above judging him. *Nothing new*, Marc thought, but the embarrassment that came with the barb was. Was that really how people saw him? "I was just worried and wanted to make sure she was handling the pregnancy okay. You know what, never mind, okay?"

There was a long pause. "Sorry, it's just you haven't seemed all that interested in Regan's health or the pregnancy. I thought…"

Gabe trailed off, and Marc was happy that he didn't finish his sentence. He didn't want to know what his family thought about him. Sure, he wasn't as involved in the day-to-day running of their business, but that didn't mean he didn't care about them.

"If you want, I can take Holly tonight so that you and Regan can go on a date," Marc offered, knowing he was setting himself up for a blow. "After the family time at the park, of course."

The silence hurt.

"Um, thanks," Gabe finally said. "But ChiChi already offered to take Holly tonight. Something about helping the grannies bake cakes for the farmers' market tomorrow. She had the same thought as you, that Regan and I need a date night. I'm planning to barbecue for dinner. Lately the smell of raw meat makes Regan sick, and I'll be damned if she decides that steak isn't good for the baby." But Marc could tell by the way Gabe spoke, it wasn't about a steak-free pregnancy—although that would suck—but that he genuinely wanted to make Regan's life easier. And if him cooking made her day, then that made Gabe a happy man.

"Maybe next week then," Marc offered, rolling his eyes when Gabe hesitated.

How hard could one little girl be, Marc wanted to ask. Holly was cute, female, and liked dogs.

Then again, so did Lexi, and she was the hardest damn person on the planet to charm. But he wasn't giving up, because while most of his friends were still eating worms and playing kickball, Marc had already mastered charming females. First out of their lunches, then into their pants.

Ah, hell. Marc stopped short. He'd been going about this whole Lexi issue in the wrong way. He wasn't looking to charm her into his bed, although parts of his anatomy would disagree; he was supposed to be making her life easier so she could get the bistro open.

Since the goal was different, he needed a different strategy.

The sun was barely up when Marc's alarm went off. He rolled out of bed and, ignoring the annoying hard-on that had greeted him every morning since he'd helped Lexi out of that window, laced up his running shoes.

He clicked on Wingman's collar and gave a sharp tug when the lazy mutt stretched out to take up Marc's half of the bed.

"Oh no you don't. You and I have a date. With Lexi. So get up."

Wingman opened one eye and immediately closed it.

"I was thinking that a run—"

Marc was about to drag all ninety pounds of dog out of the bed when Wingman's ears perked up at the mention of his favorite word—well, second favorite, right behind *custard*. Before Marc could grab his iPod or even a couple bottles of water, Wingman leaped off the bed, his tail catching the side table on the way down and sending two books, a glass of water, and the reading lamp crashing to the floor.

"Sit," Marc yelled, and like everyone else in his life, Wingman ignored his authority and headed for the front door.

"Damn it, Wingman. I said sit." Marc managed to clip the leash on right as Wingman barreled through the suite and down the hallway toward the elevator, barking excitedly. And most likely waking up every hotel guest on the top floor.

He managed to make it through the hotel lobby without anyone asking him for anything, which was why, he told himself, he was smiling like an idiot.

After Wingman sniffed every corner and peed on every tree, plant, and car tire on Main Street, they headed down the alley, giving a light knock when they came to her back door. When no answer came, he stood back and looked up. Light poured through the back window. She was home... and awake.

After a long moment of silence from inside, he knocked again—this time louder. Wingman barked his good morning. Several times. Until Marc told him to quiet down. Then the two males took their place on the porch and waited.

Marc had come over here merely to do his job as her friend, to make sure she got out of the house and breathed in air that wasn't laced with cumin or paprika. He also told himself he was a terrible liar. Marc had never liked mixing his morning run with a woman. They talked too much and complained about the sweat until the run became a leisurely walk through the park. And they insisted on wearing those skimpy shorts that were totally ineffective for working out, since all they inspired was a hard-on.

The door opened, and Marc was rendered stupid. He didn't know why. There was nothing skimpy about the men's striped pajama bottoms or pink tank top she wore, but they were effective as hell. Her golden hair was in complete disarray, her shirt stained, and her face was flushed and soft with sleep. Any other woman looking like a rumpled mess would have been a turnoff, but Lexi's dazed eyes and just-rolled-out-of-bed expression made him want to take her back to bed—and crawl in beside her.

"What are you doing here?" she yawned, obviously not nearly as affected as he was.

"Picking you up for a leisurely morning walk in the park." Wingman barked and tugged on the leash. "Well, more of a leisurely"—he paused, looking down at Wingman, who was looking back, waiting for him to say it so he could go batshit crazy—"r-u-n."

She rubbed at her eyes. "What time is it?'

"Seven fifteen." Marc guessed that Gabe didn't roll Regan out of bed for their walk. *Shit.* "I saw the light on and thought you were up."

"I was on baking duty today for the bakery. I finally got to sleep around six. And why would you think I'd want to go on a ru—?"

Marc shook his head in warning while he placed a single finger over Lexi's lips, noticing how soft and full they were. She must have noticed something too, because her breathing stopped and her eyes went big. And damn if all Marc could picture was her naked.

"Because you're my girlfriend. And walks are something that couples do together. In the park. With their dog. So go get dressed." His eyes dropped to her chest. If he looked hard enough, he could make out the outline of her nipples through her shirt. God, she had great breasts. "Or not."

Lexi crossed her arms, covering the best view he'd had all morning, and glared. "Then you need to find a girlfriend who doesn't despise mornings." Yeah, he'd forgotten about that. "It's why I'm a chef and not a baker. Night owl. And should a real boyfriend show up at this god-awful hour, he'd have brought coffee."

"Ah, cream puff, are you asking me out on a coffee date? I'm flattered." Marc leaned against the doorframe, crossing one ankle over the other. "We can go after our walk. Maybe then do a little post-morning spooning."

"No. And no. Part of the reason I agreed to this"—she motioned between them—"was because I would get time in the kitchen. Uninterrupted time."

Marc ran a hand though his hair. Natasha would have said yes in a heartbeat, and so would nearly every single lady in St. Helena. Not this woman. She was stubborn, and confusing, and never did anything that Marc wanted her to. And he liked it. How sick was that?

"Fine, we'll skip the coffee, go straight to the spooning. Although if we want any alone time, he"—Marc jerked his chin toward Wingman—"will do better if we get the r-u-n in."

He leaned closer to whisper in her ear and felt her shiver. "He'll sleep through just about anything after he's had his walk and breakfast."

"I would be sleeping through all of this if you hadn't pounded on my door." She yawned—wider this time. "Between mornings in the kitchen, the tasting, and prepping for the farmers' market tomorrow, I'm beat."

"Maybe you should hire another baker."

"Trust me, it's on my long list of things to do. First I have to figure out if the bakery can even afford it." She shrugged. "Pricilla's books are a huge mess, and I can't make sense of anything. The numbers she sent me when I came up with the budget for the bistro are totally different from the ones I found stashed in her office. Plus, she's been shorting her customers and canceling events for months. For all I know, I have to get the bistro open and start turning a profit before I can even afford to hire kitchen staff."

Marc might suck at relationships, but he was incredible with numbers. It was why, even after he walked away from DeLuca Wines, he continued to handle all of the family's books. If he could help smooth Lexi's transition from chef to restaurateur, then he was game. The extra time they'd spend together, alone, had absolutely nothing to do with his desire to help.

"I can take a look at them if you want. See what's going on and get a feel for where the bakery really is. I can also help you figure out a system that works for you. Maybe come up with a realistic plan."

She blinked up at him, and something warm and unfamiliar slid through his body. She was looking at him like he had just made her day, hell, her world. He was used to hormones and chemistry and raw sexual heat with women. But this was something altogether different, and suddenly *this* seemed like a really bad idea.

"I mean, if you don't want me to, I understand," he backpedaled.

"No. That would be great." She blushed, actually blushed, and he felt like a freaking hero.

Shit. Marc took a step back, pulling the leash as he went. "Well, we didn't mean to wake you."

Lexi rested her hand on the door, looking ready to give another excuse to turn down his offer, one that he would happily accept, when Wingman went to work. He waddled over and dropped himself on Lexi's foot, his tail slapping her shin. He looked up at her with those big brown eyes and panted a little harder for added effect.

Everything in Marc stilled. He could tell by the way Lexi ruffled Wingman behind the ears that she was going to give in and he would get that walk through the park. And when it was over he'd be in deep shit, because Marc finally understood why Gabe would blow off a day of beer and football to go for a walk in the park with his wife.

"I guess fresh air would help me focus. Wake me up. Plus, I had four éclairs this morning." She smiled, but Marc couldn't smile back. He was too busy holding his breath. "To be clear, though, I don't walk, I don't dally, and I don't like talking while pounding the pavement. If we are doing this, it's a flat-out run—"

On cue, Wingman lost it. He started barking and jumped right for Lexi, yanking the leash out of Marc's hand. He was pretty sure the dog was going to take Lexi down and made a move to grab for her when she held out her palms and simply said, "Sit."

And wouldn't you know it, the damn dog sat. Completely still, except for the quivering tip of his tail, he stared at his new mistress, awaiting her next command.

But the command that came out was directed at Marc. "Five miles. No coffee, and you have to help me cart all of my stuff over to the tasting on Wednesday night."

And like any obedient mutt, Marc agreed. Both he and Wingman watched in awe as Lexi made her way up the stairs, that perfect ass swaying saucily with every step she took.

"Give me five," Marc said to Wingman after Lexi disappeared around the corner. Wingman sat back on his haunches and pawed Marc's palm. "We got us a girlfriend *and* a date."

"Are you dating my brother?" Abby accused by way of greeting. She said it loud enough that it carried to every customer within a three-booth radius. And since it was prime time at the farmers' market, it reached the maximum number of listeners.

"Classic French pastry?" Lexi said loudly, forcing a salesgirl smile.

She strategically avoided her friend's glare, instead paying particular attention to the arrangement of mouthwatering éclairs, fluffy and custard filled and drizzled with enough chocolate to make her forget that it was only eight in the morning, on a Tuesday, and she had already been up for more than four hours.

"Two for five dollars," she said, licking a glob of filling from her finger. As heavenly as it was, it wasn't going to save her from an inquisition.

Today the DeLuca Darling wore distressed snug-fit jeans, a bright-teal top, and enough accusation to fill three churches. She also wore a slicked-up ponytail, minimal makeup, and a glare that cut through her designer sunglasses. Abby might look like an innocent coed, but even at five foot one she could be intimidating as hell. "Are. You. Dating. My. Brother? Yes or no."

"No. Yes." Lexi sucked her lips inside her mouth to keep from saying anything else. She'd promised Marc that their relationship would stay a secret, well, the pretend part, anyway. She'd also made a blood oath with Abby senior year, after daring Abby to steal the school mascot and blame it on the rival high school's quarterback, promising her that no one would find out, only to have photographic proof of Abby's crime end up on the front page of the school paper, that she would never lie to her again. And she hadn't. Ever. And she didn't want to start now.

"It's complicated."

"That's a Facebook status, not an answer. Is. Marco. Your boyfriend?"

They stared at each other for a tense moment, neither willing to cave. One night, in the tenth grade, they had had a heated discussion over which was the hottest boy band. Neither had been willing to concede, so they'd glared at each other until the sun came up.

"Fine, he's my boyfriend," Lexi started, then corrected herself. "But not my *boy*friend."

"What does that even mean?" Abby threw her hands up in frustration and opened her mouth to speak, but nothing came out—except for a high gasp.

Clasping her cheeks as though it would keep her head from shaking back and forth, Abby took a step backward with every word. "No. No, no, no, no, no. This can't be happening. You're the only friend I've ever had who doesn't go stupid around my brothers."

Lexi rolled her eyes. "I'm not going stupid. And we aren't even dating...really."

"Wow, thanks, Lex. That clarifies things. Really, it does. So clear, in fact, that next time Natasha corners me at Picker's Produce demanding to know if you're sleeping with one of my brothers, I'll know exactly how to answer."

Three ladies in neon sun visors and armed with big canvas bags looked up from the stand one over. The pudgiest of the group, who just so happened to be Nora Kincaid, set down the locally grown honey and moved on to inspect the baskets of organic squash. Not because she had a sudden craving for zucchini bread, Lexi mused, but because it was as close as she could get to eavesdrop without looking too obvious.

"Will you please lower your voice," Lexi hissed. She grabbed Abby's arm and dragged her around the table. After shoving Abby into a plastic chair and taking the closest metal folding one, Lexi leaned in and whispered, "She asked that? Really? When?"

"Yes. Ten minutes ago. While my nonna was two feet away trying to barter for a better price on the fava beans." Abby did not whisper.

Nora leaned closer and pulled out her smartphone, elbowing an eggplant in the process and sending it crashing to the sidewalk.

Lexi waved politely and then turned so that her back was to the pedestrian-filled street. In St. Helena, farmers' markets were serious business, and if Lexi wanted to discuss her business without it becoming the town's business or winding up on YouTube, then she had to keep it down. "Wait. What were you doing at Picker's? You're supposed to be supervising the remodel."

Lexi looked behind her, squinting through the back flap of the white farmers' market tent toward the bakery. Over the heads of a group soccer moms whose faces were pressed against the windows, Lexi could just about make out some scaffolding and a ladder. What she couldn't miss were the sounds of hammers and drills that had started up when the sun rose.

"I am," Abby defended. "I went to get breakfast for the crew."

"They're installing a second kitchen in a bakery. Why didn't they just eat danish and muffins?"

"Because I needed space, okay." *Now* Abby was whispering. She stole a glance toward the bakery right as Hard-Hammer Tanner slung a two-by-four over his shoulder and happened to look out the window—and directly at them. The soccer moms waved. Abby gasped, then ducked, then gasped again. She was so bent over in the chair she was practically hugging her knees. "Crap, crap, crap. Did he see me? Is he still looking?"

Yup, Lexi wanted to say as she waved at a smiling Tanner, who, ignoring his adoring fans, waved back. The man was enormous. She had always thought Marc was tall and built like a god, but Tanner looked a good two inches taller than Marc with at least thirty more pounds of solid muscle on him—and all in the right places. What also surprised her was how graceful he was for such a big guy.

After a few moments had passed, Lexi said, "You can come up now. He's on the ladder. Probably wondering why his design manager is flinging herself on the floor."

"I'm not flinging…" Her eyes darkened with suspicion. "Stop changing the subject. We are talking about you and my brother." She sighed, and her face went soft, almost hurt. "Are you sleeping with Marco, Lex? And if so, why didn't you tell me?"

Lexi considered fanning the air. It was so thick with guilt it made it hard to breathe. When she and Marc had made that promise to keep quiet about their deal, it seemed so simple. She never imagined it would put her in a situation where she'd have to be disloyal to her best friend. "Look, I am not sleeping with him." *Shit*, that was a lie. "Well, I mean we slept together, but—"

"Oh God." Abby covered her mouth. "I think I just threw up a little."

The idea of sex with Marc made Lexi queasy too, but not the kind of queasy Abby was feeling. "I got drunk, my date got handsy, so Marc took me home. He crashed at my place to make sure I was okay, and he fell asleep in my bed. With me. But nothing happened."

"Then why is everyone saying they saw you two running in the park?"

Right. That. "Marc asked me if I wanted to go on a run, so we did. And it was fun." It was better than fun. It had been one of the best mornings she could remember in forever. They didn't stop for coffee, but they sat on her back porch and shared a pint of caramel ice cream from Picker's. They talked about nothing important, laughed when Wingman farted, and scooted closer when Chad happened to walk by. Then he left and, as promised, Lexi had spent the entire day trying to make a baked pork chop interesting. "He makes me laugh. End of story."

Abby's eyes narrowed and her lips went thin. "Then this isn't some kind of twisted payback at Jeff for being a total douche? I know I told you to stick it to him, but if you're using my brother because he is Jeff's best friend, that's just wrong."

Her friend's words stung. She hadn't pursued Marc. He had followed her. And she hadn't said yes to their pretend relationship because of his friendship with her ex; if anything, that had been her biggest concern. But if her best friend came to that humiliating conclusion, then what would everyone else think?

"Marc was my friend too, before Jeffery and I even started dating." Not sure what else to say, Lexi went for honest. At least as honest as she could get without betraying Marc's trust. "I thought it was weird at first too. But Marc makes me feel good about myself. We have fun. He gives me the space I need to cook and figure things out. It's no big deal."

Abby didn't look convinced. "Okay, so what if I were to say Marco is one of the hottest bachelors in the valley?"

"So?" Lexi sat back in a chair and shrugged, trying to appear unaffected. So Marc was hot. So were a bazillion other guys. Granted, a bazillion other guys didn't make her undies catch fire every time they looked at her.

Nope. Only one guy had managed that. Not that she would admit that to Abby.

"Uh-huh." Abby sat back and mimicked Lexi's body language, only her friend actually pulled off laid-back and unaffected. "And if I were to warn you that Marc is a commitmentphobe playboy with the attention span and life goals of a horny teen."

"Why would you say that?" Lexi sat forward, unaffected going right out the tent. "Marc may have been wild in high school, but people change, Abs. I mean, only a person with some serious focus and talent could single-handedly restore the Napa Grand like he did, not to mention that he is the one responsible for bringing the Showdown back to its original glory after two decades."

That was exactly why, blood oath or not, Lexi would never say anything to Abby. Marc had a hard enough time proving to his siblings that he had his life together. Nope, she wasn't going to let them use their arrangement against Marc.

"I think it sucks that your family is constantly—"

Abby's lips turned up a little at the right corner, and Lexi snapped her mouth shut. This was a bad sign. Her friend made that face when she was scheming. And whenever Abby schemed, Lexi somehow ended up with an egg-white facial.

"Go on, I'm fascinated." Abby kicked back in the chair, her shoulders completely at ease, and gave an encouraging—and totally patronizing—wave of the hand. "My family is constantly what?"

"Nothing." Lexi stood and, afraid she would say something to rat herself out, walked back to the table, where she arranged and rearranged the danishes—three times.

"Oh, that sounded like a whole lot more than nothing." Abby slid up to the table and helped herself to a danish. The raspberry-and-peach-filled one, right in the center, which forced Lexi to rearrange—again.

"I don't want to talk about it anymore."

Instead of taking a bite, Abby licked the icing off of the top. "Then I won't tell you that you have a huge chunk of melted chocolate on your cheek and that Marco is headed this way."

"What?" Lexi whispered, her hand automatically going to her right cheek as she craned her head and...

Sure enough, walking down Main Street, dressed in black slacks and a blue button-up and looking like the poster boy for Bad Boys of Wall Street, the hubba-hubba edition, was her man. Well, her fake man. His strides were smooth and laid-back, and although he stopped to talk with Mr. Craver, the Meat in Picker's Produce, Meats, and More, she could feel his attention zeroed in on her. Her eyes were fixed on Marc when both men looked up and over at her. They both wore knowing smiles, but nothing about Marc's expression felt fake. Neither did the way her breath caught or that silly little flip her stomach seemed to have become so fond of recently.

Lexi pulled back her hand back. Clean.

She glared at Abby, who merely shrugged with an I-told-you-so grin. "I will give you one week, and then you have to spill."

"I have no idea what you're talking about," Lexi said, smoothing down her light-blue summer dress and suddenly wishing she had gone for the green one with the halter top. It matched her eyes and made her boobs look more D than full C.

"The sad thing is, I believe you. And for your sake, I hope that you figure it out *before* you sleep with him."

"I have not, nor will I ever be sleeping with Marc," Lexi snapped in the quietest possible way.

"Never took you for a fibber, cream puff," Marc drawled. Not only was all of his six foot three of pure, testosterone-loaded charm smirking down at her, he had his arm slung around her waist and his hand resting on her ass.

"What are you doing here?" She batted at his hand, which he didn't move, except to gently cup her left butt cheek.

"Making sure your pants aren't on fire," he whispered, his lips purposefully grazing her ear. Then, louder, he added, "And bringing you this." He held out a coffee cup in his free hand and smiled at Abby. "Hey, sis."

When Lexi didn't make a grab for the coffee, he shoved it in her hand. "Figured after a late night in the kitchen and an early morning in the bakery, you'd need a little sugar and caffeine to stay awake." He looked back to Abby. "She hates mornings. It's why she became a chef instead of a baker. Right, sugar?"

Rolling her eyes, Lexi took a sip to keep from saying something that would blow their cover when she felt herself flush. It wasn't the heat of the coffee that warmed her, rather that behind all the meathead BS Marc was spewing out, he was silently showing her that he listened, paid attention, and that fake relationship or not, he cared. Because a dark-chocolate mocha with a shot of hazelnut and lots of whipped cream was not only her favorite, it was the exact caffeine fix that she needed.

Problem was, the charming playboy with the badass smile and disarming dimples could easily become more than just a quick fix.

Marc's smile faded as though he read her mind. "Hey, look at me."

Unable to resist, she did, her heart clogging her throat. She didn't care if Nora Kincaid and her gossiping biddies were watching or that Abby was two feet away. She wanted Marc to kiss her, right there on Main Street, in front of the farmers' market, and in turn the entire town.

So when Marc leaned down, Lexi went up on her toes to meet him halfway. When he was close enough that she could smell his skin, feel his breath skate across her lips, he opened his mouth and—licked up the entire left side of her face.

With a horrified gasp, she pulled back.

"What?" He shrugged. "You had a huge glop of chocolate on your cheek."

CHAPTER 9

She was wearing yellow tonight. A paper-thin yellow dress with little white flowers that she filled out to perfection. It barely had straps, just skinny strips of fabric holding it up over her otherwise bare shoulders. And when she moved, hell, even when she breathed, the dress swished back and forth over those long, toned legs.

She was killing him. And so was that damn smell.

Wingman, nose shoved in the half-inch crack at the bottom of the window, whimpered. He'd been that way for most of the night, drooling over the smells wafting in from Lexi's apartment. So had Marc.

Marc's stomach grumbled, and on cue Wingman looked over with those big doggie eyes. "I know, boy. Let me finish this and then we can go upstairs and grab some dinner." He'd gotten a pretty fair understanding of where the bakery stood, financially. All he needed to do was finish jotting down his ideas.

Glancing at his computer, he noticed it was after eight. If he stopped staring out the window and focused, he could be done by ten.

Wingman barked, as though saying no, and looked back out the window. Every night, right around this time, Lexi would start tinkering in her kitchen, and Wingman sat like a lovesick pooch waiting for the pretty lady with yummy treats from across the alley to invite him over for dinner.

Tonight it was pork with—Marc sniffed the air—some kind of herby sauce.

And there he was—once again—staring up at her window instead of focusing on his work. Between trying to catch glimpses of Lexi, going over Pricilla's books, which were a complete disaster, and coming up with a business plan to help Lexi save her grandmother's floundering bakery, he'd accomplished jack shit. Lexi was only part of the problem. Guilt, for spying on a woman who was obviously struggling to keep her grandma's shop afloat, intensified when he discovered a staggering amount of unaccounted monies in Pricilla's books. Marc couldn't think past how much he wanted to pummel Jeff for putting him in this situation.

Lexi, on the other hand, had been much more productive. He watched her pick up four plates, balancing them on her arms like a pro, and disappear from the kitchen window, only to reappear in the dining room. She arranged the plates in a precise order, centering each one on the place mats she'd set out earlier in the evening. Two plates were identical, a beautiful chop of meat, the perfect proportion of what looked to be wild rice and a fancy drizzle of pink sauce. The other two plates, although identical to each other, were drastically different from the first, but even though he was squinting he couldn't make out what was on them.

She stood back and eyed each one, tinkering with the silverware before taking a seat in front of the far-right place setting. After taking just a single bite, she glared at the first dish and shoved the plate back.

Even pouting, she was cute. Tonight she was supposed to be mastering the pork portion of the menu, and the irritated look in her eye meant that she had stuck to their grandmothers' cookbook, using logic instead of instinct.

Marc leaned back in his chair and smiled at her dilemma. Lexi had always had a problem saying no. Which was why she often found herself torn between pleasing others and pleasing her need to break out of the box. Too bad that tonight people-pleasing Lexi won out, because the one who waved her finger at the rules was sexy to watch.

"Shit," Marc whispered, lounging back in his chair. Everything inside of him went still, because Lexi, with all of her polished manners and practiced properness, was watching back.

Their eyes held for a moment and neither moved. Then she smiled. It was small and a little self-conscious, but it was a smile, and he realized that she thought she'd been caught spying on him. Before he could process what that even meant, Lexi made her way over to the window and opened it.

When Marc opened his, Wingman took it as his personal invitation to leap out in Lexi's direction. Marc snagged his collar and tugged him back inside. "Sit or you get kibble for dinner."

Wingman's ears lowered. He glanced at the window and back to Marc, deciding with an irritated snort to plop his big old butt down on Marc's foot—hard.

"You're working late tonight," she said, leaning out the window far enough that her hair, tied back in a single braid, fell over one bare shoulder.

"I was just finishing up your grandma's books," he said, resting his palms on the sill and looking up at her. Even from here he could see the way her smile faded a little.

"How bad is it?"

"Bad," he said, going for honest. "But nothing you can't handle."

"Really?"

"Really." He leaned farther out the window, his stomach groaning when a gentle breeze picked up whatever she had baking up in that kitchen. "Something smells good."

"Are you trying to charm yourself into a dinner invitation?" She rested her elbows on the sill and grinned down at him.

"Well, unless you invited your entire crew up for dinner"—his eyes landed on the overflowing table set for four—"watching that much meat go to waste would be a sin."

"We couldn't let that happen now, could we," she said with a saucy smile. Cream puff was flirting—with him. "I guess I did overestimate a little."

"That is why we are the perfect couple."

She laughed. "Because I overcooked?"

He loved it when he made her laugh, which was probably why he was now drooling worse than Wingman. "And I like to eat. A lot."

"I remember. But that's like saying we are perfect for each other because I'm tall or have two eyes."

"I like my women tall, and two eyes are damn sexy."

She shrugged. "All right, I guess it's only fair. You did spend all day working on the bakery. You can break the bad news to me over dinner."

"Let me take Wingman up to my room and freshen up and then I'll be over."

Wingman barked, loud, long, and angry.

"Get out of that suit and bring Wingman."

"You might want to rethink that." He looked down at Wingman, who glared back, ready to take Marc out at the knees and make a leap for the window if things didn't go his way. "Behind that cute face and those big brown eyes lies a fluff ball of trouble."

"I don't think so. You're a good boy, huh, Wingman?" she cooed, and Wingman straightened his spine, and if he hadn't been a dog, Marc would have sworn he smiled.

"Yeah, that's part of his charm. Just when he's got you thinking that he's trained, he wolfs down dinner, drools all over your couch, and with one last doggie high five to the crotch, he's running out the door without even a thank-you, dragging your favorite pair of shoes behind him."

"He's a dog, Marc. I like dogs." She raised a brow. "And you just described yourself. Now are you coming up, or should I toss out the meat?"

It took Marc less than five minutes to pull on some clean jeans and a button-up, drag Wingman across the alley, and ring her bell. Then he felt stupid for changing. This was two friends having dinner, not a date. But when she answered the door, he felt himself relax. Because Lexi had been just as confused. She was still in that tissue-thin yellow dress that clung to her curves, all of them, but her silky hair was down around her shoulders, her lips were all shiny, and, aw hell, she looked like she was about to renege on her invitation.

"It's just dinner, Lexi," he said quietly.

"Right," she whispered, her gaze dropping to his mouth. "Just dinner."

Marc nudged his dog on the rump, and Wingman, who was sniffing every inch of the stoop and rubbing his back against Lexi's railing, got to his wingman duties and loped into the house before she could change her mind. After a sniff to Lexi's crotch, Wingman found his way upstairs, and Marc used the distraction to step inside and close the door behind him. "I brought wine."

"What a surprise," she deadpanned, but she seemed to have a hard time taking her eyes off him when she grabbed the bottle. "It's a DeLuca."

"Sure am, cream puff. And you look nice too," he whispered and gave her a kiss on the cheek, quick enough for friendly, but too close to her lips to pass as casual.

Wingman stationed himself at the top of the stairs, ears alert, tail up like an antenna, plate already licked clean, while they took a seat at the table. Lexi remained silent, her hands shoved under her thighs, and Marc realized that she was forcibly restraining herself from yanking the plate with a standard pork chop out of his hand and making him try the other dish.

He chewed his bite of chop, and the second he swallowed she asked, "So?"

"It's good. Cooked to perfection, the sauce—"

"A fig-jam glaze."

He smiled. "The fig-jam *glaze* is sweet and tart and goes well with the rice. Technically perfect." *And boring.*

"It's a braised pork chop in a fig-jam glaze over a bed of wild mushroom and pistachio pilaf. A Showdown classic." Unable to help herself, she reached across the table, snatched the plate right as he was going for a second bite, and replaced it with the other dish. "Now try this."

Marc raised a brow, chuckling when she sat back and once again shoved her hands securely under her legs. He slid the plate closer and sniffed. It was meat, but sliced thin and rolled around some kind of smelly cheese. He wasn't big on smelly cheese, but she was watching, all wide eyes and hopeful stares.

Deliberately, he took his time cutting into it, loving how her mouth opened when his did and how she was moving her lips as though the simple act would hurry him along.

The first bite exploded in his mouth, and Marc groaned, he actually groaned, over a piece of meat and cheese with a red sauce drizzled on top. All that crap he'd said a minute ago was exactly what a-holes like Trey would say when trying to impress some chick. Marc didn't know julienne from mandoline. Hell, pretty much all he knew about food was what he liked, meat, and what he didn't, anything with bell peppers, green shit, and french toast. But this, this was…

"Jesus Christ, Lexi. What's in this?" He took another bite. Groaning again, this time louder.

"A rolled pork loin stuffed with sautéed figs, gorgonzola dolce, and pistachios, basted in a balsamic and red wine reduction and served with a wild mushroom and truffle oil quinoa."

"So there's no unicorn hooves or leprechaun blood in here?"

She pressed her lips together as she shook her head, but he could still see her smile. It was too big and honest to hide.

It took a glass of wine and him eating half of his dinner before Lexi took her first bite. Another half glass of wine later and she finally started to relax. By the time he was refilling her glass for the second time, she had slipped off her shoes and tucked her bare feet up under her legs until everything but her pink-tipped toes disappeared under the skirt of her dress.

Figuring that this was the portion of the evening where he got to charm and delight her with his business prowess, Marc pulled out two files, one explaining exactly where the bakery was, financially speaking; the other was his plan for how she could save her company. Too bad she couldn't get past how bad the first one was to even get to the part where he got to beat his chest and revel in his brilliance at the second.

"So then expanding right now isn't the smartest decision," she said, looking down at the spreadsheet of Pricilla's current financials. She was no longer smiling, and Marc was pretty sure she was about two seconds away from crying. The numbers were bad, but not bad enough that they should make one of the toughest women he knew cry.

He closed the spreadsheet and leaned forward on his elbows. "What's going on that you aren't telling me, Lexi?" When she looked up at him with those big green eyes, full of embarrassment and guilt, he felt his chest tighten. "I can't help you unless I know what you're up against. No judgment, Lexi. Just a friend wanting to help, I swear."

And just like that, her entire body deflated like a popped balloon. "Last summer Pairing was having some money problems." Yeah, that much Marc knew. The shithole that was the restaurant's financial state had been a big concern of

Monte's. And Gabe's. "We changed suppliers, picked a bad one, and lost a lot of money."

"How much money?" Marc asked, although he already had a good idea. He had known that Jeff was having financial difficulty. Had told Jeff that the only way the deal would go forward with him as the restaurateur was to take out a loan, buy Lexi out, and get his company back in the black.

"Two hundred thousand dollars."

Marc gave a low whistle. That was a hell of a lot more than Jeff had admitted to needing. And a hell of a lot more than the loan was for. And suddenly Marc knew exactly where the other hundred thousand had come from. "All on changing suppliers?"

"Yeah, we had to secure six months of orders to become a new client. Plus lost business."

"Is that normal?"

"No, but Jeff said that if we wanted to play with the big boys, we had to fake it—"

"Till you make it. Yeah, yeah." It was one of the fundamental differences between them. It was also a big reason Marc had been hesitant to go into business with his friend. Marc was all about presenting your best face, even if that meant taking a calculated risk. But regardless of what his brothers thought, Marc was not the kind of guy who placed perception over the bottom line. That was just bad business.

"Wait," Marc said. "Jeff went with the new supplier?" That was so far from what Jeff had told Marc. Problem was, Jeff's story had always struck Marc as odd. Why would he buy Lexi out of the restaurant *and* give her all the equity in the house? Even worse, Lexi's side of the story not only rang true, it also sounded exactly like Jeff.

She waved her hand dismissively. "He's your friend, and I shouldn't have said anything. Plus, it doesn't matter whose idea it was. We made a bad move and lost a lot of money. We almost lost the restaurant."

"So you borrowed money from Pricilla."

She nodded and polished off the last of her wine. He filled up her glass. "Thank you." She took a sip, stopping midswallow. "How did you know? Did Jeffery tell you?"

He had to be careful here. "About borrowing money from Pricilla? No. There are three identical withdrawals from the bakery's account right about the same time." He flipped through the folder that held all of Pricilla's statements and account records. He turned to the first dog-eared page and pointed. "One under supplies." He flipped to another page. "One under petty cash, and one under utilities. And then small payments came in over the past year, were put into petty cash, and all marked *LM*. At first I couldn't figure out where the money was coming from, but then a large deposit went in the week you came home for seventy thousand." He pulled out a bank statement showing the deposit.

"It was most of what we made selling the house," Lexi said, taking the statement and studying it. "But this doesn't make sense."

What didn't make sense was why Lexi would be willing to borrow money from her grandmother to keep a restaurant going that she had already walked away from.

Jeff had come to visit Marc right around the time they started having money problems, right around the time, he now understood, that their supplier went under. He stayed for a few weeks, licking his wounds and claiming he needed time away to think because Lexi wanted out, out of the res-taurant, out of their marriage. Out. Period.

Marc had met with Monte a few weeks before and saw the potential for not only his family, but for Jeff as well if they partnered. As expected, Jeff had been on board. But before Marc would even bring Jeff in on it, he made him promise that he would wrap things up at home. Meaning that he would get his restaurant back in the black and end things with Lexi, which was a big deal breaker, because, separated or not, they were still married and Jeff had been talking a lot about his sous chef Sara.

When after a few months there had been no progress in finalizing the divorce, Marc pushed. Jeff said he and Lexi had been unable to come to terms on, well, anything other than that they were terrible together, and she wanted more money than the restaurant could afford. Since she was unwilling to sell the house, Marc suggested Jeff take out a loan and buy her out of the restaurant. Their next meeting with Monte was just a few weeks out, and his brothers were pushing to go with another restaurant, a local one that wasn't at the center of a divorce.

Two weeks later the loan was secure, Lexi filed for divorce, Jeff moved in with Sara, and the deal went forward. Yet no matter how many times he played over the order of events, Jeff's timeline didn't match up. And suddenly, Marc realized just how many other things Jeff had said that didn't match up.

"She said she was lending us money from her retirement, not out of the bakery."

This situation was so messed up it took Marc a full minute to get out of his head and understand what she was asking. "As far as I can tell, her bakery *is* her retirement, which is why I think she kept two sets of books. There's no way you'd agree to a loan that came from the bakery's account, and she also knew that at some point you'd sneak a peek at her records."

"Oh God. I screwed up so bad."

Marc knew by the way her face crumbled that he wasn't going to like what he heard. And that he was going to like his best friend even less. And he was right. After Lexi spilled the entire story about the loan and Pricilla using the bakery as collateral with the bank, Marc understood why she'd given up on the recipes so easily.

"When did you leave Jeff?"

Lexi fiddled with the stem of her glass, and Marc wanted to change the topic. This was awkward and it was none of his business, but if Lexi's timeline was accurate, then the son of a bitch had been with Sara while he was still married.

"If you are politely trying to tell me about Sara, no need. I already knew. I kind of walked in on..." She looked away, her eyes suspiciously shiny, and it was like a fist to Marc's gut.

He had to come clean. He had to tell her about Monte and the deal. He had to tell her that it was his decision to bring Jeff on, and his decision that had cost her the recipes.

Marc reached out and rested his hand over hers. "Look, Lexi, about Jeff—"

"Don't," she whispered, tears thickening her voice. "I don't want to talk about my divorce or Jeffery anymore. Not tonight. Not with you. Okay?"

No, it wasn't okay. Nothing about this entire situation felt okay anymore. But outside of his sudden need to punch something—Jeff's face, to be exact—Marc just wanted to make Lexi's world right again.

"All I can handle right now is figuring out how to fix this mess." She dropped her head to the table with a soft thunk. "God, what if Abby is wrong? The last thing I should be doing is spending the last of my money on a new kitchen. I should put it into the bakery until we are on solid ground again."

"No, Abby's right, and if you ever tell her I said that I will deny it." He waited for her to smile. When she didn't even lift her head, he laced his fingers with hers. This was not how he'd expected tonight to go. "The best plan would be to move forward with the new kitchen. This idea of phasing out the bistro build is brilliant. The kitchen will allow you to generate income faster, while keeping your debt low."

"There's no way I can make enough to pay everyone back."

"You can and you will. Look." Marc pulled out a new file and opened to the projected financials sheet he had put together. Lexi scooted closer, her knees bumping his under the table. "By catering you are diversifying your income, not to mention opening yourself up to a whole new clientele base. If you and Pricilla team up, you can cross promote and increase both of your customer bases."

And that got the first smile of the night. Lexi was slowly forgetting about Jeff and focusing on her business. "You mean Pricilla and I would both cater events. Like for the Daughters of the Prohibition menu, I should serve her cakes for dessert. And instead of just pastries for the librarians' meeting, we could offer a full breakfast menu?"

"Yup." God, she was smart. He'd been thinking of merely using Pricilla's pastries as a way to gain a recognizable name in the community, but Lexi was thinking that the benefit could go both ways. "By partnering with Pricilla, you'll get immediate branding and name recognition within the community, *and* you'll increase Pricilla's bottom line at the same time. A lot of these numbers I had to estimate, but if you look here you'll see that by taking on two medium-sized catering jobs a week, which you could price competitively, and selling Pricilla's desserts at an elevated price, you would be able to pay Pricilla back entirely, start paying down the bank loan, and still have enough money to hire her some kitchen staff."

"This says I could do that in ten months."

"Yup." He speared the last bite of pork loin and smelly cheese off Lexi's plate and leaned back in his chair, knowing that this was the part of the evening when he got to beat his chest and save the day like a freaking hero. "You'd also have built a solid customer base for the bistro's opening next summer and—"

A loud crash erupted from downstairs.

"Son of a bitch," Marc mumbled while pushing back his chair and standing. "Wingman!"

By the time they made it down the back steps, her front door was wide open, the handle covered in drool, and Pricilla's umbrella holder was on its side while her collection of umbrellas was strewn across the stoop and down the alley.

Marc turned the umbrella holder upright. Where it stayed for all of a half second before falling back over. "I'm sorry, Lexi. I'll buy you a new one."

"I feel so used," she said, picking up the closest umbrella and stacking it next to the entrance. "He didn't even give me a doggie high five before he broke down my door."

Marc smiled. "Most women would be pissed."

"Lucky for you and your checkbook, I'm not most women. And did your dog really just gnaw open my door?"

"What can I say, he's evolved."

They finished stacking the umbrellas and stood on the stoop, side by side, silently watching the light over the parking lot flicker and the old oak tree behind the Paws and Claws Day Spa move in the breeze. The evening was over, Wingman was nowhere in sight, and Lexi felt suddenly sad to see him and his owner leave.

"Thank you," she said, turning her head to look up at him, surprised at how husky her voice came out.

His slid her a sidelong glance. "For my dog destroying your entryway or for making you cry over Jeff?"

"For believing in me," she said, horrified when her voice caught.

At that, Marc faced her fully. He opened his arms wide and beckoned her with a little wiggle of his fingers. "Come here, cream puff."

That crooked smile, that simple gesture, and Lexi was transported back to high school, to every single time she had needed a friendly hug over the years and Marc had been there. Only this time when she walked into his arms, her eyes never left his and they both knew that there wasn't anything friendly about the way her body reacted, or the way his palms slid up her back to burrow in her hair.

"Marc," she whispered.

A dog barked in the distance, followed by Wingman answering, and then the sound of trash cans toppling over.

"I better go," he said, stepping back, his hands sliding down her back and lingering for just a second on her hips. "Thanks for dinner, and let me know if you need anything."

She nodded. "Thanks."

"I mean it, Lexi. The catering, the tasting tomorrow, anything. Understand?"

A symphony of barks echoed down the alley, ending with a loud yelp.

"You'd better go."

With one final wave, Marc disappeared down the alley, and Lexi found herself seated on the stoop. She tried to blame it on the wine, but she knew her weak knees had nothing to do with alcohol. Marc believed in her. Not just in her cooking or her bistro—but in her.

CHAPTER 10

Lexi had never considered death by éclair a realistic scenario. That was, until she crossed Main Street and—chafing dish in one hand, cooler in the other, and insulated bag slung over her shoulder—saw the Duval's Decadence du Jour luxury utility vehicle parked in front of the town hall, rear hatch open while a staff of five expertly unloaded the prepared feast. The Hummer was shiny and black and, with its special-order Viking cooktop, side-by-side Sub-Zeroes, and tricked-out backseat that stored enough platters and flatware to serve a complete party of ninety, big enough to take up four spaces.

It took everything Lexi had not to bolt across Hunt Avenue, hide inside the tow truck at the service station—where Stan was known to keep a full fifth of Wild Turkey in the glove box—and gorge on the two dozen éclairs currently stored in her cooler.

Natasha and crew were competing for the same job. And no one had bothered to warn her. So Lexi, party of one, stood on the sidewalk, forced to watch platter after rectangular platter of deconstructed salmon niçoise salad and Vietnamese pork crepes sail by, knowing that she was outnumbered, outstaged, and, even worse, outcooked.

Lexi set the cooler bag down, reached inside, and grabbed an éclair. She had caved under the pressure and, determined to make Marc's one-year plan a reality, gone with a boring baked pork chop and wild rice. Even her traditional round plates had porcelain envy.

"Stunning, isn't it?" Natasha said, approaching from behind. Her designer dress stated refined elegance, while her ridiculously high and expensive heels advertised sexy sophistication with an eye for quality. Natasha was a walking billboard for couture cuisine, which had Lexi questioning her traditional black slacks and white chef's jacket.

Natasha continued. "It arrived fresh from Alaska this morning. The greens and pork were brought over from this great little organic farm outside Marin. I didn't want to bore the panel with local fare or food they'd all seen before. The Showdown is the one time a year that our town gets to showcase to the world our exquisite wine and cuisine."

"By serving food from other places?" Lexi asked, some of her nerves fading.

Couture cuisine or not, Natasha had missed the point. The same point that the grannies had so eagerly explained to Lexi earlier that morning after they'd taken one look at her rolled pork loin and started whispering nervously among themselves. They'd reminded her that the Showdown was about celebrating local agriculture and tradition.

"Aren't you afraid it's a bit experimental for a group that was founded on preserving tradition?"

Natasha laughed. "Do you think it was traditional for women in the twenties to run illegal liquor?" She had a point. "Traditional can become expected and boring and gets old. And from one woman to another," Natasha said, eyeing Lexi's half-eaten éclair, "lighten up on those. You wouldn't want to add 'more to love' to your Match bio."

Lexi smiled sweetly, her last nerve officially gone. "You're so nice to be thinking of how much I'm loved. But from one woman to another"—Lexi winked, something she'd picked up from Marc—"my boyfriend has that department well covered. Good luck today."

Lexi gathered her cooler and made her way up the front steps of the town hall. As she passed under the St. Helena town flag swaying in the breeze and between the white columns that spanned the entire length of their most treasured town building, Lexi felt her breath catch and her confidence bubble up. Because there, to the left of the main entrance and several feet above an aged mahogany door with an iron grille speakeasy-hinged to the front, sat a historical placard.

The Back Barrel
Founded on August 17, 1923, with the sole purpose of serving the county of Napa, California, this is the original site of the Daughters of the Prohibition, a nonviolent, nonpolitical women's society founded on the principles of promoting patriotism, preserving local tradition, and securing the valley's future through the production, distribution, and consumption of wines, ciders, and spirited beverages of class.

This town and the DOP had been founded on the same principles that she had infused into her cooking: local pride, strong tradition, and lots of heart. And the DOP was going to take one look at her perfectly baked pork chop and realize that she was the perfect woman for this job. With the perfect menu to honor the return of their most treasured event. And how perfectly her understated elegance would highlight, rather than outshine, the wine tasting.

Balancing her chafing dish, bag, and cooler, Lexi made her way down the steps and pushed open the door.

"Hello?" When no one responded, she took a cautious step inside.

Bumping the door closed, Lexi took in the deep-red carpet, solid mahogany walls, and always-past-midnight lighting that illuminated the narrow hallway, which used to be the entrance to the Back Barrel, and found herself smiling a little. Okay, a lot. Because in the summer of 1923, two events collided that would forever change the future of the women of St. Helena.

The local prohibitionists, led by Mayor Burnhart, were cracking down and making it increasingly difficult for the men of Napa County to run wine. No wine meant an end to a way of life. So when Salvador DeLuca and Philip Baudouin were forced to dump forty barrels of premium cabernet in the Sacramento River to avoid spending the next forty years on Alcatraz, the women became fearful of what would happen to their beloved town and decided to take action. They formed the Daughters of the Prohibition.

As fate would have it, a week later, Miss Giannina DeLuca, eldest daughter to Salvador DeLuca and self-appointed sleuth of the newly formed secret women's society, uncovered that the honorable mayor wasn't running his prohibition advisory meetings out of the basement in town hall. He was running a gentlemen's club—complete with illegal spirits and illicit women. He was also running for reelection.

Mayor Burnhart had congressional aspirations and needed to please the conservatives in Washington while still maintaining a strong voting base at home. Giannina needed a headquarters for the DOP and a place to sell their families' wine.

It only took a few months for word to spread and for daughters and wives of vintners across the state to unite, and the ladies of St. Helena created one of the most extensive bootlegging operations in California. And they'd ruled the domestic wine market ever since.

Smiling, Lexi rounded the last corner, entered the old tavern, and blinked.

Several times, in fact.

Because no matter how many times she blinked, the scenery remained the same. It wasn't the massive mahogany bar that spanned the entire length of the room that caught her attention, or that there were five wine vats the size of small water towers with spigots on the back wall. No, what had Lexi balking was that the room was divided in two, with the junior league and their couture attitudes on one side, and four silvered flappers, one mobster, a fur ball in a fedora, and enough beads and feathers to stage a rendition of "All That Jazz" sitting on the other.

It was like the DOP version of *Family Feud*, only with clutch purses and family names for weapons, as the up-and-comers and the old-timers—separated by a podium and Mrs. Moberly, town librarian and the only woman stupid enough to be roped into arbitrating the evening's event—faced off.

"Oh, thank God," Mrs. Moberly gasped, clasping her hands so tightly that her white peplum gloves looked ready to burst at the seams and send the pearl buttons scattering. "The last caterer is finally here, so I call this meeting to order."

"Finally?" Lexi asked, her confidence vanishing as she took in the five, not just Natasha, but the *five* other caterers, dressed to perfection and standing behind their tables, each more spectacular than the last—all of them ready to begin serving. And none of them offering traditional or simple.

"I was told it started at five," Lexi said, checking her watch. It showed 4:49.

"The tasting starts at five," Natasha cut in. Her table, which was a complete rip-off of last month's *Martha Stewart Living*, right down to the loose cherry-blossom petals and dried-fig arrangement, was stunning. Stolen, but stunning all the same. "Food to be served at five sharp, I believe was the rules."

Meaning Lexi had ten minutes to unload, plate, and present her sample course, which was not deconstructed, modern, or in the least bit interesting.

"She'll be ready," Pricilla said, standing up and giving a decisive nod. Her dress was more giant toilet paper roll covered in scarlet fringe than flapper, but the flask attached to her ankle was authentic and most likely full.

Everyone knew that the senior league took tradition seriously and, on occasion, pulled out their mothers' dresses. Lexi had just assumed that they reserved playing bootlegger dress up for special occasions—like Halloween.

ChiChi bustled over in vintage Coco Chanel, her boa flapping behind her. When she was close enough for Lexi to smell the mothballs wafting off her clothes, she asked, "Are you dating my Marco?"

The room fell silent.

Lexi opened her mouth and snapped it closed equally as fast. How was she supposed to answer that? And here, with every busybody in town leaning in, waiting for her to deny the rumors that she had been the one to land St. Helena's most notorious playboy?

The plan was to tell their grandmas together, over Friday-night dinner. Not here, with Lexi alone and a roomful of women who either wanted to see them married with babies or on their way to an explosive breakup.

"Yes. Marco and I are"—she swallowed, hard—"dating." Did her voice just go up three octaves?

"You're kidding," Isabel Stark said, her eyes wide in disbelief. "I mean, no offense, but I thought that was just a rumor you made up to get out of dating all those losers your grandma set you up with."

"They're not losers." Lexi felt compelled to defend her tribe of lost boys, and more importantly, her grandmother's efforts. "And yes, Marc and I are together. Exclusively."

Whispers rang out, exactly what she was afraid of.

"I overheard Penny at the Paws and Claws say she saw Marc leaving her house...in the morning," someone said, though Lexi couldn't see who. They were all too busy huddling and gossiping about her.

"I heard that she already slept with him," someone else said.

"So?" Lexi snapped, daring them to say one more word. "Now if we're done, I'm here to cook." She smoothed out her crisp white tablecloth. "So if you have any more questions, they'll have to wait for later, or you could just go to Facebook and read Marc's post."

Reaching under her table, Lexi pulled out the box of decor and flatware that her *boyfriend* had carried over earlier and dressed the table. She was just finishing up with the napkins when ChiChi opened the chafing dish, which held her pork chops, and gasped.

"Oh dear—"

"You followed the recipes," Lucinda whispered. She resembled a penguin in her vintage black-and-white pantsuit with matching wing tip shoes. Mr. Puffins was striking in a black fedora and tie. But neither of them was giving Lexi the job-well-done expression she had expected. In fact, they all looked horrified.

"What do you mean, 'Oh dear?'" she whispered. "You told me that whoever made the best Great-Grandma DeLuca baked chop would win. I made the best Great-Grandma DeLuca baked chop."

"We may have overstated our decision-making power with the committee," Pricilla admitted.

Lexi's heart stopped, but her hands kept moving. *Pork chop is to be placed two inches out from the center of the plate and at forty-five-degree angle to the wild rice.* "Meaning?"

"Meaning that the Daughters of the Prohibition seem to be in the middle of a revolution," Pricilla began, glaring at the table of junior leaguers, all clamoring over Natasha's table, her new Jimmy Choos, her food. "It seems that the junior league sees the Showdown as a chance to modernize, update things a little."

"Does Natasha get a vote?" Lexi asked, forcing herself to keep plating.

"Natasha had to recuse herself since she's interviewing for the job," ChiChi said. "And someone of general-member status can't replace a board member on a night when a vote is cast."

"Since Alison Sheehan is big as a vat and on bed rest and Jennifer Logan has bronchitis, they had no one qualified to stand in. So they only have four votes tonight," Pricilla said proudly.

"And the senior league shares your views?" A quick glance toward the other ladies had Lexi scooting closer and lowering her voice. "Then we have the numbers. You three, Mrs. Lambert, and Mrs. Moberly."

Lexi felt herself relax. Even if all of the Prada mommies chose Natasha, Lexi could still win.

"That's the thing, dear," Pricilla said, and she wasn't smiling. "Mrs. Moberly can't vote. She's not even a DOP member."

"Then who's the fifth vote?"

All three grannies looked at the door and—

Oh God, no. This could not be happening. Her luck with *this* family could not be this bad.

"Ladies, sorry I'm late. I was just Skyping with my new daughter-in-law," Mrs. Balldinger sang as she waltzed into the all-in-one saloon and ladies' club, regal, refined, and ready to ruin Lexi's life.

"I had to hear all about the honeymoon. To think that after all this time my Jeffery finally found true love." Her ex-mother-in-law sauntered past all the tables, poked at Lexi's flatware, and smiled. "Let the tasting begin?"

"I messed up," Lexi said, fiddling with the hem of her pants as she sat on the bottom step of town hall and stared at the sidewalk. "I chickened out and ruined everything."

"You didn't ruin everything," Marc said, wishing he could do something to help her.

"I baked a pork chop, Marc." She dropped her head on her bent knees. "I served a baked pork chop and wild rice for the biggest catering audition this town can remember."

Marc wanted to point out that she had cooked what her clients, being their grandmothers, had requested. Learning to balance expertise with customers' expectations was a big part of finding success in the service industry. She had just gone too far in one direction. She'd figure it out. "I bet it was cooked to perfection."

"You could bake a pork chop."

"Not to perfection. But I'm more than willing to let you watch my culinary prowess. I am damn sexy in an apron." When she didn't so much as laugh, he reached out and put his hand on the back of her neck, kneading little circles in her tense muscles. "They haven't made a final decision. This could still swing your way."

She shook her head. "I should have listened to my instincts and you, but instead I got scared and went with safe. Which means I let down myself and my grandma too." She lifted her head and, as though unable to meet his gaze, went back to studying the tops of her shoes. "I need to think about moving. Maybe Paris."

Joke or not, Marc was surprised at how even the idea of her moving made him feel. Not good. "You got nervous and caved to a client. It happens to the best of us. And I don't know what they'll decide or what they're judging this on, but I do know that nothing could have happened that would be worthy of leaving the country."

"Really?" Her head shot up. "Because Natasha knows Jeff cheated on me, I was late so I didn't even get to present my plates right, then I may have implied that we are having sex, Jeffery's mom announced to the room that he'd finally, after all these years, found true love, and my dessert course was disqualified because it was baked in a shop owned by a voting member of the DOP. Now tell me how it could have been worse?"

They were silent for a moment, and she raised a brow. "Marc?"

"I'm sorry, what? You lost me at the we're-having-sex part." He shrugged. "I think that it's only fair that I be included in this implied sex, since I've already slept on your couch."

"Are you serious? You know what? Never mind." She stood in a huff, her hands flapping at her sides, that delectable ass swinging angrily.

Before she could storm off too far, Marc grabbed her wrist and pulled her onto his lap. Linking his arms around her waist and holding her secure, he lowered his voice. "Look, I was kidding. You're really upset about this, and I don't know how to make it better, and for some reason that bothers me." More than he'd like to admit. "So I went for the cheap laugh."

Lexi didn't look amused.

"This whole boyfriend thing is new to me. I'm still trying to figure it out."

"*Fake* boyfriend," she reminded him.

"Whatever." He grinned, and thankfully she grinned back.

"You're forgiven."

"Really? Just like that? Because I acted like an ass, and I think you should come to my suite and teach me a lesson."

She smacked his chest, but he noticed she didn't try to move off his lap. Instead, she linked her hands around his neck and rested her head on his shoulder. "What if I can't do this, Marc?"

He ran a hand up her back and tangled his fingers in her hair. "I don't believe that and neither do you. Because you and I both know that if you lose the Showdown, we'll find another way. So what is this really about?"

Her arms tightened, and her face disappeared in the curve of his neck. "When I said we were dating, no one believed me. Not that we are, I mean, I know that we're not, but to hear it, like they didn't think I could get a guy like you..." He felt her shrug. "Silly or not, it really hurt."

And in that moment, Marc regretted every one-night stand he'd ever had, every woman he'd led on, and every stupid decision he'd made. Because she wasn't the half of the equation that came up short. He was. But Jeff had left her vulnerable, and Marc had made her an easy target for Natasha. It had never been his intention to make her life more complicated. He had only been trying to help.

Okay, and he wanted to spend time with her. She made him feel smart and real, and when she looked at him like she had the other night, he felt like one of the good guys. He'd never really been the good guy, and selfishly, he didn't want that to stop.

"Hey," Marc said, taking her face between his hands and raising it to his.

She took in a deep breath, opened those mossy-green eyes, and bam...he felt her slide into every cell of his body. Despite everything that he wanted to say, everything that he should say, he found it impossible to talk. Maybe if he was able to keep her around long enough, he'd figure out how to become that guy, the one that he was right now with her in his arms.

"Oh God," she whispered, and he almost asked her if she was feeling the same thing. Then he noticed her face was pale and her lower lip was trembling. "No, no, no. Natasha and the junior league are coming out. And Mrs. Balldinger is right behind them."

She tried to scramble off his lap, but he made it clear that that wasn't going to happen anytime soon. Selfish intentions aside, he'd set out to help her, and that was what he was going to do.

"Marc," she hissed, still jerking around on his lap. "What part of them making fun of me in front of my ex-mother-in-law don't you get?"

He might not understand what was happening between him and Lexi, but he got women. And the best way to shut one up was with a kiss.

"Trust me?" he whispered, fisting his hands in the front of her jacket and dragging her up against him.

She stared at him for a minute and then nodded, her eyes wide and full of trust, and just like that, Marc knew he was fucked.

"Thank God," he mumbled before he captured her sweet lips and dropped one hell of a kiss on her. He felt her breath catch and her mouth stiffen under his.

"Play along with me here, cream puff," he said against her lips. "If you don't start acting like you want me, my delicate man feelings might get hurt."

"I'm not good at this," she said, turning her head slightly.

"At kissing?" Marc almost laughed, then realized she was serious.

"At, well, all of it, I guess," she whispered, the tears finally filling her eyes, and Marc wanted to beat the crap out of Jeff.

"I think you just haven't had the right partner." He framed her face between his palms and dropped a gentle kiss on her lips. "Lucky for us, sugar, I've been told I'm a great teacher. So let's start with the basics, and we'll work up to second base by the time the crowd gets to us."

"That's fast."

"No, I'm that good."

"Yeah?" Her eyes dropped to his lips. Hot need slowly filled his chest and sank down to settle in his groin.

"Oh yeah. Just relax your lips." He gave a little nip, and she nipped back.

"Like that?"

"Just like that and—"

That was all he got out before her lips started moving against his, and hot damn was she incredible. She was sweet and trusting and sexy as hell. Her lips could drive a man insane. Add to that the way she was pressing her body up to him like shrink-wrap, or the little moans she released when he got it right, but when she opened her mouth and made the first incredible pass with her tongue across his lips he was lost.

Realizing that this might be his only chance, Marc gave it everything he had.

Somewhere between her nails clawing though his scalp and her thigh rubbing up against his dick, Marc forgot that this was a game. Apparently so did Lexi, because when ChiChi cleared her throat, Lexi jumped. She blinked up at the crowd that had gathered and then back to him.

"See," he whispered, tucking a handful of hair that had come out of her braid behind her ear. "I'm good."

"Well, if you're done groping that poor girl in public, Marco, I'd like to give her the good news."

"Good news?" Lexi sprang off of his lap, but not before straightening her jacket and smoothing down her hair, which was a colossal waste of time. She looked like she'd just been caught making out behind the bleachers.

Marc smiled. She had.

"Well, yes. It seems we are at an impasse." ChiChi took a deep breath, her bell hat bobbing with anger as she shot a gaze at Mrs. Balldinger—whose smug smile left no doubt about who had voted against Lexi. "So as the rules stipulate, there must be a tiebreaker. You and Natasha will both be asked to present a new dish a week from Saturday."

"And what if there's another tie?" Marc asked.

"There can't be," ChiChi said with a smile that sent his every instinct into red alert. If the board couldn't decide on a chef, which seemed like a good possibility, then the power would default back to the customer. "Because we won't be deciding, dear. You will."

CHAPTER 11

"A re you done eye-fucking the neighbor girl? Or do you need another moment?"

Marc didn't move, but he stopped staring at Lexi, who was cooking away in her kitchen, wearing that tiny lavender apron and cutoff shorts. He knew the apron well. It had played a starring role in his dreams lately, and when she stood at just the right angle, and he squinted a little, she looked like she was in nothing but the apron. And it was a damn better sight than the e-mail sitting on his desktop.

Forcing himself to focus, Marc took one last look and turned. His two oldest brothers stood in his office doorway, and by the way Gabe was shaking his head and mumbling threats, they were doing their best to remind him that he was a screwup. And in this case he knew it was true.

"Where's Trey?" Marc asked. He'd called his brothers earlier that morning as soon as he'd seen the e-mail.

"Trey is in New York. Last-minute meeting," Nate said, calmly sitting in one of Marc's leather barrel chairs, while

Gabe plopped down, elbows on knees, eyes hard, looking slightly harassed and completely exhausted.

"One that didn't exist until this happened," Gabe said, flapping a rolled-up newspaper a few times before smacking it against his palm with a reprimanding thwack.

Marc couldn't see what was on the paper, it was moving too fast, but it didn't take a genius to figure out from Gabe's intense expression and the fact that Trey was missing that this was about one of two things: the Showdown or the Monte deal. Either way it had to be bad, because when there was family drama, Trey ran. He'd started when their parents died and made a habit of it after Abby's marriage crumbled.

"Will he be back in time for the Showdown?"

"Depends if Abby stops running these." Gabe tossed the latest issue of the *St. Helena Sentinel* on the desk.

Marc didn't need any more bad news right now, but he walked over to his desk, spun the paper around, and—"Shit."

There on the front page, nestled between "DOP Calls Tie in Taste-Off" and the ad for the Showdown, was a full-color and full-sized photo of Richard with a "My Dick Is Still Missing" headline plastered above his head.

"I'm happy she's finally divorcing the tool and moving on. But front page? The Showdown is next week. What the hell was she thinking?" Abby was a sweetheart, but when riled she had a mean streak as wide as the valley.

"According to her, she didn't do it," Nate said, and Marc raised a disbelieving brow. "She copped to the headline, but swears she only paid for a small ad in the wanted section."

"Under missing pets," Gabe said seriously. "And don't you dare laugh."

Marc couldn't help it. His sister could be a pain in the ass, and these ads running at the same time he was trying to convince people to drop a thousand dollars a pop for an "elegant and exclusive" event only made his job a whole lot harder, but the girl had spunk.

"Okay, dick jokes aside, if she paid for back page, why is she getting headline service?"

"Three months ago Kimberly Meyer was promoted from advertising manager at the *Sentinel* to editor-in-chief," Nate said, not needing to point out that Kimberly Meyer used to be known as Keg-Stand Kim: dance-team captain, all-around party girl, and Marc's homecoming date. Her name also used to be Baudouin.

"Wait, that was right after they announced that the Showdown was going to be at the hotel."

"And right after Charles threw a fit about it being held at a DeLuca property," Gabe said.

"It was also right after he became a silent partner in the paper," Nate added.

"Which explains all of the odd timing with articles about the family, placing the Showdown ads next to Abby's mess of a divorce. He's pissed that the committee picked you."

"It's pretty incredible that old man Baudouin is still this hung up on a feud that involves a dead man and a seventy-nine-year-old grandmother."

Gabe laughed. "Have you met ChiChi?"

He had a point.

"Getting back at us is one thing. But if he ruins the Showdown, it will hurt the whole town." Marc shook his head. "There is no way he would be willing to do that. What could he possibly gain besides a town boycott of his wine?"

"I have no idea, but a man who lost the love of his life and his best friend on the same day when his only crime was being honest?" Gabe gave a low whistle. "Yeah, I don't think he needs much more of a motive."

"If you didn't know about the ad, then why did you call?" Nate said, looking at Marc.

Because I didn't want to admit that I screwed up—again—over the phone.

Marc ran a hand through his hair and shifted in his seat. He didn't know why, but he had the sudden urge to see Lexi, even if only through the window. A little smile or her cute wave sounded nice. Only she wasn't there.

He turned back around. "I got an e-mail this morning from Bo Brock's manager."

"Ah, shit." Gabe leaned back in his chair.

"It was to inform me that Mr. Brock must regretfully decline to participate in the Tasting Tribunal."

"Christ, Marc. Do you have any idea how screwed we are?" Trey said from the doorway, looking both constipated and like he needed to punch someone. And from his pointed glare that someone was Marc. "Without a celebrity judge, the Tasting Tribunal will be—"

"Yeah, I get it." Marc let out a breath. "No celebrity judge, no panel. No panel, no Showdown. You don't need to explain, Trey. Plus, I thought you were on your way to New York."

"And I thought you were handling your shit."

"I am," Marc grumbled.

"Yeah? Well, then, explain to me how a guy who signed a contract would bail at the last minute," Trey challenged, taking an aggressive step forward.

Marc had been trying to figure that out for himself. The e-mail gave no concrete reason for why Mr. Brock wanted out, just a few lame lines about a serious man with serious commitments who took his job seriously.

"Take a seat," Gabe said, kicking out the spare chair in invitation, although his tone left no room for refusal.

"Do you know how important this event is?" Trey demanded, but took his seat.

"We could sue," Nate threw out, trying to get them back on track. "Who knows, maybe the threat of a public suit will scare him into coming."

"That's all we need," Marc said. "A pissed-off judge picking the winner. Not the way we want to start our first year as hosts."

"First year? You expect to do this again?" Trey asked.

Marc stopped, his chest going heavy. Sure, there had been a few snags along the way, but outside of a dog on the jury and losing the judge, he had done an incredible job, and he didn't understand why his brothers couldn't see that. Their constant criticism was getting old.

The only thing keeping him from kicking his kid brother out was that if this went south, and it was looking like it already had, the fallout would affect everyone. And he couldn't do that to his family. Especially Gabe.

His oldest brother might be a hard-ass when it came to the family name, but Marc understood. Gabe had sacrificed a lot over the years to ensure that his siblings could have as normal a life as possible after their parents died. He'd also worked tirelessly those first few years to keep the DeLuca vineyards running, and he'd eventually turned it into one of the largest wine empires in the country.

Marc had also worked hard, trying to make up for his wild youth and prove to his family that he had what it took to go the distance and make this hotel a success. He'd gotten into business school at Berkeley and, if he hadn't dropped out his second year to take a job managing a small luxury hotel in Tuscany, would have graduated with honors. More importantly, Marc had worked in several hotels around the world, taking every job possible, busting his ass to move his way up the ranks to learn as much as possible about the hospitality industry.

In his mind, he'd cut his learning curve in half, and what his brothers dismissed as dropping out of school and floating from job to job Marc saw as the best possible way to master an industry. By twenty-six he had worked in some of the top hotel chains in the world, and under some of the most successful men and women in the industry. By twenty-eight he'd opened the doors to the first in his goal of many luxury boutique hotels catering to a specific jet-setting demographic. He'd put in the time and sweat, and now it was about to pay off. Hosting the Showdown at his hotel would not only put the Napa Grand back on the map, it also would have made his parents proud.

And he was damn proud. Which was why he'd called his brothers first thing. Everyone made mistakes, but a man knew when to admit that he was in trouble and had the balls to come clean and then ask for help. Doing it alone to prove he could wasn't worth screwing this up.

"Yeah, Trey. I want to do this next year and the year after that and hold this event every year on Mom and Dad's anniversary in my hotel. And I know what seems to you like a bunch of errors and spontaneous decisions on my part is really just a clusterfuck of bad luck. I swear to you that I researched this, made sure the hotel was financially secure enough. But you all know that in business things happen. Even with the best planning and intentions, sometimes it goes wrong. That's all this is."

Marc held his breath, watching his brothers watching him, and waiting to see how they would react. If they decided to let him go it alone, he'd still come out on top, but he hoped that it didn't come to that.

"Thanks for clearing that up," Trey said, face hard. "Because we'd be totally screwed if you hadn't *intended* or *planned* on sleeping with one potential caterer while playing grab-ass with the other in front of town hall."

"You've been talking to ChiChi."

"ChiChi, Abby, Mrs. Moberly, my damn postman." Trey shook his head. "You're the tiebreaker, man. No matter which one you choose, it will look bad. I get it, they're hot, but couldn't you keep it in your pants for just another few weeks?"

Now it was Marc's turn to stand and take an aggressive step forward, around his desk and right into his kid brother's face. "Natasha is old news, and Lexi is off-limits. Understand?" He underscored his stance on the topic with a shove to the shoulder. "And since when is my personal life any of your business?"

"Since you decided to crawl into bed with the ex-wife of our business partner." Trey moved forward until they were breathing the same air and fighting over the same space. Trey was not only the youngest, he was also the shortest by two inches, a difference which he made up for with the enormous chip on his shoulder. "What part of litigation don't you get?"

"Even if I was sleeping with Lexi, which I'm not—"

"But you want to," Gabe stated quietly.

Marc opened his mouth and immediately closed it. He did want to sleep with Lexi. So bad. Even though every piece of his moral fiber dictated that he stay away, he was finding her harder and harder to resist.

"Yeah, that's what I thought," Gabe said, patting him on the back. "Now have a seat. In about ten minutes my wife is going to start calling to ask where I am. About a minute after that I'll remember that today is Tuesday, which means that Holly is at ChiChi's and my wife, who has had a long month and needs some pampering, was calling me from bed."

"Is that what they are calling it these days?" Nate asked.

Gabe shot Nate a look. "Do you want to fix this mess or let them bitch at each other some more? Because either way"—he looked at his watch—"in nine minutes I'm out of here."

A few months ago, Marc would have thought Gabe was joking. The mighty head of the DeLuca family, business god and wine tycoon, choosing to pamper a woman over going to battle for the family business. Marc and Gabe might have different styles, but the one thing they had always shared was the love of business. The bigger the stakes, the bigger the rush.

Yet somehow over the past few months Gabe had become domesticated. Then again, Gabe looked happier when he was with Regan than he'd ever looked in a boardroom, and suddenly Marc wanted to solve this problem. Not for the stroke to the ego, but because he would rather be next door tasting Lexi's new creation that dealing with this BS.

Resigned, Marc shot Trey a challenging look. Trey shot back one of his own, coated in eat-shit and with a little screw-you at the end for good measure, and then, silently, they agreed to table the discussion until later and took their seats.

"Great," Gabe said, kicking back in his chair, a big smile forming on his face. He looked to Trey. "Now, why don't you tell us why you really missed that plane?"

Trey leaned back in his chair and exhaled. "Last month I convinced Monte that the perfect place to announce the partnership was at the Showdown."

"At the Showdown?" Marc asked. "Why?"

"Because there will be a lot of press, and it could create a lot of hype." Marc opened his mouth, and Gabe silenced him with a single raised brow. When no one spoke, Trey dropped his head to his hands and mumbled, "And I think Monte is getting cold feet."

Marc stared in disbelief. "And we're just hearing about this now?"

"You're not the only one who has a lot going on," Trey admitted, and Marc finally understood. This was Trey's Napa Grand, his chance to prove to the family that he had what it took. Oh, he'd made the DeLucas millions selling their wines into new markets, one hotel and restaurant at a time. But if he closed this deal with Montgomery Distributions, he would accomplish what their father had been trying to do for years.

"Okay," Marc said, not wanting to fight with his brothers anymore. "Monte is coming, and we don't need to give him any reason to rethink the deal."

"Right."

Gabe was silent for a minute, and then he leaned forward. "Okay, Marc, you aren't breaking the tie, the Tasting Tribunal will. That puts you out of the limelight because no matter who is chosen, the paper can't blame you."

"You do know what you're saying, right?" Nate said warily. "Putting Mrs. Rose in a position over the DOP is asking for trouble."

Mrs. Rose was not only the current wine commissioner of St. Helena, and therefore the fifth required member of the Tasting Tribunal, she was also the former DOP president who'd lost her seat over a disagreement when she motioned to reinstate concealed-carry permits for active senior board members. The disagreement had included a junior leaguer who vetoed Mrs. Rose's motion, followed by Mrs. Rose shoving a gun, which was not concealed or permitted, in said junior's face.

"Which is why I think you should handle getting the judges to that tiebreaker," Marc said, liking this plan. Nate's patience and rational thought process made him the perfect person to handle the tribunal.

"What? No way."

"Marc's right," Gabe said, and Marc felt his chest swell with pride. "You manage ChiChi better than any of us. After the granny mafia, one little old lady should be easy."

"It doesn't matter," Trey cut in before Nate could object. "Without Brock we'll be at four judges. There could still be a tie."

"Three judges and a dog," Nate pointed out.

On cue, Wingman came loping into the office. Leash in mouth, he set his front paws on Marc's desk. Too distracted to scold him, Marc gave his head a pat—and stopped as everything sank in.

Son of a bitch.

Thoroughly screwed, he closed his eyes and banged his head back again the chair. "What if old man Baudouin picked his dog as a judge not to send a message to his kids, but to make sure the celebrity judge canceled and the Showdown got canceled?"

"How would he know that Brock would be scared off by a dog? Most celebrities would dig that," Trey said.

"Not a celebrity who, until recently, was using a meat supplier under investigation for cruelty to animals," Marc said.

"How come we didn't know this before we asked him to judge?" Gabe said, but Marc noticed that this time the *we* didn't imply Marc messing up. The DeLucas were in this together, and it felt good—right, even.

"Because it was never in the papers. He dumped the supplier before it went to press."

"Then how do you know?" Nate asked.

"Jeff used the same supplier."

"Oh boy," Nate said, leaning back and getting comfortable. Everyone in the room knew that this was about a whole lot more than a lost judge.

Marc also settled in for the long haul. He had trusted Jeff, taken his word for too many things, and as a result Marc had let his family down. Now he had to figure out how to give his brothers enough of the story to get a good understanding of the situation, without divulging anything that would betray Lexi's trust.

"Room service," Lexi said, stopping short when she saw that all three guest chairs were filled. "I'm sorry, I didn't know you had company."

"It's okay," Marc said, smiling and standing. "We were just finishing up."

His brothers did the same, and Lexi felt her mouth go dry. How was it possible for one room to contain so much hotness? One DeLuca was potent enough. The lot of them together packed enough testosterone to turn a convent of nuns.

Even though they all had that trademark DeLuca hair and eyes, dark and melt-in-your-mouth darker, they were as different as they were similar. Gabe was handsome in that sophisticated, corporate kind of way. Known for being the most impeccably starched and tailored of the brothers, today he had opted for faded jeans and an old college tee with glue and pink glitter stuck to the sleeve, and even though he looked tired, she couldn't remember a time growing up when he'd seemed so happy.

Trey, on the other hand, seemed irritated, which wasn't unusual. Like Marc, Trey had inherited their father's charm and panty-melting grin. Unlike Marc, though, he'd come out more hotheaded than easygoing.

Lexi wouldn't describe Nate as easygoing or hotheaded. More serious and intense, which on him was seriously sexy. He was rangy and athletic, with olive skin and work-roughened hands that spoke of long days in the vineyard, and his weighted smile advertised that their parent's deaths had hit him hard. And he was still recovering.

And Marc, well, he was everything that his brothers were, just more. Taller, bigger, brighter, funnier, sweeter, and, as far as Lexi was concerned, sexier. Although right now he didn't seem his usual charming, laid-back self. He seemed tense and frustrated and was staring right at her. They all were.

Her palms went sweaty as she took in the tight faces, felt the energy all but crackle in the room and knew that they weren't almost done, and by the way Wingman, leash in mouth, skulked over and plopped himself at her feet and how Marc looked ready to snap, she had interrupted a pretty heated discussion.

She smiled, and Gabe was the only one who smiled back. The other two busied themselves with glaring at Marc, who was glaring back, which let her know that she had been a part of that discussion.

"Um, I'll come back later." Like never. Carrying on this fauxmance in front of the town had been harder than she thought. Trying to convince his brothers would be impossible. One look at the two of them together and his brothers would know the truth.

"Nah, we were just heading out." Gabe reached down and grabbed a newspaper from Marc's desk, stopping midreach. He sniffed the air and closed his eyes, releasing a small groan before standing. "What is that?"

"*That*," Lexi said, opening the lid just enough to let the aroma fill the room, "is what's going to land me my new client."

Not just a client, she thought giddily. It was for a local Internet company, and if she got the account it would mean catering all of their events, including their weekly board meetings.

"There are four different choices." Two of which she had already discounted but brought anyway, just to see what Marc thought. It had been their routine over the past few days. He would work in his office, she would cook in her apartment, and then, every few hours as she perfected a new dish, she would bring it and a few other choices over and have him do a blind tasting. She had come to love the last part of the process. "There's enough for everyone."

When none of them moved, except to get a better whiff, she shifted the tray higher on her palm and skirted around the desk, greeting each brother by name and only stopping when she was right in front of the DeLuca who mattered most. She couldn't fool them by flirting or doing girlfriend-like things, but maybe she could distract them with her cooking.

She looked up at Marc and smiled. "You hungry?"

He conducted a slow, sensual inventory of her body, and even though she was wearing her old apron and cutoff shorts, by the time he got back to her face she felt completely stripped. God, he was hot. Especially when he leaned in and whispered, "Starved."

Needing something to keep her mind off the heat climbing through her body, she set the covered tray on the desk and eyed the brothers, all gentlemen, and all still standing. "Sit. Please."

Marc took his seat and gestured to his brothers with a grin. "Go ahead, she won't let us eat until we're all sitting."

All three brothers dropped to their chairs, eyes riveted on the tray. Lexi smiled. Big, bad Italians were just like every other man on the planet, suckers for a good meal.

Positioning herself so that Marc couldn't see inside the tray, she carefully removed the cover and slid the first two plates across the desk and stopped. Normally, had they been alone, she would have forked off a bite and, only after Marc promised to keep his eyes closed, fed it to him. He would moan and groan over the dish while she told him what he was eating. But with his brothers here, she set out the other two plates and placed them closest to Marc so he would be sure to try the best ones. Finally, she put a fork on each plate and took a step back.

Gabe took one look at the dishes and, with a few choice words and a grunt, dropped his head to his hands. All three brothers laughed.

Lexi didn't laugh. In fact, she felt awkward and self-conscious. What was she thinking serving lasagna to a group of men who'd grown up eating ChiChi's cooking? The comparison wouldn't be flattering, Lexi thought, trying to figure out the best way to excuse herself.

A reassuring hand came to rest at the small of her back. "Gabe can't eat dairy," Marc said, his eyes warm and encouraging.

"Oh. Are you allergic?"

"No, his wife is pregnant," Trey said, and they laughed again.

"At least no more Rocky Road for breakfast?" Nate offered.

"Regan claims it's divine invention, therefore doesn't count," Gabe mumbled.

"More for the rest of us," Nate said, digging into the traditional five-cheese lasagna and closing his eyes. "Oh man, this is incredible."

Lexi felt herself beam. It wasn't even her best one.

"Aw, Gabe. This is better than Nonna's," Trey said, polishing off her vegetarian lasagna roll, but not before darting a quick glance at the hallway and whispering, "She isn't here, is she?"

"No, but one more moan and I might just tell her," Gabe threatened, staring longingly at his brothers eating. Well, two of his brothers. Marc hadn't tried anything, and Lexi didn't know why.

"I could go make you one without cheese. I have some tofu in the fridge," she offered.

"He has a wife. She can make him one if he wants." Marc grabbed the cover and put it over the two closest dishes, right as Trey was about to fork off a bite.

"Hey," Trey complained.

"You have a plane to catch and a client to appease," Marc said, then turned to Nate, "and you have judges to contact."

"What about Brock?" Nate asked, his eyes flickering quickly to Lexi and back to Marc.

"I'll deal with Brock. You make sure everyone else is there on Saturday."

Gabe, who had been silently watching everything unfold, stood and smacked the paper across his palm with a big smile, which was purposefully directed at Marc. "Right now a missing judge is the last of your worries, bro. But good luck with that." He looked at Lexi, who immediately stopped fidgeting with her apron, and his smile grew larger. "Nice seeing you again."

There was so much eye-darting and implied-but-unspoken communication going on that Lexi finally felt like laughing. Men and their code. It was obvious that they weren't done talking and that whatever was so important wasn't meant for her ears. But before she could make her exit, Marc had the guys out the door and he hadn't even left his chair.

"Now," he said, taking off the lid and, resting his arms behind his head, leaning back in the chair. His long legs were stretched out, his body relaxed, and his eyes were twinkling—up at her. "Which one first?"

She walked over to his desk and sat on the edge. "I'm sorry you lost Brock. What happened?"

"Food first, questions later." With a wink he dropped open his mouth as though he expected her to feed him.

"You have two hands—use them."

"All right."

Before she could blink, he had straightened and rolled his chair so close that he had to part his legs so that they could slide around hers. Close enough that she could feel the heat from his body seep into her every pore, even though they weren't quite touching.

He put his hands on her waist and gently lifted her so she was sitting on the edge of his desk. Her breath caught as one palm slid down the back of her thighs to rest on her knee, while the other wrapped around her.

She wanted him to pull her onto his lap and finish their lesson from the other night. They had rounded first, but were interrupted before they could slide into second—and as he leaned forward, his chest pressing her thighs farther apart, she decided she might even be open to a grand slam.

"What are you doing?" she whispered, her eyes glued to his lips.

"Using my hands," he whispered back, but instead of taking her into his arms and making love to her right there on the desk, he leaned back in his chair, plate in his hand.

He took a bite and closed his eyes, but not before she saw a look of triumph. The only thing that stopped her from smacking him was that he was finally tasting her food. He slid the fork out of his mouth and, eyes still closed, said, "Tell me about this."

"The client wanted a classic meat lasagna."

He opened his eyes. "But you didn't give them that." He took another bite.

She shook her head, biting her lip to keep from smiling. "Lasagna is heavy for a luncheon, so it's *my* take on the classic meat lasagna. I sautéed the spinach in garlic and made the pasta from scratch. Oh, and I use lemon-infused ricotta."

"Homemade ricotta?"

"Of course. I replaced some of the meat with locally grown porcinis, making them the star of the dish."

"Nice. It is hearty without being heavy."

"That was the goal."

"Then goal beautifully accomplished. Next."

She leaned back and grabbed the other plate. This was the one that she really loved, but she was afraid it was too out of the box. It was shredded skirt-steak lasagna rolls in a tart peach sauce. "Question first."

Marc reached for the dish. "It's getting cold."

She batted his hand aside. "Then you better answer fast. Did you lose your celebrity judge?"

Marc sat back and sighed. "Yeah, Bo Brock pulled out this morning. Not that I blame the guy. The whole Showdown is kind of a mess."

"You call this a mess? You are doing an incredible job. You have more entries than any year to date, national press covering the event, and more than half of the tables are already sold out." Was Marc blushing? "I say losing Brock is a good thing. It will give you a chance to highlight a local celebrity, someone who is a part of the reason we are celebrating."

"Local celebrity, huh? Like Coppola or Robert Redford?"

"No. I mean, they would be exciting, but they moved here after they got famous. When we were kids, it was always someone who grew up here and was noted for doing something unique. A local-grown celebrity."

"Smart and beautiful. Impressive."

She didn't know how to respond to that, so she asked, "Were you guys talking about me before I came in?"

For a second Marc was silent. Then he gave her his signature smile. It was slow and sexy and made her heart pick up a little. "You mean were my nosy brothers asking about me being your boyfriend?"

"Fake boyfriend," she reminded him. Or maybe it was herself she needed to remind. Being anything more than friends would be foolish on her part. But she never knew foolish could feel so fun.

"Whatever. And yes, they asked. And no, I didn't tell them anything, because it wasn't their damn business." He reached out and picked up one of the lasagna rolls off the plate, making a big to-do about studying it and smelling it until she was laughing. Then he popped it in his mouth.

"This is the one," he mumbled around bits of meat and noodle.

"How do you know? You didn't even try the other ones." Not that there was any left. His brothers had practically licked the plates clean.

"You didn't want me to try the other ones. They were distractions."

"They were not." He raised a brow. "Okay, they were. But how do you know this is the one?"

"I just do." He took a single finger and dragged it through the peach sauce. "But to be honest with you, cream puff, I can think of one thing that would make it perfect."

"What?"

"This." He painted a line of sauce across the top of her thigh, then bent and licked off every last drop.

CHAPTER 12

"I don't know what you're looking for, but I'm hoping it's on the bottom shelf."

Startled, Lexi straightened so fast she nearly fell over. Smoothing her hands down the back of her dress to make sure it wasn't revealing anything important, she looked up to find Marc, wine bottle and paper bag in hand, leaning against the door of her grandmother's walk-in pantry. As always, he looked delicious in a pair of low-hung jeans and a dark-blue shirt, which pulled nicely across his chest. And, as always, her body turned to filling at the sight of him.

Wingman sat at his feet.

"Hey, boy. I've got a leftover bone for you."

Wingman stayed where he was. No tail wagging. No big, wet doggie kiss. Just a stoic stare.

"I was looking for my grandmother's special paprika," she said, giving another pat to her thigh. Nothing. "Did you see the new kitchen? Tanner's almost done. He said just another few days."

"Yup. Saw *it* and *him* earlier. He told me that you had a dinner date with Vince Jones."

Wingman let out a snort. Maybe it was a huff. Lexi couldn't tell.

"It wasn't a date, it was just dinner. He was my new cli—wait. Are you jealous?"

He tugged at the brim of his well-worn ball cap. Lexi had always had a thing for guys in hats. And this guy in that hat was a dangerous pairing for women everywhere.

"Hell yeah, I am. My fake girlfriend went out to dinner with some guy who wants to get in her pants, and I had to hear it from her half-naked contractor," he said as he pushed off the door and walked into the pantry, stopping so close that she had to rest a hand on his shoulder so she could crane her neck up and look in his eyes.

She wasn't sure if she should be flattered or scared, because the idea of him being jealous made everything seem suddenly real.

"You talked to Hard-Hammer Tanner? About me?"

"I was explaining my celebrity judge problem, and he happened to mention your dinner date."

"Dinner *tasting*. With Vince and two of his female associates to pitch Sweet and Savory Catering as their official go-to caterer for all their corporate functions. And I got the job."

"I heard." He held up the bottle.

Now Lexi wasn't sure if he was ticked about her meeting with Vince or that Hard-Hammer Tanner knew about her meeting before he did. Or if he was pissed about being jealous, an emotion that guys like Marc would see as being in direct violation of their man card.

"Did you hear that they've been trying to get on Pricilla's delivery schedule for over a year with no luck? So when I mentioned that Pricilla will be providing all of the desserts for my events, they asked if I could cater their team meeting every morning."

"Tanner failed to mention that. Congratulations." He gave her one of his rare smiles that didn't activate the dimple or come from charm. It was genuine and boyish and damn, he was hard to resist when he was being sweet. "Jerk-off also failed to mention that your dinner tonight was with the same guy you were pitching to."

Wow. Marc DeLuca, Mr. Unaffected and Unattached, was really jealous. "I didn't eat dinner, I served it. Which is why I was looking for the paprika so that I could make my famous paprikash."

"Ah, cream puff." Charming playboy back in place, he pulled her into a big hug, the cold champagne bottle dangling low enough to chill the back of her right thigh. "Are you cooking our first makeup dinner?"

She was about to say no, or shove the cold bottle down the front of his pants, when Wingman barked and took off running—away from her and through the kitchen. His leash, which Lexi saw had been looped around the door handle, pulled taut and—

"Wingman, no! Come back," Lexi hollered, making an attempt to grab the handle, right as the pantry door slammed shut.

"Crap. Crap. Crap," she muttered, closing her eyes and taking in a deep breath.

"He'll be okay, probably went to see about that bone," Marc joked.

"This isn't funny. The pantry door is broken," Lexi said, looking at the window and then down at her hips, wondering if she could shimmy out without getting stuck. Then she added up all the éclairs she'd eaten since she'd arrived back home. *Nope.* "Tanner was replacing the handle and the inside fixture broke, meaning it can only be opened from the outside, which is why I had the door propped open by the can of tomatoes."

"So you're saying we're—"

"Locked in. As in stuck in here forever, so why are you smiling?" Even though she knew it was hopeless—she had been stuck in there earlier that afternoon—she walked toward the door.

Marc intercepted her and steered her back toward the window. "I'm smiling because you're cute when you're riled. Now relax, we're only stuck in here until tomorrow, when Pricilla comes to open the bakery."

"Easy for you to say. I haven't eaten since noon. I spent all day prepping for my meeting with Vince, so I'm behind on my dish for tomorrow night and—" She paused "Wait! Give me your cell. I can call my grandma or Abby."

He shrugged. "Sorry. I must have left it on the counter outside."

"But you brought in the wine?"

"Champagne." He turned the bottle so she could see the label. It wasn't the cheap kind. Then again, nothing Marc ever did was cheap. "And I figured this would be more likely to get me invited to dinner than a phone."

"This isn't funny, Marc." She smacked his chest, trying to not smile back. Marc's charm was potent enough to break through her suddenly bad mood. "Saturday is important."

"I know it is." He stepped closer and wrapped his arms around her. And God, he felt good. Warm, strong, and totally safe. Marc had a way of making her feel like she was the most precious thing in his world. It took everything she had not to nuzzle closer and get lost in him.

"But it's also not the end of the world. So to address your concerns. First, we are in a pantry surrounded by food."

"Ingredients."

"I have champagne in case we get thirsty." He pulled back enough so that he could meet her eyes. "And I think this is just what you need. A little time away from the kitchen to really celebrate landing your first client before you drive yourself insane trying to perfect an already perfected dish for your soon-to-be second client."

She rolled her eyes. "My hopefully soon-to-be second client. Natasha's a talented chef. I won't underestimate her again."

"Who cooks from the wrong place." Marc tightened his arms just enough to bring all of his yummy parts in contact with all of hers. "You put Lexi on a plate and there is no way those judges won't choose you."

When he said it like that, confident and sincere, as though his belief in her was unwavering, Lexi's heart rolled over.

All that flirting and swagger was a front. Beneath the easygoing façade was a man who craved connection. Lexi could recognize it anywhere. It was like looking in the mirror.

Marc was lonely. He was starved for that intimate bond that only comes from committing wholly to another person, but he was terrified of giving a part of himself away. And that, more than anything, called out to her.

Lexi tightened her arms and gave in to the moment, burying her face in his chest. "Thank you," was all she said, but something between them shifted. His body relaxed, molding around hers, and as he rested his cheek on the top of her head, she knew that somehow her feelings in this fauxmance had become 100 percent real.

Marc cleared his throat and, his charm firmly back in place, took a step back. "Grab that tablecloth and lay it down. We can do this picnic style."

Lexi took in the small quarters, the locked door, the champagne, the sexy bachelor in jeans and a ball cap, and laughed. "Why does this suddenly feel like one of those 'whoops, baby, my truck ran out of gas' moments?"

He neither confirmed nor denied, only popped the cork.

"Come on," Lexi said, reaching for the tablecloth to spread it across the concrete floor. "A guy like you has to have used that trick once or twice."

"Nope."

"Not even back in high school?"

"Never needed to." Marc lounged on the tablecloth, his back against the wall, long legs stretched out in front and crossed at the ankle. He held up the bottle. "To you, for getting your first of many clients."

"You planned this?"

"Getting locked in the pantry? No. Seducing you with expensive champagne and my good looks? Yes."

"Why?" She should have known something was off when she saw the bubbly.

"Because you've had a long few weeks and a big day tomorrow, and it's my job, as your boyfriend, to pamper you." He blinked, as though shocked at what he'd said.

"We're in a pantry."

Lexi liked this new Marc, the one who seemed unsure and a little off balance.

"With champagne. Now drink up. Quickly."

She rolled her eyes. "Trying to get me drunk, huh?"

He took a long swig. "I'm just trying to empty the bottle."

"Why?"

"Can't spin it when it's still full. Now"—he patted the empty spot next to him and spread open a bag of, sweet Jesus, éclairs—"tell me about your day so we can get to the celebrating part."

"I think that is deserving of a bite of my éclair," Lexi said, smiling up at him with those big green eyes and holding out the end of the pastry.

Problem was, Marc wasn't in the mood for an éclair. He wanted to sink his teeth into a cream puff. The one sitting so close he could smell her shampoo, her skin, the sweet and spicy fragrance that was uniquely Lexi.

"You go ahead," he said. "You need all the food you can get, since you're already drunk."

"I'm not drunk, just a little tipsy." She smiled, and holy shit, he was screwed.

Not only was she a few sips past tipsy, she was dressed in one of those soft, flirty dresses that made women feel feminine and made men think of sex—which made the ever-growing problem in his jeans even harder to hide. Her hair only made things worse. It was loose and shiny and tumbled over her shoulders, brushing his arm every time she got excited about a topic and felt the need to press into him, like she was doing now.

Marc reached out and grabbed the empty bottle to keep from running his fingers through her hair, which would lead to his hands all over her body, which would lead to sex. Right here in the pantry.

Over the last several weeks, it had become apparent that not only had Jeff been less than honest about his divorce from Lexi, he'd never treated her right to begin with. But no matter how big of a jerk his friend had been, no matter how badly he wanted Lexi, Marc wasn't *that* guy. He didn't take advantage, and he didn't poach. Ever.

But if she didn't stop touching him and looking at him like he was some kind of freaking hero, his good intentions might just lose out.

"So you have the celebrity-judge thing all figured out?"

"Pretty sure, but I'm waiting for the guy to sign on the dotted line before I say anything."

"Judge found *and* you organized a tasting committee to make sure that tomorrow night is fair. All in less than eight hours." She patted his arm, and a potent shot of lust ignited in his gut and dropped lower. "And people say you're just a pretty face."

"I still have a dog on the jury."

"Which you'll fix." She popped the piece of pastry in her mouth, her tongue peeking out to lick off every single finger. "People will be talking about this for years, Marc. You brought their beloved Showdown back to St. Helena."

He felt his neck warm. "It's just a wine tasting."

"No, it's not, and you know it. Not to this town and not to you." Lexi leaned back against the wall, her head thunking against the exposed brick as she stared at the ceiling. For a second they were both silent, then her head lolled toward his. "You did this for your parents, huh?"

Marc swallowed. He did not want to talk about his parents. Not here, in this small room, where the outside world didn't exist, where the past seemed tangled with the present and the woman in front of him felt so much like his future. "I thought we were going to play spin the bottle, not truth or dare."

"I never played that with anyone but Abby," she said, her sugary breath skating across his face.

He blinked. "You played spin the bottle with my sister?" Definitely not the image he wanted, but maybe, he thought as he took in just how close her lips were to his, the one he needed.

"No, I mean I played truth or dare with Abby. I've never played spin the bottle."

Marc wondered just how many other normal high school experiences Lexi had missed out on, dating Jeff all those years. He also wondered what kind of secrets she kept. Knowing that this might be his only chance to find out, he said, "All right, I'll play, but we go three rounds, and you're next. I get to ask any question I want, and you have to answer."

She considered his terms briefly and then offered him a sassy smile. "Agreed. But I might just choose dare."

Even better.

Marc took a deep breath and let it out slowly. "I wanted to host the Showdown at the Napa Grand to prove that I could and because it will grow my hotel twice as fast. But the real reason I did it was because I wanted to honor my parents. This year would have been forty years."

Lexi leaned over and gave his shoulder a little bump. "I remember one night when Abby and I were helping your mom in the kitchen, your dad came in the room to check on dinner and..." She swallowed and her eyes went soft, but she didn't look away. "I had never seen a man look at someone like that before. I mean, he just walked in the kitchen, saw your mom in a dirty apron with spaghetti sauce on her face, and it was magical, Marc, I could feel how much he loved her. My mom fell in love a million times when I was a kid, but never like that."

Which was why she'd lived in a million places, Marc thought sadly. New marriage, new daddy, new school—at least until she landed in St. Helena. It must have been lonely.

"Pricilla always talks about her great love with my grandpa. But I never knew that kind of love really existed until I met your parents."

"Yeah," Marc whispered. His parents had had more ability to love than anyone he'd ever met. Not just their kids, but each other and life. Growing up, watching that kind of connection between two people was a blessing and a curse. There was no way Marc was willing to settle for anything less than what his parents had shared, but after losing them in high school, he wasn't sure if he had the balls to put himself out there. When you are that connected to someone and they go away—Marc didn't think he could survive that again. "Did you have that with Jeff?"

Figured he was already raw and exposed, might as well go for bust. But the second he asked the question, he regretted it. Lexi's face paled, and he watched her throat work hard to keep control.

"No," she whispered, worrying her lower lip. "I thought I had, wanted so badly for it to be real, but in the end…" She shook her head. "No. And since I don't remember you asking truth or dare, that is all you get."

"Fair enough." He moved so that their shoulders were barely touching. The contact was gentle, but the connection was palpable. "Truth or dare?"

"God, if that was a freebie, I'm almost scared to say truth," she admitted, but at least she was smiling again.

"Sugar, if truth scared you, dare will have you begging for mercy."

"We'll start with truth. But make no mistake, you don't scare me, pretty boy."

"All right. Why didn't you ever have kids?" That wasn't what he meant to ask, and he didn't even know why he did. It was just that she and Abby had gone on and on as teenagers about their weddings and babies; they'd even named them. Yet she and Jeff were married for nearly a decade and no kids.

"Um, I, we—" She might not have been begging for mercy, but he was pretty damn certain she was about to cry.

"You don't have to answer that. It's none of my business, and I'm sorry."

"No, it's okay. That's part of the game, right? You have to put yourself out there and risk being embarrassed." She shrugged as though it was no big deal, but for the first time all night she couldn't meet his eyes. "I wanted kids, but Jeffery wanted to be financially stable. Actually, you know what? I'm not going to put this all on him." She turned and looked him straight in the eye. "I wanted kids desperately, maybe too much, but he saw that there was something missing in our marriage and held off. It hurt at the time, but in the end he was the wise one."

Wise wasn't a word Marc would have ever used to describe his friend, even back when he'd still considered Jeff a stand-up guy.

"How about you? Do you want kids?"

"I assume that this is your official question. And yes." He smiled over at her. "I was going to choose truth." He leaned his head against the wall. "Part of me wants an army, the other part is terrified that I'd somehow screw it up and lose everything. Plus I have to have a, what did you call it, oh yeah, a serious relationship first," he joked, and before she could respond to his response, threw it back at her. "Truth or dare?"

She raised a brow, calling him on his avoidance, but let him have it. "Truth."

He could've asked more about Jeff, but now the guy whom Marc had always admired and envied no longer felt so impressive. In fact, he no longer even factored into this equation.

Lexi had missed out on a lot growing up, and Marc wanted to lighten the moment, give her a taste of what high school was like when you weren't tethered to a douche.

"What is your most embarrassing secret?"

"Oh God." Her hands flew to her face. "I can't lie." She peeked at him through her fingers, pure horror latching itself onto her every expression. "Can I?"

"Sugar, I won't know if you lie."

"But I would."

I know, he thought. And that, right there, was why Marc was screwed when it came to Lexi. She was loyal and genuine and honest to a fault.

"Okay, you have to turn around, though."

"What?"

She dropped her hands, her expression dead serious. "You have to turn around or at least close your eyes because I can't say this with you looking at me."

"This had better be good."

"Oh, it will have you begging for mercy," she murmured, her face the color of a good merlot.

He closed his eyes but made a big deal about it. He felt her hand fly past his face a few times, and it took everything he had not to smile or peek. He grabbed her hand midfly. "Get on with it before your buzz wears off and you chicken out."

"I won't chicken out, and I'm not buzzed."

He opened one eye.

"Okay, maybe just a little buzzed." He closed it. "Remember how senior year you took Kimberly Baudouin to homecoming? And she wore that dress with the slit up to her thong line? And remember how Jeffery and I had a big fight because I danced one slow dance with Martin Liscouski, who I only danced with because we were friends and because his date was making out with some guy from another school?"

"Yeah." Marc was starting to lose hope that this was going to be juicy. "Homecoming. Thong. Liscouski. Got it. Now get to the good stuff."

"Well, after homecoming, we all went to your house because Gabe was gone on some trip." And his parents had passed away the year before, which meant his house was the designated after-party. "Jeffery was mad about the dance and then because I didn't want to sleep with him. So he called me a tease in front of Natasha and Isabel Stark and their whole group."

Marc opened his eyes. He couldn't help it. First, because what kind of guy does that, and second, because that had been during their senior year. "You and Jeff hadn't—"

She shook her head. "Not until a few weeks later." *Which is why the prick said it,* he thought angrily. Being called a cock tease in high school was even worse than being crowned a good-time girl by Isabel and her clique.

Marc tucked her hair behind her ear. "I'm sorry he did that. I didn't know."

She shrugged, then made a little twirly gesture with her pointer finger. "Now turn around. You obviously can't be trusted not to peek."

He did. And the whole time he sat cross-legged on the floor, staring at the shelves and listening to her shuffle around behind him, he wondered if that wasn't her most embarrassing high school secret, then maybe he didn't want to know what was.

"I was upset and didn't want everyone to see me cry, so I went to find Abby, but she was making out with Chad."

"Chad Spencer?" He was going to kick that guy's ass.

"I know, gross, right? She was heartbroken over some other guy; it was nothing. Anyway, I heard someone coming up the stairs, so I ducked in your room."

The idea of her in his room made him hard. "Did you lie on my bed?"

"Only one question, remember?" She gave him a reprimanding smack on the back of his head. "But yes, I did, until you came in with Kimberly. Then I ducked in the closet. Oh God, this is the embarrassing part. Don't you dare turn around!"

He couldn't move, much less turn around. He remembered that night. Knew exactly what she was going to say, and damn if his pants didn't get that much more uncomfortable.

"So you and Kimberly started making out and"—he heard her swallow, and when she continued her voice was low and raspy—"I watched. The whole time. From your closet."

The silence stretched so thick it took everything Marc had not to turn around and see if she was flushed. Because he was so turned on he was about to burst. Which was why he asked, "Did you like it?"

She was quiet for so long he was afraid she wouldn't answer. Then he heard a slight rustling and a warm, gentle hand settled on his shoulder. He could feel her brush up against his back, which made all sorts of stupid things happen to his front.

"I'll answer, but this will be your last question. I'll still have two left, and I get to choose the last one for you. Deal?"

Truth or dare had never been this much of a turn-on when he was a kid. If it had been, he would have spent all of high school playing it instead of drinking with his buddies. Giving control over to her raised the stakes, taking it from a turn-on to erotic as hell, and they weren't even naked. "Deal."

"Yes. I couldn't look away. Now it's my turn," she whispered, her breath teasing his ear. "Truth or dare."

"Truth," he said, because he wanted her to ask him about that night.

"That first time you took me to the Napa Grand, when we broke in that day, you leaned in to kiss me, and then stopped. Why?"

"Because the day before, Jeff told me that he was going to ask you out." Marc had been considering the same thing, but his friend seemed so spun over Lexi he backed off. And had regretted it ever since. "And I didn't kiss you on graduation night and every other time I saw you because he was my friend. And no matter how many times you broke up, you always got back together. And no matter what happened, no matter how much I wanted you, you'd always be my best friend's girl."

"Oh." He heard her swallow. "Okay, since I know how you love risks, you are going bold on the last one. You choose dare."

"I do?" he groaned.

"Oh, you do." Her hands cupped his shoulders and slid forward until her fingers interlaced at his collarbone and her breasts were pressed against his back. "I dare you to finish what you started the other night at the town hall."

"Lexi," he groaned, closing his eyes.

"You promised me a lesson in kissing that was supposed to take me to second base, but I distinctly remember being interrupted before we rounded first."

He rested his hands on top of hers. Denying her this was going to be the hardest thing he ever had to do, but he knew if he touched her he wouldn't be able to stop. Ridiculous as it might sound, kissing her in front of everyone didn't seem like the betrayal that kissing her like this would be. He didn't want to be that guy.

"Lexi, we can't."

She scooted around until she was kneeling in front of him, her legs tucked up under her dress and her face inches from his. "It's a dare. You have to."

"I'm not going to betray a lifelong friendship on a dare."

He saw the hurt flash in her eyes. "You already kissed me."

"I know." That was the problem. When he was with her, everything felt so right. But being with her challenged everything he'd based his relationships on. All because when he was fourteen, his buddy had called shotgun first. How fucked up was that?

She pressed a finger to his lips. "Jeffery is your best friend. He was my first love. We dated, married, and he left me for another woman. This wouldn't be a betrayal. I'm ready to move on. And I have a divorce decree and a pair of red silk panties that trumps man law."

"Does the bra match?" he asked, feeling a boyish grin kicking up the side of his lips, as though her answer could change his entire world.

"Yes. But I agree kissing because of a dare is stupid. If you kiss me, kiss me because you want to."

"Oh, I want—" He leaned forward and pressed his lips against hers. Because if he didn't, he would tell Lexi that it wasn't the betrayal of Jeff he was worried about. It was the thought of betraying her.

The kiss started out gentle, sweet. It was the kind of kiss he'd imagined giving to her when they were teenagers. The kind of kiss that a woman like Lexi deserved. Slow and thorough, with enough heat to let her feel how special she was, how much he wanted her—how much he'd always wanted her.

He pulled back slightly and trailed kisses across her cheek to her ear, lingering for a moment and paying special attention to the little soft spot behind it, loving how her breath caught and she arched her back slightly. Brushing his mouth over her earlobe, he gave a sharp little bite to its curve before making his way back to her mouth. And Christ, that mouth of hers was addictive.

"Only second base, Lexi," he said, more for himself than her. If he ventured past simple touching, they would wind up having sex. All damn night. On the cold pantry floor.

"Okay," she breathed, but when she looked up at him through her lashes, her eyes dazed with hunger, Marc knew this was a bad move.

To prove it, he kissed her again. Only this time he didn't take it slow. He couldn't. He was too busy reaching for the zipper on her dress, her hands were busy clawing at his chest, and before he knew what was happening, she was straddling him. Her zipper was stuck, his shirt was on the floor, and they were about to get busy. Down and dirty.

She tilted her head to the side and the kiss deepened, taking the moment from high school necking to unadulterated foreplay. Her hands sank into his hair, his sank into her ass, and he molded his palms around the perfect globes and pulled her tightly against his erection.

She purred into his mouth and slid her tongue against his in a way that asked for a whole hell of a lot more than second base. Wrapping her legs securely around his waist, their bare skin heating at the contact, she squeezed, rolling her hips forward to bring all of her good parts in seriously hard contact with his. As if her grinding against his body wasn't temptation enough, Lexi had to go and arch her back, thrusting those perfect tens of hers right in range, with their nipples jutting prettily under the soft cotton of her dress.

"Damn," he whispered, his eyes riveted to her breasts. He ran his hands up her sides, rib by rib, his heart slamming against his chest with every inch gained, until he stopped just below what he'd been fantasizing about for fifteen years. And holy hell, he wanted to see her naked.

When Marc had discovered boobs, he'd had one goal: to touch as many as possible. But once he'd seen Lexi in that little white bikini she used to prance around in during summer break, all he'd cared about was touching hers. They had become an obsession.

Apparently an obsession he'd never outgrown.

His breathing nonexistent, he teased his thumbs higher up the dress, over the hard nipples, and he damn near embarrassed himself. God, he was acting like he'd never been with a woman before. His hands were shaking, his forehead was sweaty, and he was so hard that one more of her cute little hip rolls and he'd go off like a cannon.

"Just second base," he repeated, running his fingertip along the edge of her dress, tracing the gentle swell of her cleavage, savoring how soft she felt.

She moved restlessly against him, rocking her hips and letting out a little moan at the contact. She was hot and ready. He could feel her body coiling tighter by the second.

"Just a minute. I just need a minute," he whispered.

She said nothing, just moved closer, pushing her breasts into his palms. He felt her nipples scrape against his flesh and changed his mind. Touching them wasn't going to be enough. He had to taste her.

"Just a little taste," he mumbled to himself.

Gripping her waist, he dipped his head. Starting at the hollow of her throat, he worked his way down, pressing openmouthed kisses against her heated skin, over the trim of her dress, and pulling her into his mouth and sucking her though the cotton.

"You said second base," she reminded him.

"This is second." He pulled her breast deeper into his mouth.

"Second involves hands," she whispered, resting her palms on his knees and dropping her head back. The movement caused her hair to spill over her shoulder and onto his arm that supported her lower back.

"You're right. Hands."

His mouth never let up as he lowered his palm to her knee, slowly working the hem of her dress up her smooth legs, over her thigh and under her panties so he could cup her bare ass. And what an ass it was. Soft and firm and a perfect handful.

She gave a low, sexy gasp. "What are you doing?"

"Using my hands." His fingers worked their way around the front. He slid a single finger up the center of her silk panties. He made another pass, this time using his entire hand. "Just a little. Okay?"

She nodded, relaxing her legs to give him more room and whispering, "Just a little," before pressing down on his hand.

He wanted to explore, take his time. If second base with an attempt at stealing third was all he was going to allow himself, then he wanted this to last. His hand went under the panties, and Marc followed the curve of her amazing ass down and around, then slipped in from behind.

She moaned something that sounded like "Oh God, yes," with her eyes wide and so full of want that his whole body went into overdrive. "Just a little," she repeated. "Right"— she rose up and then sank back down, impaling herself on his hand—"there."

"You are so wet, sugar."

"I have been ever since I saw you watching me from your office," she admitted.

He wondered exactly which time she was referring to.

"Then it seems I have been slacking on my boyfriend duties." He slowly withdrew his finger, sliding two in its place. "I say we fix that, immediately."

She gasped. "Fake boyfriend duties."

"Oh no, sugar." He stroked ever so slowly, bringing her as close to the edge as he could get without going over. "We do this and there won't be faking of any kind."

He waited until she nodded, then picked up the pace, applying more friction and gently building the pressure. He wanted her to enjoy this, to make it last. But she wasn't making it easy. Her mouth was on his, hungry and raw, as her body vibrated with need. She was so primed all he had to do was curl his fingers, just like so and—

"Oh God," she moaned, wrapping her arms around him and burying her face in the curve of his neck. She held on tight as her whole body shook with release.

Breathing heavily, they sat there, on the pantry floor, clutching onto one another as she rode out her orgasm.

When was the last time he'd made a woman come and she'd still been fully clothed? He realized, with a grin, that this was his first. Alexis Moreau was his first.

Not that he hadn't wished he'd at least pulled the straps of her dress down so he could see that red bra she was bragging about. In fact, being with Lexi like this, and knowing that he wasn't going to get his and that he was *still* smiling like a fool, should have made him run. But honestly, right now, there was nowhere else his feet wanted to take him. And that was okay.

CHAPTER 13

Sweet baby Jesus, Lexi thought when she looked through the peephole. Marc was hot.

Still staring her fill, and reminding herself that drooling was not her best look, she smoothed down her dress—her Neiman dress that made her butt look a size smaller and her boobs two sizes bigger. It was a silky green and matched her eyes, had cost Jeffery a pretty penny, and she had been dying to wear it since she came back to town. It was her charge-it-to-my-husband's-account, Alexis-Moreau-is-back, you're-going-to-get-lucky-tonight dress. She'd bought it to impress the town, but tonight she only hoped to wow the bad boy next door.

The boy next door, who happened to be leaning against her porch rail, arms crossed, badass smile in place. Then there was the way his too-tempting pair of low-hung button-fly jeans hugged his thighs and how those dark eyes of his seemed to be staring right at her, which was impossible, since the door was closed.

"I know I'm pretty damn sexy, but could you speed up the gawking? Although flattering, it's hot out here," Marc said, smiling.

Lexi jumped back, her hand over her mouth. There was no way he could see her. First because the hole was tiny, and second, that would be way too embarrassing.

Cautious not to make a sound, she looked through the hole again. Maybe he was just making a lucky guess.

His smile widened, and he gave her a wink. "I can see you through the peephole, cream puff."

Taking three steps back, she turned toward the stairs and yelled, "Coming," hoping that it would sound like she was upstairs. "Just getting my—" She looked down. She was fully dressed, so she slipped off a heel. "Shoes. Just getting my shoes."

Stomping on the lower stairs a few times, each louder than the next, she opened the door and made a big deal of hopping on one foot while she slid on her shoe—for the second time that night. Securely in place, she looked up and smiled. Problem was, Marc was smiling back. Correction, smirking. Marc was smirking back.

"What?" she challenged. There was no way that he could prove she had been *gawking*.

"I watched you put your shoes on twenty minutes ago."

She didn't know why, but his admission made her stomach flutter. Still, she wasn't about to admit that *she* had been watching *him*.

"I changed them." Her voice went higher with each lie she uttered.

Marc dropped his gaze to her feet. "If you say so."

"What's that?" she asked, pointing to the paper bag in his hand and hoping he'd drop the subject.

"For you." He held it up, a shy smile tugging at his lips.

Oh boy, Marc was nervous—and blushing. Not good. In fact, the knowledge made breathing difficult. It also made her palms sweat.

When she didn't take it right away and his hands started fidgeting with the paper bag, the awkwardness level increased until Lexi considered shutting the door and calling off the date. Her being nervous was one thing. Him being nervous was a sign that they should put a stop to the whole situation, because it told her that tonight's date meant something to him. Which made it okay for her to admit what she'd known all day: this date also meant something to her—a big something.

"Open it," he forced out, handing her the bag.

Lexi took the bag and did as he asked, peeking inside. At the bottom sat a parcel wrapped in butcher paper. "What's this?"

Marc shoved his hands in his pockets. "Um, boar loin."

Lexi smiled. Not flowers. Not chocolates. But boar. Wild boar.

"I don't know what to say."

Actually, she did. But admitting that raw meat was the most thoughtful gift anyone had ever given her made her love life sound pathetic. Or maybe—she thought back to Mrs. DeLuca and her spaghetti-splattered apron—this was real romance.

"Mr. Craver mentioned that back in the day they served wild boar at the Showdown," he said, shifting his weight. "But that over the years it had been modernized to pork chops."

"Is that what you were asking him about at the farmers' market?"

"I ordered it that day. If you like it, he can order as much as you need."

Lexi had spent the better part of the afternoon trying to figure out what her rolled pork loin was missing. Boar would give it a gamy quality that would set her dish apart while still remaining true to the spirit of the event.

Clutching the boar to her chest, Lexi wrapped her free arm around Marc's neck and pulled him down to meet her mouth. "Thank you," she mumbled against his lips before delivering a series of soft, lingering kisses.

Breathless, Lexi pulled back, but Marc's arms were around her waist, holding her to him, the boar trapped between their bodies.

"You're welcome," he whispered right before his mouth claimed hers. It was gentle, but the heat lingered long after he'd ended the kiss.

"You'd better put that in the fridge so we can go." His palms slid down her back, over the curve of her bottom, where they lingered for a long get-to-know-you moment before making their way back up to gently cup her face. "One more minute alone and we'll end up naked. Here. In the hallway."

The drive over to his family's house was silent and so full of sexual heat it was impossible to talk. So when Marc pulled up in the driveway and put the truck in park, his fingers gripping the wheel so tightly she was afraid he'd break either the steering column or his hand, she wondered if maybe they should have had a quickie before coming over. Every cell in her body hummed to the point of frustration, and one look at the tent in his pants said he was just as bad.

"Marc—"

"I'm sorry," he said, turning to face her.

"Don't be. I mean, we couldn't be late for dinner."

"I wasn't talking about that, but obviously it's been on your mind," he said, his lips curling up into a smile that had her girly parts giving a standing O. "We still have a few minutes."

"We're parked in front of your family's house," she whispered.

"No one's out there. I promise." He unbuckled his seat belt and started to reach for her.

"Says the man who knew the pantry door was fixed." She batted his hands away.

He dodged her attempt and unbuckled her belt to pull her on his lap. He felt good. Too good. "You weren't complaining last night."

No, she hadn't. Not even when Marc, after staying true to his word of not sliding home, had turned the knob and then nonchalantly pushed open the pantry door. It seemed when he dropped by to talk with Tanner, the contractor had been installing a new lock.

"Yeah, well, our grandmothers could be looking out the window."

"Then we better steam ours up real fast."

He dropped his lips to hers, but she shoved her hand in between their mouths. Undeterred, he moved to her neck instead.

"It's not going to happen, Marc," she said, tilting her head to the side so he could get behind her ear to that sweet spot he was so good at teasing. "So going on will only make it harder on both of us."

Did she just moan or was that him?

"Tell me about it," he mumbled against her neck. His hand, which was halfway up her dress, tightened, pulling her firmly against his erection.

"Tell me what you were apologizing for."

With a sigh, Marc's lips stopped. He gave her one final nip on the lobe and then pulled back. "I'm apologizing for my family."

"Your family? What did they say?"

"Nothing yet. But they will. They're Italian," he said by way of explanation. Lexi struggled to hide her grin. She didn't do a very good job, because he added, "Laugh now, but you'll see. They're loud and opinionated and can't help but shove their noses in everyone else's business."

She gave his cheek a quick pat because he looked so serious. "I've met your family, Marc. Spent most of my high school years having sleepovers with Abby."

"Yeah, well, this is different. You aren't having a sleepover with Abby. You're having one with me."

If he hadn't sounded so frustrated, she would have pointed out that they were just having dinner. The sleepover part, although definitely on the table, hadn't been addressed. But then he ran a hand down his face and exhaled long and hard, and Lexi's breath caught, and not in a good way.

Was he regretting his decision to bring her?

"Look, if you don't want to do this, it's not a big deal." Although her heart was telling her the complete opposite. "I can just go home and—"

He kissed her silent. His lips were strong and insistent and telling her he wasn't going to stop until she agreed to let him finish. So she wrapped her arms around his neck and let him get in the last word.

"I want you," he breathed when he finally pulled back. "In my bed. My truck. The pantry. The kitchen." He gave her another quick kiss. "Especially wearing that apron of yours. Hell, I even wanted you at the damn dog park. I want you, Lexi. And I want you here, tonight, by my side at my nonna's table. Got it?"

She nodded.

"But I've never brought a girl home."

"Ever?"

"Ever." She let that sink in. He was trying to tell her something, something important, but Lexi was too afraid to listen. "My brothers are going to say shit, try to be funny and embarrass me. It's what we do."

Having brothers didn't seem all that fun. She remembered back in high school how the DeLuca boys had gotten into it with each other, laughing it off in the end. But she had always wondered if Marc, who was usually the focus, really found their games fun.

"I am afraid that they will embarrass you in the process. And I don't want you to feel uncomfortable."

And just like that her heart went mushy. For Marc freaking DeLuca.

Afraid she'd do something stupid, like cry or blurt out that she might be falling for him, Lexi gave him a quick peck on the lips and opened his door. She hopped out and offered him her hand. When he took it, they walked up to the front door.

Like she had told Marc, she had been to this house a thousand times over the years, but it never failed to steal her breath. Built in the late nineteenth century, the stone-faced Italian villa, with its ornate corbel-supported eaves and low-pitched roof, stood two stories tall with cornice towers identifying the entry of the house. Surrounded by massive oak trees and vines, it also sat in the middle of one of the most elaborate gardens in the Napa Valley—ChiChi's award-winning flower garden, to be exact.

"It's still not too late to go back to your place," Marc said when they got to the front door. The way his hand fit into the curve of her waist and his lips brushed hers, sending a yummy heat rushing throughout her body, made her want to take him up on the offer.

Then the front door flew open. And the only heat rushing was straight to her face.

Abby looked frazzled and slightly harassed. She also looked from Lexi to Marc and back to Lexi. Her eyes were wide, and sweat beaded her upper lip. Abby tended to sweat when she got mad. So Lexi took a step back, away from Abby and out of Marc's arms.

"You're here."

"Don't look so horrified," Lexi joked—kind of—and then, after studying the way Abby's left hand plucked at the hem of her shirt, practically strangling the silk, she realized that Abby wasn't mad, she was pissed.

Lexi smiled.

Abby didn't smile back. She didn't move, didn't open the door wider, didn't say, "Please come in." She just stood there, blocking the entry—sweating, her hands fisted in her shirt.

"I have to go to the bathroom," Abby announced as though it was the most natural greeting in the world. Then, to make an already awkward moment even more awkward, she grabbed Lexi by the elbow and pulled.

Marc grabbed her other elbow. "And you need her to do that?"

Abby looked behind her, uncharacteristically worrying her lower lip.

"You okay?" Lexi asked, feeling a wee bit guilty. Abby had called her a total of seven times today, every one sent to voice mail. The week was up, Abby would demand answers, and Lexi still didn't know how to explain her and Marc. It wasn't fake, but it couldn't be real, and she wasn't sure exactly where that left them.

"I'd like to bring my girlfriend inside, so would you mind moving?"

That he didn't even stumble on the word made Lexi smile.

"Yes. No. I mean, I need her." Loud male laughter erupted from somewhere in the house. "Now."

"Yeah, well, I need you to stop advertising your ex's goods, or lack thereof, until *after* the Showdown. Just like you can talk to Lexi *after* we've come inside and said hi to Nonna." Marc's hand tightened on Lexi's, telling her he wasn't letting her go. It felt nice. It also made her realize that she wanted Marc to escort her inside. She wanted to walk into this house holding hands and greet their families as a couple.

Abby eyed Marc. "Five minutes with her or I tell Nonna how you sold bootleg porn in high school to buy your truck. Is that really the way you want to introduce your *girlfriend*?"

Marc choked and let go.

Lexi looked at Marc and raised a brow. "Really?"

He shrugged. "It was a nice truck."

"But porn?"

"I'm an entrepreneur." Then he leaned in and his warm breath tickled her ear as he whispered, "Don't worry, cream puff. Even back then I was all about quality. I think I still have a few DVDs left if you want to check them out later."

Marc pulled back, and except for her nipples, which were standing up and cheering their support, Lexi didn't move. She thought of herself and Marc lying naked in bed, watching someone else naked in bed, and by the time she got to the part where she should have been turned off, her whole body was reaching DEFCON 1.

"I think my soul just died a little," Abby said, yanking Lexi by the arm.

She yanked her through the foyer, past three smiling grannies, a group of stunned DeLucas, one Hard-Hammer Tanner—minus tool belt and steel-toed boots—and into the bathroom, not stopping until they were inside the shower with the curtain pulled.

Marc wondered how he'd gone from date to third wheel as he watched his sister disappear down the hallway with Lexi, and her swaying, beautiful backside, in tow. When the bathroom door slammed with a resounding no-boys-allowed thud, he accepted that he'd have to enter the first family dinner he'd ever brought a girl to girl-less.

"What's that about?" Jack Tanner, his old buddy, asked the second Marc entered the family room. His brothers and Tanner were all seated around the coffee table, sharing a bottle of DeLuca cab. All except for Tanner, who held a longneck in his hand.

"Abby had to go to the bathroom, and apparently she needed Lexi to go with her," Marc explained while he took a seat in one of the high-back chairs.

"No, I meant, since when did you start bringing dates to your family dinner?" Tanner clarified, sharing a smart-ass grin with Trey and Nate. Gabe ignored them all, instead glaring at his glass of iced tea.

"Since Nonna would kick my ass if I missed a family dinner and Lexi invited me over tonight." He took in Tanner and frowned. Marc knew his kind. A smooth-talking, womanizing panty whisperer, just like Marc—only supersized. And he'd seen the way Tanner had been checking out his sister the other day at the farmers' market when he was sure Abby wasn't looking. "And since when do you do the hands-on shit for small remodels like the bistro?"

Tanner had started tearing apart and flipping high-end homes for fun, something to keep him busy after he retired from his career in the NFL. His company sometimes took on smaller jobs for longtime locals as a favor, and Tanner always did the initial inspection, but his crew were usually the ones swinging the hammers. Tanner was more of the seven-figure-project kind of guy.

"Since this one was a special request." Tanner leaned back, stretching out his legs and making himself right at home. "Plus my hands started getting itchy, wanted to see some action."

Marc was about to inform him that the only action Tanner was going to get was his ass handed to him if he kept smiling like that when Trey said, "Don't mind him, he isn't getting any."

"Fuck off," Marc grumbled.

"So is that a no?" Trey's grin spread across his face until Marc wanted to punch him.

Marc stood, not sure why he was so mad. Tanner was just giving him a hard time, and he and his brothers talked that way about women all the time. Well, all the brothers except for Gabe as of late. "What part of 'fuck off' did you miss? Do we need to go outside so I can make sure you get the point this time?"

"Take it easy," Gabe said, chewing on a piece of ice.

"Like you did when you tried to take me out with the remote control?" Marc challenged, referring to the time several months ago when Gabe and Marc nearly came to blows over Gabe dating Regan.

Gabe froze, a small smile touching his lips. "Didn't know we were there."

Marc shrugged. He didn't want to explain his relationship with Lexi. He couldn't. Not when he didn't understand what the hell their relationship was. Sure, he wanted to strip her naked, roll around until they were both sweaty and gasping for air, only to start over again when they finished. Problem was—and this was where it got confusing—for the first time in, well, ever, Marc found himself more attracted to the idea of snuggling than sex.

Then he conjured up the image of her in that dress she had on tonight and reconsidered his statement. Thought about the way she filled out the top to perfection and how the dress's back was cut so low that there was no way she was wearing a bra under it, and thinking became damn near impossible. Because when she'd sat in his truck earlier and her dress had ridden up, baring those mile-long legs to midthigh, his palms twitched with the need to stroke her from her red-tipped toes all the way up and under to see if she had forgone the panties as well.

He tugged at his jeans, grumbling under his breath when it didn't relieve one damn bit of pressure. All he had to do was think about her and his southern region stood to attention.

"Fair enough." Gabe nodded, a knowing flicker lighting up his eyes, and that made Marc nervous. "Does she know about the Monte deal, then?"

Trey jerked his gaze at Tanner, as though asking what the hell Gabe was thinking, talking about Monte in mixed company. As far as Marc was concerned, Tanner was a stand-up guy, had stood by the DeLuca family at a time when he could have made their lives a living hell. But he wasn't family. And family business was reserved for family. Period. So what the hell *was* Gabe thinking?

Plus, he didn't want to admit to his brothers that he was waiting for Jeff to return just one of his damn calls. Because admitting that would also make him face the fact that maybe he'd been wrong all these years. Maybe Jeff wasn't the stand-up guy he'd always thought. Maybe what Marc has seen as a good friend not judging him had really been someone who didn't care enough one way or the other.

Regardless, he needed to talk to Jeff first, have him explain a few things so that Marc had the facts straight before he went to Lexi. Because the more time he spent with Lexi, the more he began to understand what had gone down in the divorce, the more Marc got just how instrumental a role he'd played in Lexi's situation.

And if that was the case, he didn't want to tell her. Ever. Didn't want to be another guy to drop a load of BS in her life that she'd have to deal with alone, because once she knew, there was no doubt in his mind that she would send him packing.

"It's all right," Gabe said, and for a moment Marc feared that he had spoken aloud. Then Gabe sipped his tea and, after a grimace, continued. "Tanner needs to know what's going on since he's staking his company's future on this."

Yeah, well, Marc knew what the women of St. Helena said about Hard-Hammer Tanner. He also knew that the guy was not only financially set, decent enough looking for a dude, and kind of ripped, he was—Marc froze, reassessing his earlier assumption—one of Lexi's intended bachelors. What if he'd been checking out Lexi instead of Abby?

Oh hell no. There was no way Marc wanted Tanner's tool belt stinking up the air when Lexi was around.

"Well, if sitting in as a celebrity judge is too much for you, man, I can just find someone else," Marc said, standing and ready to show him to the door.

When he'd asked Tanner to help him out and fill the empty tribunal position, he hadn't thought of how much additional time the former football star with mammoth biceps and a fancy Super Bowl ring would be spending with Lexi. He'd not only be nailing her walls and fixing her pipes, he'd be tasting her damn food, something that Marc had started to consider his job.

"You lose him and *we* lose half the ticket holders," Gabe said, his voice full of exasperation and a little humor.

After word got out that Hard-Hammer Tanner was the celebrity judge, ticket sales exploded, and as of yesterday the Showdown was officially sold out. Not that it surprised Marc. Back when Tanner was in the NFL, he couldn't walk down the street without being mobbed by locals and tourists. Retirement might have softened the fanfare, but he was still a beloved town figure, and if word got out that he was off the tribunal, Marc might have to start refunding some of those thousand-dollar-a-plate tickets.

"So take a seat," Gabe said, his expression making it clear he wouldn't continue until Marc did as he said. So Marc sat. And stared down Tanner, who smiled back.

"Seems that Saul Sorrento is getting a divorce and moving to Florida," Gabe began.

"Holy shit." Nate sat up. "What's he doing with his land?"

"His kids aren't interested in running it, so he's going to sell," Tanner supplied.

Nate smacked his hands together and did some stupid happy dance in his chair, knocking over Nonna's statue of St. Christopher and nearly taking out his glass of wine. He was so wound up he didn't even notice.

Not much got their tight-ass brother excited, but everyone in the room understood. The Sorrento family owned the largest parcel of virgin soil in the St. Helena appellation region. Used as a pasture for Saul's organic cow and alpaca farm, it had never been planted on, meaning it was the perfect soil for a new vineyard. It was also the land that Geno DeLuca had been in the middle of buying when he'd won the hand of Miss ChiChi Ryo. Since Charles Baudouin had lost the girl, he made sure that Geno never got the land. But what started out as a way to stick it to a former friend had ended up making Saul owner of one of the most exclusive parcels of land in the valley. And he was finally selling.

"Wait." Marc paused, taking in the way Tanner and Gabe were sharing a knowing smile—a smile that was usually reserved for him and his brothers. "What does that have to do with Tanner?"

"Saul and my grandpa play poker. The other night he asked if I wanted to take it off his hands." Tanner's lips twitched. "Even though he's moving, he still has kids in the area and doesn't want them to get caught in the middle of the great feud of St. Helena."

"My thought was, we partner with Tanner and let him work as the go-between to secure us the land," Gabe said, and when all three brothers looked at him like he'd just committed a mortal sin by including an outsider in family business, he added, "Or we go it alone, he lists the property, and the DeLucas and Baudouins continue to outbid each other until neither of us can afford it."

Made sense. Between Abby's missing dick and the millions he'd stolen, Marc's money pit of a hotel, and the Pairing project, the DeLucas were low on liquid assets. Plus, Tanner had helped them out before when he didn't have to, and saved the DeLucas from a major lawsuit. That still didn't mean Marc felt comfortable bringing an outsider into the family business. Especially when that outsider knew nothing about wine.

"Let's say we all agree," Marc said, reminding everyone in the room that even though Gabe ran the company, their parents had set up the trust so that there had to be a majority vote from the siblings in order to go forward with a major decision like this. "What's in it for you? I didn't even know you liked wine."

"I don't." He saluted Marc with his beer and a smart-ass grin. "Allergic to tannins."

"Tanner isn't interested in the land or the grapes. He wants to be the exclusive builder for DeLuca Wines," Gabe clarified.

"If I attach myself to your family, it will mean I could lose a good chunk of the town's business. And since most of the projects I want to take on revolve around wineries and wine caves, I need to know that I've got your chunk locked in, exclusively."

Tanner was right; the second word got out that he'd assisted the DeLucas in swiping the land right out from under old man Charles's nose, his alliance with their family would guarantee a complete and total blacklist for Tanner Construction from all future Baudouin projects.

Marc leaned forward, rested his elbows on his knees, and said, "Then why help us? You could just sit back, watch our families fight it out, and maintain a healthy distance from the feud."

"I've got my reasons," Tanner said, taking a pull on his beer. "One of them being I want my company to handle the construction on that new cave you guys are digging on the south property. I know it will be one of the biggest caves in the valley and that you've already received bids from two other companies. I help you get Saul's land, and you help me move into the cave-building space."

"And the other reason?"

Tanner leaned forward, mimicking Marc's stance. "None of your damn business."

"Fine. Let's talk terms." As long as it didn't involve the exchange of a woman, Marc was willing to hear the guy out.

"Tanner's here." Abby's eyes shot to the closed door, and she lowered her voice to a hiss. "In the front room. Drinking with my brothers."

"I saw."

"He wants to hire me to teach him piano." Abby plopped down on the side of the tub as though she'd just imparted world-ending information.

"That bastard." When Abby didn't smile, Lexi joined her on the ledge.

Abby had never really dated all that much in high school. Her brothers made sure that any guy who looked interested learned how hard it was to look through a black eye. She had one heartbreak in high school, studied her way through design school, avoiding dating for the most part—until she met Richard. Which made Abby about as experienced with men as Lexi.

"Is that a bad thing?"

Abby blinked. "You have no idea who he is, do you?"

"Um, he's the hot contractor wanted by every woman in town, and he's hired you for a private one-on-one."

"He's the celebrity judge for the Showdown. His face has been plastered all over town. How can you not know this?"

"Gee, remodeling the bakery and trying to win that catering job has been a little distracting," Lexi defended. She'd also been a lot distracted by her sexy neighbor.

"And there's no way he's getting a private lesson of any kind, because before Tanner tore his shoulder, he played for the Niners," Abby explained, and when Lexi stared blankly at her she flapped her hands impatiently. "Before that, he played for USC and was one of the best running backs in college history."

"So you can't teach him piano because he played football?"

"I can't be alone with him because, before college, Tanner was the quarterback for Napa High."

"Get out." Lexi slapped a hand over her mouth. She knew he looked familiar, but, "No! Way! Hard-Hammer Tanner, as in Jack Tanner, as in class of—"

"Stolen Saints mascot, yup."

"He's the guy who—"

"I stole our school mascot, stuck it in his truck, and got him suspended from the biggest game of his high school career."

"No, I mean he's the asshole who—"

Abby slapped her hands over Lexi's mouth. "Why don't you just post it on Facebook and be done with it, that way we can be sure that *everyone* knows. Jesus, Lex, if even one of my brothers hears that, there is going to be a brawl the size of China in Nonna's front room."

"Can you get your hands off my mouth," Lexi mumbled through Abby's fingers. When she didn't move then, Lexi stuck her tongue out.

"Gross, Lex. Grow up," Abby said, grimacing, hand not budging.

"Says the girl convinced someone is outside the door listening." She frowned. "And why do you taste like lasagna?"

"Don't ask. And I forgot you're an only child," Abby said as though her grown brothers still made a habit of hiding outside bathroom doors. "I will remove them if you promise to be quiet."

Lexi nodded.

Abby dropped her hands.

"Well, it obviously didn't hurt his career all that much. I mean, you said the guy played in the NFL. Plus, he deserved it." Abby might have framed him for a silly high school prank, but Jack had broken Abby's heart.

After her parents died, Abby went into a deep depression, shutting out everyone. She was lost and scared and blamed herself for living when her parents hadn't. Jack ran into her at the right time and sweet-talked his way into Abby's kick-pants, then went to homecoming with another set of pom-poms.

"If I had known"—Lexi draped a supportive arms around her friend's shoulders—"I never would have hired him in the first place."

"He said he only agreed to do the bistro because he knew I was managing the project." Abby's body sagged. "What if he's trying to ruin my life?"

"Over a stupid prank that happened ten years ago? I don't think so." Lexi pulled her friend closer, and Abby rested her head on Lexi's shoulder, only she was so much shorter her head only came to Lexi's chest. "Maybe he just wants to learn piano."

Abby shook her head, and when she looked up at Lexi, she knew that there was more to the story. "He was one of the biggest investors in Richard's and my vineyard."

"Oh."

"I didn't know at the time. The money was a contact of Marc's, and it came through Jack's company, so I didn't make the connection."

"Until he came back to the valley?"

"No, until he told me yesterday. He said since I was a designer and he a contractor, that we were bound to work on more projects together in the future." She shrugged. "He claims that he just wanted to clear the air."

"Is he asking for the money back?"

"No. I told him that I didn't know about him investing and promised I would pay him back, but he said he would rather have the lessons."

"Maybe that's just his way of saying he knows that you didn't help Richard."

Some people in town still believed that Abby had been in on the scam, and her moving to Santa Barbara only made the rumors more convincing. Which had been hard to take, since nearly all of the investors had been close friends and family. Not that her family believed she played a role in the embezzlement, but she lost a lot of lifelong friends over the situation.

Abby rolled her eyes. "A million dollars in lessons?"

"Oh." That was a lot more than learning how to play "Chopsticks." And trying to be a good guy or not, that didn't sit right with Lexi. No matter how rich someone was, forgiving a million in exchange for music lessons sounded too good to be true. And in Lexi and Abby's world, that meant it usually was.

"Yeah. *Oh*." Abby sighed. "I just got the courage to divorce Richard. Now I have to sit in the same room with some guy who lost a bunch of money because of my inability to tell a thieving limp-dick from a good husband."

"Maybe to him a million is pocket change. Have you seen his house? It's bigger than this one."

"One million is one million, Lex. I don't care how many car and underwear ads the guy did."

"He did underwear ads? Like tighty-whities, or those sexy boxer-brief ones?"

"Does it matter? Nonna invited him tonight as a setup. For me!" Abby dropped her head to her knees. "If you had given Jack a chance, I wouldn't be in this mess and you wouldn't be dating my brother, which by the way we are still going to talk about."

"What did you tell him?"

Abby studied the grout. "That I had to think about it."

A muffled voice came through the door. It was Trey. "Christ, man, I know this is all new to you, but give the lady some space."

"Told you," Abby whispered, wiping her eyes and standing up.

There was rustling as though some brotherly shoving and maybe a noogie was taking place on the other side of the door. Then Marc spoke. "She's in there with Abby."

"Doing what?" Trey sounded completely confused.

"Not playing spin the bottle," Lexi hollered at the door, smothering a laugh.

"They're either sharing secrets or they're trying to sneak out the window above the commode again," ChiChi said a moment before the door shot open.

Dressed in an apron that read *Got Cannoli?* and a pair of red kitten heels that cost more than Lexi's entire wardrobe, stood ChiChi. Beside her was Pricilla, looking stunning in her teal slacks and a tucked-in David Hasselhoff T-shirt with a seascape of gems bedazzled around the neckline, making the ensemble evening appropriate. At least in Pricilla's mind.

"We weren't trying to sneak out," Abby defended, standing up.

"Of course you weren't, dear," Pricilla said, stepping into the bathroom and sitting on the commode. She held a covered dish in her right hand and her crocheted bag of treats in her left. She was smiling and in arm's reach of both Abby's and Lexi's mouths. Most grannies discouraged lying with a mouthful of soap; Pricilla believed more in the if-your-mouth-is-too-full-of-chocolate-the-lie-can't-come-out method.

"That's exactly what you told me the last time, right before Mr. Patterson caught you two skinny-dipping in his pool," ChiChi accused.

Abby was about to say something when Marc peeked his head over ChiChi's. "You went skinny-dipping?"

"The night she stole my car," Pricilla added.

"I had on underwear," Lexi clarified, forcing her shoulders back but failing to hide the embarrassment creeping up her face. "And I just borrowed it."

"What color was the underwear?" Trey wanted to know, popping his head in.

Marc elbowed him in the ribs and saved Lexi from answering.

"She hasn't even had dinner and you're going to scare her away." A petite woman with striking blue eyes pushed her way in the room. One hand was securely tangled with Gabe's, and the other rubbed back and forth over her pregnant belly. "The DeLucas are still learning the concept of personal space and that a bathroom isn't the place for a family reunion."

"You'll get used to it," Gabe said right as Nate and Tanner came through the door.

"Is it true you're shacking up with this guy?" Trey wanted to know. Marc slugged him in the arm, and Trey slugged back when Nate pushed his way into the room and between the two brothers.

"Leave the poor thing alone," Regan said with a reprimanding swat to Trey's gut.

"I never really knew," Lexi whispered to Abby.

"Oh, this is nothing," she whispered back. "Wait until one of them questions the other's manliness. Then it is on."

"Shame on you, Trey. Where are your manners? Sleeping in sin is one thing." ChiChi shook her head and made the sign of the cross. "Making her admit it in front her grandmother is plain rude."

Lexi felt the blush rise even higher in her cheeks. Did they know about last night? Making people think they were having sex was part of the original plan, but that was before they had done the pantry-floor shuffle.

Marc ran a hand through his hair. "Christ, Nonna—"

Pricilla shoved a summer fiesta cake ball in Marc's mouth and scolded, "Language. Plus, I don't think he's eaten the apple." Her eyes narrowed, assessing Lexi and then Marc before frowning. "Tart, pie, or strudel. What's wrong with you, son?"

"None of our business," Trey said in a mocking tone that had all the guys laughing. Well, all of the guys except Marc, who was chewing furiously. Cake ball or not, Pricilla's summer fiesta was more of a three-biter.

Lexi's chest went tight and her heart heavy at their ribbing. It didn't bother her that they were laughing or that she didn't get the joke. What bothered her was that Marc was somehow the butt of their fun. Abby was right, Lexi didn't have siblings, didn't know what it was like to be a part of a big family. But she did know how much it stung when the people you loved discounted your feelings.

"Um," Lexi began, wondering if she should just tell them the truth and show Marc for what he was: a good guy who was trying to help a friend. "About that."

Then everyone went silent, and she couldn't speak past the nerves in her throat.

Silence stretched on. Awkwardness filled the room, mixed in with so much testosterone and Italian machismo that it was hard to breathe. Or maybe it was because everyone was looking at her, waiting for her to admit that they *had* had sex.

Lexi felt like she was on center stage, and her stomach started to knot. Even though they hadn't had sex yet, Lexi was pretty sure that was on the menu for tonight. Not that she had *told* Marc she wanted him to sleep over, in the nakedest sense of the word, but she thought that the dress choice was a pretty good sign. And by the way he'd looked at her when she'd answered her door, he had gotten the memo.

"We're taking things slow," Marc interrupted, sending her one of his apologetic smiles and saving her from explaining things.

She smiled back. Lexi had never been comfortable around Jeffery's family—not surprising when his mother took every opportunity to make it painfully obvious how lucky she thought Lexi had been to snag her only son. Never once, over all their years together, had Jeffery ever acknowledged her discomfort or defended her when his family started questioning why they hadn't started a family, why they bought a house in New York, why he had married her in the first place. Yet Marc had picked up on her unease immediately. Not that she didn't like his family; she just wasn't used to having that many eyeballs zeroed in on her.

And Marc got that. He got her. Because he said, "Now everyone clear out so I can make sure my girlfriend isn't going to pull an Abby and jump out the window."

"I did that *once!*" Abby snapped, heading for the door in a huff.

"Twice," Tanner mumbled, following behind her.

"Show her the plate, Pricilla, and then we'll get out of their hair," ChiChi said, taking off the lid and exposing a plate of food. Situated in three segregated piles sat ricotta, cooked noodles, parsley, and a steaming bowl of bolognese sauce that smelled like heaven.

"What's that?" Lexi took in a deep sniff and groaned.

"Dinner," ChiChi retorted, digging her meaty hands into her meatier hips.

"Shouldn't it be"—Nate moved his hand as though tossing a salad—"mixed together?"

"Exactly!" ChiChi waddled out of the bathroom, and Lexi could have sworn she mumbled, right before she disappeared out of sight, "Deconstructed, my ass."

Marc's eyes went soft, silently apologizing for his family.

Regan stopped at the door and turned around. "You really will get used to this. I promise."

Lexi bit down on her lip and nodded. Because Regan had said it as though there would be other DeLuca family dinners in Lexi's future. A part of her wanted that, wanted to come here every Friday with Marc and share a meal with his family as though she was a part of this crazy bunch. The other part, the part that knew with family dinner and a future came the possibility for heartache, was scared. Because she was fast learning that although Marc tried to portray himself as a shallow playboy, there was nothing shallow about him. Even worse, there was nothing shallow about her feelings with regard to him.

CHAPTER 14

Three hours, two helpings of lasagna, and a slice of Pricilla's famous burnt-almond cake later, Marc took Lexi's hand and followed her to the apartment door. He watched as she dug around in her purse for her keys and scrounged up the courage to ask him in. He knew she wanted to; he could see it in the way she kept looking at him during dinner. It was the same way he'd been looking at her.

She located her keys, unlocked her door, and when she turned around, she met his gaze. It was nervous and so damn adorable it made his head spin.

He stepped forward, just enough to let her know he was interested, but leaving enough space for her to run the show.

"Thank you." She reached up and gently kissed his lips. "For tonight."

"You're welcome." Marc caught her face before she could get too far and brought it back to his. Upping the heat level, he moved slowly against her mouth, tugging at her lower lip when he pulled back. "For tonight."

Neither moved. They stood on her front porch, sharing breath and waiting for the other person to take the next step.

"You want to come up for a glass of wine?" she whispered, flashing a shy smile.

"No," he whispered back, their lips so close that when he spoke they brushed.

"No?"

"I want to come up, but not for wine."

That got a startled laugh out of her. Then she smiled and Marc felt his whole world go right.

"Okay," she began again, only this time wrapping her arms around his neck and crushing those perfect tens against his chest. He looked down to find all that soft flesh, barely contained by her dress. Holy hell, what a view.

"Marc?"

His eyes jerked to hers, which were lit with humor. "I asked if you'd like to have a sleepover?"

"Does this sleepover involve you and me, sweaty and naked?"

"It does."

"Then, yes. Thank you." He kissed her again, adding a little tongue and some hand action for emphasis. "For inviting me up."

"You're welcome." She kissed him back. Her hands were doing some action of their own.

Never breaking contact, Marc reached out and opened the front door. Walking backward, they stumbled up the porch step and into the apartment. He kicked the door with his foot, and before it even slammed shut, Lexi was up against the wall, his hands were up her dress, and there was no way in hell that either of them would make it upstairs clothed.

Things were already getting crowded in his jeans. And he didn't want to damage that dress, so it had to go.

Lexi's hands were working the buttons of his shirt. She had it undone and was sliding it down his arms in ten seconds flat, forcing him to ease the grip he had on her ass so that she could toss it to the floor.

Then she was going for his undershirt, but he had just got his hands back where he wanted them and he didn't want to let go again. So he took her mouth with his, hoping to distract her so he could get her out of that damn dress.

"Naked. I want you naked," she moaned against his mouth while tugging at his shirt, which was shoved up to his chest, her fingers curling into the fabric with frustration. He knew how she felt. Her damn zipper was caught in the fabric—again.

He gave it one more yank, and when it didn't budge, except to get further stuck, he growled, "Fuck it," and dropped his hands to her ass and lifted. "Wrap your legs around me."

She did and he nearly lost it right there. There was something about her. Something about the smell of her skin, the way he felt when she was pressed against him, the way their connection continued to grow until it blew his fucking mind.

She slid one arm around his neck and dropped the other down his chest, abs, and stomach until it finally settled over the ridge in his jeans, and damn it if he didn't buck into her hand.

When Lexi's fingers headed under his waistband, Marc headed up the stairs.

She lifted her head, which had been buried in the crook of his shoulder while her mouth did amazing things to his neck. "Where are we going?"

"Bed," he said, because he wanted this. He wanted her. Wanted to be inside of her making her scream out his name. And he wanted all of that now. But he also wanted their first time to be special and not up against some wall. Plus, it was hard to taste and touch his fill when his hands were too busy holding her up.

He made it up the stairs in record time, but before he could round the hall she had managed to unbutton his pants and was teasing those soft fingers of hers beneath the elastic band of his boxer-briefs and lower. Her gentle exploring scrambled his brain, and even though he had wanted to make love to her in the bed, that would mean she'd have to stop what she was doing down south and there was no way that was going to happen.

"The couch," she mumbled, gripping him hard.

Couch. Right. It was soft, had pillows, and would allow his hands to get to the touching part of the evening. Which was exactly what he did the second he sat down, Lexi still wrapped around his middle.

Then they were kissing again, and he forgot about everything except for her amazing lips working his. The kiss was hot and long and he lost himself in it. So when she pulled back and rested her forehead against his, he went still.

Had he blown it? Fuck! He should have taken her to the bedroom.

"Second thoughts?" he whispered, hoping to hell that she said no. When she flashed him a devilish smile and shook her head, he felt his heart resume beating and his dick go harder—if that was even possible.

"I seem to have this problem with my neighbor."

"Me too," he said, sliding his hands down to her ass and pulling her against him so she could see exactly how bad his problem was. "Seems to grow bigger every time I see her."

"Wow, that's a hard problem to have," she said against his ear, tracing a finger down one side of his erection and right back up the center. Holy Christ, her hands were magic. "Mine has to do with the window."

"Forget the window," he panted, dropping his head back as she tightened her fingers around his length and gently squeezed. He was willing to forget the window, the bed, anything if it meant she'd start moving her hand up and down.

"If I do that, your cleaning crew will get an eyeful I am sure they won't ever forget." He heard her words, but it was hard to process them when all of the blood was rushing south. She slowly moved up his length and tightened her grip before sliding back down.

"No one will see," he mumbled, his eyes sliding closed.

"You did," she whispered, her hands never slowing.

"I was looking" was all he managed to get out because she picked up the pace, squeezed to the point of pain, and he knew that he wasn't going to make it—to the bed, to the touching, to the naked part. Hell, he wasn't going to last two more seconds. Which meant he'd have to make up for it in round two, because there was no way he was going to stop her.

Two seconds, two hours, he wasn't sure. Between breathing in her skin, her mouth on his neck, and her hands stroking him into oblivion, time seemed to disappear. So did everything else.

Then, out of the corner of his eye, a light clicked on. It was from across the alleyway. Marc bit back a curse and stilled her hands. Because the thought of someone watching them, watching Lexi like this? No fucking way. She was his.

"The curtains," he said, more alert than he'd have liked. "I need to close the curtains."

"I'll get it." Lexi crawled off his lap and pulled the blinds closed. "Better?"

"Thank yo—" was all he got out before she turned around and his breath caught.

God, she was beautiful. Her hair tumbled over her shoulders in a mass of golden waves, her mouth was full and wet and so sexy he needed to have it back on him, and her dress was a mess of wrinkles from his hands. She looked like some kind of X-rated prom queen, and he ached to hold her.

"Come here." He held out his arms.

Only she didn't walk back over, instead stopping at the end of the coffee table to offer up a playful smile. He wasn't sure what she had in mind, but that naughty look in her eye was enough for him to sit back and see what she was planning.

Kicking off his shoes, he leaned back, his hands folded behind his head, and relaxed while he let her decide what she wanted to do next.

Without warning, she reached behind her and slowly pulled down the zipper of her dress. He could hear the metal teeth as she lowered the fastening, inch by incredible inch. Not feeling so relaxed, he sat upright as she let go and the dress fell to the floor in one swoop, leaving her in those strappy heels, silk panties, and abso-fucking-lutely nothing else. "You're welcome."

Her panties were purple. No wait, lighter than purple. His breath caught...they were lavender.

Her panties were lavender silk, and he'd bet his hotel that they matched her frilly apron perfectly. A fact he filed away for later, because right then he needed to appreciate those breasts. The ones he'd fantasized about since he was fourteen. Not only were they fantasyworthy, they were bigger than he'd imagined, fuller and higher with rose-colored nipples that jutted out perfectly under his gaze.

Her hands hung at her sides, letting him have his look. But he could tell that she was trying not to cover herself.

"Jesus, Alexis," he breathed. "The things I'm going to do to you."

She raised a brow, and he watched her walk closer, loving how her hips moved under the silk of her panties and wondering what the small triangle of lavender hid. When she reached the couch, he opened his arms and she went right into them, straddling his lap. Kid move or not, his hands went immediately to her breasts. He needed to touch them, weigh them, get to know each and every inch of them. First with his hands, and then with his mouth.

"Things? There's more than one?" Her arms were under his shirt, pulling it over his head and discarding it. "Sounds complicated."

"Sugar, everything with you is complicated." He kissed her left breast, right on the underneath side. "Keep my distance." Then her right. "No flirting." Back to the left. "No staring. No dreaming." He stopped, his eyes flying to hers, and he smiled. "Although I broke that rule almost daily. There was a period of time there that every morning I woke up so hard for you I'd walk around with a bulge in my pants all day."

"Those teen years must have been rough on you," she teased, stroking his cheek.

"Teen years?" He turned his head, catching the inside of her palm and kissing her there too. It felt good. Not as good as kissing her breasts. But different good. "Hell, cream puff, I was talking about since you came home."

"What other rules?"

"Let's see." He went back to her breasts, this time using his tongue. "No...absolutely no touching. Because I knew if we did"—he pulled her into his mouth, and she arched back with a throaty cry—"this would happen and I'd never be able let you go. And even if you broke up with Jeff you'd still belong to him."

She went utterly still. He could feel the doubt creeping through her. "Do you still see me as that girl? As Jeffery's?"

"No." He brought his hands to her face so that she couldn't look away. He'd been battling this attraction for half of his life, which meant he'd been battling some deep-seated guilt about his feelings for Lexi for just as long. After their first kiss last week, he'd come to terms with all of it, and he wanted her to know how he could be with her now, like this. "I figure any man who can walk away from you wasn't a fucking man to begin with."

Lexi wasn't sure what she expected him to say, but that wasn't it.

His admission was so raw and so real and so freaking hot that it made her body ache in ways she wasn't sure were healthy. And don't even get her started on the possessive way his hands gripped her hips when he said it, or how his eyes promised her the world. That made her want things that she hadn't wished for in a long time. Things that she had long ago given up hope even existed. Or at least existed for a girl like her.

"So, are you a man?"

Marc was silent for so long Lexi felt the urge to pull the crocheted afghan off the back of the couch and cocoon herself inside. But she resisted. This was important and she was no longer content to hide from life, so instead she held his gaze, which was so intense she felt as though he was seeing every inch of the real her.

After a long moment, Marc's hand slid up her spine and under her hair, gently cradling the back of her head in his palm. The little flecks of light filtering through the crack in the curtains showed the softening in his features. "Around you I am."

Before she could respond, Lexi found herself in one of the most amazing kisses of her life. His mouth was soft and sure and so gentle it melted her heart—and every last bit of resolve.

Letting go of the past, she gave herself over to the moment, to the incredible connection bubbling between them, and to Marc. It was as though someone flipped a switch and all of her fears of heartache and trust vanished, leaving a need so deep that she knew only Marc could fill it.

"Marc," she moaned between kisses, a hard task considering that one kiss fell into another, and another, until she couldn't feel or think about anything but him.

As if he sensed her walls lowering, sensed her giving in, Marc flipped her around, and before she knew what was happening, she was seated on the edge of the couch and he was kneeling between her legs.

"I love your body." It wasn't a declaration of love by any means, but the way his hands slid down her form, as though appreciating every curve and dip, made her feel cherished—something she hadn't felt in a long time.

He took her breasts in his hands and kissed one, then nibbled and licked his way over to the other, like he couldn't decide where he wanted to start and was determined not to miss an inch of skin.

He paid such careful attention that by the time he'd made his way to the hem of her panties she was a vibrating ball of sexual need. Then he skipped right over her panties and dropped a kiss on her knee. It was a nice kiss, firm and warm, and it sent little zings all the way to her toes. But that wasn't where she wanted the zing—or his kisses—to go.

"I've always dreamed of kissing you here." He pressed a love bite on the inside of her thigh.

"That was a bite, not a kiss. And of all the places, that's the one you dreamed about?"

He smiled. "My dream, my rules. I also dreamed about here." He did it again, only harder, then licked the sting away. "And here." He moved higher.

"That's a lot of dreams," she laughed, her smile fading when his tongue slid around the edge of her silk panties. It was too hard to smile while you were moaning.

"We're talking a lot of years, cream puff." He leaned up and kissed her lips. "Want to know where my most frequently recurring dream took place?"

His hands slid up her thighs, and she knew exactly where she wanted it to take place next, and just how many times she wanted it to recur. But if he wanted to play, she could too. She cupped both of her breasts and raised a brow. "Here?"

He gave each nipple a soft kiss and then said, "Although that was my very first dream, over the years it came in at number four."

"Hmm." She slid her hand down her stomach and under the elastic of her panties and rubbed her swollen, moist skin. "I bet for a teen boy who has a thing for watching windows, this would rank right up there at number one."

"Yeah," he mumbled, his eyes blazing and riveted to the triangle of silk, like if he stared hard enough he'd develop X-ray vision to see just what her fingers were doing. "Right up there, but not number one."

He ran his fingers up her thighs, and when they came back down, they had her panties with him.

"Don't stop on my account," he whispered, and she realized that she had stopped. All of her brazen confidence had fled now that she was completely naked, splayed out for his viewing pleasure, and he was still wearing his jeans.

"Maybe you should lose some of that." She pointed to his clothes.

"Sugar, *that* is the only thing keeping *this*"—he jerked his eyes toward his crotch—"from blowing the identity of dream number one. This." He leaned forward and delivered an openmouthed kiss directly to her center, causing her hips to buck against his lips. "Yeah, definitely ranks in at number two. But something's missing."

Her eyes, which she hadn't even known had slid shut, flew open at his comment. "Missing?"

"Oh yeah." He kissed her again, pulling a small noise from her throat. "In my dreams I always imagined you screaming."

His hands slid under her butt, and he raised her right as his mouth settled on her center. She nearly gave in and screamed when his strong tongue pressed against her in one long lick. This would be over before it ever started, and she wanted it to go on—and on. Especially when he used his lips, his breath, his teeth, each with the perfect amount of pressure and each at the right moment.

Her whole body pulsed with anticipation, so she pushed her heels into the edge of the couch and slapped her palm over her mouth to keep the pressure inside.

Then he delved deeper.

"Oh God!" exploded from her lips, and she bucked up against him while rolling her hips to increase the pressure.

"Oh God," she said again louder. One last buck and heat shot though her, sending her body into a frenzy as each wave of her orgasm washed over her.

Marc didn't stop; he just slowed down, applying more kisses than nips. Convinced that she didn't have a single bone left in her body, Lexi sagged against the back of couch. Eyes closed, heart still racing, she was content to sit and absorb the best orgasm she'd ever had.

In. Her. Life.

Her breath was just returning to normal when she felt Marc's tongue again. He licked her once, right up the middle, twice, a third time, slowly gaining momentum. She opened her eyes and saw that his brow was furrowed and his eyes were determined.

"What are you doing?" she asked, her voice trailing off when he blew on her pleasure button.

"In my dream you scream."

"I did scream." She even screamed again when his hand joined in the fun.

"My name." He slid a finger in, smiling at her when she clenched around him. "You scream *my* name."

Which she had no problems doing when he moved faster, focusing all of his determination on the smaller bundle of nerves. He circled his tongue right as his finger hit that perfect spot and—

"Yes, yes, God, yes." Every muscle tightened, tension built, making her back arch. "Marc, please," she begged, squeezing her thighs against his head. He slid in a second finger, sending a violent jolt of pleasure shattering her body.

"Marc!" she cried out when her body erupted again. She was so spent that when her eyes opened and she caught him smiling at her, all she could manage was a lazy grin in return.

"Was that better?" she asked.

"Hell yeah. Never once in my dream did you ever squeeze your legs so tight around my head that I almost passed out."

"I did not," she said, but didn't feel all that confident in her denial, since her thighs were tender and when she tried to move, she had to stifle a wince. So when Marc kissed his way back up her stomach, she had to admit, "I'm too sore to even move."

His eyes softened. "That's my job," he whispered against her lips and lifted her into his arms.

He carried her down the hallway and into her bedroom. The mattress was cool against her back as Marc laid her down, then sprawled out beside her in all of his naked glory. And glorious he was. His shoulders were wide, his chest wider, and all muscle she noticed as her fingers traced down his pecs to his flat stomach, enjoying how it rippled and beaded beneath her touch. She loved that she had the power to turn him on.

He rolled on his side, resting his head on his bent arm so that he could watch her explore his body. He was a big man...everywhere. And she realized that, although she had had two standing Os, he had yet to have his first.

"Take your time," he said, reading her mind. "We have all night."

"I'm done," she whispered, rising up to kiss him on the lips. She loved how he felt under her hands, but she wanted him inside of her body.

"You sure?" He kissed her back.

She parted her lips and took the kiss deeper, showing him just how sure she was. He followed her lead, moaning when she arched up so that just the tip of his erection pressed against her heat. She did it again, tilting her hips so that the tip slid in just enough that he jerked back.

"Condom," he said, tearing open the package on the bedside table and rolling it on. Then he laced their hands together and brought them above her. "And I get to do all the work, remember?"

She didn't even get to argue because he pushed inside her in one slow movement and then they were both too busy sighing to speak. They lay utterly silent, enjoying the intimate connection.

"God, sugar. You feel so right," Marc whispered into the curve of her neck, and she felt her heart open a little more. Because it did feel right, so incredibly right, and yet she wasn't scared of what that meant anymore.

Marc pulled all the way out and then slowly sank back in. The exquisite sensation made her moan; it also made her spine curl so she could take him deeper. Marc pulled back and caressed the back of her knee, lifting her leg to wrap it around his waist before pushing back in.

"Yes," she moaned.

"Yes, what?" he said, half joking but half serious.

"Yes, Marc," she played along, happy when she was adequately rewarded.

He picked up the pace, never rough or hard like she would have thought. No, everything about Marc was smooth and unhurried and made her feel cherished—beautiful. He worshipped her body with his hands while whispering sweet things to her, and every time she felt him get close, he pulled back and slowed down.

Lexi had always enjoyed sex, but she realized that she had never been made love to until now. Until Marc.

"You are so beautiful," he said, staring down into her eyes, making sure that she was right there with him, enjoying every second. She was. She enjoyed every kiss, every touch, every time he filled her.

She ran her hands down his back and grabbed his ass, pulling him closer. "More."

"Thank God," he mumbled, taking her mouth with his. His hips moved faster, deeper, and right when she knew that he couldn't hold back any longer, he groaned out her name. Her whole name.

Just the sound of her name falling off his lips, rough and raw, took her over the edge. She broke apart in his arms as he gave a final push before collapsing on top of her. They were a tangle of arms and legs, panting and sweaty, and yet Marc took care to make sure he didn't crush her.

A few minutes later he asked, "You okay?" When she didn't answer, he lifted his head. "I'll take that smile on your face to be a yes."

She nodded, and he rolled off her and went to the bathroom. Returning to bed, he immediately pulled her close. He brushed her hair aside and pressed a warm kiss on her forehead.

"I assume that was your number-one dream."

"I thought it was. But now I think I'll have a new one."

"What's that?"

"This." He tightened his arm around her waist, holding her snug against him. "Now go to sleep. Your man wants a big breakfast in the morning."

CHAPTER 15

Lexi stood at the back of the St. Helena Courthouse. Even though she was strategically positioned by the door in case she needed to make a quiet escape, she could still smell the roasted figs and baked gorgonzola wafting from her dish, which sat at the front of the room.

She warily glanced around the courtroom and felt a bubble of panic rise up. The room was large, with a domed ceiling and enough mahogany benches and paneling to build life-sized replicas of the Niña, the Pinta, and the Santa Maria. Which was a good thing, since half the town had turned out to see who would win: a disaster of a divorcée or a busty gold digger. The judges were seated, in the jury box to be exact, the plates had been served, and rumor had it that Mrs. Rose, current wine commissioner, was allergic to peanuts. Lexi didn't know if pistachios would be a problem, but she noticed that Mrs. Rose was picking out anything remotely nut-shaped.

"Why is Mrs. Rose sitting at the judge's bench?" Lexi whispered to Marc, who stood right beside her. He was wearing khaki shorts and a gray UC Berkeley tee that did amazing things to his eyes, and looked relaxed and irritatingly sure of himself. Then again, his talent wasn't on the chopping block.

He tilted his head in her direction, and for a moment Lexi thought he was going to kiss her. Something warm and soothing washed though her. Then he dropped his voice and spoke, and Lexi realized that he just hadn't wanted to be overheard.

"The only way she'd agree to give up her Saturday skeet-and-trap-shoot time was if we held it in the county courthouse with her as presiding judge. ChiChi even snuck into the judge's chamber and *borrowed* Judge Pricket's robes and gavel."

"Don't forget that Nate had to cough up a case of his new reserve," Abby added, coming up from behind to join them. She wore a cute sundress that highlighted her figure. The woman might be vertically challenged, but she was a mass of sleek curves. "He was pissed."

Lexi looked up at Marc, who winked. He *had* been about to kiss her, she thought giddily, but then Abby had crept up. Not able to look at Marc without going warm, she turned her attention to the other DeLuca brother in question.

Nate sat in the jury box, wedged between Hard-Hammer Tanner and an empty seat, with the mayor on the far end. He was glaring at Frankie, who was chasing Simon around the witness stand and glaring back.

Simon Baudouin had the markings of a dairy cow, the body of a small boar, and the face of a gremlin after a head-on collision. Showing his fangs, he skirted around Frankie with a low snort and barreled toward the jury box.

"Simon, stop," Frankie snapped.

Simon did stop, his fat belly shaking with excitement, as he gnawed on the leg of the mayor's chair. Frankie drew close, cornering him and grabbing him around his abnormally wide girth. She hoisted him up, his little legs still moving as though trying to get traction on the air, and plopped him on Nate's lap with a growl—it was Frankie growling, not the dog.

Unaffected, Simon snorted happily up at Nate and then took to gnawing on his watch.

"Seems like that's not the only favor he had to pull to make today happen," Lexi said, feeling guilty.

"Nah, Nate and Frankie have been trying to kill each other for years. It's kind of entertaining," Abby noted.

And if that wasn't enough, the DOP senior league, huddled around the prosecution's table, was shooting rubber bands at the junior league, who'd settled themselves primly behind the defense. It was like *Iron Chef* meets the Hatfields and the McCoys, and somehow Lexi's dish, and her and Marc's relationship, were at the center of the feud.

Isabel Stark turned around and saw Abby. Her eyes went wide, and she started waving, with a smile that was both caffeinated and kiss-ass. Just watching her was exhausting.

Abby nodded back. "Oh God. That woman has been calling me nonstop, asking if I need to talk about Richard, wanting to know how I'm holding up, if Nate is looking to settle down."

"According to Isabel, she's the F to your BFF," Regan said, waddling through the doors, one hand on her belly and the other tangled with Gabe's. "Hey, Lexi, we came to wish you good luck."

Abby rolled her eyes, and Lexi noticed it was not directed at Regan, but rather inclusive of. Their relationship had been rough at the start, but Abby was genuinely trying to make Regan feel welcome in the DeLuca brood. Lexi knew it was hard on her friend and was proud of the progress she'd made. It was one step closer to her letting go of the past.

"Looks like you're up," Marc said, taking Lexi's hand and giving it a squeeze. "Ready?"

"Yup." She gave a decisive nod.

Both sides had delivered all three courses. Natasha had just finished a beautiful presentation, which would be hard to beat, and taken her seat next to her friends. Now it was Lexi's turn. She was to approach the bench and stand next to the jury box, ready to answer any questions that the Tasting Tribunal might have. Only she couldn't seem to get her feet to work. Part of the problem was her shoes. She'd worn them because they were sleek and sexy and turned Marc on, which she'd thought would help her feel a little naughty and a lot kick-ass chef. She'd thought wrong. The only thing her designer peekaboos had helped was the blister forming under her big toe. The other part of the problem was sheer nerves.

It had taken three pep talks, two sex marathons with Marc, and a plate of éclairs to relax her enough so she could walk through this door. Now, after seeing that half of the town had turned out—mainly the retired half—and that Natasha had gone more traditional, Lexi decided that her appetizer was too edgy, her rolled boar loin too gamy, and her chocolate-or-bust bonbons too small and that she might not win this thing. And if she didn't win—well, she couldn't think about that right now.

She'd put herself on that plate, and that was all that mattered. Or at least that's what she told herself as the five judges studied the dish in front of them. Well, four judges studied while the fifth was busy growling at a cork-sized dust bunny and nipping at the mayor's ankles.

"Excuse me," Mrs. Rose said, her voice booming though the microphone and giving a screech of feedback. The room went silent, and all two hundred sets of eyes turned to Lexi. Who forced a smile.

Mrs. Rose was on the far side of eighty, a fire hydrant of a woman who loved hunting and guns, and when dressed in black robes with a gavel she could easily be mistaken for the Honorable Judge Pricket—who was male. Something Lexi had done once in the eleventh grade and hoped never to repeat again.

Mrs. Rose poked at Lexi's first course. "Is this raw? My Barney died eating raw fish."

"Raw?" Isabel Stark said, rising to her feet, hand over her chest. "We can't serve raw fish. There are several pregnant women from Mommy and Me coming. They can't eat raw fish." She looked at the junior league in horror. "Who serves raw fish to pregnant women?"

A series of concerned and shrill whispers erupted from the defense.

"Your husband died, God rest his soul"—ChiChi paused to make the sign of the cross—"of a heart attack."

"Which was brought on by too much raw fish."

"Last I heard they fry their fish at McDonald's." ChiChi pointed to Lexi's plate, adding, "And her fish isn't raw. It's called sashimi."

"Actually—" Lexi began to correct ChiChi, but no one was listening. They were too busy wagging fingers at each other.

"Which is raw," Isabel pointed out.

"It's delicious," Lucinda said, taking to her feet to join in the fight. Lexi doubted that the woman ever ate anything but meat—on the bone—but her support was appreciated.

"It's cliché," Natasha mumbled with an elegant eye roll.

"So is using your silicone wiles to land a man, dear, but pointing things like that out is rude," Pricilla said, sweet as can be.

"Order!" Mrs. Rose slammed down the gavel so hard a piece of wood splintered off. But to Lexi's surprise, she was the only one who jumped. Everyone else looked from the defense to the prosecution and back to the judge, waiting to see who was going to be held in contempt. Everyone except Simon, who was standing on the table and showing Mrs. Rose just how sharp his canine teeth were.

"Why don't we let the chef explain her dish," Marc said and, as casual as ever, leaned down and whispered, "By the way, nice shoes, cream puff," right before he smacked her on the fanny and sent her down the aisle.

Lexi stifled a yelp, but she was already in motion heading toward the bench, suddenly happy she'd worn the shoes.

"Well, which is it, missy?" Mrs. Rose snapped, still poking at her dish when Lexi had made it to the front of the courtroom.

"Each plate has two bite-sized potato pancakes topped with asparagus mousse and a balsamic glaze, which are all locally grown and produced. The one on the right is a more traditional take, using smoked wild salmon, whereas the one on the left uses locally caught, sashimi-quality sea bass." Lexi held up her finger to silence Isabel. "Which is raw, yes, but since I have paired traditional with the experimental, there will be something for all."

Lexi went on to explain the rest of her menu, highlighting how each course paired the new and the old, and all used locally sourced products. When she finished she resumed her place next to Marc at the back of the room, and waited.

She waited as the judges tasted and compared, waited while they huddled around the bench and held hushed conversations about her food. She even waited through Mrs. Balldinger's entire cell-phone slideshow of Jeffery and Sara's honeymoon photos. Finally, Mrs. Rose tapped the mic.

The muffled sound echoed off of the plaster walls. "Quiet, please. We have reached a decision. Would the jury please rise and state their choice."

Simon let out a low moan. The poor thing seemed to be panting as he turned toward Nate—and threw up the entire contents of his stomach.

"What the—" Nate jumped up.

Frankie praised the dog.

And Natasha stood and started clapping. "That's one vote for me."

"How's that?" Lexi asked, passing Nate a roll of paper towels from her bag.

"He ate mine first and seemed fine. It wasn't until he got to yours that his stomach rebelled."

"It's not like we can ask him his opinion," Nate muttered, wiping off his lap.

Lexi was about to ask the tribunal how they had intended on weighing Simon's vote when Mrs. Rose rapped her gavel. "Has the jury reached a decision?"

"We have, Your Honor—um, Mrs. Rose," the mayor said, standing from the first juror's seat. He was a tall man, with long limbs, a beaked nose, and a wiry mop of gray hair. He was also looking directly at Natasha as he made a big ordeal out of opening the results, which made Lexi's heart drop to her toes.

"It doesn't matter what happens here," Marc whispered in her ear, brushing a kiss against her hair. "You'll get your bistro."

Lexi looked up at him and offered the best smile she could pull off. Apparently it was already one vote Natasha, Lexi zero.

"I hope so."

"Oh, sugar, I know so." He lightly tugged her hair, and she felt a simultaneous tug in her heart. Those simple words, spoken with so much conviction, made Lexi believe. Faith was something that she'd thought she lost in the divorce.

There were no words to explain what he'd just done for her, so she gave him a gentle kiss.

"In the case of the junior league versus the senior league, the jury finds in favor of the plaintiff."

The mayor finished and no one spoke. They were too busy trying to figure out who the plaintiff was.

"Pricilla's girl." Mrs. Rose smacked the gavel. "They choose for Pricilla's girl to cater the Summer Wine Showdown."

"What?" Natasha snapped, looking at Isabel and her league. "There is no way she won. You said I had this in the bag."

"Yes, well, this town likes their food like they like their girls," ChiChi said proudly. "Homegrown and good-natured."

"I was born here. I'm homegrown," Natasha argued, crossing her arms under her chest.

"Not all your parts, dear," Pricilla said with sweet smile.

Before Natasha could respond, the courthouse doors blew open, bringing in hell with a cane.

"Overruled!" Charles Baudouin yelled, raising his cane in the air and waving it angrily.

Marc barely ducked out of the way. The man might be old as dirt, but he still had a lethal swing. He also had terrible timing. Just a moment ago Lexi had been so excited, so proud of what she had accomplished. And now she just looked confused—and sad.

"You don't get to overrule a verdict," Mrs. Rose said, standing up before Marc had the chance to tell the man to get the hell out—in the most respectful way possible, of course. "You've got to be wearing a robe to do that. And I'm the only one here wearing a robe!"

"Then I'm requesting a change of venue."

"Enough," Marc said, approaching the old man and grabbing his cane before he started swinging again. "Whatever your beef is with my family, it has nothing to do with today. Lexi won on her own merit—"

"I don't care about the caterer." Charles looked as confused as Marc felt. "I'm demanding a change of venue for the Showdown."

"On what grounds?" Marc snapped.

"On account of the fact that your family has botched this thing up at every turn. And you may have saved the food, but from where I'm sitting, you're still one person shy of a tribunal."

"Have you met my friend Tanner?" Marc asked with a smile. Tanner waved. "Local hero and former NFL superstar."

"Look at you grinning like you've already won. You're just like your grandfather, so full of sh—"

"Charlie," ChiChi scolded, and the man's face immediately reddened. "There are ladies present. And that is my grandson you are speaking to."

Charles took off his hat and covered his heart with it. "Sorry about that, Chiara. I let my mouth run away with me."

"Well, it's not the first time." ChiChi walked over to Charlie and rested a pudgy hand on his arm. The man who just a second ago had been all piss and bluster was now blushing like a schoolboy. "And sadly, I don't think you're ready for it to be the last. When you are, let me know." And after a congratulatory kiss to Lexi's cheek, ChiChi left, looking much older than she had when she'd entered.

Charles watched her leave and then mumbled a few choice words, too low for Marc, or the ladies, to make out, but his emotion was clear. He was watching the woman he loved walk out—again. Only this time he wasn't losing her to someone else. He'd lost her all on his own.

Lexi stood in her apartment kitchen wearing her purple apron, peekaboo shoes, and nothing else. The sun was slowly creeping across the valley floor, and Main Street had yet to wake. But Lexi was awake; she had never actually fallen asleep.

After last night's win, Marc and his family had taken Pricilla and Lexi out for a celebratory drink. She'd forgotten how great it felt to be a part of people's lives. Back in New York, she'd been so busy trying to keep the restaurant afloat and her marriage intact she had lost touch with all of her friends from culinary school. But here, back in St. Helena, she felt like she had connections, roots. She felt like she belonged.

After drinks, they'd picked up Wingman and come back to the apartment, where Marc had slowly peeled her clothes off and made love to her—all night. Sometime between washing each other's backs—and fronts—in the claw-footed bathtub and making out on the couch while watching late-night television, Lexi had realized that she was in love with Marc, in every way possible. She wasn't sure if he was *in* love with her, but she had no doubt that he cared deeply for her. It was in every touch and smile.

The water turned on in the bathroom, and her panties—had she been wearing any—went wet. Just the thought of him naked in the shower was enough to make her hot.

She reached behind her and grabbed a skillet, her heels clicking against the wood floor. She'd never cooked in the buff before. Then again, she'd also never had a sexy man in her shower who had a thing for her apron. The apron that she'd embroidered, in a moment of sheer giddiness, with the words *Morning, Hot Stuff*.

After pouring the eggs in the skillet, Lexi slid the frittata in the oven when a low whistle of male appreciation greeted her.

She closed the oven and turned around. Marc leaned against the doorway, arms crossed, in nothing but a towel and wet skin. Lucky girl that she was, the towel was around his neck and not his middle, which was wide-awake. She stood there for a moment savoring the view of him. Thankfully, she had closed all of the blinds, because the man was so handsome he was dangerous—naked, he was lethal.

And this morning he was all hers.

"Hey," she said, surprised at how shy her voice sounded. At how shy she suddenly felt as his eyes dropped to her morning greeting plastered across her chest.

He didn't speak, just flashed her that heart-melting grin of his and twirled his finger in the air, motioning for her to turn around. Slowly, she obliged, giving a little shake when her back was in view, before facing him again.

Without a word, he moved in. Three strides and he had her pinned between the counter and the hard planes of his body. Then he kissed her. She opened immediately and moaned when his tongue slipped inside. He tasted like toothpaste and rugged man, a combination so potent it had her shaking worse than her usual double dose of espresso.

He was warm, strong, and 100 percent male, which left her feeling very feminine. She could get used to mornings like this. The way he was pressed against her, running his big hands everywhere he felt bare skin, made her wonder if he was thinking the same thing.

When they came up for air, her arms were circling his neck, legs tight around his waist, and she was seated on the counter, the cool tile pressing against her skin.

"That was a nice way to start the day." She kissed him again.

"That was me making sure you got the good in your morning." He placed a finger above the word *Morning* on her apron and traced the word *Good* right across *her* good parts.

"And this—" He reached out and tugged the neckline of her apron lower, past her collarbone, past the swell of her breast, past the tops of her nipples, which hardened under his gaze and jutted just over the fabric. "This is a great morning."

"You hungry?" She ran her hands through his hair, still damp from his shower.

"Starved."

"I have breakfast in the oven."

"Not for that."

The top of the apron strained and went taut, preventing him from pulling it down as far as he wished. At least, she figured that was what his pout was about. Adorable frown in place, he went for the tie around her neck to loosen it.

She swatted his hand away and giggled. He didn't giggle—and he didn't move his hand, except to cup her breast, which he'd finally freed, and run his thumb over her nipple.

"Did I wake you?" she asked, not sure what to do with her hands. She'd never had kitchen sex before. But considering that they had christened every other room in the house, she shouldn't have been surprised.

"Yes."

"I'm sorry."

He took her hand and placed it on his erection and smiled. "Don't be."

Then his mouth was on her breast. The sensation of his tongue on her skin had her heart thundering against her ribs. When his hands slid up and under the hem of the apron, along the inside of her thigh and higher, her brain went into a meltdown. He pushed her legs apart. She didn't giggle this time, nor did she bother stopping him.

"I do prep on this counter," Lexi whispered, no longer embarrassed to be bared and spread for his viewing pleasure.

Marc rucked the apron around her hips and dropped to his knees.

"Sugar, that's exactly what I'm doing," he said and then disappeared under her apron and began the long process of prepping for his breakfast in bed.

"What do you mean he isn't letting Simon come to the Showdown?" Marc barked, setting down his beer. "The Showdown is the day after tomorrow!"

It was only a little past two in the afternoon, but when Frankie called him out of the blue, asking him to meet her at the Spigot and bring his brothers, he knew that this was going to be a drink-mandatory kind of chat.

"Well, that wiped the stupid-ass smile off your face," Frankie said, popping her neck from side to side. "It was starting to piss me off."

Both Gabe and Trey started laughing. Which pissed Marc off, so he flipped Trey the bird and said to Gabe, "Hey, let me get you a beer, bro. On me."

His brother had been harassing him all week about Lexi. Although Marc had admitted to being in a relationship, he hadn't said a thing about them sleeping together. As far as he was concerned, it wasn't anybody's goddamned business what was going on between them.

A point that he'd made clear to his family. Only Gabe just offered up a shit-eating grin and slapped him on the back with a welcome-to-it chuckle. Marc was still trying to figure out what the hell his brother meant.

"He figured if he pulled Simon without telling you, then the tribunal would be lacking a Baudouin," Frankie said.

"And we wouldn't have time to find a replacement the night of," Trey guessed. "Wait, your brothers—"

Frankie shook her head. "Dax is still deployed, Adam is out of town, and Jonah won't judge the Showdown no matter who asks. And if you go after any of my great-uncle's side of the family, Grandpa will claim they aren't Baudouins. Which means there would be no one to fill in and you'd have to cancel the wine-tasting part of the Showdown."

"There's you," Gabe said, and all three brothers shared a look. If they could get Frankie on their side, just for one night, the whole event would be saved and Charles couldn't do anything else to screw it up.

Frankie inhaled, only to pick up her beer and take a long swallow.

"This isn't about the DeLucas versus the Baudouins. This is about the town."

"You think I don't know that? I get it, believe me. It's why I'm here." Her voice was tough as nails, but Marc noticed the way her hands shook and how she couldn't meet anyone's eyes. She didn't look like the ballbusting, tough-as-shit tomboy that he knew and avoided. She actually looked a little unsure and a whole lot scared.

She must have seen him staring, because she grabbed a fork off the table behind them and said, "Keep staring and I'll stab you in the scrotum. Got it, pretty boy?"

Marc leaned back in his chair and put one hand up in surrender; the other was shielding his goods.

"Why is he even doing this?" Gabe asked. "Sabotaging the Showdown would hurt the town and smaller wineries more than it would the DeLucas."

"Because this isn't about the Showdown," Nate said, approaching the table.

"Great." Frankie rolled her eyes, and Marc noticed her grip tighten on the fork. "*You're* here."

"Good to see you too, *Francesca.*" Nate took the only empty chair, which happened to be right next to Frankie, who immediately scooted closer to the wall. Didn't matter. Nate leaned in, pressing all of his anger and size in her face. He wasn't as big as Marc, but he was a big man and when riled could be intimidating as hell.

So he didn't blame Frankie when she leaned back, her eyes wide and her shoulders hunched. He'd never seen his brother act like this, especially toward a woman. Hell, Frankie goaded him all the time; normally he let it roll off his back. But today—today Nate was pissed.

Gabe must have sensed it too, because he put a hand on Nate's shoulder. "Reel it back a little."

Nate shrugged off Gabe's hand, zeroing in on Frankie. "When were you going to tell me that your grandpa has been talking to Montgomery Distributions? And that all of this BS surrounding the Showdown and the judges, and a fucking dog on the panel, was to discredit my family so that Charles could swoop in and steal the Monte contract right out from under us?"

"You have no idea what you're talking about," Frankie argued.

"Really?" Nate yelled. "Then explain why Adam is in Santa Barbara, right now, looking at a piece of land that will produce enough grapes to fulfill the contract?"

"I don't know, but none of my brothers give a crap about wine, which is why they walked. I'm the only one who cares what happens to the winery."

"Then someone might want to fill Monte in on that, because he just told me he didn't want to get caught up in a family feud." Nate's voice lowered, dangerously. "Do you know how much money we've already put into this deal? There is no way you and your family will get it. Not like this. Understood?"

Frankie nodded, all of her earlier edges and attitude replaced by shock. She looked at the rest of the table, her eyes wide and almost pleading. "I know that the winery is having some money issues, but I can't imagine Charles... my grandpa"—she stumbled over the word and pressed her lips together—"I didn't know, I swear."

Nate scoffed and leaned back in his chair. Marc was still reeling at the fact that Baudouin was having cash-flow problems. Maybe this was about money and not revenge. That seemed much more credible that a love affair from six decades ago gone bad. Then again, Marc remembered the shattered look on the old man's face when ChiChi had walked out of that courtroom last weekend.

Either way, Baudouin should have thrown his cards in with every other company, gone about it the honorable way.

Frankie took the reprieve to gather her strength, and when she came back, she was spitting mad. So mad Marc had to question if she'd ever even been scared in the first place.

"You think I would pussyfoot my way into some deal rather than going head-to-head with you, *Nathaniel?*"

She had a point. If Frankie wanted to take someone on, she did it openly, wanted a public setting so everyone could witness her ripping off the poor guy's nuts.

"I'm not scared of you, golden boy. And I had no idea that Grandpa was doing this, otherwise I would have told you. I don't do sneaky." She poked his chest. Hard enough to send Nate sideways. "Ever."

She said it with so much conviction, Marc believed her. So did the rest of the table, because the tension went from nuclear to normal—well, normal for a table of DeLucas and a Baudouin.

"All right," Marc said, resting his elbows on the table in a nonthreatening way. Calm or not, dealing with Frankie was like trying to declaw a feral cat. "Help us then. Sit on the tribunal."

Her breath caught, and she looked at Nate for—support? When Nate just sat mute, she whispered, "I can't."

"Why not?" Gabe asked.

She looked at Nate again, and again Nate stared back, silent, looking as confused about what she was expecting out of him as the rest of the table.

"What's the worst that can happen?" Marc ventured. "You sit on the tribunal and he decides to show up and state that he doesn't approve of you being the Baudouin representative? We're already screwed. This way we at least have a chance of pulling off the event."

Frankie closed her eyes, and for a really long and awful minute, Marc though she was going to cry. He was reaching out to pat her shoulder when her eyes snapped open, mean as ever.

"Fuck it. I'm in. But nobody knows until the actual event starts. He isn't planning on coming, so that way even if one of my aunts calls him, he'll be too late."

"I agree."

"Thank you," Nate said, his voice low.

"I'm not doing it for you. I'm doing it for the town." She stood and shoved the chair under the table. Marc's beer sloshed over the side. "And if you ever get in my face again, I will tear it off. With my teeth. Understand, golden boy?"

Trey waited until Frankie had torn out of the bar and then said, "Sex with her would most likely cost me my nuts, but it might be worth it."

"Shut up," Nate said, stealing Trey's beer and emptying the glass in one swallow. He ran a hand through his hair. "Tell me you came clean with Lexi. That she at least knows about Jeff's role in everything and Monte liking her food."

"Not entirely." *Not at all.* "Why?"

"Christ, bro," Trey said. "You're sleeping with her and you haven't told her?"

"It's called *family* business," Marc defended, knowing it was a lie and feeling guilty as shit.

"It's called being a man," Gabe said, disappointment lacing his words.

"Yeah," Marc mumbled. He'd punked out, and his time was up. He had to tell her. Tonight. He'd tell Lexi tonight and hope that she understood.

Nate let out a low whistle. "Monte and Jeff showed up at the winery just as I was getting ready to head here and meet you guys."

"Wait? Jeff is here?" If Marc had had a sinking feeling in his gut a second ago, it had completely hollowed out at the mention of Jeff. He'd left over a dozen messages for the guy in the last week, with no response.

"Yup. And he and Monte were all smiles. After Monte told me about Baudouin trying to get in on the deal, he assured me that he'd pretty much already made up his mind and that it was ours to lose."

"What are you not telling us?" Marc asked, because he knew there was more. And he wanted to finish up here so that he could go warn Lexi, at least give her a heads-up so that she wouldn't be caught off guard. And finally man up and tell her about the deal.

"Monte is so sure he's going with us that he already selected the first phase of pairings, expected to hit stores this fall. He wants to pair our wine with specialty, high-end desserts."

Marc blinked. "We didn't provide a dessert menu."

"Apparently Jeff did." Nate's eyes went right to Marc. "And they're all available at Pricilla's Patisserie."

And suddenly Marc knew what menu Monte wanted, and exactly how those items had gotten there.

CHAPTER 16

Lexi pulled a tray of freshly filled cream puffs out of the fridge and smiled. No matter how sore her cheeks got, she couldn't seem to stop.

The smile had started Sunday morning, when Marc had her for breakfast in bed, and lasted straight through the week. It stuck with her through Monday's morning rush, Tuesday and Wednesday's three hours of predawn baking, this morning's argument over which direction the slate tiles in the new kitchen should go—Tanner thought they should go on the diagonal and Abby thought that he was an idiot.

"Tell me again why we're putting mango in my tart recipe?" Pricilla asked, elbow-deep in custard.

"Because the acid will play off the sweetness in the berries nicely." ChiChi repeated Lexi's earlier answer while brushing butter over the top of the mini shortbread crusts.

"Open your ears," Lucinda harped, picking up a napkin and folding it in thirds.

"My ears are open," Pricilla defended.

"Then maybe it's your head that's leaky." Lucinda smashed a napkin through a ring made of dried grapevines, poking Mr. Puffins in the ear and jerking him awake with a start.

Even though Lexi knew she'd have to redo every place setting that Lucinda touched, and watch over Pricilla's shoulder to make sure she wasn't purposely bruising the mangoes, her smile stuck with her—right up until the bell in the front of the bakery dinged.

"I'll get it," Lexi said as she walked through the swinging doors. Then her smile died a fiery death and her day spiraled into the seventh circle of hell.

"Hey, Lexi," Jeffery said. Dressed in dark slacks and a blue shirt—the one that she'd given him for his birthday last year—he displayed enough frat-boy charm to curdle the whipped cream.

Lexi closed her eyes for a moment and wished he would disappear, because Jeffery also displayed a plump plus one, whose chicken-soup smile, white tank, and beige shorts did little to conceal the baby bump—big enough to predate their divorce.

To make matters worse, when she opened her eyes, the newlyweds were holding hands and looking happy. Really happy. Like "we just had sex where the headboard slammed into the wall and shattered the Sheetrock...oh, and we're having a baby" happy.

The baby that Lexi had begged for, the same baby that Jeffery had said he wasn't ready to have. He had failed to mention the "with her" part. Which was fine, since she still wanted a baby but not with him—not anymore. Now, though, seeing him happily married and happily expecting while happily running a successful restaurant made her want to cry. Not that she let him know that. So Lexi went for happy too, she really did, but it came out more constipated than congratulatory.

She tried again and failed.

She'd known that she would run into the new Mr. and Mrs. Balldinger at some point. It wasn't as though St. Helena was a sprawling metropolis or that she thought Jeffery would never come back to visit his parents. She had just hoped that their first run-in would be later—like after she had won her first Michelin star, found Mr. Perfect, and had her own litter of perfect kids running around.

Even more perfect was that just on the other side of the window, her frosted bun peeking through the curved center of the C in Pricilla's Patisserie, was Nora Kincaid, with her lips flapping and cell phone clutched in her fist. And since Jeffery had on shoes and a shirt, Lexi couldn't refuse him service.

Proud that the phrase *rat bastard* didn't come out, she settled on a cordial, "What can I get you?"

"How about a hug?" Jeffery asked, his arms out wide. More accurately, his right arm, since his left hand was shoved into Sara's back pocket.

"Sorry, we're all out of that," she said, her anger rising with every second he stood there smiling blissfully. Yeah, it was a free country, and yeah, he grew up here too. But she'd given him Pairing and New York so that she wouldn't have to watch the man she'd once loved love someone else. "But we are having a special on *eat shit and die.*"

Sara went white.

Jeffery gasped.

And Lexi, remembering Mrs. Kincaid and her phone's uploading capabilities, forced a smile as sugary as the cream puffs in her hand before she slid the tray onto the middle shelf of the display case. The counter created a solid barrier between them, which was a good thing, since her hands were itching to reach for her straw and tissue paper—or maybe a rolling pin. "Two for one, actually."

"I'm sorry...about everything," Sara stammered, her face flushed with humiliation, and Lexi believed her. Not that it mattered. She was over Jeffery, over the affair and the hurt and the embarrassment, but what she wasn't over was the way her ex kept inserting himself into her life as though he still had that right. She had a dinner to cater; she didn't have time for his games.

Lexi grabbed two cream puffs, dumped them in a bag, and set them on the counter. "On the house. Now leave."

Sara tugged on Jeffery's arm. "Let's just go."

"Fine," Jeffery drawled, as though Lexi was being overly dramatic and problematic. "I just wanted to give you this." He gave Sara's tush a parting pat and walked to the counter. Pulling out a document, he extended it toward Lexi.

"What's that?" she asked, eyeing the paper and shoving her hands in her apron pockets.

When she didn't reach for it, Jeffery slid it across the counter. "This is a friendly reminder that all recipes served at Pairing are property of Pairing and that you can't serve them here or anywhere else, for that matter."

There was nothing friendly about his tone, or the way her knee begged to greet him properly.

"I haven't served anything from Pairing. I have a new menu. A better menu."

"Great, then make sure Pricilla understands the terms of the ruling. You have until Monday to remove these items from your bakery menu."

At his final words, Lexi's heart dropped in conjunction with her eyes and she took in the list. It was a printed-out e-mail, sent to Jeffery from a third party, displaying a list of required items. It included her grandmother's burnt-almond cake, her peppermint bark, Rocky Road truffles, chocolate-or-bust bonbons, and her great-grandmother's éclairs, among others.

"These aren't yours." Not a single recipe had ever appeared on the restaurant menu. "And you have no legal rights to them."

"The judge ruled that any and all items ever served in Pairing belong to the restaurant. Read the ruling." Jeffery smiled and Lexi's heart stopped.

She quickly ran through every dessert she had served at the restaurant, trying to remember a time when she had prepared any of these. She couldn't. But she could sense that she was screwed. Jeffery never showed his cards unless he was certain he held the winning hand.

Then she saw who was CCed at the top of the e-mail, recognized the name, and her heart literally stopped. Right there in her chest. As though waiting for her to catch up before it broke.

"I don't understand," she muttered, looking at the Montgomery Distributions corporate logo written in big-business blue and back to Marc's name screaming at her from the top line. She tried to take in what it all meant, convince herself that she hadn't been played, that she hadn't made a colossal mistake in judgment—again.

She couldn't. She couldn't even bring herself to speak for fear that she was right.

Mrs. Kincaid must have sensed the drama and decided to give up her window view for a front-row seat, because before Jeffery could explain, the bell chimed. But when Lexi looked up, it wasn't just Mrs. Kincaid who had come in to witness the scene, but also Mrs. Moberly, Mrs. Rose, and Mrs. Craver.

"Lexi." Mrs. Kincaid greeted her with a hesitant smile and took a seat at the far corner table. "Jeffery, and *other*."

"Don't mind us," Mrs. Moberly said, taking a seat as well and making herself busy wiping down an already-clean table. "We're just in need of an afternoon coffee and treat. But no hurry, dear; we're in no rush."

Mrs. Rose glared at Jeffery and whispered, loud enough for most of Main Street to hear, "We're here as long as you need us." With a decisive nod she took her seat and patted her purse, which according to Mrs. Lambert at the Grapevine Prune and Clip was packing a whole lot more than lipstick and her extra set of teeth.

But Lexi could survive three backseat bakers, the town's busiest busybodies, and her ex and his new wife. It was when she saw Marc, standing frozen in the doorway looking back at her, that she knew.

Her heart slowly gave one last beat for the man she had fallen in love with.

And then it shattered.

"The recipes are mine," Lexi whispered, her voice so small and so full of hurt, Marc's gut twisted painfully.

Marc opened his mouth to say that he didn't want them, that he'd never meant to hurt her, but nothing came out. The pain in his gut made it impossible to swallow, let alone speak.

The last thing he wanted to do was have this conversation here, in her grandmother's bakery, in front of her ex-husband, his new wife, and a handful of customers. But he had waited too long, and he was out of time—and excuses.

"These recipes belong to my family," she said, louder this time, holding out a piece of paper. "And no one is taking them from me." She dropped the paper to her side. "You knew. This whole time you knew."

God, his heart was breaking.

"Let me explain," he said, moving toward her and coming to a dead stop after only one step. Because Lexi backed away and held out a shaky hand, begging him to keep his distance.

"Please. Explain. Because I want to know how my family recipes, desserts that were never served at Pairing, ended up in some contract between you, my cheat of an ex, and some distribution company."

"Two years ago," he said, closing the distance between them and aching to take her into his arms, "I came to visit and you made me a batch of your grandma's éclairs."

She nodded, her eyes big and wet, looking up as if she was silently pleading for him to make this all go away. He wanted to. So badly, but he wasn't sure how.

"You joked that the ones in France were better," she whispered.

The joke had been one made out of desperation, a tactic he'd adopted early on when Jeff and Lexi started dating.

They'd spent most of the evening crammed in a booth at the back of the restaurant, talking about high school, home, the progress he'd made on the hotel. The more they talked, the closer Lexi got, until she was so close that he couldn't smell, couldn't see, couldn't feel anything but her. A bottle and a half into the conversation, she'd rested her hand on his knee and leaned in and laughed at something he said—and Marc had lost it.

After years of keeping his distance, playing by the rules, ignoring the insane chemistry between them, he went in for the kiss, promising himself that he just needed to taste her one time—when Jeffery had appeared from the back office. Marc whispered something stupid in her ear, made her laugh, goaded her into baking him some of her great-grandmother's éclairs, and vowed never to go back for another visit. At least not one that included time with Lexi.

"But you weren't even a customer," she said. "You were a guest."

"Of the restaurant," Jeffery added, and Marc wanted to punch him. "You made them in my kitchen and served them to my guest. Just like the rest of the recipes on the list."

"The *rest* of the recipes I made as a favor, for you," Lexi said to Jeff. "You said you had an important client to impress who had a sweet tooth. I assumed it was for an investor for opening Pairing West Coast. Then again, I assumed you weren't sleeping with another woman at the time."

"Either way, they belong to Pairing."

"Shut up, Jeff," Marc snapped.

"What?" Jeff shrugged like a guy who didn't have a fucking care in the world, like Lexi's world wasn't shattering while they stood there and watched, like he'd never even given a damn about his ex-wife.

"When I teased you into making the éclairs…" Marc paused, seeing how everything would look to her, in this moment. Suddenly every wild, shitty, crazy thing he'd ever done came back with such force it smacked the wind out of him. He was going to lose her. And it was all his fault. "I am so sorry, Lexi."

She looked at him for a long, tense moment. Her face crumpled, and the first tear rolled down her cheek.

"No, sugar, don't cry." He ran his thumb across her cheek. "I know I fucked up. I was going to tell you, but I got scared." Another tear fell, then another. "I'll fix this. You need to believe me."

Unable to hold back, he reached out and cupped her face between his hands. "Please, believe me."

"I'm trying, Marc," she whispered. "But it's really hard. I don't know what's real, and I'm scared that this whole thing was—"

"Wait," Jeff interrupted. "What do you mean, you'll fix this? Do I need to remind you how much money we have riding on this? Monte, your brothers, hell, my restaurant."

Jeff paused, his eyes darting between Lexi and Marc, a grin sliding across his face so slowly Marc wanted to smack it off. It was an *ah-yeah* grin that he'd flashed Marc a hundred times, reserved for poker night and mornings after at the gym. "Jesus Christ, really?"

Jeff was so obvious he might as well have given him a high five and scratched a notch in Marc's belt that read, *Alexis Moreau, Great Lay.*

Lexi snatched her hand back and wrapped it around her stomach. The look of utter humiliation on her face said she got the message loud and clear.

"I know I told you to keep an eye on her, but damn, really?" Jeff shook his head, and Marc wondered what he'd ever seen in the guy. Under all of the shine and flash was a tool. A worthless piece of shit who didn't see anything outside the realm of Jeff.

"What part of *shut the hell up* did you miss?" Marc snapped, but when he turned back to Lexi, his anger fled and all he felt was this gut-wrenching knowledge that Gabe had been right. He'd played this one fast and reckless and he'd blown it. And in the process he'd lost Lexi.

"You were *keeping an eye* on me?"

"Lexi." He took a step forward, but she backed away again, shaking her head.

"This whole thing was a big game to you guys. Just like back in high school when you set out to seduce a new conquest. The menu, my grandma's books, the bistro, the dinner at your family's house, all of it. Only this time you weren't just out to get in my pants—" Her voice caught and her eyes went round with understanding. He knew where she was going, and she was so wrong. "That was fake too. All of it was fake."

She looked around the bakery, as if remembering that there was a roomful of people watching and chronicling the most humiliating moment of her life.

"Lexi, that's not true." But she wasn't listening.

"You made me feel sexy and beautiful and like I was special."

"You are, God, baby, you are. To me, you always have been."

"You told me I could make the bistro a success. And I listened and like a stupid woman I believed you, Marc. I believed you so much that I stopped listening to the voice inside of me, warning me to take it slow. I believed you to the point that I don't think I have any belief left to give."

She reached up and untied the top of her apron, the lavender one that he loved so much. Folding it in half, she laid it on the counter and gave him one last look. A look he would never forget. He knew that whatever Jeff had done to her was nothing compared to what he'd just accomplished. Marc had played and lost, and in the process he'd completely devastated her world.

With a whispered good-bye, she walked out the door, the bells of the bakery giving a final jingle. Marc somehow made his way to the window and watched her disappear behind the alley. He rested his head against the glass when he was sure that she was gone, and that she wasn't coming back.

And that's when he finally understood. Understood that old man Charles wouldn't come to the Showdown, wouldn't try to ruin the wine tasting, wouldn't continue this sixty-year feud. Because losing the woman you love to another man could make you do stupid things. But losing the woman you love all on your own—there's no coming back from that.

A few seconds, a few minutes, hell, a lifetime could have passed. Marc stood there, looking out the window and replaying every decision he'd ever made with regard to Lexi. He was surprised when he turned around to find everyone still in the bakery staring at him, including his nonna, who must have come out at some point during the argument, because she was looking at him with shame.

He didn't blame her. He was ashamed. And angry. And he hurt so fucking bad he couldn't breathe right.

When ChiChi took a step forward, Marc said, "I gotta go," and walked out the door, down the street past the Paws and Claws Day Spa, past Bottles and Bottles: Pharmacy and Wine, and kept going until he found himself walking through his family's vineyard and somehow made it to Gabe's front door.

The door opened. Gabe took one look at Marc and took a step back, holding the door open wide. "Aw, man, come on in, you look like hell."

Marc didn't move.

"I blew it, Gabe."

"Can we fix it?"

"I don't think so." He rested his forehead against the doorframe. "She likes my dog, doesn't take my crap, and looks at me like I can be the kind of man Dad was. When she cooks…she wears this apron…" He paused and looked up at his brother and felt everything inside tighten. "And I love her so damn much that I have no idea how I'm supposed to wake up tomorrow and pretend like my life hasn't just fucking ended."

CHAPTER 17

Lexi's phone rang again, and she let it go to voice mail— again. It was two in the morning. And probably Marc. And she just couldn't bring herself to answer it.

She didn't know if he was calling to ask if she was still going to cater the Showdown tomorrow or if he was calling to apologize and beg for her back. Either way, she couldn't stomach it. If it was the first, she'd cry because he wasn't calling to apologize and beg for her back. If it was the latter, she was afraid she'd cry because she'd have to tell him where he could shove his apology. And she was tired of crying. She was also drunk.

So when the phone stopped ringing, she waited for a long beat, then decided to pour herself another teacup of Pricilla's Angelica and grabbed her needle and thread.

Earlier that evening, she had used the seam ripper to take the *Morning, Hot Stuff* out of her apron, replacing it with *Deflated Cream Puff* before she finally settled on *I Love You, Dumb-ass!*

She had just finished putting a black heart in place of the period at the bottom of the exclamation mark when the phone rang again.

Knotting the thread, she set her craft aside and downed her teacup. It was ringing for the third time when she finally looked over at the stack of three-by-five cards resting on her pillows that Abby had given her. They were a series of prompts for her to refer to in case she gave in to the weakness and answered. Most of them were so profane she would be too embarrassed to even say them, which was another reason not to answer.

By the time the call went to voice mail, she'd managed to refill and reempty her glass again. She'd also managed to spill half of said glass down her front.

"Crap." She hopped up and grabbed a pair of dirty jeans from the floor and scrubbed at the tank top until it had faint denim smudges on the chest.

A soft tap sounded at the window.

Lexi froze. Jeans in hand, breathing nonexistent, she listened. When holding her breath and standing still became not only impossible but dangerous, she tiptoed over to the window and braced herself.

Was Marc down in the alley tossing pebbles at her window? Because if he was, she would tell him just how cheesy his *Romeo and Juliet* act was—and just where he could shove his apology.

After a quick fluff to the hair, Lexi grabbed the curtain, yanked it back, and screamed.

A face was staring at her through the glass. A face with frizzy hair and pissed-off eyes that was staring. Right. At.

Her. It opened its mouth, only Lexi was too afraid to hear what it would say.

One hand over her lips, the other slamming the curtain back in place, she backed up and stumbled onto the bed. The prompt cards scattered to the floor, but thankfully the Angelica was all right.

"Will you open the window!" Abby's voice hissed though the glass and fabric.

Lexi did, and the sight made her want to cry all over again. It wasn't Marc. He hadn't crawled up her trellis, hadn't come to say he was in love with her, and even worse, she didn't know if he regretted hurting her. If he had even felt what she had. And if his chest ached to the point of suffocation.

"It's you," Lexi sighed, unable to hide the disappointment in her voice. "What are you doing?"

Abby stared. "What does it look like I'm doing? I'm breaking you out of this self-imposed hellhole."

"Oh." For some reason that made sense. "Why didn't you come through the door?"

"Because it's locked."

"I would have let you in. Plus, there's a spare key. I hid it under the gnome." Marc knew it was there. He had used it a few times to wake her up in the morning after his run.

God, she missed him.

"Great to know. Next time I have to knock for over an hour, I'll remember that."

"How are you all the way up here?" Lexi leaned out the window, around Abby, and squinted at the bright-yellow ladder wedged up against the side of the building. Then she looked at the window across the alley and wondered if he was in there. She had pulled her blinds so he wouldn't see her crying, but every few hours she checked for a sign of him. She never found one.

Maybe he had fallen asleep on his desk, waiting for her to open her blinds. She nudged her tank top lower, happy that she had forgone a bra, leaned out the window farther, and asked, really loudly, "Where did you get the ladder?"

Lexi looked at his window. No lights. No movement. Just depressing darkness.

"I borrowed it from Jack," Abby said, giving her a really weird look.

"So it's Jack now, huh? What did that cost you?"

"Three extra piano lessons, and—" Abby paused. "Why are you yelling? Are you drunk?"

"No." Lexi smiled. Then laughed. Then slapped a hand over her mouth.

Abby leaned in and immediately jerked back, her nose wrinkling. Abby had a perfect nose, pert with a few freckles, and it even looked cute when crinkled up in disgust. "Did you fall in a vat?"

"Nope." Lexi sat back on the bed and snagged the bottle of Angelica off the nightstand, shoving it in Abby's face and nearly knocking her friend off the ladder.

"Give me that." Abby snatched at the bottle, but Lexi held on.

"He broke my heart, Abs," Lexi whispered.

Abby's eyes went soft with understanding. "I know. He's an idiot, and the only thing that saved him from having to place his own 'Where's My Dick' ad is that he's my brother, and I love him."

"Me too," Lexi said, and the tears pooled up again.

"I know you do. At the farmers' market, I knew." She took Lexi's hand in her own tiny one and squeezed. "Would it help if I said that Marc knows he messed up and that he didn't know Jeffery was after your recipes until it was too late and then he was stuck between disappointing you and my other brothers?"

Lexi thought about it and shook her head. He had still kept secrets from her, and good intentions or not, secrets hurt. Sometimes they hurt worse than lies. And Lexi was tired of being hurt.

"Would it help if I said I think he loves you back, but being that he's a DeLuca with the Y chromosome, he couldn't help but screw this up?"

"That makes it worse." Lexi took in a shuddery breath and tried not to cry. Imagining a life without him had been devastating. But what if Abby was telling the truth? What if he did love her? She would be walking away from her only chance of spaghetti-splattered-apron kind of love. "I don't know what to do. This is different than Jeffery. I'm not embarrassed or angry. God, Abs, it hurts so bad." She patted the spot above her heart that felt like it was missing, like it would never be whole again. "I can't even breathe."

"Which is why you're going to go grab a towel before we both wind up drunk and crying."

"I don't want to go—"

"Grab a towel." Abby gave Lexi one last look and then started down the ladder.

Lexi wiped her face on the hem of her tank top and gave a little sniffle. When she could take in air without pain shooting through her chest, she leaned over the sill and looked down at Abby, who was on the alley floor. "Where are we going?"

"The lake." Abby held up a familiar set of keys. "Now hurry up before Pricilla figures out that I stole her car."

Lexi stumbled to the bathroom and, avoiding a peek in the mirror for fear that she would never leave the house again, brushed her teeth. She was about to leave when she stopped to smell her shirt. *Vat* was putting it mildly.

Grimacing, she shucked the tear-and-snot-stained tank and headed back to the bedroom, grabbing the towels.

"Why don't you go out the front door?" Abby suggested when Lexi stuck her legs out the window and nearly tumbled down the ladder.

"This is more fun," she hollered back, tossing the towels to the ground, hoping they landed on Abby's head while silently counting each rung of the ladder as she descended.

"Um, Lex?"

"Don't talk to me. I'm counting!"

"Yeah, well, you might want to count your way back up to your room and get some clothes on."

Lexi got to the bottom rung, number fifteen to be exact, and hopped off. "No way. Last time we did this I played it half-assed and look where that got me. Married"—she counted off each infringement on her fingers—"divorced, in debt, jobless, and with a broken heart, courtesy of my fake boyfriend."

The last infringement counted for five on its own, which brought her loser grand total to a whopping 90 percent.

Abby gave her a long look and cracked a smile. "Well, you don't have to worry about half-assing it this time, because I can see your whole ass."

CHAPTER 18

Marc stood at the back of the ballroom, watching people mingle and chat and fill out checks big enough to pay for a year of medical and educational needs for the entire town. From the way the mayor kept grinning and pumping the hands of the guests, Marc knew that even though the night was only half over, they had already reached their mark. Just like he knew that he should be out there welcoming his guests, drumming up support for next year's event—doing his job.

But the only thing he could do was think about Lexi.

He knew she was there. Her first course had been served, and devoured, and now the waiters were bringing out the entrées. But Lexi hadn't come out of the kitchen. And Marc, not wanting to make this night any harder on her, had kept his distance.

The summer his parents died, Abby had locked herself in her room for three months and posted a sign that read *Need Space*. Earlier that afternoon, Marc had seen Lexi in the lobby of the hotel talking to Abby, and when he gave her a little wave, she gave him a look that pretty much read the same as Abby's sign. The only difference was that by the time school rolled around, Abby had taken down her sign. He didn't think he'd get that lucky with Lexi. Hers looked to be permanent—with regard to him.

"I just overheard the mayor talking to the press about how great tonight turned out," Nate said, walking up beside him with Trey in tow. "Said it was the best Showdown St. Helena has hosted in recent years."

"It's the first Showdown St. Helena has hosted in recent years," Marc mumbled, tugging at his bow tie and knowing it wouldn't make one ounce of difference. He felt like he'd been slowly suffocating all night.

"Good thing the bar wasn't set very high, then," Trey said. "Just means next year it won't be hard to beat."

Marc didn't say anything. He didn't know if there would be a next year, not at the Napa Grand, at least. At the rate his chest was struggling to expand, he didn't know if he'd make it to tomorrow.

"Some dumb-ass said I have to sit at the head table," Frankie said from behind. All three men turned and stared in shock. Someone actually moaned; it sounded like Nate.

"What?" Frankie said, looking from one brother to the other. "Oh right. I'm late. Sorry," she snapped, and that was the only Frankie-like trait about her. Gone were the black leather and steel toes, and in their place were fitted red silk, strappy heels that brought her to at least six feet, and enough skin and cleavage to make Marc wonder if the whole tattoo rumor was just that—a rumor.

"Francesca," Nate stuttered. The assured, never-show-emotion, ever-so-logical brother actually had to snap his jaw shut and wipe off the drool. "You look great."

Frankie bent her knees enough to meet Nate's eyes, which were currently glued to her chest. "They're called boobs, Nathaniel. They come with being a woman."

Nate looked up and flashed a rare smile. "I know what they are. I've just never seen yours before."

Marc had to pause. He wasn't sure if Nate was flirting or sparring.

Either way, Frankie's eyes went hard and her lips thinned. "Just tell me where I have to sit or I'm gone."

"At the front table," Marc said.

"See, the dumb-ass was right," Gabe said, walking through the crowd and resting a hand on Frankie's elbow. "Would you like me to escort you there?"

Frankie blinked. And took a step back, as though thrown by the gesture. "If you're being nice because of the dumb-ass comment, I'm sorry. It's the DeLuca hair and eyes. They're so dark I just assume they're full of shit." Her eyes narrowed and darted around the room. "And if you're offering because your wife made you, tell her I've been walking since I was seven months old, so bite me. Oh"—she looked at Marc—"you have ten minutes to start the tasting, because I'm thirsty."

Nate's eyes zeroed in on Frankie's ass and didn't let up until she had disappeared into the crowd.

Trey whistled. "Definitely worth the risk of castration."

"Shut up," all three of his brothers said in unison.

Gabe gave him a long look and placed a hand on Marc's shoulder. "You got the papers?"

"All ready to go." Marc patted his breast pocket, and the contract his assistant, Chrissi, had delivered to him earlier in the evening. "Are you guys sure? There's a lot riding on this. If it goes bad, it's going to go really bad."

It was the only thing Jeff had been right about. The play they were about to make was bold and risky and all Marc's idea. He was willing to risk everything if it meant making things right, but he didn't want his brothers to suffer if his plan imploded.

"You believe in this?" Trey asked.

"Hell yes," Marc said. It was the best idea he'd had in ages. It was how his father would have handled this situation. And that made Marc feel confident in moving forward. "But it has just as much chance of succeeding as it does of falling apart."

"Will there be another girl?" Gabe asked.

Not like Lexi, Marc thought, shaking his head.

"Well, there'll be other companies." Gabe clapped him on the back, and they headed toward Monte's table a united front, DeLuca dialed to high and badass brothers cranked up to one hundred proof.

"Plus, we're Italian," Trey said as they passed the front table and made their way around the ballroom.

"Meaning what?" Marc asked. "We're leaving the gun and taking the cannoli?"

"No," Gabe said. "Meaning you don't fuck with our family, our wine, or our women."

By the time dessert rolled around, Lexi had avocado mousse dried to her left butt cheek, choux pastry permanently attached to her scalp, and enough ganache on her jacket to pass for a chocolate bunny. She also had a heartache the size of Montana and a hangover that made oxygen toxic.

Arranging the chocolate curls on the last plate of cream puffs and éclairs, Lexi picked up the tray and gave herself a gold star for the day. She'd decorated the ballroom, prepared a three-course meal for over a thousand, and managed to avoid Marc for most of the evening. The first two she'd managed with the help of her grannies and Marc's kitchen staff. The last she'd managed all on her own.

Seeing him after his morning run in the lobby had been hard enough, and knowing that as head chef she had to deliver the desserts to the head table made her stomach drop painfully to her toes. But she had to do it. It was the reason she had swallowed the hurt and started prepping the minute Abby had dropped her off at home last night—drenched and naked and ready to take control of her life.

The town was counting on her, Pricilla was counting on her, and she was counting on herself. It was time to grow up and start living the life she'd dreamed of. Even if that dream life didn't include Marc.

Lexi dusted the hair out of her face, and after shoving a miniéclair in her mouth for strength, she pushed through the swinging kitchen doors, ready to present her family's pastries to the world. She had meant what she said yesterday. Her grandmother had entrusted her with these recipes; they were *her* legacy, and she would spend every penny she earned tonight fighting for them.

Lexi rounded the beverage prep station and was headed toward the main dining room when she came to a stop. Because there, just two feet away and on the other side of the pass-through window, stood Marc and his three brothers, deep in discussion with an older man she didn't recognize. All the DeLucas were dressed in tuxes, all looking beyond handsome, and all exuded so much male swagger that the tall silver fox, who in any other circumstance could have doubled for the Most Interesting Man in the World, seemed to be suffering from DeLuca intoxication.

Lexi felt for the guy. Those brothers packed a powerful punch. In fact, they looked like a sexy group of Italian mobsters, giving the poor man a choice between a single gunshot to the head or concrete shoes. And he'd be so dazzled by their charm that he'd say yes and yes.

A month ago, Lexi would have gone for the gunshot to the head. Quick, painless, and, if done right, wouldn't ruin her clothes. The new Lexi, the one who streaked down Main Street screaming the theme from *Rocky* at the top of her lungs, the one who wasn't ashamed of the woman she had become, would go for the concrete shoes. Because concrete might be heavy, but she would rather go standing up than just lie there.

She should move on, deliver her tray to the tribunal table, and then disappear back inside the safety of her kitchen. Eavesdropping was wrong and rude, which was why she stashed her tray on top of the ice machine, pressed her body against the wall, and squatted down low enough that she could peek over the ledge of the pass-through but remain inconspicuous.

"That's it?" Silver Fox said, flipping through some papers.

"Yes, sir. And this is a one-time offer," Marc said. He sounded so confident and so sure of himself that Lexi felt her traitorous heart stand up and cheer. His brothers flanked him, letting him run the discussion but making it clear that they had his back. It was what Marc had worked so hard for. His parents would have been proud.

"You will get the distribution rights for all DeLuca wines," Marc went on, "in the markets that are specified in the contract. They will be paired exclusively with Pricilla's pastries, *if* Lexi and her grandmother agree, so I suggest you make this deal so sweet that they can't say no. Because understand, if they say no, or if you bring in another supplier to pair with DeLuca products, the deal is off."

"What about Jeffery and Pairing?" the man, who she assumed was Montgomery, asked, obviously stunned by the turning of the tables.

"He is no longer an approved partner for DeLuca Wines," Gabe said. "Any company that deals with him will find getting partners in the valley difficult."

Lexi almost fell over.

Montgomery played it cooler, and just nodded. "And I have until when to decide?"

"If we don't hear from the Moreaus that you have reached a deal that works in their favor by next Friday, then we will start negotiations with Hunt Foods and Distributions."

Lexi didn't know who this Hunt was, but by the way Silver Fox straightened when Marc mentioned his name, she assumed he was the Baudouin to Silver's DeLuca.

"You guys play hardball," Montgomery said.

"That is not our intention, sir," Marc said, respect clear in his voice. "You chose DeLuca because of the food that was served to you at Pairing." *He did?* "Those dessert recipes as well as all of the desserts served here tonight belong to Alexis Moreau and her grandmother. It's only fair that they benefit from their hard work."

"I didn't know," Montgomery said, and Lexi wanted to find Jeffery and shove him in a tub of curdled cream. That's why he'd wanted her to make Pricilla's desserts several months ago. The first time he'd asked for a few desserts, he said it was for an investor, and another time he'd claimed they were for poker night, but she'd bet her éclairs that it had all been for Montgomery. The rat-bastard sneak had been cheating on her and using her for her recipes.

She stood up, momentarily forgetting she was eavesdropping, then dropped back down, this time all the way to the floor.

"And that's my fault," Marc said. "This is my way of making this right."

The talking turned to numbers, and Lexi tuned them out. She snagged an éclair off the tray and sank back against the wall, wondering, over a cream-filled bite, if Marc wanted to make other things right. And if he did, could she forgive him for what he'd done?

Two éclairs, a cream puff, and a handful of ice chips later, she realized that she could. All she needed was to stop being so scared. Life was crazy and risky and it didn't always apologize when it was rude—and that was okay.

Lexi smiled and grabbed another éclair.

"I hope you brought enough to share with the class," said a sexy voice from overhead.

Lexi tilted her head back and stared up into the most beautiful eyes she'd ever seen. Marc was leaning on the passthrough, his forearms leisurely resting on the lower sill, bow tie dangling from his neck, and he smelled so good she wanted to cry.

His eyes were red-rimmed and his smile raw, and she'd bet he was about as miserable as she was. So she held up the last bite—the best bite—and offered it to him.

He didn't reach out, didn't take it, just opened his mouth.

Lexi stood up and gently placed it inside. He didn't nip or lick her fingers; instead, he pressed a gentle kiss to the tips and then straightened.

"I saw you went for a jog last night."

She froze, her face heating. "You *saw?*" She was going to kill Abby.

A little smile tugged at his lips. "Not live, unfortunately. But Mrs. Lambert was working late and heard a commotion. She was going to call the cops when she saw a very drunk, very naked woman streaking past. She whipped out her cell and filmed it. You can watch it on YouTube."

"It's on YouTube?" *Oh God.*

"Yup, watched it ten times." His smile faded and his face went serious. "I am so fucking sorry, Lexi. I screwed up and I got scared, but I never played it fast or loose with you. You have never been a game or a challenge."

"Marc," she began, but he placed a finger on her mouth.

"Please let me finish. I have to say this. I fell in love with you when we were fourteen and snuck into the hotel. I didn't know what it was at the time, but I knew I'd never felt it before and I never wanted it to go away. Then Jeff came along and I lost you. And then my parents..." He broke off and swallowed. "When Jeff went to New York, I didn't know if I was willing to take the risk of loving someone only to lose them again, so I told you to go after him, and it was the biggest mistake of my life. Well, it *was* the biggest mistake, until I stood by and let him take your recipes and said nothing."

"Is what you said to Monte true? Did you really get my recipes back?"

"Not all of them, just the desserts. I pointed out that since he failed to disclose in the divorce proceedings that there was a deal in the works while you were still married, it might be in your best interest to renegotiate the terms of the settlement. Then I threatened to explain to the judge that your desserts were never on the restaurant's menu and that he'd set you up."

"Thank you, but I'm sorry that you got stuck in the middle," Lexi said softly, knowing it was true. She was beyond angry at Jeffery, but she knew how much it must have hurt Marc to lose his oldest friend. "I never wanted you to have to choose between us."

"Screw the middle, sugar. And as far as I'm concerned, you are my only choice. Ever."

Marc took a small step back and dropped down to one knee and looked up at her over the pass-through.

"What are you doing?" she whispered, terrified that she was misunderstanding his intentions.

"Taking the biggest risk of my life. I don't have flowers or candy or a ring, and you have every right to tell me to go to hell, but I'm offering you my love and loyalty and everything that I am."

He took a breath and just looked at her, and what she saw in his expression made her chest swell.

"You look like your dad right now," she whispered.

He rose to his feet and tangled her hands with his. "That's what I figured out when I watched you fold up your apron and walk out of the bakery. I'm just like my dad, sugar—when I screw up, I screw up big. But when I love—"

Lexi reached through the window, grabbed him by the undone ends of his bow tie, and kissed him. And good Lord, he kissed her back.

It was then that Lexi knew exactly what it felt like to be loved.

"I love you, Marc," she whispered against his lips. "And I've got an apron at home to prove it."

"Wait." He pulled back enough to look her in the eyes. His were weary and hopeful and so full of love it made her breath catch. "Is that a yes?"

She nodded.

"God, I love you." He kissed her nose, the corners of her mouth, her lips. "And your apron, do you know how much I love your apron?"

By the time they eased back, her hands were tangled in his hair, his were suctioned to her bottom, and they were both stuck in the pass-through. Marc tugged and Lexi pulled, but it was no use. The width of his arms around her hips had them wedged in.

Lexi laughed. "We're stuck."

"Right where I want to be." Marc flashed that bad-boy grin that had everything inside of her melting, especially when his hands started making little circles on her backside. With a quick peek at the tray on the icemaker, he asked, "Any éclairs left?"

Lexi took account and shook her head. "Nope, but there are some cream puffs."

"My favorite," he whispered right before he captured her lips with his and took a nibble.

Sneak peek at
Autumn at the Vineyard

It had taken eighteen months, some tricky negotiating, her entire life savings, and a lot of ballbusting—but Francesca Baudouin was finally a vineyard owner. Well, she was the owner of fifty acres of prime St. Helena appellation soil, which would take another five years of sweat and, quite possibly, selling off a few of her vital organs before it became a quality producing vineyard.

But Sorrento Ranch, the most sought-after property in the valley, and all of its belongings, was hers. She bought it right out from under the DeLucas' noses. In part because Mrs. Sorrento played darts with Frankie and her great-aunt every Thursday night, but mostly because she knew selling the land to either family involved in the great DeLuca-Baudouin feud would piss off her ex-husband.

"One more inch and I'll shoot," Frankie said to the four-legged garbage disposal in front of her, whose mouth was currently wrapped around the plastic casing of the water tank. She stomped her ballbuster, steeled-toed combat boot in his direction for added emphasis.

The alpaca's beady eyes narrowed and dropped to her feet. Extending its lips in her direction, he made a loud raspberry sound and then went back to nibbling. Yeah, ballbuster or not, hooves beat boots.

But Frankie wasn't about to let some hardheaded mule with shaggy hair and buck teeth stick it to her on her first week in business. Being the youngest of four, and the only girl, Frankie was a pro at dealing with stubborn males who excelled at ignoring her completely, while messing with her life wholeheartedly.

She cocked her rifle.

"The only thing separating you from becoming next season's sweater-set is my trigger finger, Camel Boy." Because the only thing separating *them* from fifteen thousand gallons of rainwater was the thin plastic seam-binding on the water tank, which "Sweater-Set" had managed to chew loose. She didn't want to deal with the cleanup and couldn't afford a new irrigation tank. "I mean it, one more bite and the only identifying male trait you'll have left is stupidity."

That got his attention. In fact, the animal straightened and fluffed out the fur around his face, making him look like a cross between a camel, a koala, and Clifford the Big Red Dog. When he wasn't destroying her property, he was kind of cute. In a big, dumb, oafy kind of way.

Sweater-Set was the sole remaining alpaca from Mrs. Sorrento's alpaca farm. The rest of his hooved brethren were living it up at Alberta's Paradise Alpaca Farm and Pet Sanctuary. Sweater-Set hadn't even placed one hoof in the back of the moving truck when the rest of the heard gathered their spit and took aim. The poor thing had been kicked out of his own family, and before Frankie or Alberta had been able to catch him, his fluffy butt had disappeared, and Alberta had left instructions to call when Frankie had the runaway secured. That had been four days, two patio chairs, and a motorcycle tire ago.

"See," Frankie said, lowering her rifle to the ground and picking up the cushion from Mr. Sorrento's old recliner in one hand and a rope in the other. "That wasn't so bad. Now just come over here and I'll give you a treat."

Eyes glued to the nubby avocado-green cushion, the alpaca took a tentative step forward.

"Then you can go to your new house." Another step. "Where they feed you gourmet hay and mud tires, and there are kids around all the time to play with you." Step. "And you'll get to see your family."

The alpaca stopped, squared its body, and let out an ear-piercing bleat, which sounded like a cross between "wark" and Chewbacca screaming, right before he sank his teeth into the plastic casing and pulled. Hard.

"Sweater-Set!"

"Wark!"

"No—"

The tank split at the seam, and before either could move, a wall of water came crashing down with enough force to topple Sweater-Set into Frankie and send the two of them skidding back several feet.

When Frankie stopped moving and the water had receded into a pool of mud and algae, she shoved the hair out of her eyes and took stock. She was flat on her back, with a stick wedged into her right butt cheek and a drenched Sweater-Set sprawled out over the top of her.

"Move," she said, shoving at the animal.

"Wark-wark!"

"I warned you! But did you listen?"

Sweater-Set let out an apologetic nicker and dropped his head to Frankie's chest, his big brown eyes looking up at her through his lashes.

"You could be halfway to Paradise right now," she cooed, giving him a little rub behind the ears. "Just think, in a few months it will be grooming season and all the ladies will be prancing around in nothing but sheered skin. Plus, you'll have your family."

This time the nicker was almost sad, so Frankie, ignoring that he smelled like wet dog and calling a temporary truce, dug both hands in his thick fur and began scratching his cheeks. "Yeah, I get it. Family sucks, but I can't let you stay here. In a few months I'll start planting my vines, and you'd eat them."

Sweater-Set huffed, a burst of hot air hitting Frankie in the face.

"Liar." Frankie worked her fingers around his temples and into his head. Sweater-Set's eyes slid closed in ecstasy. "You already cost me a water tank, which I can't afford to replace, by the way."

Sweater-Set's only response was to nuzzle Frankie's chest and hum loudly.

"So there's no way I have the budget to keep replacing everything you decide to sink your teeth into."

Hum. Hum. Hum.

"I hope he bought you dinner first."

With a groan, Frankie turned her head and, wishing she were standing so she could glare at him without having to shield her eyes, swore. Upside down or not, there was no mistaking the man who was currently towering over her—or the way her stomach gave a lame little flutter when he lifted his mirrored glasses and delivered a heart-stopping wink.

"Afternoon, Francesca," he said with enough practiced swagger that it made not rolling her eyes impossible.

Nathaniel DeLuca was six-plus feet of solid muscle and smug-male yumminess, and he smelled like sex. He was also extremely Italian, annoying as hell, and for whatever reason, every time he entered Frankie's space she felt all dainty and feminine. Which pissed her off even more because at one time she'd trusted Nate with her heart and her deepest secret.

And he'd broken them both.

Thank God she had on her ballbuster boots today. Too bad they were currently covered in mud and alpaca fur, and pointing at the sky.

"Go away, *Nathaniel*," she said by way of greeting.

Sweater-Set hummed louder, arching into her hand as Frankie scratched down his spine.

"And leave a lady in need?" Nate said, coming forward and squatting down to pluck a maple leaf off of Frankie's forehead. "Nonna ChiChi would have my ass."

"I know you're used to your women poised and proper. But I've got this handled."

"I didn't know you paid that much attention to my women, but now that you mentioned the difference..." He plucked a branch from her hair and flashed his perfectly straight teeth in her face. His smile, like his personality, was lethal, and his entitled attitude was 100 percent DeLuca. "I won't have to worry that you'll cry when I tell you to stop exciting my alpaca and get the hell off my property."

ACKNOWLEDGMENTS

To the most wonderful agent in the world, Jill Marsal, who I couldn't imagine taking this journey without. Thanks to my editors Lindsay Guzzardo and Becky Vinter, for believing in my work and supporting me throughout the process. Lindsay, although I am sad that this is the last book we will collaborate on, I wish you the best of luck in your new venture. And to the entire Montlake team for being so fabulous to work with.

A special thanks to Britt Bury, Hannah Jayne, and Jacee James for all of the brainstorming and plotting and for being amazing friends. And to my coven of Rougers, I am honored to be included in a group with such amazing writers and women!

Finally, to my daughter Thuy and my husband Rocco, for allowing me to follow my dreams and high-fiving me the entire way!

ABOUT THE AUTHOR

Marina Adair is a national bestselling author of romance novels. Along with the St. Helena Vineyard series, she is the author of *Tucker's Crossing*, part of the Sweet Plains series. She lives with her husband and daughter in Northern California.